I0822879

STITCHED ON MY HEART

Also by John Martell

The Unmerciful Sea

Midnight Radio

Stitched On My Heart

John Martell

ISBN 979-8-9880171-9-6
First Hardcover Edition
Cover design by Josh Sledge

Why do you see this body with all its scars,
when your name is stitched upon my heart?

CHAPTER ONE

August 2001
Marlowe Beach, North Carolina

Erick Sunstrom turned off the radio in his Jeep. The news that had blared continually from the speakers was trying to compete with the roar of the wind and the tires, but it failed miserably. The constant flapping of the little bimini top didn't help. It wasn't like the news mattered right now. "Hurricane Michelle is still plotted to make landfall sometime overnight between the North and South Carolina borders. With wind speeds of over 110 mph, it is expected to hit the coast as a strong Category Two…" was being repeated every five or ten minutes before Erick switched the radio off. It was the same announcement he had heard for the past six hours, with only small variations of time and speed. Until the next update from NOAA, the announcers on the radio and TV across the east coast would have to repeat themselves endlessly with dire warnings to their listeners that they should listen to the dire warnings that the announcers repeat.

A few moments of relative silence from the idle banter of a radio DJ turned weather forecaster would be a welcome respite.

It let Erick be alone with his thoughts for a moment.

The green Jeep Wrangler hummed monotonously along the old canal road toward his family's beach house home. The road headed toward the North Carolina coast, up from the south where the old George Washington Highway came up from the South Carolina border into the North Carolina coastal lowlands. Erick knew that most people would be leaving the beaches by now. They would head inland away from the coastal islands if they hadn't left already. The more modern Highway 17 that led to the west would be filled with the late summer tourists and a few locals, or possibly be already empty of cars, since the radio had been screaming at everyone blindly to get off their collective asses and leave the coast for the past day.

But no one would be on the canal road. It didn't go in the right direction for the tourists. The narrow two lane road was lined with pine trees on one side, and a slick black water canal on the other. Once the road got closer to town it turned into Sunset Drive. "There won't be much of a sunset tonight," Erick thought. The trees and green swamp grass were the only things he passed on his way to the coast, and they paid no attention to Erick as he sped along.

If Erick wanted anything on this trip, it was to avoid traffic, as well as contact with any people in general. He also wanted to avoid contact with rain and wind, which were not going to be conducive to driving in an open topped Jeep. What he wanted was to get in and get out as quickly as possible, before the first raindrops hit. Though that now seemed unlikely.

Erick made himself relax. He slowed his Jeep down, let the noise of the wind lessen and quiet. He was alone. Nothing bothering him. No problems. The drive was nice, not as desolate or empty as some of his journeys, that was for sure. The Jeep just hummed along on the black pavement. The soft top flapped in his ear. And no one, not a soul, was talking to him or looking at him. It wasn't exactly like being on a sailboat, but it was close.

Erick smiled. Just slightly. He didn't even notice he did it.

It had been a long drive. Longer than anyone would realize. Erick glanced at the map shoved unceremoniously in a little storage pocket. A worn corner that had become soft from the multiple times it was folded flapped haphazardly in the wind. He had come from Atlanta, from his parents' home. "If that's home," Erick thought, "then what am I doing here?"

Before that he had been in Florida.

Erick had been down on the Atlantic coast of Florida, in Fort Lauderdale, to meet with his hired shipbuilders to go over the last additions of a new build for his ocean going racing catamaran. The racing version was a brutal design, one made solely for speed. It was the pinnacle so far of Erick's still growing racing career. She would be fast, he hoped, with an incredible reach, and a sparing lightness that meant she would lift out of the water and fly if the crew didn't keep her well heeled. Just the thought of taking her out, sailing her until she sped over the water, breaking her, and bringing her back together, even if it was just in Erick's imagination right now, was enough for him to slowly put his foot farther and farther into the accelerator. It took Erick a moment to rein himself back into reality. That reality was that he was steadily rocketing toward his family's other home to outrace the approaching storm from the southeast.

He had been in Florida five days ago, when Hurricane Michelle had been nothing more than a teasing glint in the eye of a hot blooded Atlantic Ocean. She was just one of many low pressure waves that had passed off the African coast. But this one hung on, grew, spiraled, and finally took steady aim for somewhere on the U.S. east coast. When Erick was in Florida, Michelle was still too much of a wanderer to have narrowed her gaze to a landing spot. Florida, Georgia, the Carolinas, they all seemed equally likely.

Erick had watched, like everyone had, to see just what Michelle would do. She swirled, enticed by the shores, a deliberate and sultry sashay that seemed to mesmerize the coastal residents, including the plethora of surfers who prayed to the gods of the sea, whomever that may be, over a shrimp po'boy and a bottle of cheap beer. Erick understood. Even the name, Michelle, oozed a sexy sensuality, a whisper in the ear that meant things, hot, steamy, dirty, and well skilled in getting her way.

Erick had decided to get out of her way early, in order to beat any evacuation from the Florida coast. That was a nightmare he actively wanted to avoid. It had been a long drive to Atlanta and his parents' home.

Erick had only arrived in Atlanta when his father had again questioned him about his choice of vehicles. Erick's father owned a near flotilla, "fleet?" Erick wondered what the term would be on dry land, of European luxury car dealerships, and was a high up muckity muck with Stuttgart. Ever since as a young man in the Navy when he had seen his first 300SL Gullwing, Conrad Sunstrom had fallen in love with fast sorts cars. He had parlayed a decent amateur racing career first into a repair center, then a dealership, then more and more dealers. Now the Sunstrom name was synonymous with fast and luxurious vehicles on billboards, sponsor signs, and racing cars across the south.

And boats.

Erick's father had generously offered to pay for the sails of many of Erick's racing sailboats, as long as they were silver and black and had the big Sunstrom logo on them.

He had also offered Erick the use of a brand new Gelandewagon, also in silver, about a year ago. Erick had gotten used to the continual turnover of new and newer cars in the family garage. When he was young, Erick hadn't liked the occasional disdain of other teens, not his friends, thankfully, who had "worked" for their dented and salted rust buckets to judge him for driving his family brand. So when Erick had to get a new vehicle, he had bought the exact opposite of an overland wagon. The Jeep was All-American, simple, easy to work on, spartan, and notoriously unreliable. But it was all Erick's, no one else's, and it served him well enough.

But it never stopped his father from offering Erick a new car every time he was home the same way other parents offered their kids a sandwich when they visited.

He didn't blame his father. Erick understood his father's passion, and appreciated both the concern and care his father had always offered. Erick's mother Jane had pointed out how much Conrad had done for Erick, and how it always made his father happy when Erick took his help. "He likes being involved in your life, Erick," she pointed out. "He's never made any demands on you, you know that?" Which was almost always true. Conrad Sunstrom had always offered, always asked, but had never actually forced anything on his son. As much as he was involved in the business, when Erick was younger, Conrad had always been at the weekend sailing events, skipping car races just to watch his young son putter around in low wind in a bay, happy to see him win or come in fourth.

So it wasn't a sense of spite or a thumb of the nose to Conrad Sunstrom's career as an automotive bigwig, nor was it a judgement as a parent. Erick really bought the Jeep because he liked it, and mostly to show his father that he was now successful enough to do it all himself. Conrad Sunstrom had already succeeded as a father, teaching his son and guiding him. Now it was time for Conrad to just be a dad. It was a little difference, but important.

“The Jeep’s fine, Dad,” Erick had insisted. “If I show up in a G-Wagon, people are either gonna think I’m a rich boy or I am untouchable. Either way, I don’t want to scare anyone off. I’d rather have them underestimate me than overestimate me. Plus,” Erick continued, “the Jeep’s kinda cool.”

It was the same argument the two often had, but by this time Conrad’s heart was no longer in it. He loved his son, and had no need to win this competition. Jane had pointed out to Conrad that he should be happy their son still showed up to see them. At 30 years old, Erick could have just run off and stayed away, his life strewn to the four corners of the world.

But Erick still couldn’t stay in Atlanta. This time, his parents gave him good reason to leave. “I was going to go over to the beach house to close it up, but your father has this big deal coming at the race track…” Jane had trailed off. She knew Erick would volunteer to go to the beach house. He probably would jump at the chance to go to the coast, especially the place he considered his home. Erick only had an apartment outside of Atlanta just for the mailbox. A storm was coming, and the house needed to be closed up for the end of the summer.

Erick had just done a six hour drive from Florida to escape a hurricane and an evacuation that didn’t come when Michelle began to track north along the coast. Now he was doing another six hour drive to the North Carolina border and home.

“I haven’t been home in…,” he had to think hard about it. Erick went back in time to his visits, “Spring of ‘99, but that hadn’t been for long. 1997?” That was a strangely pleasant time, laced with oncoming sadness. He had been in the house for a week or two in the fall of 2000. It had been a long time. Erick still had things there. There were clothes, probably more than he had at his apartment, and what little stuff he had collected over his life, including his sailing trophies. Erick’s mom had gotten rid of a lot of his high school junk, or stored it in bins that she occasionally had shoveled off on him over the past decade. But the beach house was still his home, where he grew up.

Now the mixed salted trees, pines and coastal hardwoods that had been twisted and shortened by the gales that blew from the subtropical coast, all flashed by in a familiar blur out the side of Erick's Jeep. He had done this drive so many times that he knew the patchy forest by heart. Each tree, each bump, went by in predictive fashion. The road went from smooth to an asphalt patchwork. Erick knew it meant he was getting closer to his home.

A worn blue sky was still being burned by a late white sun in the west. It would be a few hours before it set and got truly dark. Erick tried to figure out how long he had before he would be stuck for the night. The sky to the east was already a scudding gray with white clouds, which meant rain was coming sooner than he wanted. Erick knew he must hurry, then. It didn't matter where the eye of the hurricane touched down. The skies would darken, the wind would blow, the ocean would boil, and the sand would fly. But by the time all that started tomorrow, Erick Sunstrom would be long gone, back to Atlanta, well before the heavy stuff hit.

The road under his tires changed from a smooth roar to rough and bumpy. It meant he was getting near Bodin, the county seat, and the only real town along the coast. It tried to be a cute village, a mix of old and new, but the little town had grown as much as any town on the coast of North Carolina had. Tourism and money had taken their toll. Now strewn with a mix of art galleries, gift shops, and the occasional watering hole, it had become more and more homogenized even though every shop that opened claimed to make the town more special.

Erick didn't care. Bodin wasn't his home. He had spent his summers on the beach, and when he was younger had never trusted those Bodin kids who spent their summers in the swampy still canals and bays instead of on the shore. Things changed once Erick went to high school in Bodin. He became best friends with many of the teens from the island. And he remained friends with most right up until well into college.

All Erick wanted to do when he got to Bodin was to turn right onto the big new bridge that had been built over the Intracoastal Waterway, then make the turn to the south and down the beach road to his family's house on the coast. It sat at the southern developed end of Marlowe Beach, on Snow Island. Marlowe Beach had developed and grown, too, but it mostly was more beach rentals, new grocery stores, and tons of restaurants, buffets, and bars. Marlowe Beach had certainly changed over the years since Erick had first come for summer vacations when he was 12, not for the better, probably. But it had been his home for a time. Erick had loved the beach and coastal life when he was younger. It had just been a while since he had been there, really had the sand between his toes.

There wasn't going to be much time to go for a walk on the beach. Erick was going to make the turn onto the bridge, speed over, get to the house, close the windows and bring in the garbage cans, and get the hell outta Dodge before the water started to rise. "No issues, just get over to the island."

He almost made it.

Most of the islands had been evacuated of tourists the day before. The locals would have decided what they were doing sometime earlier in the afternoon. If they were staying, they would then go to pillage the local grocery stores of all the water, bread, and peanut butter. The ABC stores would have been next, and those, too, would be closed soon afterward. The police and fire departments would have a mild case of dread for those that were stocking up, because it meant there were people staying.

With news of the increasing winds, the locals all had a limit to their daring. 100 mile per hour winds coming straight off the coast would mean ocean overwash and big waves on the shore. In sleepy little Bodin, the town would have other problems. The rain would bring flooding in the downtown.

Bodin flooded even in heavy rainstorms to the point where the shops would be closed as trucks made wakes in the flooded streets that would wash into the doors of businesses and houses. Then old men and women would curse the drivers for being out in the storms and the drivers would flip off the old men and women.

While the rain was bad in Bodin, a hurricane was an order of magnitude worse. The old time locals would have all put their antique dinner tables on concrete blocks and left for higher ground by now. Anyone still there was going to be at the mercy of the storm until the roads cleared and the police could get back out. There was always someone who thought they would be okay, they could ride it out. Then the power would go out, and the trees would fall, and the water would rise, and they would realize that they are in over their heads, hopefully not literally.

So it was little surprise that the police were getting ready to block off the bridge to Marlowe Beach. The big orange blockades were on the side of the road, not yet in front of the bridge. A few cars passed by on the outgoing lanes. Erick sighed and slowed down. As much as he liked his beach home, he had other things to do that were much more important. He hoped to get in and out without having to talk to anyone. Erick wanted to get to the house, do the needed chores, and get out to get back to Florida and get his catamaran done. Erick wasn't ready to come back home for any length of time. Not yet.

A police officer waved him to stop. Erick stared at the man, wondering if he recognized the officer. They were about the same age, though the two could not look more different. A glance at the name tag, and then at the man's face, and Erick recognized him only a few seconds after the cop recognized Erick.

"Erick Sunstrom! I did not expect to see you pulling up here. And in a Jeep? What's up with that? Where's the Mercedes?"

Erick looked at the officer, a soft, slightly thick young man his age, but looking older with a face of old acne scars and a low dark brow that hid a bit of his eyelids. His simple bowl cut of fourteen years ago when he had been in high school with Erick had been replaced with a short crew cut. His hair was still black, but receded a little bit, making him look both young and old.

"Scott Parker!" Erick hadn't seen Scott since high school graduation. Erick had last heard Scott was working at the fishery on the south end of the islands. Scott had obviously moved into law enforcement. Scott's father Sam was famous, or infamous, along the island as the local town manager. He was gruff and impersonal, and all the kids thought he hated them all, but he really was just of a different age, where everything that needed to get done had to be done with a bit of a gripe. He had been, in a word, crusty.

But Erick had liked Scott. Scott had once called him "bud" when he came into school, and Erick had been stunned at the casual kindness. Scott was the first reason Erick had changed his opinion of "those Bodin kids." They hadn't really been buds, though they certainly never had any bad interactions. Erick had once bought a bunch of Cokes for everyone on a hot day from the 7-Eleven. A few days later, he tried to buy some for a few other kids, including Scott, who refused and paid for Erick's drink instead. "You got it last time," he had said simply. Scott had left a good impression on Erick. He hoped it would still reciprocate right now.

"Ha!" Erick tried to laugh off the crack about his Wrangler. "There's nothing wrong with a Jeep," he said, hiding a cringe. "There's a reason you don't see an S-Class out on the beach sand.

"Look, I know you are getting ready to close the bridge. I just need to get over to my parents' place. I'm gonna close the shutters, tie down the trash cans, empty the fridge, and turn off the well pump. Then I'm outta here. Seriously. I just need a half hour." It was an exaggeration. It would take a half hour alone to drive to the house and back. Erick hoped there wasn't much else he would need to do. Besides, the hurricane was hours away. The winds were just starting to pick up, and the sky was closing up, but the rain was holding off. If Erick got out of Dodge as he planned, he could outrace the rain and be one state away by nighttime.

"Well, we technically haven't closed up yet," Scott almost winked. It was true. He hadn't moved the big reflective orange barriers out into the road. They sat just to the side of the bridge next to a pile of dull brown sand bags, piled in a heap, waiting to do the solitary and unglamorous job of sitting on cheap steel bars to keep the barriers from blowing down the road or floating away in a current. The knots at the top were tied up into squished ugly faces, all tired but resigned to their fate. "You gotta go close up the Castle, huh?"

Erick winced again. He looked away to hide his face as he laughed into the approaching wind. He hated how the locals called the big old beach house the Stuttgart Castle. But it had been the biggest, fanciest old beach house on the island. It only grew in legend as every year more and more of the prestigious, seductive German cars appeared in the old tabby concrete drive. "Yeah," he tried to laugh it off again. "I gotta close up the Castle. Mom asked." He hoped to appeal to Scott's better nature by invoking the Mom clause. You always did what Mom asked. If not, you weren't a good son. Scott better not want to look like he was a bad son. Scott's mom would be disappointed, and his dad would be cranky.

"I get it, bud. Yeah, go ahead. Just don't get stuck there. You ain't got no top," he pointed at the little bimini cloth that barely covered the front seats. "You don't want to be out in the rain in this thing."

Erick almost laughed in Scott's face at that one. "If you only knew," Erick thought. A hurricane rain in the Jeep would be a tiptoe through the tulips compared to some of the things he had been through. "I'll be out soon. If not, you can come get me at gunpoint." Erick nodded to the service revolver on Scott's hip.

"I'm not gonna do that," Scott insisted. "If it gets that bad, you're on your own. Just ride it out until it's over. That old house of yours has been here as long as the beach itself. It's probably the safest place here." Scott then paused before waving Erick on.

"Hey, Erick," it sounded strangely serious to hear his name from Scott's mouth. Like Scott was moving into adult speak, with a real warning about the approaching storm. "Listen, you should just know. I saw someone else down there. Eliza is in town. I think she is doing the same thing to her dad's place. I was going to go by and see if she needed help, but now that you're here…" He let the statement trail off.

Erick got quiet. That was serious. "Yeah…" he almost thought about turning around and letting Scott, dull, soft, crew cut Scott, go over for him. Just give him the key, a can of Coca Cola, and a hundred dollars, and turn the Jeep around and run. Instead, Erick pushed the clutch and shifted into gear. "Thanks.

"I'll see you soon."

CHAPTER TWO

July 1987
Marlowe Beach

Erick looked out over the fresh water sound that stretched to the horizon, along with the barest sliver of land miles away. It had been a clear day. A high pressure cell had sat on the islands like a big ugly bird nesting uncomfortably on a sparse straw mat. The sun burnt down from an empty blue sky. Everything was hot, thick, a sickly sour soup of brackish water that splashed and stuck to his body. Erick knew that across the coast, people would be looking to the west and begging for a cloud. Just a little rain, a breeze, a bit of shade. Even on the beach side of Marlowe the ocean had been pushed out to shallow long waves. The sound hadn't even offered Erick the chance to cool off like he could in the ocean. The shallow water just sat there, soaking up the sun, getting warmer and warmer.

Erick was celebrating his upcoming September birthday a little early. Most kids his age would hope for a car for their birthday. Erick was still 16, and he already had his pick of cars, as long as it was from a Sunstrom dealer. But his gift had already come, and there was nothing on earth that would hold him back from using it.

Except probably a lack of wind.

Erick had been introduced to sailing as a kid in his summers at Tybee Island, Georgia. His father had immediately bought him a little Opti as soon as he had finished his first week long lesson. The little boat was perfect for a kid, small, easy to master, fairly maneuverable, and it didn't take up much room. Erick had fallen in love with the boat, and with sailing. Other kids might have been watching *Miss Budweiser* on TV, the screaming hydroplane unlimited series powerboat, but they offered no appeal to Erick. He had long been nonplussed by straight line speed, having grown up around the fast cars his father fielded on racetracks across the south. But Erick had admired the ability of the cars to go fast in the slow parts. It was a known bit of magic for racing. Just thrusting a car through air at higher and higher speed meant nothing if the vehicle couldn't turn and stay on track in the twists and turns of Daytona or Sebring. There was a mantra in auto racing. "You gotta go slow to go fast." It meant to drive a less forced race, to drive smoothly, even if it felt slow. The driver would then find the lap times would drop, and the car was actually going faster. But Erick had been close to the drivers, famous and journeyman, amateur and professional, and had heard the more intimate and complex explanations between people who understood without explanation. He knew, you have to go fast in the slow parts, too.

Erick loved to go fast in the slow parts. Sailing did that.

Anyone could send it with the wind at their back, but tearing through a reach on a windsurf board or a slick hulled fast sloop, that was happiness.

But there was something even faster.

So there Erick sat, looking across the horizon to the west, eyeing the changing weather. Darkening clouds promised wind, maybe rain, maybe lightning, but definitely wind.

Erick had gotten his birthday present early, in late summer, and there was little his parents could to do keep it from him. The beautiful Hobie 18 bobbed under him. It was already familiar in Erick's hands and feet. Even in the low wind, the boat was so lithe that it moved along with the quiet tinkle of water under its twin hulls. Erick hadn't even had it long enough to give it a name.

A little over a week ago it had arrived from France via Florida on a truck to Marlowe Beach. Erick saw the twin hulls, usually a gleaming white, and laughed at the speckled silver over the glass. It still had white tops, a concession made to the builder to keep them cooler in the sun. When he saw the silver and black color, Erick had said to his mom, "Well, I should have known Dad would find a way to make it look like one of his cars." Erick half expected the beautiful blue and yellow mainsail to have the Sunstrom emblem centered on it. Still, the color made the cat stand out with the shiny silver twin hulls.

Erick had assembled it himself and taken it out the same day, just to do a break run to make sure it worked. He had sailed in the Intracoastal Waterway between the soft grassy islands that had long ago hid pirates and pirate treasure. The waterways were much more valuable than any hidden treasure in the sands.

Now, Erick wanted his real birthday present. The sailboat was great, but what Erick wanted was to catch a big wind and let the cat fly, then crank it into a reach and see how fast it would get going. Then tack back and forth, chasing faster and faster wind. Then, after all that, he was going to send it down one of the cuts between Bodin and the barrier islands just to see how fast he could go.

That was what he wanted for his birthday.

Erick didn't expect any thing more; there should be no surprises for him, no one to jump out of a darkened room and start singing, no smiling aunt pinching his cheek, no card in the mail with a five dollar bill. This was enough, more than enough. Everything.

The dark clouds made dark water that raced toward him. The dark patches in the sound showed the direction from which the wind came. It was still too hot to make rain, but the wind, that's what Erick wanted. Erick hoped for high winds, and he got what he wanted as the breeze blew out his candles and granted his wish. The wind hit his mainsail and jib. The cat lifted out of the water like its feline namesake would snatch a bug in the air. A snap of the sail and the catamaran began to run, easily reaching a water shredding 12 knots. The little jib snapped taut and added sail. The twin hulls skimmed across the water. Erick let it run before coming about to set a reach, just to see it turn. "Going fast in the slow parts." It barely settled before leaping back up to speed. He ran a reach, then worked the rudders as he close hauled the little boat toward the approaching wind, just to see how close he could get before the sails luffed and he was in irons.

Erick turned back to port, just enough to be close hauled, then he slowly let the cat turn to beam. Finally, he got the wind behind him and let the fast little cat run. He felt like he was close to 20 knots flat out.

It had already been a long day, out hunting for wind that only now had come in the afternoon. Erick was tired and hungry. The water from the sound clung to him, thicker, pungent, not like the scratchy salt of ocean water. It lingered with a taste like an old washcloth. He was thirsty and hot. Fortunate for being sunkissed most of the summer, Erick felt his shoulders dry and almost crinkled, but at least not burned. It was after four o'clock, and he needed to get home to get cleaned up and eat dinner.

In the swift cat, there was no problem with Erick being in a hurry. He pulled in the sail, gathering wind and putting the spurs to the boat. Erick buckled himself, then placed his feet on the starboard hull and began hiking out, weighting the pull of the wind in his sails against his body as the starboard hull lifted out of the water. Erick twisted his face away from the bow, spitting the filmy, fishy brackish water off of his lips and face, shaking it from his eyes under his sunglasses. He felt his hair twist in the wind, long, curly, a golden blond that hung down to his shoulders. Even wet, it still fluffed out in the wind. He shook it again to keep the long locks off his hot and sweaty forehead. Erick would get teased about his hair at school, with hints of Bon Jovi or Whitesnake references by dull witted boys with dull black haircuts. Erick's mom had likened him more to one of her musical idols, Robert Plant, which Erick took as a great compliment.

At least here, alone, no one bothered him. Erick could sail and wave his hair with no concern of pleasing anyone else, or putting up with the sophomoric antics of sophomores and juniors. Erick had no one to prove himself to but himself. So Erick let the cat fly, along with his hair.

Erick eyed the winds behind him. The dark skies mixed with white clouds. If there was going to be rain, it would not be for hours. Gray and white clouds mixed, promising a bit of shade, maybe more wind, but there were no sheets of rain to blot out the far horizon yet. It would be an easy sail back across the cut and into the Intracoastal, where Erick could then sail to the dock across the road from his home. Erick leaned out, just a bit more.

The cat grew taller, and the sail dipped a little lower. Erick found his balance. It was a risky move, hiking out in high winds, but Erick needed to find the boat's limit. Back stretched, knees straight, legs tight and straining, head back and eyes forward, the cat moved with purpose. Erick moved the line by inches, or fractions of an inch, to tighten and loosen the sail as the cat lifted or lowered. He was now moving fast in the fast part. He kept his eyes forward, only glancing at the sail for ripples, letting his hands and feet tell him where the sail and hull were. The starboard silver hull gleamed under his worn out summer Top-Siders, which clung to the hull even though they were soaked through. Erick's mom would complain about their smell and he had to start leaving them on the dock, but they were closer to crew than gear for Erick. His toes squished in a familiar bit of wet filth, and the cat moved slightly at the flex.

Everything was working perfectly. Erick was flying an edge, both figuratively and literally. He felt one with the cat, the wind into his back, the sails filled tight. The mainsail was full, not even a ripple in the high wind. In his teenage mind, where everything was subconsciously sexual, the tight sail looked like a silk bikini, pulled tight over a girl's summer body. The smaller jib was just as tight and smooth, pulled taut like a bikini bottom over the few forbidden spots that delighted the boys even more than the uncovered suntanned skin they always thought they were allowed to see at the beach. Erick's father had often joked, though he was half-serious, that to a teenage boy, even algebra would give them an erection. To Erick's sixteen year old mind, sailing his cat with the tiny and tight bikini sails, it was closer to pornography. Or more accurately, erotica, though in the teenage boy's mind, the two probably were interchangeable.

Erick was too young to understand the many symbolisms going on as he sailed his cat. Erick kept the boat flying on edge as he aimed for an opening between two low balds, twin piles of dirty sand that were piled up to make a canal, Cockle's Cut, that he knew would open to a small bay, and then through a more sedate marshy path to the Intracoastal Waterway, and his family dock beyond that.

He took the entrance at speed on one hull. His cat would barely fit in the narrow cut. It was just wide enough for him to sail through. He would be across the cut and out into the little bay with its hidden beach in moments. Under his slippery feet the cat purred with the sound of water being cut by the bow. Anyone coming the other way better hope to be able to go under him. Erick wished there was a way to pull up the starboard daggerboard that hung in the air under him, but he wasn't about to let go of the mainsheet. Any accident now would send the cat tumbling into reeds and shoreline, resulting in a torn up set of sheets, a snapped mast, probably a cracked hull, and a very likely broken up Erick Sunstrom. His father would be upset, but would understand.

His mother would probably never let him sail again.

"I just better not crack this up."

The early birthday wish was an omen that Erick wouldn't recognize at the moment he thought it. Sailors know omens well, but Erick just had not experienced enough of life to know one, for good or bad. Or even to realize they can be both, at the same time.

The strong west wind was giving out, just as Erick was about to reach the little bay that separated the two waterways of the sound and the Intracoastal. He planned to sail into the round bowl of water, gently drop the flying hull into the shivering silver waves, then take a fast but leisurely turn to slow the cat down, and finally settle in for a soft run to the Intracoastal and home.

He just didn't expect another boat to be there.

CHAPTER THREE

July 1987
Marlowe Beach

Eliza Rhodes lay on her thin pink towel, alone and hidden in the small secluded bay off Cockle's Cut. The beach, if anyone could call it that, wasn't much of a beach, just a smooth dry silt sand, a mix of dull white and fine gray powder, with a scattering of the dead twigs, dried sea grass stalks, and weedy bamboo that broke off and tried to stick itself through her towel to poke and scrape at her thin waist.

What the little bay and beach did offer was privacy. It was a little mermaid's perch for Eliza to sit in the sun, alone, away from others, no prying eyes, no talking, no gossip, no fears or worries that intertwined into the life of a high school girl at every moment of Eliza's day. She just got to sit on her towel, alone, listening to the radio as it put out annoyingly cloying commercials for restaurants in between the singsong twang of a DJ and the occasional song she liked.

Eliza liked coming out to the bay on occasion. She had a little boat, a Boston Whaler Newport, a craft so ubiquitous that it had been constantly in demand for the past eight years. Eliza had run it aground onto the shallow water. Even on the soundside beach, the boat was so light that Eliza could turn it around and pole it into deep enough water with no effort from her 90 pound frame.

The boat was her father's. Butch Rhodes was a manager at the local fishery, the seafood processing plant, and it was expected that he have a worker's boat, not something fast, no water ski racks, no big motors, just a small side console and an outboard motor. The boat wasn't that important to Eliza. But in a place where there was only one set of roads going north to south, with the highest speed at a blistering 35 mph, and Eliza being too young to have a license anyway, everyone got around by a boat of some kind. Kids on Marlowe Beach had boats the way kids in the mainland had bikes.

"Kid…" Eliza heard the word in her head and then abandoned it to the winds. That's why she was out here. Eliza was working on her tan, in more than one way. She was fifteen, going full into the teen years, just old enough to be part of the teenage life on the islands. She was starting her sophomore year in school, which meant on the islands she would move from the smaller middle school into the slightly larger high school that served only the last three years of a teenager's education.

Her friends had teased Eliza about going into high school looking like a middle schooler. She couldn't help it if she was thin, and she was short, too. She just was a petite girl. Everyone else was skinny, for the most part, but she was noticeably thin compared even to her girlfriends. And girls could be cruel, even close friends, without even meaning it.

What made things worse was the controlling attitude her parents had on her. Eliza wasn't allowed to wear a bikini at the beach, only in the back yard of their old house, or around other girls. Her friends teased her for having a pale belly while they were getting brown over the summer. A two piece swimsuit wasn't ladylike, according to her mom, and just wasn't appropriate, according to her father. It didn't matter that girls in bikinis were encouraging targets for her 8th grade brother Tommy. He could check out the girls all he wanted, but Butch Rhodes had made it clear, nobody would look at his daughter that way.

So Eliza came out where she could be alone, took off her shirt, and lay down on the pink beach blanket to get a tan on her less exposed parts. At least no one would see her here, and it wouldn't get back to Eliza's parents that she was out exposing herself in a bikini.

Eliza was going into high school, and she needed to have a little bit of trust, and a little bit of self-determination. She just wanted a little chance to grow up, just a little. Not to be seen like a middle schooler, and a sixth grader at that, with her trim body. She wasn't looking to grow up, just be her age, like the other girls.

Eliza could hear her mother Mila's voice, "You don't have to be like the other girls."

Eliza didn't even want to think about what her father would say.

She flipped over onto her chest after feeling her skin start to bake. Sweat had pooled in her collarbone and in her bellybutton. She felt it all pour off onto the towel. Eliza undid the strings on her top, and in a fit of spite, pulled her bikini out from under her and set it next to her shirt. "No one is around," Eliza told herself. "It isn't like there's anything for them to see, anyway."

Eliza was looking forward to high school. Longer days, more people, even a modicum of freedom. Just going to the local football game and not being with her family, being able to walk around with her friends and talk to other people. Eliza knew what she meant by "other people," and didn't know why she had to think that silently, secretly, alone on an empty beach hidden in the middle of an uninhabited island, away from her parents. She meant "boys," but it was still built into her head not to think that.

Eliza had her own share of desires. She had seen the surfers just off her beach. Her parents had just moved from their old house in Bodin to a bigger, taller house on the beach side of Marlowe. It was new and nice, with a tall A-frame living room full of glass to look out over the Atlantic Ocean, and it let Eliza stare at the beach from behind the glass. Sometimes she would stand and watch the surfers, older, late teens or early twenties, maybe some old men in their thirties, and occasionally the fat old guy on a long board with gray hair and a beard in baggy Jams. And when it wasn't behind glass, it was behind a different wall. She was always with two or three other girls from school, silly, giggling, one was starting to seem a little, well, trashy, at least by Eliza's parents' standards. Or with her annoying brother, who would comment loudly every time Eliza would glance even sideways at any boy on the beach, just to make sure their father heard him. She never got to be alone. There was always a window to watch, but the window was always closed.

Eliza had noticed her new neighbors must have had a son, but hadn't met him yet. There had been no open window for that. Eliza's father had been a little, "a lot," judgemental, Eliza realized, when the neighbors had moved to the beach last year. The family had fixed up an old house and done some major renovations, while preserving the original look of the big cottage. Eliza's new house screamed modern, with serious angles and new windows, including a big circular one to light the stairways. If anything, her family had built the eyesore while the older houses looked more appropriate and beautiful. Eliza just chalked it up to her missing her home in Bodin, and her father being proud.

There was no way Eliza's parents could close the window on her now. Eliza was old enough to go to high school, and she had made it clear that she wasn't going to that little private church school in the woods to the south of Bodin. Eliza had put her foot down on that, a rare moment of stubbornness and defiance to her parents. She really, really, didn't want to go to a high school of thirty people with no sports, no cheerleaders, no dances, and no… anything else.

Eliza rolled back over. She hadn't bothered with suntan oil. She would just brown naturally. She felt the pool of sweat that had gathered in her lower back swish and pour down her suit, then into the towel. The air was hot, thick, with little wind in the sheltered bay. The dark clouds and wind that hung far out over the sound just weren't finding their way through the trees and blue sky. All of her was hot, all over, and she liked it. She looked down at her tummy and legs. In the bright sun, everything looked strangely monochrome and purple. Eliza couldn't see if she was tanned; the sunlight blinded her just enough to not be able to see well. She reached for her sunglasses, but all they did was make everything darker. But Eliza knew, she *knew*, she got wonderfully cooked, and she would look good when she finally went back to school.

While Eliza sat up admiring herself, she heard a strange noise coming from the sound side. It wasn't the familiar fast sputtering drone of a motor boat. She would recognize that immediately. This was something unfamiliar. It was a strange, unnerving ripping sound that was a mix of a scream and a whisper from the trees on the other side of the bay. Eliza saw nothing through the trees but the sound grew louder.

Eliza stared, rooted and ignorant to what was happening, as the twin silver hulls burst through the opening of Cockle's Cut. For a fleeting moment, she thought that a plane was crashing through the water, until she saw the sails appear at a steep angle to the narrow waterway. It took time for her mind to realize it was a catamaran, as it began a slow turn. The twin hulls began to point toward her, then they rotated farther into the bay in a wide but rapid arc. Eliza saw a man, young, blond, long hair, shirtless and soaked from the bow wake spray, as he stood on one hull. Before he glanced up, she quickly grabbed her shirt to cover herself, forgetting until this moment that she was topless. But she was also mesmerized by the sight.

The sailor seemed mesmerized, too, but at just the wrong moment. He glanced up, finally noticing the boat on the shore, and then the girl beside it, covering herself as best as she could.

Eliza watched, hoping the man, now realizing it was just a boy, hadn't seen her. But she knew he had. He didn't smirk, though, or smile a lecherous grin. He seemed just as stunned as she was. Eliza could tell that because he immediately dropped the line and sent the catamaran tumbling over into the water. The boy fell over backwards, with a slight yell, before disappearing over the side.

Eliza pulled on her t-shirt and began running awkwardly through the shallows to get deep enough to dive into the water and swim out to see if the boy was still alive. There was no one else there to help. It was up to her.

She wondered just what she would find when she got there.

"Please don't be dead," Eliza prayed. She didn't know what she would do if she found a dead body.

Then Eliza realized what she had been thinking about right before this had happened. "This is a strange way to answer a prayer."

CHAPTER FOUR

July 1987
Marlowe Beach

The cat was behaving just the way Erick wanted. He felt it under his feet, controlled, but not tamed, which was the way he liked it. He ripped the single hull across the water, flying on top of the other hull as he entered the little bay. This would be the end of his trip. The rest would be merely parking. Erick would gently touch the flying hull down, turn in a wide arc, slow his cat, and make his way through the more intricate and narrow creek to the Intracoastal and then to his dock. Everything was going perfectly.

Right up until he saw the girl.

The boat wedged on the beach was a surprise, but the girl…

She was an angel.

Erick didn't even notice she was barely dressed until he started to slip. But by then, it was too late. It was all too late.

All Erick saw as the cat began to tip, and then he began to fall, were the two wide brown eyes, round but with soft upturned tips, like they were surprised and smiling at the same time. She was incredible looking. Short light brown hair, wavy and curled, a twisted mess from laying on the sand, a small part pinned down making it look a bit like she just woke up. Dark skin, a slight olive color under the summer tan.

And, God, those eyes.

They looked right through him. Even on a day full of blue skies, dark clouds, heat and wind, all Erick saw was stars.

He almost didn't care when the cat came crashing down on its mast and sails, sending him backwards over the side. Erick became more aware of his precarious situation only when his back crashed into the daggerboard and he felt a snap and a sharp stab in his shoulder. He had only a moment to wonder if he had been stabbed through the lung with the broken board, and he was going to bleed to death in the water of the bay.

The only problem was that he would never know her name.

"Who is she?" was Erick's only thought as he held his breath and fell into the water.

Erick began to sink.

"Well," Erick thought as he sunk into the water, "I'm not dead."

That was a good sign.

His shoulder hurt, like he had a cut there, but he wasn't in serious pain. Erick kept his eyes closed underwater, afraid to see it turn blood red, as he kicked himself up to the surface. He struggled with his first breath. He hadn't had much time to take in air before he had crashed into the water. Kicking his feet, Erick flipped himself onto his chest, doing a rather pathetic doggy paddle to hopefully reach his heeled cat. His shoulder hurt, but hopefully it might move. Erick was sure if he reached out to do a single full stroke, his arm would tear off at the horrid wound and flop around uselessly, spurting blood until the sharks showed up. If the cat was broken, he wouldn't care if he did have a severed arm. Erick couldn't show up back home with a torn off arm and a broken sailboat. His parents would kill him.

Then he remembered the girl…

Something splashed around the side of the cat. Erick couldn't see anything behind the trampoline. The sharks were coming in fast, he joked to himself. Instead, Erick saw a tiny, thin arm cut through the water, pulling the rest of a girl's body forward. It was her!

"Are you alright?" her voice, it was smooth, soft, warm, like a slow song, not entirely fitting with the lithe body or pixie face, or those eyes. Erick felt himself sink a little.

"Stand up," she said.

"Huh?" Erick gulped and spit water. It tasted warm, cloyingly still and tannic, a swampy tea.

"Stand up! It's only four feet deep."

Erick stopped treading water and put his feet down. The sandy bottom reached up to his toes, and the water above rose only to his chest. He felt a little foolish. He had wrecked his boat and was splashing like a kid.

And staring at the girl.

She had come out to save him. All five feet of her, probably 100 pounds sopping wet. In this case, being sopping wet didn't add much more than a few ounces to her frame. Erick couldn't take his eyes off of her. Some people would say she was cute. Short hair, tiny thin body, those bright brown eyes. To Erick she was more than that. More than just cute, more than pretty, she was beautiful.

"You're hurt," she said.

Erick followed her gaze, taking his eyes off of her for the first time. Under his arm a trickle of blood turned into a river as it mixed with the sound water. He had forgotten the deadly stab wound from the daggerboard. A gash disappeared down his shoulder blade to his back where the skin had been split open.

It was a surprisingly gory cut for something that didn't seem to hurt as much as it should.

"Oh, that's nothing," he tried to shrug it off, but the shrug hurt, too. He couldn't help but stare. "I'm alright." He forgot the cut as soon as he looked away, back at this girl who had come to save him.

She noticed his gaze, a sort of dumb sparkle, which made Erick smile shyly. She took it differently, Erick realized, as she looked down at her own body, wondering why this cute but bloody and soaking wet boy was staring at her. She was wearing a short shirt, but had jumped in to save him without putting her bikini top on. She glanced down, all of a sudden realizing how exposed she was. She tried to shrink into the water, with limited success.

"Kinda takes the mystery out of the relationship, doesn't it?" It was all Erick could do not to laugh.

CHAPTER FIVE

July 1987
Marlowe Beach

Eliza swam back to her beach, hid behind the boat, and wrestled to get her top back on under her t-shirt. "This is so embarrassing," she thought, not even thinking about the dumb boy that came flying in too fast on a boat and then crashing off the side. Of the two people in these events, she should have seemed to be the more capable one. She did swim out to pull a dead body out of the water, after all.

The boy took his time to follow her to shore. Once she was dressed, as little as it was to put on her top, Eliza came back around the boat to find the boy trudging through the shallow water to the other side of her little Boston Whaler. He smiled, but grimaced when he stumbled and his arm went out to catch his balance. "Come here," Eliza called, trying everything to forget the past few moments while at the same time trying to remember every bit of it. "I've got a first aid kit on the boat."

Eliza turned him around to examine the wound. It was, not ugly, she decided. A gash had started on his shoulder, deeper than she would have thought, but then it quickly eased off to a bright scratch that looked out of place on his smooth, tanned back. His shoulder wrinkled from his tan as he wiggled his arm. "It seems like it still works," the boy said.

"Stop doing that, you're making it bleed again."

The boy shut up. She wasn't used to giving orders, much less having someone listen and take them. "Let me wipe this off and put a band aid on it." She grabbed a slightly dirty first aid kit from the side of the boat, never used before despite the many wounds her father or brother had gotten from fishing lures and rope burns. Pride led to bleeding and infection in her family. Eliza wiped off the cut with a folded paper towel, then tried to clean it with an alcohol swab, but she wanted to hurry up and get a band aid on the cut and turn him back around. Two small strips went across the deeper cut to squeeze it together, but the boy barely flinched. Nor did he complain with her holding his shoulder firmly to press the band aids onto his cut. Eliza resisted the urge to pat them with her hand.

The boy turned, and again stared at her. "Thanks," was all he said, as he tried to reach over his shoulder to rub the cut.

"Don't touch it!" Eliza took his hand back, "you'll ruin the work I just did. So, what's your name?"

"Erick, what's yours?"

"Eliza."

"Eliza…" the boy, Erick now, began to stare again. "That's a cool name." He kept looking at her like he either saw something curious right behind her head, or he wanted to say something.

"Thank you," Eliza suddenly became a little shy, and looked away. "Are you alright?" She didn't know what to ask, so she asked the same question again. It reminded her just how undressed she was. Eliza had come out to escape from other people just so she could wear a bikini without her mom or dad getting on her, so she could get a tan, so she wouldn't look like a freshman or middle school kid, so she could meet a boy at high school. "Well…" Eliza realized, "I got an early start on that." She still had a hard time making eye contact with Erick.

"So, um, can you give me a hand with the cat?" Erick asked. He stared out at his keeled sailboat, its mast dipped into the water, the sail beginning to fill. "It is kinda your fault I put her over."

"My fault?!" Now Eliza had a reason to look at him. "Maybe if you had been going a little slower, not trying to show off."

"Show off?" Erick laughed, looked away, then back at Eliza again. The laugh was good natured though. Eliza didn't think he was laughing at her, more like at himself. "I didn't even know you were here! If I hadn't seen this drop dead gorgeous girl staring at me, I wouldn't have been distracted," at least he didn't say 'half-naked,' "and I wouldn't have put her over.

"But yeah, maybe its more my fault. But can you blame me?"

"Well," Eliza thought, "I guess there are worse ways to meet." She twisted her arms and looked at her feet. She hadn't painted her toenails. Her father didn't like that. "He said I'm gorgeous," her mind raced. She went ahead and took the compliment, and the blame. "What do you need me to do?"

"Okay…" Erick seemed to get confident. Eliza noticed that when he was around his boat, he was in his element. "Actually, I've never done this before."

"Fallen off, or lifting a boat up?"

"Well, both," Erick said with a dumb big smile. He was delighted to admit it. "I just got this thing this week. I've tipped over before, but it took some work. But pretty girls weren't involved in that. Wait, I don't mean that girls weren't involved in making the boat keel over, I meant…"

"I know what you mean," Eliza wondered if he was doing this on purpose. Erick looked like the kind of boy that expected every girl to fall for him. That long hair, the green eyes, the big smile, the tan… She realized she kind of was falling, too. "Just tell me what you want me to do."

"Well," Erick thought, "Get on the side where the mast is. I'll go lift the sail to get it out of the water if you can lift the mast just a little. Then I'll go over to the hull and pull the starboard side down. When I do, let go and get out of the way. That mast will pop up quickly. I don't want it to hit your face."

Eliza swam out to the end of the mast and stood in the shallow water while Erick shook the water out of the mainsail. Then he went around to the other side. She could see him climb the hulls through the mesh trampoline between them. He was thin, slightly muscular, mostly in the shoulders. He looked like a swimmer. "Or a sailor," Eliza realized.

"Okay, push, then let go!"

The cat lifted up, its mast flying toward the sky. The upper hull crashed with a soft splash into the water as Erick flung himself backwards out of the way. He came back up, rubbing his shoulder.

"Are you alright?" It was the third time she had asked him. Eliza needed a new line, or this boy needed to be more careful.

"Yes, I'm fine!" He put his arms up, a gesture to admire the work they had done to right the ship.

"You know what?" Eliza said, thinking hopefully, "Maybe you should let me take you back. I'm not sure you are ready to sail that thing just yet." Eliza meant it to say he shouldn't sail with a cut open shoulder, but she worried he might take it as a slight. The look on his face said otherwise.

"Sure, why not? You can give me a tow to the waterway. I can probably make it back to the dock after that."

Eliza hoped Erick would ride back with her on the Newport, but he meant to steer the cat through the narrow and twisted channel tied to a line. He rode on the cat, his hand lightly on the rudder, making sure the boat didn't end up ramming her motorboat from behind. Once they got into the Intracoastal, Erick signaled she could untie and let him go, but Eliza didn't want to do that yet. "I can tow you the rest of the way in. Where's your dock?" She saw Erick's face light up at the suggestion. He didn't want to get away just yet, a good sign.

"I'm about three miles down."

"That's near my house! We just moved in recently." Eliza tried not to sound too excited, but she knew she failed. "I'm about halfway down the beach road." This was getting better. Eliza had to ask, "Do you go to school here?" Pleaseohplease don't say you are in college, she begged.

"Yeah, I'm going to be a senior this year. We just moved here last year, it's only my second year."

That might be why she didn't recognize him.

"What about you?"

"I'm going to be a sophomore. We'll be in school together." He had only been here a year…

She couldn't turn around any more. Eliza kept her head forward, watching the calm waters of the Intracoastal. They rode in silence. Eliza couldn't turn around. She knew he would see the big dumb smile on her face.

Eliza slowed her boat as she got near her family's dock. Erick spoke up, "No, it's the next one, one down." He pointed about a tenth of a mile down the waterway at the long dock with the fancy white picnic table and chairs on the land side. Eliza pointed at the nearer dock, "No, this one is mine."

Erick stared at the dock, then the big new house across the street, with its giant A-frame living room, and offset stairway with a giant round glass in it that looked like a weird chimney. Then he looked down at his dock, and across the street, to his family home, the old cottage with the big wrap around porch and the wide old tabby drive. It was sunk into a natural swale behind the dune. The big new house stared down at his cottage with its one big circular eye.

"Wait…" Erick looked dumbfounded, then his mouth began to twist into a bright white delightful smile, right into Eliza's eyes.

"You're my neighbor?!"

CHAPTER SIX

August 2001
Marlowe Beach

The last person Erick wanted to see was Eliza Rhodes. Erick hadn't even thought of her possibly being around, not during a storm. Hell, he hoped that wasn't her name anymore. Maybe she had gotten engaged and married in the two years since he had last seen her.

Had it been two years?

Two years and two months, not that he was counting.

And to be fair, he hadn't actually *seen* her then. Not the last day he saw her. And not now, at least not yet.

Erick scratched at his chest where it itched, even though it didn't really itch. "It's just your imagination," he told himself.

The roads through Marlowe Beach ran north to south, with a gentle line of houses on the beach road, and a scattered number of shops, stores, and offices on the wider main bypass, the "Big Road" as the locals called it. Most places were already closed down and boarded up. The Big Road had all the color from the mishmash of businesses with their signs and emblems. There were a few new places since the last time Erick had been down. A real estate agency had taken over an old medical office. A gift shop had turned into what looked like a pool and spa dealer. Most of the places looked familiar, even though they all looked a little gray and desolate in the gloomy sky. The parking lots were deserted, except for the Food Lion that had a few cars left in the lot. Erick wasn't about to stop there. They would be out of bread and milk already. "Everyone and their milkbread," Erick pictured a bowl of milk with a slice of bread in it, which was the go-to meal for people during a hurricane, for some reason.

Erick turned onto the beach road where the Big Road ended. It was a slower drive, but more scenic. The beach road, too, was empty of cars. He drove past the other empty beach houses, then past the I Wish It Was Empty house on the hill that looked down on his old beautiful beach house. His two story family home appeared out of the dune, with its wrap around screened in porch, the big green shutters sticking out on posts over the white framed windows, the old roof shingles, brown the color of wet sand. They complimented the painted wood shake siding that was the color of shallow ocean water, white with a hint of light green. The big old wooden plank steps that led up to the screen door were a gloomy gray. He would have to repaint them and put on a new roof soon. Erick knew every inch of the place, every bit of color. He could close his eyes, walk through the house and still see every inch of it.

He made a desperate point to keep his eyes on his house, and not look up at the house next door. "If I don't look, I don't see her, I don't make eye contact, I don't have to think about her." Then Erick felt a little foolish. There was no one to see him, and he wasn't fooling anyone, because there was no one to fool. Erick looked over and saw a nondescript car parked in front of the house, and nothing else. He just hoped she wasn't looking out a window. The open Jeep with just the little bimini canopy did nothing to hide Erick from anyone glancing his way. With only two houses before a narrow undeveloped strip of beachfront dunes, it was obvious where Erick was going. He would stick out on the empty road for anyone to see.

A mist was already forming in the air. Erick would have to put the Jeep in the garage while he worked, and then put the full top up before he left. More work. He had hoped to get onto the island, get the garbage cans in, make sure the windows were closed, and leave. But closing up the house always took longer than he thought. Everything took longer to fix than you thought, he knew. "Mom left the shutters open," he noticed. "But it looks so nice like that," she would say. She was right. The old beach house had Bermuda shutters, hinged from the top so that the windows got more shade from the overhead sun. When the shutters were propped open, they kept the house cool but let in soft light, and gave the house a dynamic shape, like the windows were sleepy eyes looking out at everyone slyly. With the big flat shutters closed and locked down, the place looked mausoleum-like. Just a big block. With the shutters out, the place looked alive and welcoming, like a bunch of arms open to tell everyone to come inside for a big shaded hug.

"That's what the place was like when I was younger," Erick remembered.

He drove up the rough cracked driveway. It was made of tabby concrete, a mix of beach pebbles with a bit of cement binder. It looked like a packed solid version of the beach, filled with sand, shells, and polished rocks, so much better than the black top paved public beach accesses down the block or the boring white concrete strips of newer houses that had been going up for the past ten years.

There was no time to go romancing the driveway. It was getting cloudier by the moment. Erick's desperation to get the house closed and get out of there grew. He felt uncomfortable, like he wasn't allowed to be in his own home. It was a feeling

Erick had felt for the past year now. He knew it wasn't the storm coming. Erick drove his Jeep hastily up to the garage. It was too small to hold the Jeep in its entirety. The garage had probably been made for a Model T, or a horse drawn carriage. Erick pulled up just enough so that the front seats were barely inside the garage and the swirling misty rain would stay off the seats. He took his keys, threw his small travel bag with his cell phone and change of clothes onto a dry shelf, and walked up the garage stairs to the kitchen door,

The family always went in through the garage door, next to the kitchen. The big wooden door at the front of the house with its wavy old glass was just for visitors. Erick opened the door and was met with the wonderful smells of an old wooden house. It was full of salt, and woody cologne, and a bit of mustiness that had to be there. It wouldn't be an old house without it.

Whenever Erick came home, he would go through the door, down the hall, turn left at the big old living room and dining table, and then out the back door. It led to the back porch, the walkway to the sun deck, and then to the beach. He always wanted to go to the beach to see it, whether it was a summer day, a cold winter wind, or a gloomy nor'easter churning the ocean. It was his beach. Erick had seen the beach recently, only a day ago, in Florida. But this was *his* beach. Of all the sand, of all the oceans, this was his favorite spot. He had been around the world, and seen some of the nicest coasts in his travels. None of them had this beach. He had printed his feet in this very sand for days, months, and years.

But this time Erick didn't want to go outside. He didn't like what he might see. Erick stood in the hall, dark, alone, quiet. "I'm not going to be held hostage from my own beach because I'm worried about someone seeing me," he told himself. "I'm going to check out the waves." It's what you did when a hurricane came to your beach.

"*My* beach."

Maybe go get the trash cans in first.

Erick turned down the air conditioning, even if he was only going to be here for a half hour. It was already hot and still inside, and it was going to get humid, and he wasn't going to suffer in the heat. Then he opened the front door to walk back down the driveway to drag the big wheeled cans back to the garage. Erick slipped on a windbreaker, tucked his head into the collar, and watched his feet as he walked down and up the drive.

He'd have to move the Jeep to put the trash cans inside.

He would do that when he left. Erick tucked the cans in a corner in hopes they wouldn't get caught in the swirling winds to be sent scuttling down the beach road when the heavy rains came.

Back inside, Erick felt at home, but also alone. He had no one to prove himself to, no one to dare him. "What the hell," Erick thought, and went out the back door. He wanted to see his beach.

A raised walkway led to the old sun deck where Erick jumped up on the bench to look out over the ocean. The waves were starting to show up, more gray-green than blue. They would get much worse, soon. The waves would wash up the beach all the way to his dune. They would probably cause some erosion. At some time in the future, he was going to have to build a walkway and steps over the dune, but Erick was going to fight that until the bitter end. People were supposed to run over the dunes to the beach, like kids in flight. Steps made you tired before you even got to the sand.

The ocean was a dull green, a flat salted version of the color of his home's shutters. The waves were full of white lines of foam and whitecaps. The breakers began to reach down to the ocean floor, where they were able to gain height, start to curl, and then bring their weight down with a shuddering crash on the sand. It was a frightening meeting of land and sea.

Sailors don't like big rough waves, but what they really fear is that place where the sea and shore meet.

In the old days, ships would be pushed ashore, snatched up by the low shoals, broken on their keel, and everything, sailors, cargo, supplies, were spilled into an uncaring sea where they were all brought to shore by waves like this, to be torn apart. The ocean didn't care who or what it cast away when the storms came.

Erick stared intently to the east, directly into the waves. He wasn't generally superstitious, and gazing into the abyss wasn't tempting fate or anything to him. Erick heard the stretch of a door spring, and then a distinctive slap of a thin wooden screen door closing over his left shoulder. He made a point not to flinch, then turned to the right and stared at his shoes as he carefully measured each step back to the house.

Hurricane Michelle was coming, and he had more important things to do.

Inside, the house still seemed quiet and still, even as the air conditioning worked to cool the humid beach winds. The windows let in light fitfully. It would only get darker as the evening went on. There was an almost silent gloom to the house, a morbid aloofness of the house looking over Erick's shoulder, as if to see what he had in his hands. Only the intermittent hum of the refrigerator from off in the kitchen stopped the place from the roaring silence that an empty room can feast upon the ears.

Erick thought about turning the TV on, but the incessant chatter and continual radar updates would make him stop to watch. He cut on the radio instead. The hopeful singsong voice of the local DJ still prattled on about the storm, but sooner or later, the guy would turn the page to an upcoming blood drive or fishing tournament. "He'll have to play some music sometime," Erick said to himself.

Erick stood in the middle of the living room, listening to the radio, wondering if he needed a list. It really was just close the shutters and lock up, Erick thought, but there was always more. Bring the rocking chairs in. Get the mats from outside, they always blow away or get soaked. "Did Mom leave anything in the fridge?" he wondered. That was his first distraction. Erick realized he had been driving for half a day now, with only breakfast and a bag of gas station peanuts in him, and the day was getting late. His stomach growled at him in answer to the thought.

Erick searched the refrigerator for any food that needed to be eaten. His mom had been there a few days ago. He could tell she meant to get back. There was an opened milk, some ham, "Ugh, ham..." Erick didn't like ham. Turkey slices. "Turkey will do," Erick said to the empty kitchen, looking for approval. No one said no. Some toasted bread from a frozen loaf in the freezer, a couple slices of Provolone cheese, and a healthy dollop of Duke's mayo, and Erick had a dinner that would suffice. He had eaten worse, and less. But he had also eaten much better. There were cans in the pantry if he needed to stay longer.

"Nope," he said to himself, "Get this done, get on the road, get to a hotel in South Carolina, and have a big freakin' breakfast at Denny's if I have to." Denny's had been the preferred morning stop for his family, especially his father, for years. "Because Waffle House is not a place for a luxury car," Conrad had said, jokingly.

People in Jeeps ate at Waffle House.

Erick ate on a paper plate over the sink with a bottle of ginger ale to wash it down. He ate solemnly, watching the forming clouds over the Atlantic from the kitchen window.

The beach house had outdoor stairs that went up to a guest or maid's room on the second floor. The steps fortunately blocked his view out the kitchen window to the north as he ate over the sink in silence. The radio gave up on the chatter and finally blared a Matchbox 20 song. Erick threw his plate in the mostly empty trash can. "That's one more thing," he added to a mental to-do list. “Take the trash out.” There probably wasn’t anything that would smell in the waste baskets across the house, but it would be a good idea.

Erick sighed. “I might as well get on with it,” he said out loud, just in case the ghosts might tell him otherwise. Unfortunately, the house was not haunted. Erick gathered up the trash bag, then wandered to the bathrooms to collect the little plastic grocery bags his mom liked to accumulate. Tied in little tight knots, they all got thrown into the big kitchen bag, which he sealed up.

Erick hefted it easily. It was just a few boxes from the kitchen, Erick’s plate, and a hefty amount of tissues that his mom had thrown away. Hardly the stress of heaving an anchor up. Erick took the bag one-handed out the garage door, slid carefully around his Jeep, and walked out into the raging mist to throw away one more thing that was stalling him from leaving. He lifted the trash can lid and tossed the bag unceremoniously inside. Then he stood there, the beach boy, the sailor in him, and did what every man has done whenever a storm approaches; he stared out into the storm as he got rained on.

The rain was only a mist for now, but still, he should have been smart enough to come in out of the rain. Erick stared to the west, over the long driveway, across the empty beach road, into the soft chop that was forming on the Intracoastal Waterway. On his hurried trip in the mist out to get the garbage can at the street, he had purposefully kept his head down. He hadn’t looked around, or just didn’t bother to notice. Across the street from his house, hidden behind tall shrubs, was a small pier. It had been a dock for his boats over the years, with a little boathouse for storage, and an old but well maintained boat ramp, chained off to keep anyone but the owners, meaning only him, from using it. Most locals had their own boat dock property, and if they didn’t, well, tough luck for them.

Erick stared out over the road at his dock. There, seen through the spiked arborvitae, on the soft grass, he saw a little wooden boat, just a tiny 12 foot dinghy, with a mast sticking up bare into the wind. It was his boat. He had built it himself long ago, when he was still a teen, over several months. Erick had made a point to keep it in good shape over time, as any good sailor should for a craft that special. She was sleek, and cute, with dark wood bent in just the right places, a sharp keel and narrow transom. He had worked tirelessly for months in the winter to have her ready by early spring when he was in high school. Erick had kept her in care ever since. His mom even liked to take her out for a row, as she must have done recently.

And now she was sitting on the grass, not even tied to a post.

"Shit."

CHAPTER SEVEN

August 2001
Marlowe Beach

Eliza had emailed and called her friends to let them know she was coming down from Massachusetts to see her family. Of course, it was her dumb luck to come home right before a hurricane was going to hit. Eliza pretended the hurricane was the reason that none of them had made any plans with her. Well, one had called, before Eliza had left, just to say they were busy with their family, and probably wouldn't have time to go out or anything. "Kids, you know?" Eliza still didn't fathom how one of her best friends from high school was married with an eight year old. Another one was a single mom of a four or five year old girl. *That* had not gone over well with Eliza's father.

Eliza had lost touch with many of her friends from high school when she went away to college. She had gone to East Carolina University and graduated with a degree in marine science. It was a half-hearted attempt to follow in her father's footsteps since he ran the industrial seafood processing plant on the south end of Bodin. Eliza had no desire to run a business or manage commercial fisheries. Or worse, be her father's underling or secretary. Eliza found more interest in scientific studies. She had also wanted to get away from the small island that had gotten smaller, socially, every year. Eliza had finally moved to Massachusetts to study and teach in Falmouth at Woods Hole Oceanographic Institution after working there as a researcher several years ago. It was satisfying work for her, "well, satisfying, maybe," especially since it took her mind off of other things. It kept her away from home, to her satisfaction, and to her family's annoyance.

Eliza's father would miss her; Butch would let Eliza know that on the occasional telephone call. Then Eliza's mother would miss her as well, but in a different, slightly judgy way to remind Eliza that she needed to come home to see her father. Eliza's brother Tommy was a little more blatant. While he didn't seem to miss her, he would constantly point out that he stayed, got married, and went to work on the same island they all grew up on. Tommy was silent on Eliza's choices, but that was the point. By saying what he had done, he was leaving a big empty space for what Eliza had and hadn't done.

Eliza's mom often put some soft but constant pressure on her for more grandkids, which only made things worse. Eliza's family had not been very supportive of most of the boys she had dated. If her father had anything to do with it, Eliza would have been married to the son of one of his coworkers, where she would be a stay at home mom. Never to leave the island for more than a trip to Disney World.

Eliza had already planned to come home before Hurricane Michelle had formed. It was partly to promote a new sustainable consumer guide for commercial fishing and restaurants that she had started in the past year. It was an Atlantic Ocean copy of what the Monterey Bay Aquarium was doing with their Seafood Watch, based on a lot of research that Eliza had compiled. The little regional cards listing safe bets for seafood were still piled in her car. Eliza had pointedly noted that even though she came up with the initiative, her name wasn't anywhere on the cards. Eliza had hoped for something to brag about to her parents.

Eliza hadn't seen her family in a while now. Her father was closing in on retirement. Tommy had his own home, with a wife on her way to complacency and a son that didn't see enough of his father. Eliza's mother was still insistent on whatever she felt like she should be insistent upon, depending on her mood. Eliza loved her family, to the point of occasionally letting them manipulate her. That had made it harder to keep coming home. But it was getting easier for Eliza to escape from her family, especially with the distance between North Carolina and Massachusetts. "I'm closer than I used to be," Eliza realized as she opened the door to her family's beach house. Closer was a relative term. Massachusetts was far away, a full day flight or a two day drive, but it was much, much closer than she had been over the years past.

Eliza had volunteered to go board up the house while at home. Butch had said between his creaks and coughs that he would do it, he was fine, but then her mom looked at her, and Eliza suddenly felt a powerful urge to get out of the house for a while. Going to the home she grew up in during an approaching hurricane suddenly seemed appealing. It had been a while since her parents had moved out of the beach house. When Eliza moved away and her brother got married and bought his own home, the big two story house on the beach just wasn't a good fit for her parents anymore.

Now Eliza was actually "at home." The beach house was where she grew up. It was new when she was a teen, but had gotten old quickly. It was dated with 1980s style, an angular design of straight wood and big clean windows without any shutters or any other break in the big flat walls. It was like a kid had stacked blocks at different angles to design a home. Eliza had loved it as a teen. She had a room that didn't share a wall with her thirteen year old brother, and a great view of the beach.

The beach was wonderful. Her girlfriends from Bodin would come over for the day, or for a sleepover, and they would play on the beach or watch the storms roll in. When they got older, they watched the surfer boys come up from the beach access to the south.

And of course there was the big old beach house next door.

She remembered when it was full of life and fun, loaded with shiny cars of all kinds. Now it was empty.

Someone must have been over there before the storm, she knew. The shutters were open and the trash cans were out at the street. Eliza thought about going and getting them, but it wasn't her place to do that. Hopefully a police officer would drive by and take the cans in, to keep them from flying out into the waterways or down the beach road. Just so Eliza wouldn't feel like she had to do it herself.

Eliza unlocked the door and went inside. She was just going to put up the storm panels over the windows. Unlike the old houses that had the Bermuda shutters that hung on by old corroded hinges and prayer, mostly prayer, her house had big impact plastic corrugated sheets that could be attached to each window. They looked neater, let in a little light, and were much more protective of the windows. They would screw on with bolts and wouldn't come off in 150 mph wind. If it got above that, well, the house would come off the foundation first, Eliza guessed.

The problem was that the big sheets were cumbersome and awkward. It would take time to put them up on the windows, especially since the wind was already picking up. She went to the shed that used to be loaded with rafts and boogie boards, but now was just dusty storage for long unused fishing poles and jars of nails, along with about thirty of the big wavy opaque gray sheets. They were light, but that just meant the wind would lift them more easily. A couple fell out of her hands as she got them out, and the shed door flew back open with a bang.

"Sh…" she tried not to swear. It wasn't in her lexicon, but she had heard it enough. Be around anyone nautical and someone will know how to swear. But not at this house. Even if she were alone, the winds would carry the word to her father's ear and he would frown at her language. It didn't matter that Eliza had heard him say the same word time and time again, when he thought she wasn't listening. She pulled the mild oath back before it escaped and put it deep down inside her. Eliza held up four of the sheets in front of her face to shield her from the east winds, which also meant she couldn't see down the hill to the neighboring house. Then she carried them into the screened back porch.

"This isn't going to be easy," Eliza said to herself. One of the sheets fell and rattled. In the back of her mind she thought she heard a familiar sound of a screen door slam. But it must have just been the wind.

Eliza attached the four sheets to the windows on the back porch, then went back for more. She decided to get all of them, doing multiple trips from the shed to the back porch. Then she could take them to the windows one by one. At least then they would all be out of the wind.

Eliza went to do the front porch next. Eliza knew she couldn't help herself, so she looked over at the old brown and blue and green and gray beach house next door, just down the sand dune from her lofty front porch perch. Eliza almost immediately noticed something sticking out of the garage. She saw the trash cans had been moved while she wasn't watching, and a truck, a Jeep, was wedged mostly inside the little carriage sized port.

Eliza's heart fluttered, a little nervous, just knowing someone was there. She tried to rationalize it, and thought quickly that the most likely thing was that the Sunstroms had hired a local person to close up the house and bring the trash cans in. It seemed like what they would do. Anyway, it was a green Jeep Wrangler parked there. No Sunstrom would be seen dead in a Jeep. Or any American car.

Eliza looked at her dull Camry in front of her own house. It was a car that was meant to go from one place to another without getting her wet in the rain, nothing more. Erick had once joked about…

Eliza pushed the memory from her mind and attached the next hurricane screen. She would have to go outside to do the two windows on the south facing side, but there was no other way to get them on easily.

Eliza did her best to carry the small wooden paint ladder and two screens to put up. The wind was not cooperating with her as it twisted the gray squares in her hands. No matter what her exercise workout had been, she was still whisper thin and a plaything in this wind. The screens twisted her wrist until they forced her to let go and fall into the salt grass below her.

"Shit."

CHAPTER EIGHT

August 2001
Marlowe Beach

"Shit."

Erick stared out at his little boat. "Mom must have been using it, and Dad pulled it ashore.

"Now I gotta do something with that, too."

While he pondered his next problem on the list, Erick heard a dull rattling crash. At first, he thought that a shutter or window broke on his house, but the sound wasn't right. It was an odd, dull quiver, nothing like the wonderful creaking his beach house would make. It sounded plastic, wrong for the setting.

Sounds, especially weird sounds, set him off. There was always something singing on a sailboat when things are going right. But when something went wrong, it went wrong fast, with an odd harmonic that gave Erick only enough warning to maybe duck or hold his breath. It was in his reflexes, and nature, and a little fear, to look toward a sound that didn't belong on the wind. Erick glanced up and to the north, where the sound came from.

Far off up the hill, standing gingerly on a cheap wooden folding ladder, was the delicate figure of Eliza Rhodes. She was looking right at him. She heard him swear just as she dropped the hurricane screen with a dull clang on its corner, and looked over her shoulder right at Erick. There was no place to hide now.

Erick was far enough away that Eliza couldn't see him sigh, or slump, after being seen. He hoped so, at least. The rainy mist was a gauzy fog, which whitened out the distance as well. Erick tried to stay neutral, like he did when he was racing. On land, everyone was genial, fun loving, drinks all around from the winners. "Most of the time." On the water, everyone was a competitor. Not necessarily an enemy, but they might as well be. Unless the boat went over, which was a whole different thing. There were no glares, no dagger stares or yelling and cursing, just everyone coming to the rescue no matter who it was. That was the rule of the sea.

"Well… it is supposed to be…" Erick scratched at his shirt, then dropped his hand.

There was enough salt in the air from the blowing winds that Erick felt like he was out on the water. Was Eliza a ship in distress? Did it matter? One thing was for sure, none of the ugly salts he ever competed against looked anything like her.

"Hey," Erick called out, trying to keep the remorse out of his voice, with only partial success. He hoped it got lost on the wind.

"Hey."

"Do you need a hand?" Erick called over the wind. It was something that sailors knew to do in high winds to make themselves heard. Eliza stood teetering on the ladder, holding her wrist. Erick watched her stare down at the ground, her feet shifting on the ladder, as a gust blew her brown hair into her face and mouth. She spit it out gracelessly and smiled a foolish grin. Other people might look silly or goofy. On her, it worked well.

It always worked well on her when she smiled at Erick.

Erick saw her, every bit of her, the round high cheekbones, those big round brown eyes with the upturned ends, slightly wide mouth and perfect teeth. If she tilted her head a little, Erick felt like he was the one falling off of that ladder, and he was on solid ground.

“Yes,” she finally yelled back. “I think I do.”

Erick began the walk to Eliza’s house. He followed the remnants of the old path they had beat into the dune when Erick was a teen. Erick plodded over, head down unwilling to look up to get his hopes up or get his hopes dashed. This was nothing like the times he would walk over to Eliza’s house, unsure of who would meet him at the door. Or the times Eliza would come running in her swimsuit and shorts, only to have Erick meet her halfway, unwilling to let her walk the whole distance without meeting her to hold her hand.

CHAPTER NINE

October 1987
Marlowe Beach

A big old pickup ground to a halt in front of Erick's home. If there was a more bland and unassuming vehicle on the whole island, Erick didn't know what it was. This thing made a 1970s Plymouth seem exotic. It was just a big dull brown pickup. No one could even tell it was actually a Chevrolet C truck. The name alone was so unassuming as to make the truck nearly invisible. If there had been a Chevy bow tie badge on it at some time, it had long ago fallen off.

Behind it came an only slightly more stylish Datsun hatchback, which was possibly older than the truck. Both were so old, rusted, and beaten, it was hard to tell the model years. The cars were good for only two things. They would move from place to place, and they had some capability to carry stuff, in this case, surfboards. That was all that mattered to the teen boys that got out of them.

Paul Davis and Tye Meyers lifted their boards out of the back of Paul's truck. "C'mon, dude," Paul yelled, "Let's get to the beach! We ain't gonna have days like this much longer!" Erick grinned at them as he walked up the sand path to Eliza's house. It had only taken a few months for him to beat a path through the grass and sea oats to her driveway. It was October, and the weather was surprisingly warm, with a hot sun bringing a late summer day to the early fall. Marlowe Beach was graced with tropical weather well into autumn, with some days that became downright hot. Today was one of those days. The Gulf Stream was a freight train that rolled warm water right up to Erick's beach, with big curling waves breaking slowly offshore to a lowering tide, which meant it was starting to barrel. The teens that surfed were desperate to say they got in the tube so they could brag about it on Monday. Teenage surfers were bigger liars than fishermen. But they never corrected each other. It was part of the code.

John Grey got out of his beat up and rusted Datsun. It was yet another salt wounded used car, but it was his, and that was a big deal. He undid a surfboard from his soft rack on the roof. "You comin'?" It was a simple enough question. They wanted Erick to go out with them. They didn't want to seem like they were teasing him for choosing his girlfriend, giving up a day of big waves to spend with a girl. Only one of the three even had any semblance of a girl that liked them, and Erick still didn't understand what John's semi-girlfriend Jill, a cute acne scarred junior that looked like she was half his size, saw in the lumbering goof, but Erick didn't question their relationship, either.

John, Paul, and Tye all came over to his house because it not only had a good beach, but they also could eat for free and have a bathroom. Erick's house was unofficially labeled "party central," even though the worst that they had ever done was have about twelve kids over to watch an R rated movie while John tried to sneak some of Erick's father's beer. Everything to a teenager was overblown and exaggerated for effect. They were all sure they were having the most raging party ever.

Erick shook his head at the question. He simply jerked his thumb over his shoulder at the path. The other boys saw Eliza walking down the path to Erick's house. Erick turned and walked, then jogged, to make sure he got halfway there before Eliza did. The two met and held hands, then turned and walked together back toward Erick's house. The path wrapped around the dune that Eliza's house sat upon. They had discovered that the path had a spot where it turned that they were out of sight of Eliza's home. As soon as they got there, Eliza stopped, wrapped her arms around Erick's neck and lifted herself up to kiss him. She tilted her head and kissed him again, then snuggled against his neck. She felt Erick sigh and soften when she put her head on his shoulder. Erick always did the same thing every time; Eliza had gotten to expect it, and like it.

The two had found their little spot, a secret from Eliza's father. Erick's parents were rarely home, and Eliza had quickly learned that Erick's father was typical of most men, quietly encouraging their sons to pursue and date girls. Erick's mom was likeable and sweet, even if she seemed a little worried about Erick. Again, typical. Eliza wished her parents were as typical.

So they had found the first place they could kiss without being seen, and it had quickly become a refuge and ritual.

The boys made cooing kissing sounds, but their heart wasn't in the teasing. No one was going to make fun of a boy who had a girlfriend in high school. Teen boys were desperate, as well as stupid, but they were not that stupid. Erick had what they wanted, and they weren't going to make fun of him, not that much.

He had the beach house. He had the car. For the other boys it was a badge of honor to drive a cheap beater. There were a few students who had their moms buy them new cars when they turned sixteen. And the other students generally made fun of them behind their backs. No one really liked the few stuck up kids that got whatever they asked for. The guys knew Erick didn't have much choice in the matter. He drove a 560 SL, in silver, of course.

And Erick had the girl.

Plus, he was a nice guy. It was hard to hate him.

So Erick's friends left him to his girlfriend, sitting on his lap as the two smooched in the swale of a dune on the beach, hidden from the judging eyes of Eliza's parents.

CHAPTER TEN

August 2001
Marlowe Beach

No one was coming to meet Erick this time. He had to do the walk alone. No friends in the driveway, no longing smile from Eliza, no soft look from his mom out the window, none of that. It was just a slow uphill slog through sharp seagrass that scraped at his shins. When he was younger walking the path was like skipping on clouds. The feeling of salt grass or sea oats as they dried in the sun, whipping back from his outstretched hands, that was a part of his home.

"I wish this damn path had grown over," was all Erick thought now. If there wasn't a path back to Eliza, he wouldn't be able to take it. Erick had worn the path down so bad that he and Eliza had changed the shape of the dune. Man's triumph over the course of nature. Erick knew that sometimes nature came back with a bitter vengeance and bit you in the ass.

He could have waved and gone back in. He could have just looked away.

"I could have stayed in fucking Atlanta," he told himself. But he hadn't. Erick loved his beach, his home, about the only home he had. He loved his family, his mom and her needing him to help out, his father for being cool enough to understand that Erick liked the solitary adventure of coming here. "Then why do I feel like I shouldn't have come back?"

Erick wasn't getting his hopes up. He reminded himself of that with every step. That's not what he wanted. Maybe he just wanted to know why this was the first time in over two years that Eliza had spoken to him. "Maybe I don't. Maybe I don't care." Erick felt the bile rise up in him, and tamped it down. He had never been an angry person in general. Erick had worked through enough pain and anger in the past two years that he had no place for it now. Erick kept trying to delude himself of all the feelings of dread, or think of reasons to turn around, that he found himself at the little white fence that bordered the property line without remembering how he got there.

It was a throwback, an old low fence, whitewashed, a beach style, only about two feet tall, with long four inch wide planks that ran in an X from low post to low post. It was only a few feet from Eliza's house. The fence had marked the far edge of the Sunstrom property from long before they had owned the land. It desperately needed painting. The fence was white in name only. The paint peeled to reveal a dull gray wood that probably was ready to rot off. The nails that held the slats in were rusted to a leaking reddish brown, and probably had a whole complex of tetanus disease living on the broken sharpened ends. One of these days Erick would just pull the whole thing up and be done with it.

"Or, more likely, I'll hire someone to do it, preferably when I'm far out on the ocean. And not here."

The wind picked up with stronger gusts, and now there was a sheet of real rain in the breeze. The graciousness of a cloudy sky was fighting with the gloom of an approaching storm, and Erick knew which would win. He stepped over the fence carefully, and walked up to Eliza, still on the ladder.

She had just stood there, watching him, waiting.

He picked up the corrugated hurricane screen and handed it to her. "Hey," he said again, this time more quietly.

"Hi, thanks." Eliza looked down, expectantly, waiting for Erick to say something more. Then she took the sheet and wrestled it up to the window as she leaned onto the outside of the house. The ladder teetered and looked like it was going to fall. Erick took hold of the sides to stabilize it. "Thanks, I've done this before," Eliza said.

The words immediately came out wrong. She simply meant that she had put up the screens before, and she usually just tipped the ladder into the house to reach the window. She immediately realized the way she sounded. "I mean, I know, … I mean, thanks."

Erick just stood there, holding the ladder as she leaned over. It wasn't her fault. She hadn't spoken to him in two years. Well, Erick thought, hiding a slight frown by turning into the winds with a grimace, not speaking to him in two years probably was her fault. His chest itched, but he held onto the ladder in the wind.

Erick watched in silence as Eliza screwed on the covers. The screens slid into metal grooves, and thin handles were spun into them to make them fast. Eliza's legs were even with Erick's eyes. Even the shape of her thighs were familiar, through the stretchy dark fabric of blue jeans. Somehow she always made even the most humdrum of clothes look sleek on her. Erick didn't want to stare, so he watched Eliza's hands as she deftly attached the screen. She looked down through her arms at him and smiled, just as Erick realized he was looking at her bare waist, and up her loose shirt.

Erick looked back down at the house, at the legs of the ladder, anywhere else, as Eliza came down. "The wind's picking up already. I don't think I could have done this alone.

"So, how are you?"

So far all they had said to each other were multiples of "Hey" and "Thanks," so Erick knew this had more meaning than just the usual platitudes. "I'm fine," he said, lifting one arm. "I'd say 'never better,' but we know that's a lie." He smiled as if it were a joke. "I mean, you'd think by now my parents would have taught me to come in out of the rain, but no…"

Eliza laughed at the little joke as Erick held out his hand in the rain. He was getting soaked even though the rain had just started. It wasn't a hard storm yet, but it only took minutes for Erick's hair to go from his wavy blonde shag to a weighted down mop that darkened when it got wet. Erick shook his hair, running a hand through it, then shook harder, like a dog. He knew his hair looked like crap when it got wet.

"Well," Eliza almost paused, just a sigh half caught in her heart, then continued, "I'm glad you are doing okay."

"That's not what I said," thought Erick. It was hard to say which was better and which was worse, being okay, or being fine. He shook his head one more time, just to get the stupid thoughts out.

"Let's get the other screen up and get out of the rain, then," Eliza said to throw out a task and distraction at the same time. She saw the look on Erick's face.

Erick moved the ladder while Eliza got the other screen from the ground. They made idle chitchat about the relative benefits of hurricane screens and the old shade shutters of Erick's house. Eliza showed him how they worked, banging on one once it was up. "Nothing will get through these things," she said. "They will stop anything from getting in."

"Come inside," Eliza invited Erick when they were done. "I'll get you a towel."

"I don't want to get in the way," Erick said, jerking his thumb back over at his house, still open, windows uncovered. "I'm just here for a half hour," he insisted. It had already been longer than that since Erick had arrived. He knew it would take longer, much longer now, to get the house closed up. Erick tried to get out of staying at Eliza's house. It wasn't his best attempt to deflect. He didn't try very hard.

"I could use a hand with the rest of these things," Eliza offered putting up the other screens as a compromise excuse. "You can tell me what you have been up to."

Erick saw her glance down at his hand. He had forgotten to do the same thing with her, and pretended not to notice. "Alright," he acquiesced. "But I gotta get going before the storm hits. I don't want them to close the bridge on me. I just got here."

Eliza led Erick through the front porch into the living room. "Yeah, they told me the same thing when I came here." The wind whipped around the house as if in response, making a deep whirring sound. Eliza's newer house was tighter than Erick's old beach house, which whistled and sang off tune when the wind came through the doors and cracks. The strange disaffected hum from outside made Erick uncomfortable. Eliza looked out the windows at the rain that began to splatter. "I hope it's not too late already."

Erick stared out the window, too. It was just an outer band, a bit of rain, the locals would say. The heavy rains wouldn't get here until tomorrow. The wind began to blow the tall sea grass down in waves. Erick always loved how the storms blew the grass flat, then have the blades spring up in a lull in the wind, only to be bent down again at the next gust. The grass would bend, giving in to the wind, but never break. Their roots ran shallow but wide. Sea grass was resilient, living in the summer heat, salt air, and dry sand. It flourished at the coast, where the water met the land. "They won't close the roads just yet," Erick was sure. This wasn't even a squall, just some wind, carrying the water from an outer band of Hurricane Michelle out of the sky. But it would not be a fun drive in the Jeep. "I may have to stay, though. I'm not looking forward to driving in this slop."

"You've seen worse," Eliza almost sounded teasing, but it was meant as a compliment.

Erick shrugged it off. It wasn't really something he was comfortable with Eliza bringing up. She didn't get to decide what was worse or better, not now. "Everyone here has been through worse than this." Erick could wait for a break in the storm between the rain bands of Hurricane Michelle, if they were wide enough. The radio in Eliza's house, as if it had a small mind reader stuck inside, began the news blare with the same singsong voice, predicting a faster pace, with mostly rain and wind being the main features. "Heavy rain starting later tomorrow morning, with winds approaching 90 miles per hour, to lessen overnight to 35 miles per hour, with possible gusts up to 55 miles per hour the next morning before clearing out in the afternoon. We're going to be in for a rainy night or two, neighbors, and I'll be closing up at nine o'clock to get to higher ground. But we'll be up and running tomorrow morning with all the news and road conditions if we can." Erick half listened. He kept wondering if he was going to be stuck here. Erick looked over at Eliza, looking coy, curious, and a little scared.

"Riding out the hurricane at the house won't be so bad, I guess. Back before we moved in, Dad brought us over to see Hurricane Belle when me and my sister were little. It passed by right offshore. I saw one wave wash all the way up the dune."

Eliza laughed. Erick always loved telling stories about his house. She had heard so many over the years. "That one I hadn't heard before."

"Oh, it was great!" Erick brightened with the memory. "That was the first time Mom ever served us out the kitchen window. You know how the window over the kitchen counter opens to the back porch? Well, we rarely had a screen in it, and me 'n Astrid were just sitting out there, staring at the clouds, listening to the ocean, rocking in the chairs, and Mom opens the window and starts shoving baloney and cheese sandwiches out to us. I got my own whole bottle of Mountain Dew."

"That's where you got your addiction," Eliza said.

"Mountain Dew, it's not just for breakfast anymore!" joked Erick. "Man, I haven't had one of those in ten years!"

Eliza laughed again, a sweet authentic giggle that she used to have in perpetual use around Erick when they were teens. It faded out as she thought back to when ten years ago would have been for each of them.

Erick quickly talked over the budding silence. "Well, looks like I'm stuck here, for now at least. You want me to help you with the rest of these window things?"

"Sure," Eliza brightened at the offer. "Are you sure you want to stay though? I don't want you to feel like you're stuck here on my account." It was the slightest of lies. The house was going to get dark quick with the big hurricane screens up. She felt her mood lighten with one of Erick's weird little jokes.

"I should have known I wasn't going to get out," Erick replied. "I got here too late in the day to get everything I needed to do done." Another wind gust whuffed around the house, like a dull ghost at a party he wasn't invited to. "I could go over to Bodin and get a hotel room, but my Jeep would still be soaked. It's better off in the garage here. And it isn't like that house is going anywhere from a level one hurricane." The locals had a spoken but unwritten rule; you rode out anything under 100 mph. Erick knew it could still be bad, but like Eliza had said, he had been through worse. "I'd just have to come back again and clean up anyway."

"You're going to stay here tomorrow?" Eliza asked.

"Yeah, looks like it."

There wasn't much in the way of conviction in Erick's voice. Staying, especially now that Eliza was here, felt more like conviction in the prison sense rather than confidence. "That's kind of a mean thought," Erick told himself. It wasn't like he was spending the night here. Erick had his own bed, his own room, his own house. And if he had to, he would just leave. Damn the storm, and go. "That's a good way to disappear and die," his conscience whispered to him. Sailors had gone out in the winds, spit in Neptune's eye, and never come back. You don't sail on Christmas, and you don't go out in a gale.

"And you don't let women on a pirate ship," Erick had to fight not to say the last part out loud.

Eliza stared at Erick as he stood in silence. "You're doing your monologue again, aren't you?" One of Erick's eccentricities was to tell a tale to himself, and then after a moment blurt out the punch line, expecting everyone to get it. Eliza had sat and listened to him when they were younger, him explaining a stupid reference to a TV show just so she would get the joke. Her parents had limited much of her TV watching, mostly by controlling the remote themselves.

"Yeah, sorry, dreaming about pirate ships in the night, as usual.

"Let's get these things up so I can finish my chores next door."

"Okay, we'll do this. I can help you next, if you want."

Erick shook his head. "No, it will only take a minute to close my windows up, and I have a few things I need to do myself," he thought about the boat. "What the hell am I going to do with that thing?" But Erick kept that thought to himself, too. Eliza had already caught him daydreaming once. She didn't get to always know what was running through his head.

Just because she stared at him with those damned bright round brown big open deer eyes, all wet like you could swim in them.

CHAPTER ELEVEN

August 2001
Marlowe Beach

Eliza and Erick gathered up the hurricane screens and took them upstairs. Eliza showed how to get the old bug screens out of the windows and put the big sheets in by sticking them out the open window, then tightening down the latches from the inside. "It's a lot harder than doing it from the outside, but I'm not climbing out on the roof right now." She laughed again, that same sweet giggle. The wind lashed out a gust, pulling on the sheet. Erick grabbed at Eliza by the waist. It felt so familiar, about the same size, certainly the same curve. Eliza still had her narrow waist, and straight hips. "Nope," Erick thought to himself, and he hooked two fingers in her blue jeans belt loops and tugged to anchor her down. Erick didn't need that, didn't want that, the physical contact, the intimacy it meant, but he also didn't want to explain how his old girlfriend ended up pitched out of a second story window during a hurricane.

“Thanks,” Eliza puffed her mussed hair and smiled. She put her hand on Erick’s shoulder. She was silent for a moment, looking for something to say. “I could have ended up a kite.”

Erick simply tugged her back and let go, then walked to the other window. “I’ll do this one. Why don’t you get those leeward windows done? Just shut that window we just did first so the wind doesn’t blow through the house. You’ll be okay on your own.” He wasn’t about to get stuck in a darkened bedroom with Eliza in his arms. Instead he handed two screens to Eliza and pointedly turned his back, focusing on the other window in the bedroom.

Eliza walked out of the room silently. She didn’t know why Erick had offered to help her, especially now that he seemed so off-putting, while at the same time cracking his silly jokes with a smile. He was strangely confident and uncomfortable, all at once.

Eliza realized just how quiet the house had gotten. “That’s probably the reason why he’s acting this way,” she thought. Talking would mean … talking. Silence was uncomfortable, but easier. Eliza wasn’t sure if she wanted to ruin what little good magic there was left. It would mean dredging up a lot, especially what she had done two years ago. Eliza had done her best to acknowledge it to herself, and ignore it. “Kind of like what he’s doing now,” she realized. Eliza dropped the two screens on the carpeted floor with a dull flop. “What are you doing now?” she yelled, a little too loud. The house was getting sealed up, and it absorbed the sound of the storm until she opened a window and the wind came across the opening. “Are you still sailing?” She waited for an answer, wondering if it would come, or if she would simply hear a thump as Erick jumped out the second story window to the back porch roof and then to the wet sand and to his house.

He had done that before. In more ways than one, actually.

Instead, the answer came back quickly, as Erick came out of the room, finished before she had started. “Building, actually.

I designed a new cat. I'm putting that engineering degree to good use finally. I'm a helluva good engineer, you know."

Eliza stared at him dumbly. "This was another of his weird sayings," she guessed.

Erick saw her confused look. He got that on occasion. Sometimes people just smiled and thought he was being cocky, others nodded with that vague, "uh huh…" and moved on. "It's from our fight song at Georgia Tech. I forget that most people don't know that. We're famous for our engineers."

"Uh huh," Eliza continued with her work. Erick just stood back and watched from eight feet away.

"We're trying to find a way to mix carbon fiber and other materials to make a faster boat, but be marketable for retail. It's slow going, but we are close to a final product. Hopefully it will be ready and proven by March for the races."

"Are you going to race?"

"Hell y… of course, she's my girl," Erick grinned.

Eliza smiled again at the comment. That was one of their sayings, at least she thought so. Erick would say that about his little boats. When they were together in high school, he used to say it about her.

As uncomfortable as it was, with Erick with her, Eliza felt happy, oddly so, at having Erick back in the house. She was away from her family, and even though she was on the edge of a hurricane, and stuck in a darkened house, it was a bit liberating. Eliza always felt like Erick fit into her life well when they were together. He was being nice, nice enough, she guessed, not bringing up any past. That was part and parcel of their relationship…

"*You don't have a relationship*," a little voice in her head reminded her. "*I haven't seen him in two years. And he's still in love with the first bit of wind that hits his face.*" Eliza felt like the voice was a mix of hers and her parents, with her high school friends thrown in for a good bit of spite. Things had changed, no matter what she would think right at this moment, with Erick, smiling, charming, aloof, looking like he wants to shake her by the hips or just jump over the railing of the stairs and run away. Just to show Eliza what it was like.

Well, she knew what it was like. Eliza started to remember how it felt to harbor a grudge. Maybe he should jump that rail, she thought. It would be easier, probably best, just to do these windows and then let him go. Board everything up so she couldn't see out of them, maybe take a chance that she could get home. "Ugh," she thought, grabbing another screen, "I'll have to tell my parents I saw him. That won't be fun."

The rest of the screens went up, and the house got dark. Without even the dim light of the early evening coming through, the rooms were dull and dismissive. Not dark or fun for hiding like the way shadows keep secrets meant to be discovered. Just a cloudy translucence where everything was there, a glaucoma that sat over each room. Eliza began turning lights on everywhere, but the yellow tungsten color of the bulbs gave a dated appearance to the place. There still was the 80s furniture, rounded crate chairs and a sofa that was meant to last, but not to tell a story.

"Do you want something to eat?" Eliza glanced at the clock on the mantle. It too, looked like it was something meant to be nice but just looked like it was something "nice" bought from a catalog. "It's past dinner time, at least for me it is."

"No, I already ate," said Erick.

"Baloney and cheese?"

"Turkey."

"You're moving up in the world."

"It's all Mom left me, unless I want to unthaw some shrimp." He listened to the wind, since he could no longer stare out the window. "I'm worried that's gonna happen anyway."

"Drink?"

"You don't have any rum in this place, do you?"

Eliza laughed. Ten years ago, she would have frowned. Her parents wouldn't dare have alcohol in the house. They still wouldn't, but ten years ago she wouldn't have laughed at the mention. "How about a Mountain Dew?"

"No, I gave that stuff up. It gave me heartburn. Any chance you got a ginger ale?"

"No…"

"I'll have an ice water."

Eliza poured two glasses of water. It wasn't really a way to celebrate a homecoming. Erick was distracted, like he wanted to say something, and Eliza knew what it was, and she desperately didn't want him to say it, so she said nothing.

"Look, Eliza," it was the tone and words Eliza feared. But Erick merely wanted to go home. "Thanks, but I really gotta get going over at my place. I have to do the shutters there, too. And, well, I got other stuff. Are you going to try to head home? I mean, it's going to be a mess here, and you might get bored. I hope the power doesn't go out." To add emphasis to his words, another gust wailed around her house. "Thanks to the weather gods," Erick whispered in his mind. Someone was on his side right now. He just wanted to get out. He felt trapped behind those closed off windows and hardened screens. It was like being deep in the hull of a ship.

"I understand. Are you sure you don't want me to come over and help?" Eliza asked, hopefully.

Erick just shook his head as the radio blared more news out. They sat quietly and listened. The lanes on the bridge to Marlowe Beach were closed to oncoming traffic overnight due to high winds and potential flooding on the west side. The police didn't want anyone going to the beach at night. If anyone was going to leave the beach, they should do so now. "I may just stay and ride it out," Eliza said. "It beats another night with my parents."

Erick said nothing. He ticked a box in his head with the comment. Eliza was here alone. She had come to visit her family, but didn't want to be with them tonight. Erick glanced at her left hand. He knew now what he would see without looking or asking. "God, why did I have to even think that?" He waited for the weather gods to send him another warning, but nothing came this time. The storm gods were notoriously fickle.

"Well, be careful. I'm gonna head back." He walked to her front door. As he opened it, without looking back, he called out, "If you need anything, you know where I live."

"Why did I say that?" Erick wondered as he walked out into the wind. A gust blew around the corner of Eliza's house, sending a raindrop into his eye. "Okay, I'll admit it. I deserved that one."

CHAPTER TWELVE

March 1988
Marlowe Beach

March had been cold, and long, and boring. March was always a terribly long time. Eliza just wasn't old enough to realize it until this year. March was too far away from the end of school and summer to get her hopes up. Basketball season was well over, which only meant to her that her first year of being a junior varsity cheerleader was pretty much over, too. Erick had been busy with baseball and his senior year at school. Every day was coming home at 4:30, doing her homework, having dinner, and maybe seeing Erick during the week. They barely even saw each other at school with different class schedules and lunches.

And when Erick had been coming home, he was working on his cat in the boathouse. She didn't know what he saw in the thing. He rarely sailed throughout the winter. It was cold, with choppy breezes. Eliza loved being around him, but not out on a sailboat in February. She didn't even know what it was that he had to do to the thing all the time.

He was locked into that unheated shack all winter, since after Christmas.

They went out on the occasional date, sure, to the movies, burgers, and often her family would encourage her to drag Erick out for rollerskating, which he hated, but did for her.

But March was half over, and for once, having something half empty, in this case a month, was a powerfully positive thing. March came in with cold winds and harsh storms, just when everyone on the island had been locked inside since the end of December, with nothing to do. The island effectively closed down for two months, and everyone was cooped up inside. And they all were getting a little sick of each other. So when the third week of March came about, and the sun came out, and the temperature hit 70 degrees, there were a lot of pale bodies and squinty eyes that appeared on porches and beaches to finally enjoy a day outside.

Erick came over that morning.

"I have something to show you," he said, cryptically.

"What?" Eliza lit up, but kept her smile a sly one. She tried her best not to bounce on her toes in the doorway as her parents looked on.

"It's a surprise," he told her. He waved at her parents, "I'm just taking her next door," he called out. Erick was both mitigating the continual fear from Eliza's parents that somehow a teenage boy was going to run off with their daughter and start a life somewhere, and avoiding any hint that they were welcome to come along. They would find out soon enough what it was. But not as soon as Eliza.

"C'mon," Erick reached out and grabbed at her hand, almost pulling her with him. It was so unlike Erick to do that. Erick got excited about his passions, Eliza knew very well, but he never liked to push and pull. They would often end up intertwined with each other, hands and arms wrapped together so much it felt like a knot that couldn't be untied. But he always was with her, not in front, not behind, not pushing. Eliza skipped and ran to catch up with his step.

"What is it?!" she asked again. She hadn't seen him this excited in a while.

"I told you, I can't tell you. It's a surprise." Erick just kept walking, slowing his pace a little in the sand path. When they got to the turn on the dune, Eliza let go of his hand and tried to put her arm around him, to pull him close, to feel her boyfriend next to her, but even then Erick didn't stop. "No one has seen this yet," he almost begged forgiveness, "I wanted you to be the first."

Instead of heading into his house, or to the beach, Erick took her down the long tabby drive to cross the road to his boathouse. She could see his silver and black and white catamaran sitting peacefully in the water. It looked no different than usual. "Are we going sailing?" she asked. "I'm not dressed to get wet, Erick." She sometimes had to scold him when he jumped into things without asking her first. He meant well, she knew, but sometimes…

"No, it's not that," Erick stopped outside the boathouse, and put his hands on Eliza's hips, looking down at her, his face one of sheer delight. Eliza melted a little. Erick was just so cute when he smiled at her. When Eliza smiled back she watched Erick's reaction, always the same. Eliza had noticed it whenever she kissed him, that when the two got close, face to face, and Erick looked at her, his shoulders softened, his chest fell as he exhaled softly, even his eyes went from his squishy almond shape to sleepy and wet, while the green inside flashed with gold. Eliza had noticed it the first time they kissed, but had not realized why for so long. Erick was comfortable, relaxed.

Eliza felt the same way. When she had told one of her friends about this, a secretive bit of teenage innocence meant to be steamy but sweet, Eliza's friend had just poo-poo'ed the comment and said, "Jeez, you two are in love." She had said it all long, and syrupy, almost sarcastic, "in *luuuvv…*"

She may very well have been right.

"Alright," Eliza said, slowing Erick down just enough to pull him close for a kiss she felt she well deserved, "Show me."

Erick opened the door to the boathouse. It was a wide shack, typical of the type for this side of the Intracoastal Waterway. Open on the bottom with a lift for a boat, along with two narrow walkways on each side so that people could climb in a boat, it also had a wide and flat deck on the land side, usually just a place for throwing life jackets, sails, paddles, whatever nautical detritus was needed but not wanted to be stored just yet. Erick usually kept the place pretty shipshape, but it was a bit of a mess, with a cloth tarp and some cans out, along with a table and tools. But that wasn't what took up the bulk of the space.

In the middle of the deck, in the mix of dark shadows and filtered sprinkling light that came from underneath as the sun tickled the water below, was a beautiful wooden boat, a short sailing dinghy. It was brand new, though it looked old, no, vintage, no, classic, that's the word, Eliza knew it immediately. The boat had a narrow shape, with an upturned bow, and a tiny stern. It was brown, stained and painted in two colors, with dark brown going to a wavy light sunkissed yellow from stem to stern. The gunwale was painted an ornate mix of white, with a twisted silver and brown braid, like the pinstripe on a classic car. Eliza stared at it, then the tarp and paint, taking in the smell of fresh cut wood and stain.

"You built this?"

That was what he was doing in his spare time over the winter. Freezing his little butt off working on this little dinghy.

"Yes," he said proudly. "It's a peapod. See how it's narrow and it turns up at the bow, like the shape of a snow pea.

"But, c'mere, I want to show you this," he took her hand again, but this time waited. Eliza held him there for a moment, taking in the work he had done. As if this wasn't enough. She was incredibly proud at what Erick had made. The boat was a work of art. Then, Eliza took a step forward, with Erick, to go to the stern.

On the back, shining as if the paint was still wet, was her name on the stern. It read "Or Eliza".

Eliza laughed at the joke. It was a play on one of the little pet terms they had. At Chirstmas, Erick had played Fur Elise, joking that it was "For Eliza." Over the winter, when Eliza and Erick had a chance to go out, or to meet with friends, he often was teased because he made a choice of being with her over his guy friends. "It's either you or Eliza," he had said, "and none of you are *that* cute." They had all teased him, saying that it was "Eliza or else," and the term "Or Eliza" was created.

She loved it. It had always been "Or Eliza," the few winter months he spent hidden away in here notwithstanding. Erick always made sure she felt special to him.

"You named it after me!"

Erick beamed, "Of course, it's good luck. And I'll never, ever rename her."

Eliza pulled Erick close, kissing him roughly, excitedly, the way teens feel when their life is just a bunch of desperate moments of joy between all the times they have to spend growing up. "Of course you won't," Eliza said, and she kissed him again, in the quiet, with only the lapping water softly cheering for them.

CHAPTER THIRTEEN

August 2001
Marlowe Beach

Erick hadn't turned on any lights to his house when he had left to help Eliza. Now the place was dark and gloomy, with the fitful winds that blew and stopped as Erick crossed the path back to his house. Erick once memorized the steps, like following a pirate's map, counting the paces south and east, "North and east," he told himself, for that was the way to Eliza's home. Now he was leaving. "It's just backwards now."

Not that it mattered. He would know his way even in the dark. There was still a sliver of sunlight to the west. Erick could see the big palmetto at the front of his driveway swaying, waving to the storm winds.

Inside, Erick tried to do his mental list again. He had gotten almost nothing done and it was after 8:00. "I came here to close the shutters and take the trash cans in. And I'm still here." No more stalling. Erick went upstairs to start closing the shutters.

The windows were old originals to the house, but the frames had been replaced by his parents when Erick was in college. Erick had loved how the big old wooden frames rattled up and down. They used soft ropes attached to weights to help them slide. The frames had to be waxed on occasion to keep them from sticking, especially in the summer heat. But it was one of the fun things about living in a great old beach house. It had character, stories, feelings. The windows didn't always work right because they had been opened and closed so many times that they were worn and scarred, then rubbed smooth. But his mom said she had enough of struggling with them, so his father had brought in a crew to replace the weights and fix the frames. Erick had been gone the whole time, and hadn't been there to complain. Not that it mattered. Back then, it wasn't his house. He had left and had no say so in its upkeep.

But now, Erick was glad to have the windows fixed. They opened smoothly, stayed up halfway, and didn't come crashing down on his fingers. Erick lifted the new plastic screen which allowed him access to the older Bermuda shutter. Each shutter was a large rectangle of plywood, hinged just above the window, held out by a long white painted wooden dingbat that had wedged ends to jam into a block. Each side had a hook and eye so that the wooden slat wouldn't fall off if a little wind tried to lift the shutter. Erick only had to unhook the near end of the brace from the window, pull the shutter in, then use two hooks on the side to hold the shutter down tight. It was an incredibly simple and efficient design. Erick closed the screen and window, then moved to the next one.

After doing eight windows on the ocean side, the upstairs began to feel closed in. The west windows still were uncovered. Even though it was dark and Erick couldn't see outside, just having them open felt less restricting to him. Close the shutters and nothing could get in. But it also meant that the ghosts of the storm could be lurking just outside, ready to claw their way through when they saw their chance. Erick shuddered at the delightful blood chilling thought. Erick had often made up stories to scare his sister. Astrid had been so oddly macabre in her love of scary stories, even though she often complained to their parents that she couldn't sleep afterwards. "How she ended up normal is beyond me," Erick thought as he walked by her former room. He wondered what Astrid would say to him now.

"Go over there and make things better," probably.

"Shut up."

"You know I'm right."

"Yes, you usually are."

"Usually?!"

Erick thought about calling Astrid, but now wasn't the time. His cellular phone was still in his bag, in the Jeep. "Don't go grocery shopping when you are hungry. Don't make decisions when you're sad. Don't gamble when you're drunk."

Erick left the front windows uncovered, "at least for tonight." It would give him something to do tomorrow. "Besides the boat," Erick remembered the bigger chore. "It's something I can do instead of being bored watching TV all day." Yeah, that was the reason he wanted to stick around.

Erick turned on a few lights, just to keep the ghosts out. Then he went back downstairs and finally gave in and turned on the TV to the Weather Channel. Most of the live coverage was in Myrtle Beach. "Cantore always gets the fun spots," Erick joked. But there was also a camera farther north in Wrightsville Beach, which wasn't seeing much yet. Still, it was better than Erick's view out the back window to the porch.

His beach house had a giant single pane of glass behind the dining table, about five feet square. Erick was stunned it had never been broken. It overlooked the back porch, which sheltered the window from the worst of the winds. About the only thing that got thrown against it was salt spray, really. The coating was a filmy translucence over the entire glass right now. Erick knew he could clean it, but the glass would just get dirty again in a half hour.

Erick wandered the house, turning on a few lights, then turned on the outside front porch light. It was brilliant yellow. Not bright, but very, very yellow, like a dandelion flower. The bulbs were meant to provide light, but not attract moths and bugs in droves. Erick had his doubts. The yellow glow only made it out to the front steps. Beyond was now a darkened, stormy no man's land. He just needed to be outside for a while. "I might as well go to bed now," Erick glanced at his watch. He had hoped it would be at least 9:00. What progress he had made surely had chewed up the hours, hadn't they? But it was barely 8:45. It seemed wrong to go to bed that soon. "I'm not a freakin' child," Erick said.

The front porch was screened in, which helped keep rain out. The rain had stopped now, and probably wouldn't get bad again for another twelve hours. "I still could leave." But then how would he take care of his boat? If the Intracoastal flooded, and it would, the little boat would be beaten at its moorings or lifted and washed away. It was an old boat, but he didn't want to lose it.

Erick stepped out onto the front steps. He stared out over the driveway. Up the beach road he could see a street light, all bright white, gleaming down to a spot on the empty road. It was the only light he had. He couldn't see his boat, or the boathouse, or the end of the driveway.

Closer to the north, up on the hill, was Eliza's house, towering over him. Every window was closed, but bits of light crept out of the cracks around the hurricane shutters. And there on the porch was the unmistakable outline of Eliza, a thin, hazy black shadow on a similar yellow background.

A wind whipped around the house, pushing him gently in the back.

"Okay, you win."

CHAPTER FOURTEEN

August 2001
Marlowe Beach

Erick shook the rain off his windbreaker on Eliza's front porch. The multicolored Nautica jacket was still new, with crisp colors and crinkled lines that hadn't softened with time. It was a new look for him, but it suited Erick well.

"I'll take it," Eliza offered.

"It's fine out here," Erick said. "I can just leave it on a chair. It's still a little wet."

Eliza took it from his hand. "It'll get all blown away out here. We've had plenty of water in this place." Eliza gestured into the well lit but sealed living room. "I'm glad you came back over. I was bored about a minute after you left."

"I'm the entertainment, huh?"

"No!" Eliza didn't mean that, even if Erick seemed to imply he was hurt by the comment. "I meant that it was nice, having you around. Again." She threw the last word out softly, into the wind, hoping it would only be a suggestion that Erick would think he heard. What she wanted to say, what she wanted to ask, was much more, but she kept worrying Erick would ask her questions that she couldn't answer, not yet. She didn't even know the answers herself.

"Okay, I'll give you that one. I was getting a little lonely, too. It's tough when I don't have anything to think about and do. I still haven't finished the prep for this hurricane yet." Erick shrugged. Eliza smiled, thinking what Erick knew. He was stalling to stick around. At least she hoped so.

"*Do you, really?*"

Eliza didn't even bother to answer the voice in her head this time.

The TV glowed the same weather news that Erick had been watching at his house. "Myrtle's gonna get it," Erick commented. Everyone on the coast immediately becomes a meteorologist when hurricane season kicks in. "Sucks for them."

"Yeah," it wasn't much of a response from Eliza. She, like much of the coast, had a love/hate relationship with Myrtle Beach. With the huge high rise hotels and massive tourism, the place was jam packed every summer with millions of tourists. Marlowe Beach was a sleepy coastal Mayberry by comparison. But at the same time, Eliza's father would still go across the border for fireworks at the end of June every year And it was a fun, wild place.

"You want to play a game or something?" Eliza was at a loss for what to do now. She had gotten Erick back over. Eliza didn't want to be alone in the house, with the windows closed and the early bands of wind and rain outside. "Where do I go from here?" was the first thought she had. When they were dating a few years ago, the night would go from walks and intimate talk, plans for the next month, holding hands, tangled arms, which would lead to more intimacy, tangled tongues in a dark corner that led to passionate hurried sex before they were both too tired to do anything. Eliza knew, with Erick's standoffish stance, that wasn't happening. Not that she wanted that right now, either.

"*Don't you, really*?"

"What do you want to play?" Erick asked. He seemed amiable. Erick had always tried to find a way to agree to doing things with her. Eliza remembered the times she had taken Erick to her family church gatherings, and he was always pleasant and charming, helpful, the diligent outsider. Even though Erick never felt like he fit in. Probably because he didn't.

"How about Yahtzee?" It was something that Eliza could play well. Erick was notoriously better than anyone else at a lot of games, but Eliza thought she could hold her own with him at Yahtzee. It would give her a chance to talk, lighthearted, but close.

"Dice games? In this house?" Erick raised his voice in mock derision, "I'm shocked, *shocked!* To find that gambling is going on here!"

Eliza frowned, a serious pout this time. Erick was making fun of her and her family now. Yes, her parents had been strict, conservative, and a little judgemental. Eliza had been away from them long enough to see the world, thanks to Erick in no small part, she had to admit, and Eliza knew that some of those wicked sins she had heard as a kid were not so wicked. And Eliza also knew, deep down, that her family was no less guilty. There were lots of splinters in other people's eyes. Eliza had heard about them all from her parents when she was younger. It still hurt no less when someone plucked the plank from her eye. "You don't need to make fun of me."

Erick smiled, then, seeing her serious face, went through a mix of frustration and anger, before settling on the look of a parent over a petulant child. It wasn't any better than the other looks he gave Eliza. "It's from a movie, Casablanca. It's a funny line from a film. We watched it once."

Eliza didn't remember that, but she knew the film. She should. Everyone knew the name, but she just didn't remember watching it with Erick. He was occasionally bringing her over to his house in the evening to watch a film. It was always an excuse to sit on the sofa and make out. Her parents were a little more lenient by then. She was going over to the house next door, not out to a party, and adults were there. What her parents didn't know was that Erick's folks always went to bed early and left them in a darkened living room, showing an old black and white film, while Erick would slowly half undress her, kissing her stomach and hips and...

"I remember that film!" It slowly came to her. Eliza had been nervous, as usual, and Erick was slow and gentle with her, never taking off her clothes or her underwear. He just left her half dressed, with delicate teasing kisses. He had later explained he never wanted to do anything without her permission, and always hoped she would just undress herself. Eliza couldn't explain she was still timid, especially with the fear that Erick's parents might walk in on them. They had been slowly moving to more and more intimate moments, but then they both got interested in the film. Erick had nestled on his side, wedged against the couch so Eliza could stay stretched out, still half dressed, in the early summer late night heat, as they watched the film to the end. Once the movie was over, it was late and Erick had helped her button up and walk her back to her house.

It was such a strange and titillating memory to come back right now, Eliza thought. Erick had been such a typical horny teenager, but he had waited for permission that never came, then just kicked back and actually watched a movie, never moving on his temptation of a girl in her bra and panties laying right next to him.

"We could see what's on TV," suddenly a film in a dark room sounded a little better than playing a board game for two.

She turned the channel to Turner Classic Movies. "What is this?"

Erick made a soft "ooohh..." sound. "Rebel Without A Cause, that's a good film. We missed the beginning, but you'll like it. Star crossed teen lovers struggling with their place in the world. James Dean, Natalie Wood."

Eliza left the room to make popcorn while Erick sat down on the sofa opposite her TV. She still had the big tube TV in her house. Erick's father had recently replaced the ones in their beach house with big LCD flat screens. Somehow it looked okay on the older TV. Erick never heard the sound of microwave popcorn popping nor noticed Eliza until she sat down. Erick slid over to one side of the sofa to give her room.

"I'm not going to bite you," thought Eliza. She handed Erick his own bowl. Eliza turned off the lights, in hopes of creating a more theater like feel, while staring at the TV eight feet away as the wind whistled outside.

The movie was beautiful and sad. Eliza had to ask questions to know what was going on, who some of the characters were. "Is that the guy from Gilligan's Island?" and Erick answered them all. "Yes. He played Thurston Howell, the rich guy."

Eliza slowly worked her way closer to Erick. The best she could do was rub shoulders. Like they were old pals. She knew now there would be no snuggling, no casual undressing, and certainly no teenage style intimacy. Erick didn't try, and Eliza never had tried. This was as far as it would go, physically. At least until she said something about what had happened with them.

"This makes the hurricane not so bad," Eliza bounced off Erick's shoulder, then she flinched inwardly. She didn't know if she would hurt him that way. But he didn't say anything, just smiled. But he also didn't do it back.

"What are you going to do, you know, after all this?" It was a start.

"I've got to get back to Florida soon. I think in a week or so we should be ready to test the cat."

"And after that?"

"See if there is interest in sales. Maybe arrange some regional match races, something to promote it. We may do something next May."

Eliza was silent. She meant, after everything else. After they had met again. After all the other afters. What was he going to do? Chase another boat? Another race? "Have you ever thought of coming back here? I mean, I know you liked it here."

"Oh, yeah, well, I had my reasons for liking it here." Erick pointedly looked at the screen. "But, well, … What can I do here?" He stopped for a second, but wasn't about to let Eliza get a word in. They had discussed this long ago. "You don't know my cousin Grant, do you? He's younger than us. He just graduated college. And he's got a job, a business manager for some regional company, I don't know. When he graduated I asked what he wanted to do. And he said he wants to retire and work as a docent at an aquarium taking care of turtles. It's a very specific wish. Working with turtles. I know it's an important job," Erick had seen the volunteers who sat on nests at the beach at the end of summers, "but that's his dream. He's already figured out what he wants to do in retirement, and he wants to do it when he's my age.

"I don't have any turtles to save."

Eliza didn't have an answer for that. She didn't know what Erick's dreams were, either. He never seemed to have any that were not more than three months out. Eliza wouldn't mind working at an aquarium taking care of turtles. "Do you ever think of working with your father?"

Erick looked at her for a moment. He had already discussed this with her, years ago. Even when he was a teen. "What, as a driver?" Erick started to say, "I don't have a deathwish," but stopped. That definitely wouldn't go over.

"And I'm not interested in selling cars." Erick then realized he planned to do exactly that, selling a boat design, to be raced. "Okay, maybe I'm a little hypocritical. And I know, I do love it here." he looked around the dark confines of the room.

Eliza watched Erick, his neck twisting in the dark. She caught the hint of light skin under dark, under the collar of his shirt. Erick looked scruffy, but his facial hair was still that golden blond she remembered. A cute nose that looked more afraid than curious, and green eyes that sparkled in the white light of the TV. Eliza had seen Erick stare out and dream with those eyes, wondering just what he was looking at. Whenever Erick did that, he had a soft smile just starting on his mouth.

"I know you do." Eliza smiled too. "Why don't you come back? You already have a home here."

"And do what? I'm not one to open an ice cream shop." Erick tried to lightheartedly mock the fun dream of moving to the beach and selling tie-dye shirts or running a burger stand. But he didn't want to scoff at anyone who did. Eliza had worked at an ice cream shop. "And, like I said, I don't have my turtle."

"Well, tell me what your turtle would be," this was getting somewhere for Eliza that she hadn't gotten Erick to go to before.

"I don't..." Erick started to say "I don't know," but he hated the expression when people used it for things they just hadn't thought about yet. He paused and said, "You know that old hammock I had on the back porch? That's probably it. Sit in that thing, drink ginger ale and Hawaiian Punch, eat a mango, and choose which foot I use to push the hammock to make it swing."

"That sounds perfect," Eliza gave Erick a small squeeze on the arm, then let go.

Erick's eyes twinkled again, Eliza saw them brighten. "I used to take the cat out over to the other side of the waterway," he nodded to the west, out in the dark across the beach road, "and just beach it on a smooth part of one of those islands. Then I would lay on the tramp and watch the stars, just to get away from the lights.

"You remember meeting Terrance, my old partner? We sailed onto Portsmouth Island once and slept on the cat. It was incredible. There is no light out there. None at all. You could see satellites going over and the Milky Way, and ships out on the horizon. Little spots of sea fleas glowing on the beach where they ate all the plankton. It was incredible. The world felt so big, and you're just a small part of it. A glowing bit of plankton in the sea. If I had to retire, I would want that, every night.

"That's my turtle."

Eliza saw Erick sparkle with a bit of happy joy. "He deserves that," she thought. Eliza wanted to ask more, like, "Do you want a family to share it with?" "Can you find that now, here?" and deeper down, "Am I in there somewhere, or was that all lost two years ago?"

"But that's not for today or tomorrow. I got to get through this storm, then get the cat finished, and then see if we can build it in higher numbers and sell it. That stuff's for later.

"How about you?"

Eliza wasn't ready for the question. She had only just started back at her career two years ago. There wasn't really much in the way of advancement academically, outside of getting tenure, and socially… "Listen to me," she thought, "I sound like Erick, all step by step business." The only thing she had accomplished was the new seafood watch cards, and that hadn't gone very far yet.

"I don't know," she admitted. "Wood's Hole is nice, and I like the research aspect. But saving turtles at an aquarium might be fun. Just where is your cousin now?"

"Ha, don't get your hopes up. So you don't want to come back here?"

Eliza had to think about that. There was a lot of emotion in the question. It wasn't just a cut and dry yes or no. "I love it here," she admitted. "It's certainly nicer for swimming, and I don't mind the mild winters. But I like being on my own," that didn't sound good, she thought, and tried to cover it up, "not having to deal with my parents' opinions. I love them, but I can't seem to do the right thing for them."

"Tell me about it," Erick sympathized.

Eliza wasn't sure who Erick might be referring to, his parents or hers.

"You could probably work at the aquarium here, get a job at Fort Fisher. Southport's nice." Erick thought that the cute little coastal town of Southport seemed like a nice place to live.

"You could… " Eliza stopped. Erick wasn't going to work at the fisheries. He wasn't going to run a jet ski rental. It was a weird feeling to have seen Erick do almost anything he tried to do, and then not know what he *could* do.

"Yeah… I could." Erick agreed to something that Eliza wasn't sure she had said. It was better than "No, I couldn't."

It was a start. The two sat in silence watching James Dean and Natalie Wood escape to an empty mansion to play husband and wife. Eliza pressed up against Erick and slowly rested her head on his shoulder as the storm began to wind up outside in the dark.

CHAPTER FIFTEEN

August 2001
Marlowe Beach

"Don't go."

It was what Eliza had said that night to Erick. The movie had ended with Jim and Judy getting the family they wanted, at the price of poor Sal Mineo's Plato biting the dust. But that was just the life of a teen. The screen went dark, then an introduction for the next film. Erick had gotten up to leave.

"It's only going to get worse tonight, and I'm finally a little tired." Erick had worried earlier in the evening about going to bed too early. Now it was 11 o'clock and getting later by the moment.

But Eliza asked so nicely, with those brown eyes in the dark, lit only by coming attractions for a Marx Brothers film, "Don't go. You can stay the night. If you want."

Erick had no desire to spend the night at Eliza's house when he had a perfectly good empty bed all alone in his dark old place. Erick thought for a moment, then realized his choices were limited. Go back out in the wind and darkness. Sleep over, in Eliza's parents' bed, or worse, her brother's. He certainly wasn't going to stay in her room. Of course the storm gods sent a howling wind and hidden lash of rain onto the back porch.

"I don't want to be alone in this wind, not tonight. Please."

"Okay," it was too easy for Erick to acquiesce. "Get me a couple sheets and I'll sleep on the couch."

Eliza had seemed both relieved and disappointed. It had meant that the evening was over. No more sitting on the couch for the two of them. She had stalled as much as possible, but Erick even turned the TV off and made the room black.

It was a fitful night, but Erick had slept on worse. And better.

Erick had gotten up early the next morning, even without the morning sun coming over the horizon. It was dark and still inside, with the shutters hiding the outside world. A lull in the storm meant Erick was in the clear for a moment. There would be no breakfast in bed, especially since there was no bed. He slipped on his clothes quietly, grabbed his jacket, and equally quietly slipped out the door without waking Eliza upstairs. It was not quite six o'clock in the morning, and the sky was still dark and gray.

Breakfast and a cup of very hot and strong coffee, along with a morning glance at the weather, "Outer bands are already lashing the South Carolina coast…" yeah, yeah, Erick could see that from the downstairs windows. He also saw the boat. "Damn." If he didn't go do something about that, the old wooden sailboat would float away, get caught in the reeds miles north, or get smashed to splinters on a dock somewhere. It was still worth saving. Or if nothing else, at least preventing trouble for others. No one deserved to have a boat jammed on their pier.

Erick felt the desperation hit him. Still tired, "I'm used to that," he tried to convince himself, he felt his face, with a couple days of stubble moving its way into a beard. Erick felt like he still had imprints from the sofa cushions' coarse texture printed on his face, too. He needed a shave and a shower. He settled for a quick trip to the bathroom instead.

A small but heavier band of rain swashed over the island. "I'll wait this out." If he went upstairs to close the rest of the shutters, it would kill a little time. Erick liked the idea. Back when he closed up the windows when the family vacationed here, before they moved in, before the air conditioning had been fitted, the house would become all hot and desperate. Erick remembered the days when he was young and they had to close up on summer nights when the thunderstorms hit. He'd kick the covers off and lay naked on top of his bed, sweating and restless as the house shook from the thunder.

By 8:00, one band of rain cleared, and the next followed. Hurricane Michelle was just offshore. Erick had to go take care of the boat.

Erick wandered out of the house, wondering if he should change out of the clothes he had on for the past two days. The crinkled linen shirt was meant to be a a casual dress shirt, not something to wear while working in the rain. But now was not the time to go through his limited clothing choices. Erick started walking down his driveway.

He had two choices.

He had three.

He had four…

"Okay, I have multiple choices," Erick sighed. He wanted to just go back to the house and watch the weather until the power went out, but that didn't seem like one of his choices right now, not soaking wet in a late summer rain that shouldn't be this cold on a warm day. He also wanted to wander over to Eliza's and see if she was up yet. But that didn't seem like a good choice either. Erick stopped and let the rain distract him. He sniffed. It was one of his favorite things about a hurricane.

The big storms came up from the tropics. No matter where they became a named storm or a hurricane, the low pressure would blow up from the tropics. It would snatch up palm branches and birds, and all the wonderful tropical smells that went with the warm Caribbean islands. Half was his imagination. Erick thought he smelled jerk chicken and conch fritters sometimes, but it was just the thick green smell of tropical plants and warm salted water that stirred his soul and called to him. Erick could close his eyes and see twisted dark wood and geckos on a porch, and a big blue bay loaded with sails. "I would have made an excellent pirate," he thought. "But I probably would have just bought a house in Tortuga and slept in a hammock and gotten drunk on rum every day." When he said it to himself, it didn't sound that bad. When he thought about actually doing it, he got restless.

He opened his eyes, and the rain stung him.

Erick stood in his driveway while he contemplated his choices. Okay, he could go close the shutters, wait out the rain, and then get the boat. Or get the boat and close the rest of the shutters. He could go back, close the shutters and leave. He could stay. He could… "What were the other choices?"

The rain began a little harder now. It still wasn't bad. Erick could stand in this all day, really. It beat a storm at sea. Most locals wouldn't even close their shops for this. At worst, someone might run to the car to get an umbrella they forgot.

The sun was now up, hidden behind the rolling clouds of rain and wind. It made the clouds a dirty mix of dark and light. Bright white clouds, wonderfully puffy, sleepy, that were cut by ugly dark gray swaths of gloom and storm. Erick looked up at them. They were wonderful creamy daggers of death and destruction that hinted at what was to come. They tried to stab at the puffy white clouds, but the white clouds easily parried and dodged. Floating up and away, escaping with their lives to brighten someone else's day somewhere far, far from here.

Erick was halfway down the drive before he realized he had made a choice. "The boat it is," he guessed. Crossing the street was easy; there wasn't a car to be seen. Surprising that no one was out now. He figured some fool would want to drive around in their pickup truck, "just to have a look around," they would explain later to the news crew. Or the tow truck driver. "Everyone already has their milk and bread," Erick joked.

"Nothing like a bowl of milkbread during a storm." He walked across the three lanes after looking both ways, a habit born of living in a tourist town.

His little peapod sat, none the worse for wear, just up the embankment, only feet from the rising water. Erick's mom still took it out for a row, or the occasional sail. Erick thought she did it because she missed him, missed his lessons he gave her, the times they spent together when he was younger. "She must have pulled it up with the trailer winch," he decided. His mom had seemed delighted to learn how to careen a boat.

She had taken it out once, years ago, while he was away at college. Then had tied it back up inside the boathouse when a storm came up. The little wooden boat was shaken on its lines and broken loose. It ended up being thrown against the pilings and dinged up. When Erick came home, she had apologized profusely, but Erick had just said, "It's alright, Mom. You did the right thing to tie it up. Now I get to do more work on it. Sometimes we do everything right, and it still goes wrong." He had spent a good part of his fall break repairing the broken gunwales and putting a new coat of lacquer on the little sailboat.

But ever since then, she wasn't willing to put it in the boathouse.

The water was already coming up on the boat ramp. It was only a few feet from where the sailboat rested on the grassy patch next to the concrete. Erick went in the boathouse to discover the lift wasn't working. That was probably another reason Erick's mom had left it out. "Great." He couldn't just leave it out on the bank. It would float away or get beaten on the dock.

The boat was about all he had left from when he was a kid. His cat had long ago been sold, replaced with faster craft, and then those were sold when he moved into the professional world. But the little peapod, that was special. He still loved the little thing. He had worked hard on her, and she meant something to him. He needed to do something.

CHAPTER SIXTEEN

August 2001
Marlowe Beach

"I shouldn't have let him go."

Eliza had woken up with a start. She had realized the time, after 8 in the morning, and Erick would have been wandering around the empty downstairs, puttering or watching TV. Instead when she went down, Eliza found the house empty. Even the sheets were nicely folded on a chair. Outside it was raining, she guessed, from the sound of the wind.

Eliza imagined Erick was back at his home, alone, too. Soon he would close up his shutters and his house would be as closed off as hers. Dark, sealed away from the storm, ready to ride out the worst of it, alone.

She sat around, listening to the radio, playing the dull sounds of oldies music. Someone at the station had decided that the Eighties were long ago enough to call them Oldies and begin playing the plainest of the songs, music that everyone had listened to because it was the music played the most on MTV. At least Eliza guessed that's what it was. Eliza didn't get to watch MTV very much when she was younger. Eliza made toast and an egg. It would have been wonderful to try to find a way to make it something fancy, but it was just toast and an egg.

Bored, sullen, feeling a little sorry for herself, Eliza went on the back porch first, but the wind and spray coated her. The ocean side porch was unscreened, just a couple slats to keep her and her brother from falling. In her brother's case, more likely, from jumping into the sand below.

The front porch was screened in. It had rocking chairs. And it faced away from the approaching storm. She could also see a little of Erick's house. Eliza could sit out there and wait until the hurricane got too bad, then she'd go inside, watch a little TV, wait for dark, and go to sleep, hopefully to sleep through the storm, and wake up early to an overcast sky clearing out to the north.

Instead she watched Erick walk across the street.

"Not smart enough to come in out of the rain," she joked to the winds. From this far she couldn't tell what he was doing, but she assumed he was going to store her boat. She was surprised he still kept it, but she was always glad he did. "Well, not always," she thought. Sometimes she had hated seeing the little sailboat, sitting there, tied up to the dock, alone, fading, unused. The stern had gone from glossy and clean to a murky and cheerless gloom. Eliza watched Erick take off his shirt. He was just a bit of a shape at this distance. It was too far to see him from the wet screen surrounding her porch all the way across the street in a rainstorm. He began pulling the boat toward the water, standing on the grass in his old Sperrys and shorts. Erick had looked cute in the Ocean Pacific shorts of their youth. The longer green shorts he wore now seemed unfairly grown up for him as he tugged the boat into the water.

Almost on cue, Erick took off first his shoes, then his shorts, to wade into the water in only some dark colored boxers that wrapped around his thighs. Erick went to one side of the sailboat and began to rock forcefully, splashing water in the boat. Eliza couldn't believe what she was seeing. He got out of the water, hefted a dull white sand bag, and tossed it unceremoniously into the boat.

With that, Eliza grabbed a raincoat, her mother's, from a closet and wandered out into the storm.

It was a rainy five minutes until she reached Erick, standing waist deep in ugly brown water that was churned from the bottom of the Intracoastal. He was leaning heavily on the side of the boat, pushing the gunwale down into the waves. Seeing Eliza appear in the rain like some spectral figure in a rain slicker, Erick stopped, let the boat bob slowly up from the weight of the water, and stared, wide eyed.

Eliza stared back. It was the first time she had seen him, like this, shirtless, in over two years. Eliza hid her face from Erick, a bare whisp of her wavy brown hair hanging loose from under a deep hood of her mother's rain jacket. Eliza hoped the hood kept her eyes hidden enough that Erick wouldn't see her stare. He was still fit as ever. Erick was always thin, trim, with broad firm shoulders, and a narrow waist. He, like any sailor, needed to find the perfect balance of being lightweight, but also strong and fit for his size. The wide shoulders and smooth chest were nothing like a football player or weightlifter, but he still looked almost perfect to Eliza. He had his late summer all over tan, the late summer blond hair, the all around good looks that still made her swoon a little. He looked exactly like he did when she first saw him at 16, only 14 years older, if that made any sense.

She stared at Erick, standing there, who looked a little dumbstruck at the woman in the raincoat who came to warn him to get out of the rain, like a ghostly wraith that walked the beach before a hurricane. He was almost perfect.

Except for the thin white gash that ran across his tanned chest. Eliza was glad the rain and the hood hid her eyes, because they looked crestfallen at the long thin scar, still there after two years.

"What?"

Erick called to her. He stood still, the only thing not moving in a whirlwind of little waves, raindrops, and a bobbing old sailboat. "What's wrong? You're looking at me funny."

Eliza shook herself from the misty sobriety she was in.

"What are you doing to *my* boat?"

CHAPTER SEVENTEEN

May 1999
Avalon, Catalina

"I've already given up going to Hawaii. You can't ask me to give this up, too."

Erick sat outside a rinkydink café in Avalon on Catalina Island, staring out at the bay, with lines and lines of floating mooring buoys, all in rows, like magical parking spaces for the boats that loved to do a day sail or a weekend trip to the quiet vacation island. Right now there were more masts than cabins on the water. It was the end of the evening for a race from Los Angeles, at the Los Angeles Yacht Club in San Pedro, to Catalina. Considering the trophy that sat alone in their room at the Hotel Atwater, a century old inn looking out over the bay at Avalon, Erick felt like there should be more happiness in his life at this moment.

He sat across from Eliza, looking stunning without trying. Her hair fell in long rings over her eyes in soft bangs. It only made her eyes more soft, more brown, as they sparkled in the last of the afternoon light before the sun went behind the mountains of the island. It would get dark quickly, but the lights of Avalon would twinkle on like lanterns, opening up the evening to the sailors that had come for the day and night. It wasn't a massive party town, not like Miami, or any other hard drinking port for sailors. It was a great place to wind down from the day, especially a long day of sailing, or waiting.

Erick had raced a two person cat across from Los Angeles in a blistering 4 hours, winning his class. Eliza had boarded the Catalina Express catamaran alone. While both boats were by definition multi-hulled, the two couldn't have been more different. While Erick soaked himself in the cold Pacific, the Express took only about an hour, blistering the time the sailboats took, and taking the passengers across in smooth, enclosed comfort. Eliza had unloaded the bags and checked in before Erick had probably left the harbor, she guessed. Eliza had looked out the window of the speedy passenger ferry but had barely caught a glimpse of any sailboats, and quickly bored of the open empty ocean.

"But do you have to go to Spain?" Eliza asked over bowls of milk white clam chowder in big, clunky ceramic bowls. At least it wasn't a giant round piece of bread. The Californians delighted in hollowing out a sourdough roll and dumping overly creamy clam chowder into the middle so that people could carry them around instead of having to do the dishes. She only stirred the chowder to let it cool. They always served it too hot. She was hungry, and the other options seemed so… Californian. Bison burgers, sushi, halibut, which was an amazingly boring fish that every restaurant couldn't seem to get enough of, and vaguely Mexican dishes that seemed to have all the fun taken out of them. At least she could get some tuna. She understood tuna. It was a universal fish, happy wherever it was. Especially in her tummy.

"It's the King's Cup Regatta," Erick tried to explain, but the names meant nothing to anyone outside the insulated clique of sailboat racing. Eliza rolled her eyes. She was tired of the names Erick threw out. She knew they were important to him, these races, but she just didn't see the importance to her. Erick saw her make a face, and tried to explain. "It's a race series in Mallorca. They have been bringing back the big fast boats in the past seven years. So many people are hot for the cats, and the big old monohulls will be there, too. If I go, I have a chance of making another international series. I don't have to be racing in Miami, or, or..." he waved dismissively at the tranquil harbor at Avalon, "this stuff."

Eliza suddenly felt defensive. She had just been dismissing the strange food of the California coast, so different from the flavorful and crunchy tastes from her home on the Atlantic coast, and now she was ready to speak up for the little town on the quiet island, perhaps because it was a gilded mirror of her own home town, so far away, but still similar. "What's wrong with 'this stuff?'" she mocked Erick's wave. "This is quiet, it's pretty, it's peaceful, it's not a bad place for a home."

Erick looked over the harbor, the boats bobbing at mooring buoys, the round white casino off in the distance. Then he turned, slowly, back to Eliza.

She had come with him to San Diego first to see him sail, then to Los Angeles, while he met with TransPac teams. He knew he needed to sail on the big monohulls when they did the long open ocean races from Los Angeles to Hawaii. If he sailed on a team, it put him in contention for a position in an America's Cup trial team. But his heart hadn't been in it. He preferred the fast cats, and the monohull racers had too often knocked the faster multihulls, ever since 1988 when a Stars and Stripes catamaran had fended off an America's Cup challenge from New Zealand's gigantic monohull.

Now here Eliza was, still here, with Erick. Eliza had never been more beautiful, he thought. He stared at her in the soft evening light, seeing her pleading brown eyes hidden under the loose ringlets of brown. Eliza hadn't changed since Erick had first seen her. She was taller, certainly, her eyes sparkled with a squint that was new, he had noticed, her skin was less taut in her twenties than at fifteen, but to him, she still looked perfect.

What Erick noticed most was that Eliza was there. In the seat, across from him, concerned, speaking out to him, asking him to make a choice. Eliza had given up part of her life so that they could be together. It was no small task what she had done. Erick had spent most of his adult life simply chasing the wind, with the freedom of knowing he always had a place to fall back. It didn't entirely matter that Erick acted like he didn't have the option to fail. Erick never wanted to go back, hat in hand, to his father, but in the back of his mind, he knew he could. Erick knew that the money, the house, the sponsorship, it was all there, either for the asking, or for the taking, no matter how much he swore he wanted to succeed on his own. Generational wealth was a blessing without a curse.

Falling in love was nothing but a curse.

Eliza had given up her time at Woods Hole as an instructor and scientist. She had taken a leave of absence and followed Erick to Miami, then to San Francisco, to San Diego, the Caribbean, now LA and finally to this tiny little village in the Pacific Ocean, to be sitting an arm's length across from him.

But Eliza had to make that choice, and do it both personally, and in a public way. Eliza had to give up her life, just starting out, too, like Erick's, to cope with a world that was not hers. Dealing with competitive sailors takes a thick skin, and many of them didn't even have that. They just lash out at each other, angry, ugly, behind the veneer of a beautiful sail and a summer wind. Erick had tried his best to separate his relationship with Eliza from the more coarse and ugly parts of the sport.

The other part of her choice was just as ugly. Eliza's parents certainly weren't happy with her chasing after a rich sailor kid with rich parents. This was the first time she had effectively said no to her father, and while Butch had not been pleasant, her mother was the one who brought in the shame. Dishonoring her father's wishes, living together before they were married, even though Eliza's father didn't want her to marry Erick in the first place, all the parental control came out when she announced she was taking a sabbatical.

She was supposed to come back to Bodin and take over her father's job, which somehow, with the rough and tumble men that ran the fisheries, their collective uncouth stares when she was a teen, the horrid misogyny and open discussion of spousal abuse, was somehow better than following her boyfriend to exotic locales and dealing with sunburned rich sailors who threatened to sue if a boat turned in front of them.

But Erick knew it took all her might to come with him, to leave her career, and especially defy her parents. He wouldn't dare ever tell Eliza what her brother and father had said to him the last time they met. It had been a dull threat, one only worthy of the base notion of men who were used to getting their way in the little town, but the comment "I think you should leave her alone" was followed by dark stares, the promise of dull violence from dull men who probably didn't know just who they were dealing with.

Erick had gotten around on his fists before; he had to, it was part of the sailor's creed, to protect your crewmates and ship, but he wasn't one who was quick to violence. Erick had hurt someone, bad, years ago, and had seen just what damage can be done, both physical and social. The other guy started it, and deserved most of what he got, but to Erick, no one deserved that much injury. He and his crew had made it clear to the guy that it was best left alone, not to pursue any issues, and the punk kid got the message through some well meaning but stern men.

So the one thing that Erick knew he couldn't do was get in a fight with Eliza's little brother and her father. Whether they beat the crap out of him, as seemed to be their unsaid promise, or he handled it all himself, there was no going back from a broken jaw or a concussion or spitting up blood by her father. Eliza wouldn't understand the basis of "He started it." No matter what, no matter how hard it had been for Eliza to move on from her family, their relationship would never survive that.

So Erick kept quiet, and Eliza made her choice, and now they were together on a beautiful bay looking out over the cooling air of the Pacific. Eliza was right, this was a beautiful place, a great place to retire and do nothing, just sit in a hammock, day sail, drink rum, grow a beard…

All the things that Erick may want to do. When he turned fifty. But not now.

"Look," Erick started again, "I… we…" he stammered, looking for an answer, staring at those deep brown pleading eyes, knowing that he should give in, but something else held him back. "I'll tell you what. The Palma races are a big deal, and I have already made commitments. I mean, there are going to be big names there, *big* names, with lots of money. If you let me do this, just let me see what comes of it, let me see what I can build from this." Erick didn't want to say that it might mean international travel, pulling her to all corners of the globe, but to Erick it might mean success, monetary success, to be his own man, not to have his fatherr show up to pay for every event or sail he needed. Then they could talk about a life of their own, free from their past. Erick wanted to say, "then we can talk about marriage," but he was afraid it would ruin the magic. It was too nice a night for something else that serious.

They finished their dinner with nothing decided except that they would walk around Avalon until late that night. "This is such a pretty place," Eliza sighed, holding Erick's arm in a twisted braid as they walked up St. Catherine Way in the dark. The lights cast a warm glow of yellow tungsten bulbs that only made its way onto the streets, but kept the skies dark. They made their way to the big round casino, a gathering place built by William Wrigley back in 1929. Eliza stared at the giant ornate structure, amazed at the intricate design. “So, they gamble here?”

Erick said, “No, it’s an Italian term. It just means a gathering place. It’s a dance hall and movie theater now, like the old Lumina was up in Wrightsville Beach.” The Lumina was a long gone dance hall on the coast up from their home. Eliza had often wished she could have gone dancing in a big dance hall like that, just the two of them, when they were young. She had to settle for roller skate nights and VCR parties.

Eliza stared up at the building, almost 12 stories tall, as it dominated the landscape of cute hotels and homes nestled into the mountainside town. This was so different from her home, so different from anything she had seen before.

In the distance, the noise from the bars in Avalon echoed with a distinct rowdiness of the sailors celebrating their wins or lamenting their losses. Eliza and Erick stood under the towering casino, drenched in the soft spotlights that lit up the building.

Then Eliza reached up to Erick’s neck and pulled him down to her mouth. She kissed him passionately, with her youthful abandon, wanting to crawl into his arms as he wrapped his hands across her waist and lifted her awkwardly to him. They didn’t care who saw them, because no one was looking. Everyone else had something else to do on the entire island. Erick and Eliza were alone, but together, a moment that was more than good enough. They didn’t want to let go, afraid of losing that moment. As Erick kissed Eliza, he took in all the senses that she poured out on to him. He knew her scent, not a perfume, but her, a warm sweetness that matched her tanned skin. Eliza’s breath was warm and heavy, feeling her begin to pant as she kissed, making a small gasp of air but afraid to remove her lips from his.

With almost a moment of sadness, Eliza pulled away, letting her forehead touch his before she slipped down his body as he released her and her feet touched the ground. The two intertwined their arms again, and without a word, began a too long walk back to their hotel, pausing only in the darkness between the light posts to kiss and nuzzle each other's necks.

They avoided the celebrations still going on as they snuck past tourists and sailing stragglers coming to and from the hotel to make it up to their room. Inside, the air was still and chilled from the near silent air conditioner on the wall. Neither bothered to turn the light on; they were intimately familiar with an intimate process. Eliza held Erick close, still dressed, warming herself to the heat radiating from his excited chest. Her fingers reached to unbutton his shirt, slowly, unwrapping Erick like a present she wanted to savor in the discovery. Undone, Eliza rested her cheek on Erick's chest, letting his tufts of hair tickle her. Eliza had become accustomed to the way his chest curved, the way her cheek and jaw and ear would nestle into the valley between his pectoral muscles.

Erick held her there, his hand softly tangled in her hair. Eliza sighed, a signal for him to release her as she looked up, soft eyes and red lips begging for her next kiss. Eliza gripped Erick more tightly this time, pulling him to her so that when their lips finally loosened, they came away with an audible smack. The darkness covered them. Only a pool of yellow light filtered through the window shade, but it was more than enough for the two lovers to guide themselves toward the more delicate, intimate, and desirable parts of their bodies, covered and unavailable to anyone else but each other.

Erick quickly undid his pants and kicked them off. It was the only indelicate part of undressing that they never found a way around, so Erick did it quickly while Eliza looked away. Then she unbuttoned her skirt and let it drop more ceremoniously; Erick always liked to see her move her small hips as she undressed. Eliza stood in silhouette as Erick admired her body. Every time he saw her, it was a mix of similar delight in the familiarity of Eliza's body, and a continual discovery of just how physically beautiful she was. Eliza's panties hung over her slim hips, almost as if magically staying in place, a bit of darkened lace placed just above her smooth abdomen and thin waist only partly covered by her loose shirt.

Eliza smiled happily. She could see Erick's face in the soft light. He still held a boyish visage of stunned amazement. It felt like a compliment over the thirsty lust that other men seemed to have. Eliza, conversely, couldn't help but stare at Erick in his tight boxer briefs, with an already significant bulge stretching out the front. Eliza stepped toward Erick, her hand sliding down his chest toward his growing erection.

Erick slipped his hands around Eliza's waist, then lifted her shirt over her head. Her short hair, in curls and waves of salted stiffness, tousled as she lifted her arms. She grinned, knowing it was another of Erick's rituals that he loved as he uncovered her body.

They nestled together again. Eliza felt Erick's warmth, along with his erection pressing against her, a more sexual moment than just romantic. He turned Eliza around, holding her at the waist from behind, then moving his hands up to her bra to undo the snaps. Eliza held it, her arms crossed, for a moment as if to deny him the view of her small breasts, then dropped it to the floor. Erick kissed her, hard, on the back of her neck, his tongue licking at her shoulder. Eliza felt her knees weaken from the kiss. It was a release, as if a message, to send an end to any tension she had. It was the first notion of permission that she, and her willing body, gave to Erick, who always waited for that moment. He kissed her below her hairline, then slowly began tracing a line in the darkness down Eliza's spine, lower and lower. Erick let his tongue carve a path of esses down her spine until he got to her lower back.

Eliza waited for the moment. She knew Erick would get where he was going on her body, but the price was the pace, a slow and wonderful promise that he would get there. He always did. Eliza leaned forward, arching her back and offering herself to Erick, while taking his hands and placing them on her breasts, another permission given.

Erick kissed her, lower and lower, until he finally made it to her panties, where he pulled them down low enough to find the base of her spine. The nerves tangled and tingled there for Eliza, but with Erick's patience, she was now ready as he kissed her, holding her hips tightly as she slowly wiggled.

Eliza turned and removed her panties, then quickly tugged down Erick's boxers, his erection springing out. It was enough teasing for her, enough foreplay. Erick could find a way to explore Eliza for hours if she let him, so she pushed him to the bed, then jumped over him to lay next to his nearly naked body. Erick immediately began caressing her thighs, waiting for the next part of their ritual. They kissed as Erick trailed his fingers, up and down her inner thighs, higher and higher, until Eliza lifted her hips. It was her sign that he could touch her. It only took moments for Eliza to be ready, and she pulled Erick by the shoulders over on top of her.

Most of the hotel would be out still celebrating, but the few that were in for the night would understand the noises coming from the room. Everyone was having a great time, some in different ways than others. Young men would laugh, knowing nods to each other after having seen Erick's beautiful skinny girlfriend, as they honored his conquest with sly high fives and gratuitous comments. The older sailors would have their own remarks, kept to themselves, knowing both the need for sexual release and the great fortune to have someone special to love. Many of them knew both that feeling and the loss of not having someone special in their lives.

Inside the room, Erick and Eliza finally lay next to each other, asleep, exhausted, Erick still in his shirt.

CHAPTER EIGHTEEN

August 2001
Marlowe Beach

Erick almost laughed at Eliza as he flexed and pushed down on the gunwale again. This time he flinched, stopped, and exhaled an exhausted breath.

"I'm going to sink her.

"It's the only way I could think of to save her."

Eliza looked dumbfounded. "So you're going to *sink* it?"

Erick shrugged, his shoulders flexing under the pressure of the boat. "I'm going to flood her and let her settle to the bottom. That way she won't float away as easily. And when the hurricane passes, I'll pull her up and pump her out."

"Won't all that water be bad for it?"

"I can fix her. It might take some effort, but it will be worth it." Erick lugged two more sandbags out into the shallows, splashing up to his waist, and threw them in. "It's better than seeing such a good boat get lost in a storm." He proceeded to tip over the gunwale again. This time water flowed in more freely. The little sailboat was tippy. The rounded hull made the boat great for sailing in light breezes, but unstable as it keeled. The boat bounced back, and Erick put more pressure on the gunwale.

Eliza bit her lip under the mask of her hood pulled over her face. She saw Erick strain, his muscles flex in his shoulders. She would have under other conditions found the scene surprisingly sensual. Erick with his strong shoulders, narrow waist, not overly muscular in some scary way, but fit, athletic. It was one of the more baser moments of their times together when Eliza would watch him take off his shirt to move or lift something. She had forgotten that feeling for the past two years.

And now it meant something else. Eliza couldn't take her eyes off the thin white scar that cut across his tanned chest. All she thought now was that she hoped nothing bad would happen to him.

"Do you…" she didn't know if she could even wander out into that water, "do you want any help?"

"Ha!" Erick laughed, showing his smile, white shark teeth, but with no threat behind them. Eliza almost relaxed seeing him smile at her. "Not unless you have an extra swimsuit on." He nodded at her jeans, which were getting soaked in the rain. "No, I can do it. It's my problem, anyway, you shouldn't have to fix it."

"Well, you did help with my windows," Eliza pointed out.

"It's not really the same," Erick stopped for a moment, taking in the temporary reprieve of his little boat sinking. "This is a big task." He pushed once, and this time the boat flooded, filling with sound water before beginning to settle. Erick fell backwards, avoiding the little boat sinking onto his legs, and watched it as it settled about two feet onto the soft muddy bottom. Then he stuck his head under the water and pulled up a rope. Erick trudged silently up to the shore and tied the line to a large piling on the pier. Even if the dock was washed away, the pilings would stay. “She’s not getting away from me easily, I’ll tell you that,” Erick said as he tied off the line.

Eliza met him at the water’s edge to help him out. “I’m good,” he waved off her hand. “I’m a little filthy,” Erick joked, smelling himself. “This sound water, and all that muck,” he pointed at his bare feet, now soft and covered in silt from being in the shallow water.

Eliza didn’t care. “Compared to a commercial fishery, you’re probably a field of flowers.” She tried to use it as an excuse to get close and pretend to smell him. Eliza remembered how Erick smelled, always with a hint of cologne, woody, or sometimes the sharp aquatic green scents. He did it to hide the continual odors of a dock or sailboat, with the dense creosote and diesel that permeated the marinas. “Just a little splash,” he used to say, and always ask if it was too much.

Either it was too windy, or the scent had washed off, or Erick just didn’t do that anymore. Eliza noticed nothing. But the wind was blowing away from her. It frizzed her hair and made her hood flap. Eliza was getting soaked as the rain continued to blow. The wind was not letting up, but getting worse.

Erick walked away, over to the boathouse, without looking at her, leaving her standing alone in the rain. Eliza had reached out to him, literally, and he had gone the other way. Suddenly she felt cold and alone. The rain was beginning to bite, soaking into her shoes and jeans. Eliza turned and left. Her mind told her to go home and get out of these clothes to dry them. To change into something else that she didn’t mind getting wet. The back of her mind told her something different.

Escape. Before he came back out and she had to face him.

Eliza turned and walked up the road to her driveway.

CHAPTER NINETEEN

August 2001
Marlowe Beach

Erick had seen Eliza try to get close to him as he climbed onto the embankment. He was dirty, wet, and smelling of that permeating swamp odor that the shallow brackish water carried. If Erick wanted to get close to her, if he wanted Eliza to get close to him, now was definitely not the time or place. Not in the middle of a rainstorm that was continually stinging his bare chest. And especially not standing nearly naked in only his workout boxer briefs. There was no one out in the rain, but the last thing Erick wanted was some guy in a big truck to drive by and see him in his underwear sharing intimate glances with his ex-girlfriend.

That wasn't exactly true. The last thing Erick wanted was to share an intimate glance with his ex-girlfriend.

"That's not entirely true, either. Is it?"

Storms brought out the loneliness in the minds of lonely people. Erick knew that all too well.

Erick went into the boathouse to gather his dry clothes and a towel. At least he would be semi-decent and have a chance to wipe off the grime and most of the sound water. Erick just paused for a moment. "This is not what I wanted," he said out loud. With the storm winds picking up, and the door closed, he knew Eliza would not hear him. What did he want? Or, what didn't he want? Eliza was at least trying to be, what, decent, nice, that old ex girlfriend who ignores the past and tries to be friends? "Yeah, I definitely don't want that," Erick shook that fear out of his head. He wasn't going to be happy knowing Eliza had moved on, that she's engaged or had a guy up in Massachusetts, or worse, dating some local that "kinda remembered" him from high school.

Erick stood still thinking, unaware of his place in the lonely boathouse. He stared at the water washing underneath the walls as it splashed through the empty slip. It was gray, with flecks of shining white where the little whitecaps rushed into dark shadows. It looked like an old mirror that had lost its silver. Erick stared, empty eyed, through the water as he drew pictures in his mind of Eliza and other women in rapid succession. Suddenly, with a start, his vision cleared from the purple myopia of staring at an empty spot in the boat slip. Erick's arms were above his head, resting on the towel that he used to try to wring out the icky sound water from his hair. Erick had just stood there, in his briefs, letting himself dry in the breeze. He remembered he had left Eliza in the rain without a word.

Erick quickly dried his shoulders and chest. He ran his hand over the long scar that went across him diagonally. It still was disappearing, thankfully, but it was always more prominent when he had a tan and when he was wet and his skin was soft. Eliza had never seen it before. It was probably a bit of a shock to her.

Erick dressed quickly, threw the towel over his head, and went back out into the rain. He would have to shower and change after sinking his boat.

When Erick came out, Eliza was already halfway up her driveway, with her back turned to him. She stood out in the rain like a ghostly little sprite. There were legends on the beach of a man who walked the shore, dressed in an old rain slicker, who came up to people and wordlessly warned them of an approaching storm. Eliza in her bright yellow raincoat, its hem flaring out like a little skirt as she clutched the front closed, looked like some rad neon 80s variant on the genre. Only this time the spirit looked more like a wraith walking away from its victim.

"At least this time I get to see her walk away," Erick thought, standing alone in the rain.

CHAPTER TWENTY

June 1999
Palma

Eliza lay on the coarse sand of Platja de Ca'n Pere Antoni, adrift in a sea of people foreign to her. The beach was a popular spot in the old section of Palma, La Seu, the huge cathedral that was central to the city, as well as the big open tourist port. Across the water stood the Porto Pí lighthouse. To her back, past the big retaining wall, and just beyond the wide shore city road, stood towering palm trees, stately enough to give the city with its Spanish and Moorish history an even greater flash of the exotic. Just past them, towering over the impressive trees, were the resorts, edifices of rectangular extravagance, where the wealthy and pretend wealthy came to play or be feted by hoteliers that fawned over their guests with a regal countenance.

Eliza had been here a week, and was still both in awe and severely uncomfortable with the place.

The beach was beautiful, she had to admit that. The water was clear and shallow, warm, almost shockingly so, even for Eliza who was used to the heated summer of the Gulf Stream churning like a salted freight train just outside her family's beach house door. The air was hot with bright sunny days all week long. With the yellow sun and blue sky, Eliza found it sometimes unbearable, until she realized that most of the visitors and locals hid from the heat of the midday. She wondered if the priests had prayed for a cloud and ever got one.

But the sand was sharp and gritty. It reminded Eliza of the fake beaches put up in mountain lake towns so that the sand wouldn't get washed away. It was too pebbly for her. Eliza couldn't nestle her toes deep into it like the old yellow sand on Marlowe Beach. There were no shell fragments, no bits of polished sea stone, no microscopic cubes of glinting quartz nor opaline shine from an oyster shell flake. It was just as if someone had put a beach there, and then left.

The palm trees were tall, too tall. The fronds swayed in the occasional breeze, dusting the sky like feathers on a wand. They provided the color to the tropical beach feel. And occasionally the shadows did chase so slowly across the shore, but the respite was short lived. The trees were pretty, wildly exotic in a way that made the coastal palmettos of her home seem plain in comparison, but they were too few in number. It was unnatural to have the giant trees so sparsely growing, so well manicured.

Across the bay, through the sea of masts that littered the harbor where hundreds of sailing boats moored, Eliza saw the lighthouse, the Porto Pí. It was a short, stubby little thing, a rectangular box on its end with a church steeple point where the light would be. It barely cleared the horizon across the water with all the sailboats in the way. Again, it was nothing like the towering lights of her coast. Cape Lookout on an abandoned and empty shore would stare down at the diminutive harbor light, and Cape Hatteras, with its black and white candy stripe, would make the little Porto Pí seem like nothing more than a storage shed.

And the people. Eliza kept having to remind herself that she was the one out of place, not the other way around. Eliza had a darkened summer tan, enhanced by the week in Palma, and her skin was naturally a slight olive cream, never truly pale even in winter. But the locals and tourists were all brown, with rich raven black hair. The men oozed a confident masculinity that made her profoundly uncomfortable, which was only made worse by their lascivious stares at the long dark haired women with long legs and curved hips so different from Eliza's sandy brown curls and boyish figure. Eliza had worn colorful board shorts and a bikini top, which even that was a daring risk to her personal modesty, but felt out of place as the women walked by confidently in black bikinis, and then the men in their small Speedos did, too.

It was such a different world. Eliza had expected it to be a little like Myrtle Beach with the grand hotels and tourist attractions, with some old history, sort of like what she had seen in San Diego the month before. But this was more like a fancy movie set of the Riviera mixed with Las Vegas tinsel and flash. The whole setting made her uneasy.

The language barrier had haunted her. Eliza knew little to no Spanish, and what she heard was thick with strange syllables and sounds, unlike the chatter of the waiters at the U.S, Mexican restaurants. Her father had continually commented that they should speak English when he heard them talking to each other, but he would put on a pretend Spanglish and say "Gray-see-as" with his thick drawl. But here, everyone spoke a distinct flowing Spanish, thick with their tongues softening the esses into th's. Eliza understood none of it, and was confused by the rich Spanish food and the copious amount of red and burgundy wine that people consumed.

Erick had helped, or at least attempted to help. He guided Eliza to pick food she would like. Milder dishes without the strange earthy sweetness that so many spices gave each meal were the choice of the day, each day, as she slowly took risks with some food. Often Eliza pecked at Erick's plate, who offered to switch with her, every evening. She finally agreed and found the food to her liking. It was about the only thing she had succeeded in embracing.

Eliza had asked about the names, where platja de C'an Pere Antoni came from, or what was La Seu. Erick explained that platja was just the Spanish word for beach, and c'an is just house. "It just means it's the beach by Father Anthony's place," Erick had shrugged when Eliza asked who Father Anthony was. "Who knows?" After a while, she gave up on the translations, especially when Erick had to be gone for longer periods of time.

What should have been a romantic week in an exotic summer vacation city off the coast of Spain had turned into an exercise in loneliness. The only thing that mitigated it for Eliza was that she suspected Erick felt the same way, too. He would come back from his meetings, or the training sailing, tired, and slightly edgy. He never complained to her. Erick kept it quiet and bottled up, but Eliza could tell there was something not right about the whole event. Erick was never happier than when he was sailing, or on the beach, or just under a summer sun. Eliza had seen how Erick lit up as soon as they crossed over a bridge, or set foot on a dock. But that wasn't him now.

He had finally spilled it, at least as much as he could for Erick. "These new 40s are brutal," he exclaimed, laying on the bed one evening after a final practice. The racing community had begun a new series of catamaran races with 40 foot long foam and carbon rigid cats and trimarans in the past few years, and the boats had come into their own with massive speeds. They had also proven to be problematic with control, living on a ragged edge of containment by the crew. But Erick had expressed a more personal problem. "These crews, these sailors, we've got five people per boat, all moving in unison. When one of them slips, everyone else gets the shi…" he paused, knowing Eliza didn't like his colorful sailing brogue, "crap ripped outta them.

"And these guys are cutthroat. I've never seen so many men just ready for a fight. Sailing has always had that douchey element," he wasn't sure if that was offensive to Eliza, but let the word slip into his rant, "but usually, well, it's honorable. As long as we aren't sailing against those New Zealanders." Eliza never understood Erick's dislike of the Kiwi sailors, but then she never asked, and didn't really care. "I've never been on a dock where so many people are aching for a fight. We might as well go out there with sloops and cutlasses."

Eliza let the rant go. Erick had been nothing but diligent in his duties to her when he had the time. The times were getting shorter and shorter, closer to the weekend with the races coming up. And he had been meeting with teams, with builders, and sponsors. Erick was creating some interesting new ideas in the sport, and his pedigrees, both as a Sunstrom and as a sailor, were drawing interest. Eliza had been a little surprised when Erick had introduced a representative from one of his father's car companies to her, and even more surprised that it was a strikingly beautiful severe blonde woman only a few years older than Erick.

Eliza felt the growing heat of midday as she watched the regular beach goers, along with several new weekend visitors, gather up their towels and head for the comfort of the cool resorts, ready to wait out the hotter part of the day. Eliza had less time. She needed to be at the marina in two hours. It wouldn't take long to get there. Erick would begin the heats later that afternoon, and sail into the sunset.

By 2:30, Eliza was dressed up and standing under the shade of Erick's VIP canopy, along with a few other women, spouses and girlfriends of the crew. There were few of either, she realized. The skippers liked to leave their wives at home, or in the casinos, or the resorts. The younger sailors Erick's age preferred to chase the local women that came out to look at the handsome and fit sailors. Eliza had long ago forgone the rites of jealousy of those moments when the sexy and provocative women in short dresses or barely there San Tropez coverups would flirt with Erick. He always would disembark, his head down not to make eye contact, pretending he didn't hear them call out the first time, and then with a wry lopsided smile, he'd give them an "aw shucks, thanks" grin, very American, almost cowboy, which seemed to both turn off half the women and charm the other half into desiring him more. But he would go to work, stowing lines, or carrying a bag with almost nothing in it, just to cover his head, until he found her. Then Erick would drop whatever he had and pick up Eliza and swing her around, a banner for everyone to see, even though he never looked anywhere else but at her. That was usually when the women went off for more easy prey on other boats.

But now Erick was at work, and Eliza was again alone in a sea of people. While Erick was out on the water warming up the crew before the first heats of the afternoon, Eliza stood around on the scaffolding seating under a sponsor's banner. Big names in European fashion littered the marina. Watches seemed to be big in sail racing, with Breitling, TAG Heuer, and Rolex all bringing sponsorship in one way or another. Eliza wondered where her Swatch was that she had ten years ago. Clothing brands were also plastered across the boats and sails, with Tommy Hilfiger, Nautica, and Sperry showing up. Eliza noted the one striking automobile manufacturer, BMW, sporting its racing colors on an otherwise clean white sail. It was noticeable especially to her because of Erick's family history with some of the European builders, and also because of the severe blonde woman who occasionally stared her down from behind large dark glasses. Erick had introduced Eliza to her as Alina Auffenberg, a sponsorship official who had worked with his family some, and with him back in 1995 during the races in Miami. After the terse greetings, Auffenberg had done nothing more than occasionally glare from afar at Eliza. She chalked it up to some Teutonic stoicism on Auffenberg's part. Eliza still felt slightly uncomfortable around the tall German. Auffenberg certainly had the look down pat, with long severe blonde hair, cold blue eyes, and an athletic build that looked more like the sailors on the marina than sultry feminine. The other sailors didn't seem to mind, and paid her attention until they, too, got a cold shoulder from the woman. She was a few years older than Erick, but seemed almost motherly compared to Erick's youthful exuberance.

Eliza was glad the woman didn't bother to engage in any chitchat. Auffenberg frightened her, just a little.

Eliza noticed that the older sailing skippers, normally rough and coarse, some would try to describe them as salty, even were quieter with their colorful and vulgar talk around Auffenberg. Erick had said to chalk it up to her being the money person, and you don't anger the sponsors.

Eliza took a cold ice water, waving off the proffered champagne, to watch the beginnings of the race. Eliza felt like she should have taken a glass, as the sparkling drink was the main sponsor of the boat Erick sailed, but it was too hot, and she hadn't liked how the alcohol and bubbles made her feel. Eliza wished she could just get a Coke.

Eliza sipped the cold water, and someone handed her a pair of small binoculars so that she could watch the race better. A man, one of the private sponsors, "the money," as Erick and others would say in whispers long after they walked by, smiled graciously as he handed the binoculars and let his hand drift down her back before Eliza stepped forward to avoid more intimate contact. It was another thing that Erick had taught her. It was also another thing that had made Erick upset. She had seen him shiver inwardly at some of the men he met, and had quickly led her away at the few social business meetings they had attended together. After the second time, Erick had just suggested she go out on her own, or stay at the hotel.

The man seemed to take the hint, but still lingered nearby, as he said, "Class flag is up!" Everyone stepped forward to the end of the stand to watch. Eliza used the moment to slip away and go to the other side of the VIP suite. She was closer to Auffenberg, but father away from the groping hands of "money."

Eliza knew there was still five minutes to go, so she waited in the background. Eliza was neither sponsor or "money." She wasn't even a wife or a team member. Just a girlfriend. Eliza waited until she heard the one minute horn, a long wailing blast, then worked her way to the corner of the stand. She found Erick's sail in the midst of a flurry of masts and cloth, standing out with its notable green and champagne sunny yellow. Eliza watched the tip of the masts as the boats raced to a bubbling starting line, only visible to those on shore by the two big buoys marking the edge lines. Erick's boat was near the front, and moving fast. A short horn sounded, and Erick's boat crossed the line, behind two others, but moving faster up the outside.

CHAPTER TWENTY-ONE

June 1999
Palma

With the one minute horn sounding, Erick felt like they were in a decent place in the midst of the fleet of 40 foot catamarans and trimarans that battled for position at the start of the race. His boat, as every sailor had to think of the boat as "his" boat, was fast, but ragged. Erick could run it faster than any other boat on the water. The problem was that almost all of the boats out there could run faster than the others, if they found the wind first or best.

"Pressure starboard," Erick said in a deep, low voice. He kept his head down, speaking to the wheel. Erick was the driver, a deft and proven hand on the wheel of the big cat. He only looked up to see how the sail was filling. Erick didn't want to draw any attention to where he looked. He simply glanced up at the big green and gold sail with the sponsor logo of a stylized champagne bottle. La Couverture Verte was a new

French champagne vineyard. The wealthy owners wanted to promote their product and cru, so they bet on plastering a banner all over the sailing community and its rich clientele. The main issue Erick had was that they insisted the team be made of as many French sailors as possible. With an international sport, and many of the better sailors already on crews, it meant a limited number of men to choose from. It also meant that Erick had to deal with a crew that didn't speak English very well. They had also not appreciated his rather limited attempts at communication with his college level Frenglish.

The cat had been under the helm of Jean Laurent Fleury, who now was the team tactician. He began to respond to Erick's soft but determined comment on approaching wind, but then stopped, and said instead, "Good eye." Fleury had been the driver, the helmsman, as well as the tactician, which meant he handled the boat's helm and made decisions on tactics and overall strategy of the race. He had taken a poor team and turned it into a mediocre one, driving up from the back of the pack to middling. The cat was edgy, fast, but hard to put on the ragged edge, especially while trying to keep an eye on both the competitors and the wind. Erick had been made helmsman after he vastly outperformed the other tryout, a bow crewman/trimmer. Erick had also outperformed Fleury. It was an easy decision by the money people to put Erick on helm as the driver, but it had not sat as well with the French crew who had wanted one of their own on the wheel.

They still performed, and the tension eased some when Erick started winning the occasional heat. He took the once last place boat, then middling, and put it consistently in the top three. The sponsors didn't want to hear any griping when their logo was nestled in between major clothiers and watchmakers on camera.

Erick wasn't concerned about that now. The boat was moving, going well, and fast. He had seen more wind from starboard, and had aimed his cat toward the edge of the starting line, tracking just inside the committee boat with thirty five seconds left before start. The other boats battled in the middle of the fleet, trying to find the wind while positioning themselves near the portside pin that marked the inside starting line. Already the protest flags flew, along with the calls of "Protest" coming from the boats. Erick had kept his boat clear of most of the mess, especially from the Australians and the New Zealanders. They still seemed to harbor some animosity toward any Americans for the slights at the America's Cups back in the 80s. Erick gave the Kiwis a particularly wide berth, not letting them pick a fight, while forcing them to tack away or lose wind.

The boats would mostly aim for the inner line, nearest to the first mark based on the general direction of the approaching winds by a few feet. But what they earned in distance they would give up in speed. The slight starboard shift, barely a hint of slate in the shining water of the bay, meant that Erick was running closer to the wind, now in fourth or fifth place, with a wide open line to the start. By the time the Kiwis were able to respond by turning to take the position, Erick was running fast, with his sails filling in first on a fast tack. His cat began to make speed, passing the other boats far to his port. Fleury counted down, and the short horn sounded a second before Erick took the start line. He was in third place, and by far the fastest boat in the fleet, taking the lead by the first tack and flying a hull to the first mark.

Erick had passed the fleet on the outside, and could now control the race, covering off any tacks by the other cats. Erick put the second place boat, the Kiwi trimaran, behind him. Fleury looked at Erick and simply smiled a smirk through thin zinc covered lips. Erick had made Fleury look good, and the Frenchman wasn't going to complain in either English or French.

After La Couverture Verte took the finish line in first place for the heat, the champagne flowed at the dock. Erick and Fleury took their congratulations quickly, and left for a more intimate conversation.

"We won't be able to do *that* again," Erick said.

"I'm impressed we were able to do it once," Fleury felt like he had just found a thousand francs on the floor of a casino and hoped no one had seen him pick it up.

Erick shrugged. "We get another chance for points," the heats gave the teams points, which qualified them into the finals, with only three of the teams competing. "We beat the Kiwis in the tri, no matter where we finish, and we'll point into the finals. It might be a good idea to get into the mix and see what we can do as a team. We have speed, but we are just so unbalanced compared to that tri. They can run fast and safe."

"They make me nervous," Fleury said. He hadn't liked the rough hewn celebrations throughout the week. The Kiwis were holding up their end of the deal by drinking and celebrating into the night on off days, but Fleury didn't like anyone who couldn't hold their drink and behave civilly. His sunburned forehead was normally taut and smooth, but this time it furrowed into red rows, leaving pink lines as he relaxed.

Erick laughed. "Hey, they don't call it break gear for nothing!" Erick had little concern with roughing it up in the mix of boats before the start, as long as he got a chance at the open air. "You'll keep us filled in, and we will have a good shot at the cup."

The second race started about the same way as the first, except that the cats were more spread apart, and favoring the starboard line near the committee boat. Fleury had the cat running well up the middle of the pack while others jockeyed for a tight run to the first mark, still leaning toward the short line. The Kiwis and their big trimaran attempted to cover off Erick's boat.

Erick had to heave to, putting the boat almost at a standstill, when the Australian boat had cut across their path. Fleury flew a protest but there was little likelihood of anything being called. There was no impact, and Erick and the trimmers got the sail filled and cat moving, losing three positions. Erick ran his cat below and alongside the Australians, as some glared and cursed. But they could do nothing else. The Aussies were ahead, and any move they made would make them lose speed and position. Erick looked again to starboard, but the line was so well set that it was directly perpendicular to the first mark. Fleury saw the glance and ordered a tack, sending the cat swiftly moving across the Aussies' wake with ten seconds left. The Australians could counter, but it would put them at a slower pace as soon as they got to the line. They both would lose speed and position. The horn sounded, the Australians crossed the start on a tight line to the first mark, in second, behind a surprise push by the Cartier team in first place. Near the committee boat, the Kiwis crossed in third, almost virtually tied with Erick's La Couverture Verte on an opposing tack.

The race was on.

Fleury immediately ordered a tack as soon as they were in open water. He wanted to have the cat going in the same direction as the other boats. They were on a starboard tack, while the Cartier team and the Aussies ran off to port. The Kiwis were quickly bearing down in front of Erick's cat, which meant they would have to bear off anyway. An open run, with all boats on the same tack, would mean an interesting turn at the buoy, but if Fleury got around the first mark, they could run down the Cartier boat, and hopefully run away from the Kiwis. A second, and a finish above the New Zealand boat, would assure a start in the finals, which the team and sponsors desperately wanted.

"Come about," Fleury said as softly as he could over the rushing water and wind, in English, before shouting "Paré à virer!" loudly across the cat. The crew came alive, running across the mesh trampoline as spray kicked up. Erick and Fleury accomplished the tack before the Kiwis had time to respond, even if they wanted to.

Ahead by less than a boat length, the Kiwis kept to their own tack, which meant the two would either race to the first mark or the Kiwis would tack away. Fleury knew they wouldn't do that. The Kiwis wanted to rob La Couverture Verte of her wind. But the tack had been so sudden and fast that the French boat got clear air. Erick put her up on a hull, with the crew already climbing the flying hull, hiking out and gaining speed. The Kiwis tried to tighten their port tack, but it just slowed them, making the New Zealanders pass just astern of a distancing La Couverture Verte with its crew standing as if at attention as they sped away from the frustrated Kiwis. A protest flag went up, but was immediately waived off by a pursuing committee boat.

Erick made for the first mark, ready to turn to port and do a fast downhill run with a freshening wind. If the Aussies had any issues with their turn, they would be in Erick's grasp. But Fleury reminded Erick to make a clean and clear pass. The Cartier boat and the Aussies had right of way, and anything they did to slow down La Couverture Verte would put them in the grasp of a now angry group of Kiwis.

Erick took the order. Fleury was right. They were in a good position, and didn't need a skirmish with the New Zealand boat. They certainly had a good third place, possibly second, and maybe another win if the Aussies made a mistake. The Australians rarely made any errors, but anything could happen in a sailing race, especially at these speeds. Erick took a slightly wider turn, to make sure he made no contact with the first marker buoy. It cost him distance, but he kept the cat moving, and it launched away, the sails filling in with a snap before the squirrel crew member helped run out the big spinnaker. It filled with a dull pop, and the whole boat leapt forward, distancing itself from the still turning Kiwis. The downhill run would be fast. There was no chance of catching the Aussies or Cartier. All the boats got the wind at the same time. It also meant that they would lose no distance, either. It would be a tacking battle on the next upwind leg that would decide the race.

Everyone held position on the windward run. The backmarkers hunted for gusts before the front runners would get them, hoping for even a gain of feet and seconds, but with no luck. The boats would run to the next windward marker, where Erick would spin his cat sparingly around the big bobbing buoy before running out another starboard tack. Speed was key, as well as a bit of risk. Or, in Erick's case, a lot of risk. He had to let the cat fly, but to do that he needed room on the water. The wide starboard tack would free him from the Kiwis, who would either follow on their own tack or more likely turn closer to the mark but give up speed. Which was exactly what they did, earning less distance to the next mark but at a slower time.

Fleury watched them intently as Erick kept La Couverture Verte flying on a low risen single hull. As soon as the Kiwis tacked, Fleury ordered the response. Now the two boats were coming at each other, with La Couverture Verte in the right of way, only a few boat lengths ahead, but flying a high hull on a long run. They would have to tack once more, then take the turn to a final downward leg to the final buoy and then the finish. If they could just hold off the Kiwis on this turn, they would have third place secured.

La Couverture Verte raced to the center of the course, with the New Zealand boat aiming for the same spot, only a few seconds behind them, but from the opposite direction. As they got close, Fleury made a point to wave off the Kiwis, noting his boat's right of way. "Come about when they get to our wake," he told Erick, who already knew the plan.

"Paré à virer!" Fleury shouted just as the Kiwis came behind them. He wanted to turn into the New Zealand path, forcing them either to slow or to tack. The Kiwis did neither. The New Zealand boat surged into the position of La Couverture Verte, forcing Erick to let go of pressure and turn back toward port. It slowed his boat massively, but he and the trimmers pulled the sails, taking in more wind and lifting the boat again, moving fast. But when speed was lost, it could never be made up. The Kiwis had distance and their mast well ahead of Erick's boat. Fleury immediately flew a protest flag, and the committee boat flew a penalty to the Kiwis.

It wouldn't matter, Erick knew. The Kiwis would be forced around the buoy in penalty, but there was no way La Couverture Verte would be able to catch Cartier, now in second behind a superbly flying Australian team. Out of spite, it seemed, as the Kiwis now were yelling over the sea as if they could be heard, the New Zealand boat immediately turned another tack and cut off the wind to La Couverture Verte. Erick adjusted his line, but now he would be too close to the mark, and would have to tack again. Fleury sighed, "Come about. Paré à virer!" He saw the glaring and gestures of the Kiwis, and just wanted to get in without a fight on the water. He would take the upwind mark while the New Zealanders circled it in penalty, then run to the finish and worry about the consequences in the steward's booth. The Kiwis were cooked after that move, anyhow.

Erick pointed out the Kiwi protest flag. "Look," he pointed with his shoulder, as he kept two hands steady on the wheel. "Great, they're racing under protest." Fleury answered, "They won't be upheld, not after all that," he gestured back where the white water of their crisscross paths had already disappeared. "The committee already penalized them. If they think they will win on the dock, they are in for a rude surprise. And they better not try it again. They probably are qualified for the finals, but if they pull anything, they will get banned. These stewards already don't like the Kiwis." Even in a gripe, Erick liked the way the Frenchman spoke the words, as if it all was just a pleasant afternoon drive though the French countryside.

"Let them take the mark, don't get caught up," Fleury warned. It looked like the Kiwis were already widening their path as if to open the tighter inside around the mark, in hopes that La Couverture Verte would take it and the Kiwis would again cut them off. "If we can run them down on the windward leg, we will do so, but sail safe," Fleury ordered. "We have more to lose than they do."

Erick took the order to heart, but he also heard, "run them down on the windward leg." After a wide but fast turn, the two boats were only a few lengths apart. Erick immediately got the spinnaker flying and took his cat up on a hull to let it fly. He and the crew hiked out, all stressing their legs and abdomens as they leaned against the incredible pull of the pressure in the big green and gold sail. He put it high on the ragged edge, risking a tip, but gaining speed on the fast but lower trimaran. The long run was a knife's edge fight to find speed when the wind was the same for both boats. The Kiwis tried to run La Couverture Verte to the boundary but gave up speed for it, and the Kiwis had to steer back into the wind fully, now only slightly ahead.

Fleury took a sighting on the other boat as they were three fourths of the way down the last leg. "We've overtaken them. Make sure we have a good line to the last mark." Erick just nodded, then, as an afterthought, threw out a simple "aye." He wasn't necessarily comfortable with the position, especially as the Kiwis tried to bring back their boat in front of Erick's cat. If they got ahead, New Zealand could spoil Erick's line. It probably wouldn't matter, as the Kiwis would be disqualified anyway, but Erick and the rest of the crew wanted to have the best finish possible. To beat the Kiwis on the water after they refused a penalty would be worth more than a first place.

"Pare à empanner!" Fleury gave the order to jibe. Erick both understood and knew the command was coming. The whole crew knew it, but it was good to stir them up, get some yelling on the last turn. They were flying a hull, ahead of the Kiwi trimaran that would have to slow to make the turn.

Erick was waiting until the last second to bring the hull down, an eye on the mark before his turn to the finish. Fleury watched behind them. The Kiwis were doing a crash attempt to speed by on the port, still lifting one of the three hulls. They had no choice but to touch the hull to slow down. They already had a penalty, and couldn't make the mark and turn at such a speed.

The Kiwi skipper didn't bother to slow down. Both boats still flew a hull, but Erick was dropping his as soon as Fleury shouted a warning. "*Merde*! Look out!" was all he could get out before the hull of the New Zealand boat crashed across the lower hull of La Couverture Verte. Too late, the big trimaran turned to port. It only added to the carnage. La Couverture Verte was already lifted partly out of the water. The two masts hit like a clash of swords, pulling the already tumbling catamaran over on its side. The power of the impact was so severe that the big catamaran had one of its hulls crashed, with bits of foam and carbon reinforcement exposed or flying off. The mast flexed, then broke at the base. As La Couverture Verte went completely vertical, its crew went from last ditch efforts to save the craft to holding on for dear life. Two men clung to the upper hull, hanging by their hands as their feet dangled. One of the crew had already slipped down the trampoline and into the water. He was trying to swim away as the rest of the boat towered over him. It was a terrifying aura of the giant boat ready to capsize and trap the poor man underneath.

Jean Laurent Fleury had already fallen or jumped off the upper hull, away from the rising boat. He had been jettisoned by the impact. He was unprepared and fell awkwardly, slamming into the water on his back. No one would hear the high pitched scream he made, nearly starving him of breath once he tried to swim back to the surface. He inhaled water before he reached air, and found himself struggling to cough and breathe while clutching at his shoulder, torn from its socket and useless to help keep him afloat.

Erick had been holding on to the wheel with a deft but light grip. It had slipped from his fingers as his boat began to turn on its side. Erick tumbled out of the small helm, twisting his back and legs in the process. Then he felt nothing but air. There was nothing to grab, nothing to hold onto, no place to plant his feet and push. He was at the mercy of gravity and water, and he knew it. There was nothing to stop his fall.

Until there was.

CHAPTER TWENTY-TWO

June 1999
Palma

Eliza has seen the entirety of the accident from her place in the VIP stand. From her binoculars she had seen it all, but seen very little. It was just a mash of sails and masts, then Eliza saw the gold tip of Erick's boat go down. She couldn't see much detail, but Eliza saw two people fall, and she knew, she just knew, one was Erick.

Eliza hadn't seen Erick brought to the docks by the rescue boat. The little motor boat had gone farther down the marina, close to the ambulances. Eliza never saw Erick, nor the tactician, the Frenchman, who had also been injured. By the time she had made it down to the end of the marina, only the crews of the boats who were being treated on the site were still there. Eliza tried asking about Erick, but the Frenchmen didn't seem to understand, or they just couldn't express themselves in English.

It took an agonizing thirty minutes to even convince someone to take her to the hospital. And even longer to break through the language barrier there to explain just who she was looking for. Erick had been in the *urgencia*, the emergency room, at the Hospital General de Mallorca. Then he had been taken into surgery, and now he was in an induced coma, hours later.

Eliza had hated every minute of the experience. No one would tell her what had happened at the marina, though it seemed that some were blaming the New Zealand boat. Like any of that mattered now. When she had finally arrived at the hospital, Eliza almost thought she was in the wrong place, with its classical stone castle features. It looked more like the cathedral only blocks away on the waterfront. "How would he get any care here?" Eliza had wondered. The nurses looked like nuns.

When Eliza asked anyone for help, all she got was the same singsong lilt of European Spanish that made her all the more uncomfortable. Eliza began to hate the language. No one would tell her anything.

She wasn't even allowed in the room with Erick. She wasn't family. Even though it was a revolving door of team managers and sponsors, the "money" opened doors that she couldn't, Eliza was left alone in a busy and cluttered hallway, filled with moving patients, doctors, nurses, and whatever they called the orderlies here. Even the young assistants who cleaned the rooms and moved the trash were beautiful wholesome looking Spanish girls, Eliza's age and younger, with the severe raven black hair and kindly smiles that said nothing to Eliza, who sat red eyed for hours waiting for someone to tell her something in English.

Finally, Alina Auffenberg came in and sat next to her. Her cold Germanic stare was rimmed by redness, and she looked tired, stressed, but not nearly as bad as Eliza felt. "Has anyone told you of his condition?" she asked Eliza. It was all Eliza could do to shake her head wordlessly without bursting into tears again.

"Erick has broken ribs from hitting a supporting line on the boat when he fell. He lost a lot of blood, and the impact cut his chest. The biggest issue is that something happened to his heart." She said it so coldly, as if to hurt Eliza.

Eliza felt her own heart sink into blackness. She was afraid to ask, but needed to know. She hoped it would be something that wasn't so bad, that it really was just some broken ribs and bleeding. Those things seemed to be injuries that people recovered from. "Is he going to be alright?" Eliza couldn't help but make the question sound like a plead, because it was.

"We don't know," it was a terse, uncaring reply. At least, it seemed Alina didn't care how Eliza took it. It was as if Alina was trying to keep Eliza from being informed. But Alina did get up to find a doctor and bring him over. He looked distracted, unconcerned by Eliza's predicament, but he responded to the German's direct demand. He spoke English fluently with a decided Spanish accent. If Eliza hadn't felt like she was going to throw up at any moment, she would have found it charming. As it was, she barely noticed, and understood only every other word. "Are you …" he looked from Eliza to the more poised and taller Alina, "how are you related to the patient?"

"I'm his girlfriend. Please, just tell me, is he going to be alright? What has happened to him? No one has told me anything!"

The doctor looked at Alina, then the closed door to Erick's wing. Alina gave him a resigned nod. "He has a myocardial contusion. It is a bruise on the heart. We currently don't know how bad it is. This happens on impact injuries like this. It happens in car accidents."

"Is he going to be alright?!" Eliza fought back tears in a scream that was part plea, beg, and demand.

The doctor was noncommittal. "We don't know, not yet. It is something that will take time to determine. Right now we want to make sure his chest and lungs stay clear. He needs help breathing right now, and his other injuries are serious. We will know more in a few days. *Lo lamento*, I'm sorry." He left with only a final glance at Alina, as Eliza had buried her face in her hands.

Eliza couldn't handle this, not here, not now. No one told her anything, no one talked to her, and she wasn't even allowed to see Erick. Eliza wasn't family; she was just "the girlfriend." All the time Eliza had been in Palma she had been just the girlfriend, sent to the corner when the big boys talked. She had been pawed by "the money," left alone on the beach, and isolated by a language. No one even offered her food or a drink of water. The team had sent a revolving door of people to the hospital, visiting Erick. Eliza suspected Erick was an afterthought when the crew came to see the tactician, the Frenchman, who was being held overnight. But now Eliza was alone, and Erick was alone.

Erick had continually left her alone. She had followed him to California, only to follow him to Spain with the vague promise of things changing. Or not. All Erick really had said was that things would be better, as if being the captain of a boat that he controlled was better. Erick would have more control, and more demand, and Eliza would be more alone. More travel to places that spoke a different language with food she didn't understand.

And now Eliza was in an uncomfortable plastic chair in a hospital filled with strange clinical machines, horrific stretchers, and bitter smells of all types. And Erick had left her alone, again.

Eliza was exhausted. She didn't even know if she could ask for a place to sleep. Her body ached with twisted pains up and down her back. Her eyes felt like they were on fire from crying, and her stomach was churning, even though it was empty. Nighttime set in late, and by then no one was around from the team sponsors. Eliza got up, left the hospital, and hailed a taxi to go back to her hotel. The taxi driver was the only person who tried to make her comfortable by asking her how her night was. He even got out of the taxi and watched her go inside, calling out “"¡Cuídese!" to her as she went through the lobby doors.

Eliza went to her room to wash her face and try to sleep. She felt as sick as before, and couldn’t rest. Eliza realized that Erick’s parents hadn’t been contacted. She didn’t even know their number in Atlanta. Erick had never written it down. Eliza got up and went through Erick’s backpack. She found a few business cards, which had the dealership number. Eliza hoped that someone would still be there that could give her their home number. It would be around six o’clock in the evening there right now. Eliza struggled in the near dark, with only the filtered light of the street lamps coming through the closed curtains, to work the phone. She finally turned on a harsh bright desk lamp to read the multilingual instructions to make an international call.

Over the long line from Spain to Atlanta, Eliza got a strangely comforting voice with a soft southern accent, “Sunstrom Luxury Automobile, how may we help you with your vehicle?”

“Um, yes…” the soft singsong happiness threw Eliza. She wasn’t ready for sunny words. “I’m Eliza Rhodes. I’m, uh, dating Conrad Sunstrom’s son. We’re here in Spain, and well, Erick has had an accident, he got hurt, and I’m trying…” Eliza didn’t want to tell this stranger too much, but didn’t want to have to tell some poor secretary the news to break to the boss and his wife that their son was in the hospital.

“Oh, honey, I’m so sorry!” The lilted magnolia flower of a voice dripped with southern honey to Eliza. It was the first kind sound she had heard in English, and the only ones she had heard besides the kind stranger in a taxi. “Someone called them this morning. They are already on their way out there. I got them the flight myself. They are probably over the Atlantic Ocean already."

Eliza melted in her seat. It was one thing she didn't have to do. And she realized that someone told Erick's parents in another country on the other side of an ocean before they told her what had happened.

"Are you okay?"

Eliza barely heard the words.

"Are you okay?" The Georgia drawl was soft, and long. "Okay" came out as "Owe-kay-eee?"

"Yes," Eliza said between sobs. "Yes."

Eliza hung up the phone before she started crying again.

Erick's parents were over the Atlantic already. It was an unbelievable feat until Eliza remembered that Atlanta was mostly airport. They would fly to Heathrow, in England, or directly to Barcelona. Then they would have to get to Mallorca. Eliza and Erick had taken a ferry. But the Sunstroms would fly in. She knew.

Eliza and Erick were supposed to fly back to the US tomorrow. Eliza looked at her watch under the harsh glare of the white light of the desk lamp. "Today," she said. "We were supposed to leave today." It was already after midnight local time. It was part of the deal of her coming along. They would leave the day after the races. Eliza had been gone long enough.

"Too long." Eliza had been uncomfortable the whole time she had been in Palma, and now she was alone. When Erick's parents got here, they would have questions she couldn't answer. Erick had left her alone and unsure of her place.

"He did this before," Eliza remembered, now angry at what she had been put through. Erick had been injured, and she had been hurt. People were there for Erick. No one was coming for her. What if Erick never woke up? It was a horrid thought, but the doctor hadn't seemed hopeful. Eliza tried not to think it, but the thought came unbidden. "What if he died?"

Eliza had spent years with Erick, while he chased the winds and his dreams. And now he left her alone in a strange country. It just wasn't fair. He had done this before.

An hour later, she found the same taxi out front of the hotel. "¿Te encuentras bien?" the driver asked. "Ci," Eliza handed him her bag for the trunk. "Do the ferries to Barcelona run overnight?"

An hour later, she slept in a cabin on a big passenger ferry to the mainland of Spain. As she fell asleep, Eliza wondered if she would see Erick's parents going the other way when she arrived in Barcelona.

"They probably wouldn't even recognize me."

CHAPTER TWENTY-THREE

August 2001
Marlowe Beach

The rain had found its way around her mother's poncho and had soaked into Eliza's jeans. Her plain Keds shoes were wet, too. Not sloshing wet, just damp enough to get into the soles and feel icky. Eliza knew they wouldn't dry out, not now, not for a few days. "I've still got power," she thought, "I could throw them into the dryer."

"I could also get into the car and go home," her mind told herself. Eliza tried not to listen to her mind. It would mean she was just running away again. Eliza kicked off her shoes, then pulled her jeans off, unraveling them inside out off of her thin legs. Walking around in the house in a shirt and underwear still seemed wrong. Her parents had insisted on some form of modesty all of Eliza's life, and now, even though there was no one else in the house and the windows were blocked off, it still felt strange. Like she needed permission, and the ghosts of her parents, still alive only a few miles away on the other side of the islands, were not about to give it.

Eliza's brother Tommy had run around in his goofy little boy underpants all the time. And then when he was older he was constantly shirtless. But Eliza had to cover up her swimsuits when she was inside.

Eliza walked to the laundry closet and threw her shoes and jeans in the dryer along with a few clean towels to soften the load. She kept one towel to dry her legs. Wrapping the towel around her waist, she went to the living room and turned the TV back on. She wasn't about to let the announcer see her in her underwear.

The storm drivel was the same, only a little closer now, with more rain, still expected to make landfall nearby. It was the same thing they had said over and over, only now they had a few reporters in Myrtle Beach and Charleston and someone in Wrightsville. They always went to the fun spots.

Eliza went upstairs to her room to find a change of clothes. She kept a few pairs of shorts there just to have something if, "when," she came down and stayed at the beach. She hadn't been down from Woods Hole in the past year, and that trip hadn't been for long. The shorts were cute, little tropical flowery boardshorts in blue and white. Eliza didn't remember them being so small, or else she had gotten… "No, that can't be it," she told herself. This time, her mind knew to keep its big trap shut.

Eliza felt strangely comfortable. She was back in summer clothes, at the beach. Never mind that summer was all but over and there was a gloomy hurricane just offshore. And Eliza was no longer a sunny teenager without a care. She looked at herself in the mirror. She certainly wasn't fifteen anymore. "Thank goodness," she said to the mirror. She had changed, her eyes were both wider, and a little more narrow, with the upturned lids turning a little more up when she smiled. She was still thin, but had gotten taller, and yes, okay, she finally got a bit of curve. But she was still the same sunkissed olive brown girl, woman, that called the house her home… She did the math… "Fourteen years ago?"

Half a life.

That wasn't the way to look at it. She had a life ahead of her. Not half her life wasted. It hadn't been wasted, really. No one should look at what a kid did, or the recklessness of teenage years, and hold it against an adult. Eliza had been a good girl and a doting daughter. And she had been trying to be the adult she was supposed to be. Eliza looked at herself, and saw past her figure in the mirror. She looked, well, still cute, still pretty, but Eliza looked more at who she was right now, experienced, successful, following in her father's wishes but also on her own path. The things she had been through were like what others had experienced. Eliza had traveled, worked, failed, been disappointed, succeeded, respected, and liked.

She hadn't nearly died.

Her mind whispered it.

She looked great.

She didn't have a scar across her that ruined her.

Stop saying that.

She had been in love.

She had run away.

He did it to me! More than once!

He's next door.

If Eliza didn't get away from that mirror she was going to take it down and throw it into the churning sea.

Fine.

I'll show you.

Yes, you will.

CHAPTER TWENTY-FOUR

August 2001
Marlowe Beach

"Did the water always smell that bad?"

Erick couldn't help but sniff at his own odor. The water from the sound and Intracoastal had an aroma of earthy, swampy detritus, dependent on where it came from. The tall sea grasses that grew into islands had water that was rich and salty, with a strange sickly sweetness that was not entirely unpleasant. But step just a few feet away from the grass onto the muck of a clear spot, and the wet clay and sand silt bloomed with a stinking rot of decay. There always was a dead crab somewhere in the area, and the scent was a giveaway. The flowing water all around was difficult to describe. It had earthiness, and crisp cool, and damp washcloth, and still hot water in a plastic bucket, all in one, that gave it a distinctive aroma.

Erick just smelled bad. It was a bit of everything all over him. Even the walk back to the house in the rain did nothing to wash off the stench. It was a familiar smell to him, but that didn't mean he liked it. A gust of wind driven rain blew into his face, carrying a bit of the sea in the droplets. The sharp tang was like the storm offered him a piece of salt water taffy to wash out his mouth. "Thank you," he said into the wind to the invisible Nereids that offered him this gift. The Nereids were ocean nymphs, daughters of Nereus, the Old Man of the Sea, who often granted sailors wishes for good fortune. His fifty daughters were known to aid sailors in their needs, especially when unexpected. Everyone needed a god to follow, and Erick had decided to embrace a bunch of cute girls who liked sailors and swam in the ocean.

He just hoped they couldn't smell him.

Erick walked through the open garage, squeezed past the Jeep, and grabbed his travel duffel out of the back from under the seat. The bag was wet, but it was waterproof. He'd need a couple changes of clothes for this trip. Instead of walking into the house, he simply cut through the garage door to the back, where the outdoor shower waited.

The shower was a masterpiece in simplicity and practicality, as well as being unbelievably hedonistic to a teenager. Erick wondered if his parents understood that, in the way every child assumes their parents to be dispassionate lumps of clay without an ounce of desire in them. The shower was built under the set of outdoor steps that led to the upstairs guest room. The steps would allow a person to go down the outside of the house to get a shower if they needed one. The shower itself was nothing more than a set of treated planks and a pipe with a showerhead plumbed onto the outside of the garage. Three walls were put up for a bit of decorum to hide anyone scrubbing themselves to a pink pulp with a bar of Dial soap encased in scratchy, coarse sand. There was a door that could be locked with a hook and eye, the same simple tool used to hold every screen door and shutter in place across the old beach house. Two more plywood walls had been put up, creating a sheltered spot to stand for dressing and undressing, so that no one's clothes would get wet in the shower. The walls went down just past the knees of the person inside the shower, which made for an exciting and titillating game for kids to look at the ankles of whoever was in there and wonder if they were naked or not behind the thin walls.

The shower was at some times a communal place, where any family member could stick a leg in to rinse off the sand, or take turns running some of the fresh iron rich spring water through their hair. Erick would often battle with his sister for dominance of the shower when they spent summers there. But when he had become a teen, the door would be locked. It was a place to steal away, but still be in public. Sometimes the ankles and feet would be the usual two, sometimes four, with the smaller ones on tiptoe as a desperate teenage couple would gather a moment to themselves after a day at the beach with everyone around, just to have one passionate kiss, alone, together, under the hard steel water that tasted so good on their lips.

There was no one waiting in the shower for Erick. Just a long, faded towel, so wonderfully scratchy, that would soak up all the well water off his body when he was done. Erick undressed, unconcerned that anyone would see him. The walls kept onlookers out on the best of days. No one would be watching him get undressed in this storm.

Erick left his soaked boxer briefs in a pile while he hung up his shirt, which was soaked from the rain but at least not from the fresh water fragrance all over his body. It could just be hung up and dried inside later. He threw his travel duffel strap over a protruding nail that should have had his name over it.

Then Erick turned on the hot water and waited, naked, as the wind whipped his ankles from the openings under the walls.

CHAPTER TWENTY-FIVE

May 1988
Marlowe Beach

Prom night on Marlowe Beach was a cluttered mash of teens struggling to find their own way to dinner, photos, then the dance, and then… something. Some students would have the keys to their parents' rental home, just a cheap cottage on stilts, where they all planned to sneak away, in plain view of anyone who passed by. They were partially excited by someone hopefully sneaking a bottle of their dad's vodka out of the house, avoiding both parents and police as if it were the heist of the century. Others were hyped about getting a limo, with the same idea, only with a hidden traveling bar in the back that somehow would go unnoticed by the driver that was hired by the kids' parents. A limo was still a step above the Honda Prelude that mom insisted their sweet darling had to have, that the snotty prick boys drove.

There was all the discussion of where to go out to eat, as if this was the one time all year they weren't going to the Hardee's over in Bodin. Almost everyone wanted to go to Davis Fine Seafood, which was the closest to fine dining, because it had tablecloths and candles. But there were only so many tables and so many reservations, so, someone was going to be disappointed. But there were still enough fancy restaurants to go around, and they would all fill with rental tuxes and fluffy dresses early on Friday night.

The tuxes and dresses would be another competition in teen one-upmanship, mostly from the boys. White jackets were popular. Some of the boys thought it would be cool to wear their Wayfarers with white coats, and a few were willing to take the risk of wearing a pink tie and cummerbund. The daring of them knew no bounds.

It didn't matter what they wore, because they were all sure they were going to get drunk or laid, finally, after years of talk. The vast majority of the boys would be disappointed. And an even larger number of the girls would be, too.

Erick hated prom. But it was important to Eliza. She was excited to go, to be on a fancy date with Erick. They had tried and tried to date all year, but sports, Christmas, Spring Break, family, too many things got in the way for the two to do anything more than the occasional movie or mini golf. So, prom it was.

Erick had a classic black tuxedo. His father had insisted. Conrad had told Erick that sometimes you needed to look your best. Especially when you spend a lot of time looking "not your best." He hadn't meant it as a slight to Erick. Conrad explained to his son that when racing drivers were done with a race, everyone took their picture, and the drivers were hot, tired, lines on their eyes where the goggles were, their hair was soaked and oily, they looked exhausted. Because they were. Conrad had been to so many endurance races where he had seen his drivers, ecstatic with a win or a podium, deflated with a loss, but always dirty, grimy, almost haunted.

But at the awards ceremony, they showed up in their best, the black suits and crisp shirts, and they looked good. It was as simple as that.

Erick wanted to look good for Eliza. He didn't care about the Armani tuxedo, except that it fit him better than the rental tuxes that everyone else had.

Eliza was a different story. Erick knew her family didn't have his money. But Erick never liked flaunting their wealth, even though he didn't have a choice, Armani tux to the point of that argument. But he couldn't offer to buy Eliza a dress, either. It didn't matter to Erick. He would be happy if she showed up in jeans and a t-shirt, but it was prom, and prom was important to Eliza.

"Are you sure you don't want the S-Class?" Conrad had asked as Erick got ready to drive from one house to the neighboring one. This was certainly a time that he could not trudge through the sand and sea grass over the dune. Erick still wore his old white boat shoes, since they were easier to drive in. Erick would slip on the dress shoes before dinner. "No," was all Erick said. He didn't want to explain that he didn't need to make that much of an appearance. His convertible was flashy enough. Some of the teens would be trying to air out their father's pickup truck. They didn't have the choice of multiple expensive German and British luxury cars in their driveway. It would prove to be foretelling later on in the evening.

Erick drove down the driveway, up the beach road all of about one hundred feet, then turned into Eliza's drive, where he pulled up, got out, and waved to his parents who still hadn't gone in yet.

Even with the smaller convertible, Erick felt a little uncomfortable. He knew Eliza's parents were more working middle class than his. Eliza had told Erick how her mother had found a dress from a cousin that would fit her, and it looked pretty. All she said was that it was pink, and so Erick had slipped a couple of pink handkerchiefs in his pocket in hopes one would better match her color. He never really thought about how Eliza had to find a used dress that fit her, and she had to take whatever she could get.

He never had a chance for his poor teen brain to process the thought, because Erick was stunned when he saw her. Eliza floated out on a sea of frilly lace under her dress, a foamy light pink, with an impossibly tight bodice and flowery straps on her shoulders. She wore dainty white lace gloves that gave her a mix of an innocent princess playing dress up and the 80s glamour of Madonna. Eliza saw Erick smile and light up at her appearance, and she spun around like a little girl showing off her dress. In a moment in Erick's eyes Eliza went from a stunning vision, to regal, to adoringly cute, then a hint of sexy, and finally to smiling bright eyed Eliza.

His girlfriend.

The girl he loved dearly.

There were the photos, the poses, Eliza's little brother trying to get into the photos. Giving Eliza the wrist corsage, Eliza pinning the boutonniere on Erick's lapel. "Oh, really, I do *not* care," Erick told her when she worried about sticking a pin in the jacket. "I'll turn this thing inside out for you if it'll make you happy." More photos, Erick holding the door to the 560. It was still sunny, but Erick had left the top up. He didn't want to mess up Eliza's coiffure. His own blond hair was filled with almost as much mousse as hers was with gel. It would take a hurricane to get their hairdos to move.

Then it was a short drive back to Erick's and more photos, pretending to do the same thing over again. And finally, back in the car. "You know," Erick smiled slyly, "We don't have to do this."

Eliza stared at him, quizzically. "You don't want to go to prom?"

"No, I mean," Erick pointed to the road ahead. "All this stuff, the pictures, the formal dress," he tugged at his collar. "I have a full tank of gas. We could just keep going."

Eliza laughed, and reached across the center console of the little car to wrap her arms around his, as he rested one hand on the transmission shifter. She didn't answer, just leaned over and sighed for a moment, the thought of running away, just for a weekend, going somewhere where they could be away from her parents and their friends who talked about them.

"Where would you take me?"

Erick thought for a moment, as he turned down the cassette playing in the stereo. For a moment, he, too, was caught up in the idea of escape. He was graduating soon, and for a brief second he thought about just going away. "Wilmington would be too close," he started with the obvious. "And, really, I don't want to live there anyway. The Outer Banks?"

Eliza made a snarling face. "It's just another version of our beach."

"Okay," Erick paused as they stopped at a red light. "Chapel Hill is nice."

"I've never been there. Isn't it pretty far away? I don't think I'd like being that far from the beach."

"You just said you didn't want to go to another beach!"

Eliza snickered, a dusty laugh that was wonderfully patronizing to poor Erick, who just couldn't understand the nuance of her opinions. "I just don't want to go to *that* beach!" she said. "I still would like to go to *a* beach!"

The light turned green, and Erick slowly accelerated so as not to shake up his passenger, all full of delicious contradictions. He thought, silent, as she watched. Not Myrtle Beach, too close, too touristy, Not Charleston, too old, and it smelled funny. The big cities inland offered almost nothing to two teenagers running away, and who really wanted to actually *be* in Raleigh, anyway? Then Erick hit on it.

"Have you ever been to Hilton Head Island?"

"No, where is it?"

Erick got dreamy. "Oh, wow, it's great. It's on the coast of South Carolina, way past Charleston, actually near the border with Georgia, near Savannah. It's this great beach, where the palmettos grow like weeds. They have this big orange lighthouse, and a big harbor, golf for the old people. Great beach houses. The beach is wide and flat, hard packed, kinda like Carolina Beach, or Oak Island. It's warm in the winter there. We could go, get a house, tie up a hammock on the back porch, and sleep outside every night.

"Just the two of us."

Eliza squeezed closer, her dress getting squished by the seat belt. She didn't care. She wouldn't need the dress after tonight. "That sounds wonderful. Let's do it."

Erick just laughed. They pulled up to the beach roller skating rink. "Well, I think we better do our prom photos first," Erick said to her. "I don't know how your dad would feel about us running away tonight, but I guarantee that our moms will get mad if we don't at least get a good photo first." Erick slipped into his dress shoes and went around to open the door for Eliza. Before they took a step, she wrapped her arms around his neck and kissed him. She didn't care if anyone saw them. For one moment, Eliza just rested her head on Erick's shoulder, holding him. It was her favorite comfort, and she held him softly, like a child holds a blanket. Erick had his arms around her small waist, pulling her close, just close enough to let her know she could stay there as long as she wanted. He would never let go if she didn't want him to.

A soft sigh, and Erick began to relax his grip. That was usually the sign. But Eliza pulled him close again, even tighter. Eliza kissed him again. Another couple came out of the rink and waved. Erick quickly let go with one hand, waved, and nodded, then he placed his hand gently onto her back. If Eliza didn't want to let go, he would just hold on. They didn't really need to take prom pictures.

Eliza looked up at Erick. He had a small streak of red on his lip from her overly bright lipstick. She took his handkerchief out to dab his lip, and the second folded pink cloth came out with it. "Why do you have two handkerchiefs?"

"A gentleman always carries an extra handkerchief, in case he needs to give one to a lady." Erick cocked his head. Everyone knew that.

A truck roared up to the entrance of the roller skating rink, clanked to a stop, and the loud music blaring from it stopped. Eliza and Erick watched Ray Daniels get out and wait for his date, Julie Dixon, a junior with a pile of curly brown hair held up behind white Wayfarers, to struggle out of the passenger side in her prom dress.

"Okay," Erick thought, "maybe not *everyone* knows that."

After the photos, Erick drove Eliza to dinner. He had gotten reservations at a more romantic, and dark, and adult, restaurant, 1900, a hidden escapist fine dining establishment that was in every way the opposite of the fancy restaurants that the other teens were going to. This place was intimate. Soft light hid the clientele as they watched from behind Moroccan walls. Sconces cast dim colored shadows across the room. Erick led Eliza to a small table nestled into a nook, far from the bar. To Eliza, the other diners looked like exotic visitors from foreign lands who had come to do nefarious deals under copious amounts of spicy dark red wines. The place reeked of danger and sex.

"I love this place," Erick said. It had been the one choice he had made. He asked Eliza to prom, and it was his job to choose the place they ate. "It's mysterious, like something is going on that we don't know about."

Eliza felt out of place. She was in a pink girl's prom dress, not in haute couture, nor a white frocked refugee. Erick looked... older... under the bare whisper of a waving candle.

He looked like he was planning something, and had to look over his shoulder every time someone passed to make sure they weren't listening.

"Get whatever you want, okay?" Erick's voice was casual, almost dismissive of the haunting room they were in. "The scallops are good. The steak here is outstanding, actually."

Eliza looked at the big menu, wondering if they just had a burger. She chose a chicken over a smoky pasta, as she was unsure as to what else to get. The menu was very expensive. Erick had ordered abalone, which Eliza had never heard of. "It's a west coast shellfish. You know those shiny shells you see in the gift shops with that mother of pearl? That's abalone." Erick ate the strangest things on the menu. "You want to try it?"

Eliza looked at the big dumpling shaped thing, covered in a creamy sauce, made a face and shook her head.

Both of them began eating in silence as they picked at their food. Erick didn't want to do anything wrong. He stared at his plate, and wondered if he should have just gotten the scallops. Or if they should have gone to a burger joint drive in. That would have been cute. Eliza in her pink dress, him in his boat shoes and tux, happily spilling mustard on them, getting ice cream and sharing it.

"You don't have to finish that, okay?" Erick wondered if Eliza was nervous. It was a big night, and even though both of them had to be in early, as Eliza's father had set a rather strict midnight curfew for his daughter, Erick and Eliza both felt a sense of desperation about them. For different reasons, they both wanted to get to the next part of the night, and the sooner it came, the better.

Erick got the bill and paid with cash, leaving a pile of twenty dollar bills on the table. Eliza asked if he needed to wait for the change. "No, that's good, with a decent tip."

In the car, they drove back to the roller skating rink. It finally was getting dark, with a dull sunset over the Intracoastal Waterway being hidden by approaching gray clouds. Erick drove past the entrance and parked his convertible, much to the chagrin of the sophomore boys who were there to play valet. He wasn't about to trust a fifteen year old boy with his car. "Aw, c'mon, man…" was the plea, which told Erick he did the right thing. The boy half smiled, half smirked at Eliza. They were in the same year, but the status of showing up for prom in a fancy car against standing waiting for someone to let them park their parents' late model Mazda was a giant chasm. Erick for the most part ignored the glances at his girlfriend, especially by the younger teens. Eliza wouldn't even notice. She never heard what the boys would say about her behind her back.

Prom was... prom. The junior class had decorated the roller skating rink and the outdoor veranda. The theme was some vague tropical paradise, with coral and pineapples and fish, and lots of blue and green. Two of Erick's buds had been part of the decorating crew, and the junior class was really proud of what they had done, he knew, even though most of the students just didn't care. Erick saw his friend Brian and date Lanie, and went over to tell them he liked the look. "You did a good job, man," as the two shook hands like they were adults making a deal. Lanie immediately squealed at Eliza and complimented her dress. Eliza beamed and gave her hips a twirl. Erick said, "You two look great. That's a nice dress, and Brian, dude, you clean up well. You look like Don Johnson." Brian held out the white tuxedo jacket and did a pose. "C'mon, sweetie," Erick took Eliza's hand, "we gotta go show you off to my friends. I don't know who will be more jealous, the girls or the guys."

It took time, as the girls in Erick's clique had to all stand up and show off their dresses each time a new couple came along. Eliza liked the attention. She noticed how the other girls would compliment each other, and did the same thing. Eliza knew most of them well by now, having hung out almost exclusively with them for the school year. Eliza scanned the crowd, but saw only one of her friends her age there with a junior who had probably asked out of desperation, and the girl had said yes for the same reason. Being able to say you went to the Junior-Senior prom as a sophomore was a powerful coup, one that could be lorded over the rest of the class for the remainder of the school year.

Erick didn't care about the others at the prom. "No, man, I'm not going to be able to go out. Eliza has to be in, I mean, I gotta respect that, and I've got a regatta I had planned since this time last year. I have to go up to Wrightsville tomorrow. I should be there now, but, hey, priorities." Erick lifted up Eliza's hand in his. She hadn't let go except to dance and drink punch. Erick didn't care if she ever did.

The night went as expected for almost everyone at the prom. The music was loud, the band played tons of covers, everyone got excited when they played Michael Jackson, and all the kids plotted on what would happen later on. Erick could see a few of the guys were nervous, thinking that they would be out late with dates they considered friends, not "dates." The girls were more confident, rolling their eyes when their boyfriends made stupid innuendo about getting drunk later on, as if that was appealing. Erick ignored it all and Eliza took no notice. They only had eyes for each other. Any chance they got the two walked out to the veranda. Already the crepe paper had been blown to ragged bits, with tiny tabs held on miraculously by bits of clear tape. The night got darker, and so did the corners, where the more intimate couples could steal away for a pretend moment of discretion.

Erick and Eliza wrapped their arms into a knot as they held hands. Eliza wanted to twist herself up into Erick and not let him go. Erick nestled his leg against hers, hopefully her leg, as he could barely find Eliza's thin frame in the fluffy lace dress. The two found a dark corner where they could afford some space from everyone else. The students defined an unwritten rule that each couple had to be one post of the veranda away from another. It was dark enough that they couldn't be seen there, nor heard, if they were quiet.

"Are you having fun?" Erick worried.

"Yes," she answered. To Eliza, it was a stamp of approval, not an answer. She was almost walking on air. Even as the winds whipped up her dress.

"Whoa, I hope you don't fly away!"

Eliza tightened her grip. "You'll just have to hold me down," she wrapped her free arm around Erick as she pecked at him.

"I'm not letting you go," he joked, kissing her back.

Eliza let go of Erick's hand, and worked her way inside his jacket, around his back, trying to find any way to hold him closer to her, with less in the way. They kissed sweetly, with the occasional parting of the lips for a more discreet, passionate exploration of each other. Erick tasted the rosy fruit punch of the prom on Eliza's lips. Eliza smelled Erick's woody cologne mixed with the earthy aromas of food and sweat from dancing in a black jacket. Salt winds kissed their skin, washing away the scents for a moment, so that the two had to keep going back to each other to find the familiar fragrances that they were so intimately used to.

A slow song came out through the windows to the veranda. Every time during the night, Eliza had led Erick to the floor for a slow dance. It was a rite of passage for teens to cling to each other and live out the fantasy of the song being played in their heads, imagining the world where they lived the words, forever and ever. Erick would feel Eliza with her hands wrapped behind his neck, interlaced fingers, as she pulled slightly downward. She would rest her head on his shoulder and sigh, while he held her at the waist, and the two stepped clockwise in unison to the slow music.

At this moment, deep in the dark on the veranda, it was yet another soft pop hit, one of many that the band played, mixed in with the upbeat tunes that made everyone scream.

The soft melody of a rather choppy version of *Endless Summer Nights* started up.

Eliza wrapped her hands around Erick's neck, as she always did, as the two swayed to the soft rhythm. It took only a minute, but she stopped, and this time looked at Erick. His green eyes almost glowed under the soft mixed lights flashing inside, but hidden in the darkness. Erick could see her almost pleading with him, a nearly terrifying feeling of desperation. "We should have kept driving," was all she said, then kissed him, hard, pulling him tightly, with more ferocity than the soft pop song called for.

The song ended, but Eliza kept her hands clutched tightly over Erick's shoulders. Another song came on, a loud Bon Jovi effort, and from the inside came the requisite cheers of adolescent boys. Erick stiffened, now a little uncomfortable with the grip Eliza had on him. He straightened, and in an effort to unclench her grip, he tried to take her hand to lead her back to the dance floor.

"Wait," she asked, "just a moment."

Erick stayed, content to please her. He knew the night was important to Eliza. She just didn't want it to end yet. It took a moment, but Eliza relaxed, let herself go, and the two slowly walked back into the rink. It was hotter inside, still without the gusts of winds coming off the shore, and the lights were erratic as they flashed out of tune with the music. By ten o'clock, Eliza looked at Erick and asked if they could leave. "Let's get out of here," she insisted. Erick understood the command. It wasn't time to go home yet, but neither wanted to be there now. A few more dances, some "see ya laters," a distinct wink to a friend, and the two walked out of the roller skating rink turned teen party palace for a night into the wind and cooling gloom of the night. The car was a far distance now, as the band played *Careless Whisper* in the distance.

If they had any option, Eliza and Erick would have run off to an empty beach house, but teenagers, wealthy or not, have no options in getting a hotel room or renting a house. And Erick had to get Eliza back by midnight, which meant he had to be on the way home before midnight. Time management was a bit of a specialty for any teen, even if they have to set their watch back a few minutes to be on time, and Erick was no less good at it than any other. But it also meant that the clock ticked in his head.

Eliza had no such worry or warning. She just wanted time alone with Erick.

Erick pulled into a distant beach access parking lot. It was empty, windy, cold, and early enough that no one would come looking for any teens on the make in a car in the dark. The cops had better things to do, especially if no one was really breaking the law.

Erick put the car in park and turned it off. After the loud band the silence of the car with only the soft roar of the wind on the convertible top was an annoying whine far off in the distance. He leaned over the center to kiss Eliza, who leaned in, already unbuckled, pulling Erick to her. She didn't care if he was twisted over the low center console. Erick struggled to get turned, but didn't fight it. He wanted Eliza as much as a seventeen year old boy ever could. She sat in the passenger seat, all fluff from her waist down, as she lifted her legs to tug off her shoes. Her dress seemed to overflow the bottom half of the little car, while her dress top wrinkled and fell lopsided over her small frame.

Erick had long given up the pretense of fashion and had slipped his bow tie off. His shirt had been undone at the collar, and Erick magically had unbuttoned the next button to open it further. Erick would have taken the damned jacket off, too, if he had only thought of it before he had gotten into the car. But Erick had no desire to take the time to remove his jacket, or anything. He didn't want to ruin the moment by looking away from Eliza.

Eliza looked at Erick excitedly, but unsure. She felt strangely passionate. It was a need to be with her boyfriend, the first boy she had ever kissed. But all her life had been guided that good girls don't do this. Whatever "this" was. All Eliza wanted was to be close to Erick, and even in the little two seater, the distance was too much. Erick sat up in his seat, pulling his knees up to lean farther over to her. Eliza pulled him more. If there was a way, Eliza was going to yank that boy over onto her lap and squeeze him until he broke, then kiss him and make him better.

Erick did his best, leaning over his seat, holding himself up with straining muscles, until he gave in and leaned back. "Hang on," he said breathlessly. Erick could have opened the door and gone around, but it would mean going out into the cold, opening the door and letting the wind in on Eliza, and he wasn't going to do that. Instead, he flopped himself over the center, across Eliza's lap, and wedged himself against the passenger door, with his feet, shoeless, propped up over the dash.

Eliza turned her body to let Erick nestle against the seat, with the window handle jammed into his back. "Have you done this before?" Eliza teased.

"No, … not that you would know," Erick joked back. To be honest with himself, he realized he had never had another girl inside his car besides Eliza. Outside of his mom and little sister, at least.

Eliza smacked Erick lightly, then pulled him close by his open shirt. She kissed him hard, making him shut up. Eliza prowled her hand under Erick's jacket, then under his shirt, feeling his smooth skin. Her hand slid up to his shoulder, squeezing it. And Erick responded, wrapping his arm around Eliza's hip. Eliza tried to lift her leg over Erick's, desperate to intertwine herself more fully onto him. The fluffy frills of her dress puffed up, almost to the dash, making her leg slip under the polyester and taffeta.

Erick ran his hand up her leg. He was titillated by her smooth stockings, even through the layers and layers of white lace that hid her body from him. As the two made out, one or the other helped lift another layer of Eliza's dress. Eliza knew she should be demur. That's what she was taught. She was the good girl. No matter what Erick said, boys will be boys, and Erick was another boy. But Eliza wanted to be with Erick. She didn't know how she was going to accomplish what she wanted to fulfill her desires right now, especially in the tiny confines of his little two seater.

Eliza had wondered if he would surprise her with a hotel room. Or going off to a back room of a friend's beach box house. Eliza wasn't sure if that was how it was supposed to be, but she and Erick had been together, dating, but vaguely, as school had always gotten in the way. Or church. Or her parents saying no. Or his parents saying no, less often. This was about as good as the two could do, wedged into the passenger seat of a little car hidden at a beach access in the dark as a cold wind blew over the beach.

Erick couldn't hide his excitement. He had always tried to be decent, keep those stupid teen urges to himself. At least not try to brag to his friends about how desperately he wanted her body, even when they occasionally commented on Eliza's cute little butt. Eliza let her hands run softly up and down Erick's body, over his now uncomfortable suit. The cummerbund had been nothing but a twisted and binding strap across his waist. Erick undid it, almost magically, by reaching behind him and snapping the buckle undone.

Erick realized that as much as he wanted Eliza, physically, and even though she was giving off some pretty unmistakable signs she wanted, something, something more that her tongue counting his teeth as she seemed to be doing at the moment, this was just not right. Not that it was wrong. They both wanted each other, even if Eliza wasn't sure how to say it, or know just how far she wanted it to go. But it was just not right. Not the right time or place. The car was small, the seat would only lean back so far. Erick wasn't in beach shorts and a t-shirt, covered in sand and salt. The tuxedo cut into his body with every twist. He would never tell Eliza, he wasn't about to complain, but the jacket was digging into his armpit, and the window handle was jammed severely into his lower back. He wanted desperately to kneel down in the wheel well and count every layer of Eliza's dress until he knew how many there were. But that, too, was against him. Erick could feel the layers, every time he slid his hand up Eliza's knee, then found another thin bit of gauzy cloth. And underneath all that, the smooth stockings, and a hint of a garter belt, and lace strings from her panties. She was, underneath the delight of a cute prom dress, hiding the risque elements of intimate apparel that every teen boy only fantasizes about seeing.

But all those things were barriers to her. And barriers for Eliza to him. There was no way the two would find a way to undress each other, in the slow and deliberate way that young lovers want to do, pretending they were presents that they took turns to unwrap, peeling off a piece of tape or a ribbon a bit at a time.

Eliza watched as Erick looked down her figure, caressing her calf, then knee, then thigh. He kissed at her leg, and she wondered what was next. Or hoped. She wasn't sure.

Erick was bent, almost doubled over, and then he finally lifted his head with a soft groan. He nestled his head into Eliza's shoulder, and just wrapped his arm around her. His other hung uselessly behind the headrest. He didn't know where else to put it.

"This thing was not made for this," he said. Eliza tried to rub his back, but she couldn't reach it. Erick glanced at the clock under the tachometer on the dash. They had been struggling to get close, even though they were way too close, for over an hour.

Eliza looked at Erick in the vague light of a far distant streetlamp. "You look tired." The way she said it was more a sound of resignation than concern. She did her best to make him comfortable. "Let's get out and go to the beach," she suggested. She didn't care how cold and windy it was. There was room to move. Or at least room to stretch.

A gust of wind answered her. Erick looked at the soft convertible top as if it were the ceiling of a haunted house with a ghost walking on the floor above. "It's too cold," he said, tugging at the shoulder straps of her dress that had fallen tantalizingly off her shoulders and down her arms. He knew what she was implying, but there was no way, not on a sandy windblown beach, and definitely not in the cold.

"We could go look for a party, but I doubt anyone is out yet. The dance is probably just ending now. But, honestly, I really don't want to go, and I know your father would have a fit if I took you to a house with alcohol. And you know, someone would run their mouth. Or take a da... picture of us with a stack of red cups in the background." Erick felt resigned to being turned away at all the barriers put up to him. He wasn't going to undress his girlfriend in his car for their first time, and he wasn't going to get her in trouble with her parents if they went to a party for half an hour.

"Let's just stay here," Eliza answered. She lifted her hips, silently hinting for Erick to sit in the seat, as she slid into his lap. "This is perfect."

Erick kissed her lightly, then asked, "Did you have fun? I mean, I know it's not the entire prom experience."

"I loved it."

"I love you." Erick squeezed her tight and kissed her again, unaware of what he had said to Eliza. It seemed just right to him. He slowly became more aware as Eliza began to melt, her body warming, then with a soft shudder she squeezed him tight. Erick had meant it, at first, in the way that someone says "I love you" when a friend really comes through for them,

"Oh, wow, I *love* you!" Then Erick realized that he really meant it. They may have been just teenagers, but from the first moment Erick had seen Eliza, the moment he fell off his boat, he had been in love, and only thought of her through the whole school year.

"Can I tell you something?" Eliza asked, her brown eyes wide, soft, and bright.

"Sure."

"You're the first boy I ever kissed."

Erick only smiled. It was a silly comment, something a kid would say, hardly believable, but sweet. Then he realized both how young they were, and how far they had gone, as well as how desperately far they wanted to go, to the point of wrestling in a two seat car. Erick wondered what would have happened if he had taken the big S-Class with the back seat. It was a lot for a teenage boy to take in, stuck in the darkness in a gale.

"You're going to be the last girl I ever kiss."

They would give in, and drive home early. Both had to be up the next morning, and wouldn't see each other until Monday at school.

Eliza would undress with some help from her mother, who asked how the date went. Eliza tried to keep herself from seeming too excited, describing the night, knowing her father was listening in the hall. Once Eliza got changed into shorts and a t-shirt, she climbed into bed, letting the darkness hopefully calm her fluttering heart. "He said he loves me." She heard her own voice in her head, sounding so immature, like a little girl squealing to her friends. But Eliza knew Erick meant it.

Erick circled around and came home to a fairly calm and slightly proud set of parents, who plied him with similar questions. "It went fine. I don't know if she liked dinner, but it was a lot of fun. I'm just glad I got to go on a real date with her. I wish it didn't take a prom to do it." Erick took his jacket off, showing a disheveled unbuttoned collar. "I don't know how you stand it," he told his father, as he dropped his dress shoes to the floor by the closet.

"He looks so good," Jane said, taking Erick's jacket. "That's how I stand it," Conrad told him. "To please her." Erick understood a little better now. "You need something to eat?"

Erick, like any teenage boy, could eat a refrigerator empty in a few hours if he tried. But he really was tired. It had been a long day and night. Erick felt the exhaustion of dancing all evening, the discomfort of being pinned in the side of his car seat for an hour and a half, and the hopefully hidden sexual frustrations of doing what he thought was right. "I think I better just go to bed," Erick said. He wandered to the stairs and up to his room.

Erick could see the lights on at Eliza's house as the wind whipped the sea grass into waves. They blinked out before midnight, with only the yellow glow of a bulb on the back porch still shining softly. Erick had liked the nightlight ever since he had met Eliza, almost a year ago. "God, I love that girl." It wasn't a testament. It was a realization.

CHAPTER TWENTY-SIX

August 2001
Marlowe Beach

"I shouldn't be doing this."

It wasn't the voice in her head that told Eliza she shouldn't be tramping over a hill in a hurricane to go see her former boyfriend. It was her. This wasn't smart. On so many levels.

That voice had talked her into this, and then Eliza convinced it to agree with her. Eliza was at the point where she didn't know which way she was going. Except that she was going over the hill, back to Erick. She needed to see him before the storm got worse, before they were trapped inside.

"Before he leaves again," she said to herself.

Before you leave again, the voice in her head tried to say over a gust of wind.

At least it had stopped raining for a moment.

Hurricane Michelle had found its way just offshore, and would hit within a few hours, to the south, near the border between North and South Carolina. The little town of Calabash would probably see the eye go over it. Over Marlowe Beach, all that meant was that there would be rain and wind, and waves, and no let up until the storm was done. There would be no peace in the eye of the hurricane here. Eliza counted her blessings that she still had time, in between the rain bands, to tromp across the wet grass and sand path. There wasn't much of the trail left now after years of disuse.

She went around the side of Erick's beach house. It was still a habit, to come around the side and then up to the back door. No one had gone in the front door there when she was younger. As Eliza got close, she heard the outdoor shower running. A gust of wind carried the sound, then carried it away. Eliza walked around the shower, to the outside entrance, the little dressing area. Eliza didn't know what she should do. "Go inside the house? Wait for him on the sofa?" She thought that was too forward, now. When she was a teen, Eliza could run up the stairs to the back porch, her feet pounding a signal that she was there, and just come inside. Like she lived there. Erick's little sister Astrid would squeal, and then Erick would shoo her away, and Erick's mom would tell Eliza to get a drink, because it was hot. They treated her like she was family.

But Eliza couldn't go in, not now, not be waiting inside on the sofa like when she was fifteen.

Another gust of wind, and then a splash of rain with it.

Eliza couldn't stay outside. She would get soaked, again. She hadn't bothered with her mom's poncho. It was wet, and unflattering. She wasn't her mother.

"Erick?" she called out. "It's me…" "Who else would it be?" she told herself. "God, why do I still act this way?"

The shower ran unabated, no answer from inside. Then, in a moment, "… hey… I just need to get cleaned off."

"Can I wait here? It's starting to rain."

"... yes ..."

In the shower, just on the other side of the thin plywood wall, Erick leaned against the shower pipes. He held the hot and cold faucets. The hot was warm to the touch, the cold chilled, but the mix coming out the cheap plastic shower head was perfect, just the way he liked it, a bit of overly warm water, filled with iron from the lens of water brought up from a shallow well by the pump in the garage. Erick just let the water run over him, beating on the top of his head, making his hair droop over his face, hiding it.

Erick looked up, letting the spray wash over his face. He grabbed a bottle of soap, an old Dr. Bronner's liquid that he had started using about ten years ago when he got tired of scratching himself with a cheap bar covered in sand. He liked the smell. The peppermint usually made him feel good, invigorated. Erick smacked a handful onto his face, rubbing it roughly over his stubble, closing his eyes to wash his face clean. Erick hoped the peppermint worked this time to brighten him, or at least wash away what had been there. "Maybe she'll just go away again," Erick thought, as he rubbed the soap across his chest. A bit of cold wind washed through the opening under the shower wall, sending the water spraying back up for a moment as it defied gravity in a tiny vortex. It was, even after the many times he had experienced it, a strange feeling. It reminded Erick to put a copious amount of soap in his hands and wash more intimately. Erick hated how the sound water would trap itself in the most obscure places of his body.

Eliza sat quietly, just outside the shower door. She could see Erick's feet as he turned in the shower, but that was all. She looked around, but the little room offered no other place to rest her eyes. Erick's clothes, what little he had on were there, wet and ingloriously in a pile. So was his duffel, and an old towel. She almost laughed, thinking it was so much like a man, all he needed was a cheap towel and a change of clothes. But that wasn't fair. Erick had been put in a position to come to his home to close it up, and now he was stuck.

"*He's naked behind that door, you know.*"

"Shut up," she told herself. She knew. Erick would have to come out, to her. She had him cornered, unless he just stayed in the shower until she left first. The wind picked up harder now. They were getting closer to the main part of the hurricane now. Eliza felt the wall bow inward with the pressure, as if something was pushing her back to get her to stand up off the little bench.

"*He's right behind the door.*"

Erick washed his hair. It was the last of his mechanical, ritualistic pattern. Wash the body, then the hair, rinse, and let the soap run down him. Then a moment of peace. Just a minute of the hot water pouring down him, just hot enough to make a little steam. Especially now. Erick could feel the cold wind on his feet. Hurricanes carried with them warm, thick, humid blankets of air. But when they blew with the stinging heavy raindrops, they felt cold. Chilly little stingings as the wind blew droplets hard onto the skin. Then the power would go out, and the houses got hot and still inside and you had to get back out into the rain, just to cool off again.

Erick didn't have to get out of the shower, not yet. Eliza had said nothing, made no sound, as he closed his eyes and scrubbed his nails into his hair, feeling the little bit of silt that washed into his head when he sank his boat. The sand came out, but he scrubbed a little more, until his hair squeaked. "Maybe she left," Erick hoped. "Maybe not," he hoped, too.

Things would be so easier if, when he opened his eyes, Erick could turn the water off, go to his house, wait out the worst of the hurricane, and maybe leave before it got light tomorrow morning.

Erick opened his eyes, and Eliza was waiting by the opened door.

Eliza stood naked, waiting as she watched Erick under the shower. It felt wrong, and unfair, for her to come in when he was naked and vulnerable like this. But Eliza needed to see Erick this way. Eliza had watched as Erick's chest moved. He was still thin, but fit, taut, with his wide rounded shoulders and flat abs. Eliza used to like to see him like this. Then she stared at the scar across Erick's chest. It was a rude and unfair line, not even straight, but jagged and crooked, that went from under his right arm, across his chest, and then curved up over his collarbone to disappear before it got to his neck. The scar was thin, like a minuscule pink valley over Erick's body. Long, but fine, a kite string that wrapped over him, or the shadow of a bandolier. It was just an imprint. It was there, but it looked like Eliza could just reach out and pull it off Erick, like a wet piece of lint that had rolled up and Erick hadn't noticed.

Erick opened his eyes to see Eliza standing there, waiting for him.

For a moment he did nothing but stare at her. The two had snuck into the shower so often as teens, for a few moments of transgressions, that it felt almost common, as if they had stepped back for a time when they were back in school. Or the second time, when they were older, and darkness hid more adult, heated passions.

Erick reached out to Eliza and pulled her under the shower. Eliza gasped from the heat, while Erick turned the hot water down to a lukewarm trickle. Then Erick took Eliza's hand again and pulled her to him. Erick let his body warm hers so that Eliza became used to the hot water. Eliza had always liked the coolness of the shower after a hot day, unlike Erick's attempts at a sauna.

Eliza wrapped her hands around Erick's neck, letting one hand slowly go up his chest, just so she could feel where he had been torn apart, two years ago. Eliza had to know. But Erick didn't flinch, or didn't notice, or didn't care. In a moment, she had Erick locked to her, a soft but passionate kiss under the shower. Erick hadn't been distracted by her touch.

Erick turned Eliza around in the shower, pressing his chest against her back, and Eliza took Erick's hands to let them explore her naked body. His touch was familiar, but now more gentle and hesitant. The wind stirred the shower now, making the shower water do spirals on the wood floor at their ankles. Eliza put her hand up, behind Erick's head, and let him kiss and bite at her neck. She shivered when the wind hit her. Erick turned up the hot water. He kissed Eliza lower and lower on her back. It was a familiar map, but to a different place. Eliza turned again, slowly facing Erick, who ran his tongue across her hip. Then Erick lifted her leg, propping it on the tiny ledge at the bottom of the shower wall, so that he could find a much more intimate spot.

Eliza closed her eyes and bit her lip, as Erick held her by the hips. She tried desperately not to gasp or moan, even though no one would hear her as the tropical winds poured out over the beach. But her body gave way.

Erick was joyful, in a sort of kind relentlessness. His knee hurt, propped on the wooden floor. His neck hurt, bent backwards, and he didn't care. Eliza was above him, eyes closed halfway, but seeing nothing as she moaned and shuddered. Erick didn't want her to hurry, even if it meant bending and breaking him. He let her rock slowly, then passionately, a little harder each time. Erick caressed Eliza's thigh, just to reach toward her hand, then guide it to the back of his head to hold him tight against her. He let her enjoy herself for moments, then minutes, and minutes more.

Eliza felt herself build in passion, a relentless pressure that she remembered from the many times before. She gripped harder, pulling Erick closer to her, knowing that Erick had long ago given her the indulgence to do what she wanted, desired, and needed. Eliza couldn't hold back as she finally released herself in a shivering, rocking orgasm. It was familiar, but new, a new position, and certainly a new place, in the winds of a hurricane just offshore.

Erick felt Eliza finally force herself onto him, rocking her hips hard. She moaned softly, a shaking, shivering cry. Then an intake of breath, she held it, and again. Eliza twisted Erick's hair, holding him tight, a little too tight, for a little too long. Eliza remembered through the red haze of half closed eyelids of Erick's encouragement in the past. It was a familiar part, when he did something right for her, without worrying what it did to him.

Eliza felt a fast and electrifying quiver through her body, then a hard shudder that made her knees buckle as she barely kept balance in the wet confines of the shower. Then another, softer, more exhausted. And then, finally, the wonderful debilitation and lassitude that is satisfied by a loud and palpable exhalation of breath in a moaning pant as Eliza leaned against the side of the shower for support, with Erick still beneath her on his knees.

Erick finally stood up, holding Eliza by the waist so she wouldn't fall. She dug her hands into his neck for support, then found her favorite spot on Erick, nestling against his chest. The water still poured over them, unstoppable. In the garage, the well pump began a rhythmic tattoo as it engaged to bring more water up from the ground.

Eliza felt Erick's body, warm, still the same as it had been two years ago, before the accident. She felt him against her, still firm even with the water cooling his body. Eliza pulled herself to Erick, hinting at more.

Erick obeyed by scooping Eliza up awkwardly and letting her wrap her legs around Erick's hips. Eliza held on tightly with her arms and legs wrapped over Erick. There was little Eliza could do in her position, but all she had to do was be close, hold on to him, or grip the shower pipes for balance, and he did the rest.

Only after they both had been satisfied did Erick finally turn off the shower, now running cold from an empty tank. Eliza took the one towel and wrapped it around them both, in a failed attempt to keep them warm as the winds blew through the shower. She placed one hand on his shoulder, and traced a bit of the scar down his chest, before lifting it off in embarrassment.

"I just needed to know you were alright," Eliza said.

Erick held her close in the cooling outdoor shower. "I am," he said, quietly, "I am, now."

CHAPTER TWENTY-SEVEN

January 2000
Puerto Viejo de Talamanca

Erick had felt like a well tanned bouncing ball in the past year. After his accident, he spent two miserable weeks in the Spanish hospital, with his parents doting over him every day. The team had stayed until he regained consciousness, then had the decency to stay a day longer to give perfunctory good wishes, and left a representative for a week to make useless demands of the hospital in broken Spanish, occasional English, and flying fluent French. Erick would have laughed if his ribs hadn't been killing him. Catholic nuns and adoring young *voluntarias* both made his life better and more difficult, bathing him, as well as doing other more intimate care. The dark haired doe eyed Spanish girls who gave him the occasional dreamy look did nothing for Erick. He knew that even if he had any desire, his ripped open chest and every ragged gasping breath was not sexually appealing at the moment.

After two weeks, it was clear Erick's heart was not damaged. It was about the only part that wasn't. The broken ribs, messed up shoulder and the terrible rip across his chest were the most visible wounds, which meant Erick was bandaged across his chest and had a sling across his shoulder to immobilize his collarbone. Once Erick was stable, then came the first argument. Erick wanted to go home, just to find out what had happened to Eliza. No one even said anything about her. It was like no one noticed she was gone. Erick had asked with his fractured Spanish in a rare quiet moment if anyone had seen the thin brown haired/blonde girl he was with, but the staff all seemed as one to not even remember seeing her. They saw so many people, and they were more interested in treating the injured or sick.

The team had offered a recovery in the Champagne region of France, with therapy in between glasses of wine, it was implied. They weren't so much regretful of the events as they seemed to blame the Kiwis for knocking out the boat and injuring the crew. The team was trying to show off how much they cared, making the injury and recuperation a reward to lord over the New Zealand boat.

Conrad Sunstrom took the incident in a bit of stoic stride. He had seen accidents in auto racing, and knew this wasn't as bad as it could have been. His son was alive, so, yes, not as bad as it could have been. Jane had been more concerned. But she had been happy to see her son on the mend. The two of them insisted he go to Germany, where they had the resources of their name and brand to get the best care available. "The Germans were *German*," Erick had heard his head tell his beating heart, "efficient, caring, but cold, nice… *German*." All Erick wanted to do was to get better as soon as possible, hopefully well enough that every spoken word wasn't a gasp of pain.

Stuttgart it was.

There was outpatient treatment by sturdy German caregivers in a clean German rental home with a quiet and efficient, yet again, servant to clean the house and cook the very German meals.

Erick missed the red wine and tapas of only a few months ago. He had to get out of there.

Better but still wounded, with the repairs done to his body, not so much his mind, Erick wanted to go back to the beach, just to do some slow therapy to get his body back into shape. He had gotten soft and thin as his body softened his muscles from disuse, and his naturally creamy skin started showing through his tan. Erick certainly wasn't going to get much of a tan in October on Marlowe Beach. And there were no real therapists or trainers on the island. His parents asked him to come to Atlanta, but he had other plans.

Erick really needed some time alone. He was wounded, on the mend, but had not heard from Eliza since his accident. He didn't even know where she was. She had been traveling with him for the past year. Erick had planned, or at least hoped, to put together some form of controlling interest in a sailing team, to give him a sense of security, a plan. Then he was going to propose to Eliza. Erick had even purchased an old Masreira ring from a jewelry dealer, just as a placeholder until she could pick out a more appropriate one. The delicate gold leaves evoked spring and a delicious gossamer evanescence, which was what Erick always felt around his girlfriend, as if things were going to change with every gust of wind.

Now, Erick didn't even know how to contact Eliza. He even pondered calling her parents, but he had enough pain in his life. Erick wondered how that conversation would go, "I don't know what her father would tell me, 'Go to hell,' 'I told you so,' 'You're not good enough for her,' 'Stay away before you hurt her again.'" All of them seemed like accurate, if unfair, choices.

Instead it was winter in a shack in Costa Rica. The weather was going to be getting colder in North Carolina and in Georgia. On Marlowe Beach, a coastal low had turned into a fall nor'easter, blowing the ocean into people's backyards across the coast. It hadn't gotten better from there. A winter ice storm blew through Atlanta, then went up the coast, flooding and chilling the mid-Atlantic coast. While others suffered with aches from their age and injuries in the cold air, Erick had stared at the same tropical water day in and out as he stretched, swam, lifted weights to finally get some tone back. Then Erick would cook himself in suntan oil to a tasty brown on the palm tree infested beaches. It was an interesting life, one that almost let Erick forget what had happened to him. Even his scar, a strange jagged diagonal across his chest, had finally started to heal some, with liberal doses of a sticky honey poultice that attracted the local flies in bunches but definitely helped smooth the wound across his heart.

Erick's former partner on the Miami sails had come to visit him at the time. Terrance Creedy had sailed with Erick back in the 90s. It sounded so weird to say that, but to Erick, Terrance was from a different time. Even though it was, "five years ago?" Erick couldn't quite believe it. Erick felt like he had aged three years in the past six months. When Terrance had shown up, Erick wondered just how many years Terrance had aged in the past five years.

Terrance was balding more than he had been back in the day, and had a bit of a gut, a bit more than back in the day. But Terrance had always looked like a thirty-something carefree amateur sailor, because that is what he had always been. He just was very, very good at it. And Erick loved him dearly. They got along incredibly well for two very different people.

"So, how's the family?" It felt funny to even say that. Erick thought it sounded like something an adult would say to another adult, not two sailors who laughed their way through storms and waves.

"Good, it gets easier, well, I don't know if easier is the right word, more like experienced, with the second one." Terrance had a three year old and a newborn.

"Sheila okay with you coming down here?"

"Yeah, she's probably happy to get me out of her hair," Terrance laughed as he scratched his balding dome under his ubiquitous short brimmed hat. This one was yellow, but Terrance always seemed to have a rainbow supply of the little cloth caps, all ready to match whatever boat he was on for the day.

The two spent the day just talking, mostly, as they sat on Erick's porch overlooking the Atlantic waters. Erick explained the accident, and Terrance had the obligatory sailor tantrum swearing at the New Zealand sailors. It sounded funny coming from a dad, Erick thought. Terrance had been incredibly light-hearted and easy going when they sailed, no matter what the situation. Whenever they sailed, if there ever was a disagreement, it was rare, and the apologies were quick and rote, hardly worth the breath, the two were so forgiving of each other.

When Terrance finally asked about Eliza, Erick just shrugged. "I haven't heard from her since the accident. I don't even know where she is. She may be back at Falmouth now. I tried there after the accident, but they wouldn't give me any information other than she wasn't there then. It's like she doesn't want to be found."

Terrance shrugged and looked around, waving his arms at the empty paradise. "Yeah," he commented, "Who would do such a thing?"

Erick laughed. Terrance may be right, he may be wrong, but Erick had escaped from reality for a while. It wasn't like Erick had made himself easy to be found, either.

"What do you want to do now?" Terrance had asked.

"I was thinking…" Erick began.

"Bad idea," Terrance joked as he took a swig of Imperial beer.

"I know," Erick laughed again. His chest and ribs had long ago stopped hurting, but it felt good to laugh like that again. "Anyway, you ever do a cross Pacific sail? I feel like I might want to do that. I've been wanting to go to Point Nemo." The spot far off in the Pacific Ocean was the most isolated point in the world. It was so far away, anyone sailing there would be closer to an astronaut passing over than any person on land.

"Point Nemo?" Terrance almost spit out his beer in an act of incredulity at the suggestion. "Are you nuts? There's nothing there. You hear about Isabelle Autissier? She went there. Her boat capsized there last year and she sat there until another sailboat rescued her. Just sitting on the hull for a day and a night.

"Why would you want to sail all the way out there? It seems like a place people go to die, if you ask me. Don't they crash spaceships there?"

"It seems like a good test," Erick flexed his arm, showing off his tanned and firming up shoulder.

"A good test?!" Terrance opened another beer. "Come to Miami this spring. Here's a good test right here," Terrance flexed his own bicep as he bent the bottle to his lips, sending half the beer down in a series of gulps. "Dude…" Terrance shook his head, unable to find the words, then looked at the half drunk bottle, "I'm going to need more of these if you're gonna talk shit like that."

Erick smiled at his friend. He had needed someone to tell him straight, and clear. Terrance didn't always have all the answers, but he knew bullshit when he heard it. "I guess I just need something to think about. I don't want to end up fat with hammock rope imprinted on my ass."

"And bald," Terrance said. "Don't forget bald."

"Not gonna happen, Creedy!" Erick got up from his chair and went inside for more beer. "I'm fighting it all the way!" Erick shook his long hair for emphasis. He hadn't had a haircut in months now.

"You look like a surfer dude, not a sailor," Terrance teased. "You should get a windsurfer board. Go up to Hatteras, surf with those Canucks."

Erick snorked.

"You can go to Tampa. Sheila can get you a great deal on a condo!" Terrance's wife was a flourishing Florida Realtor.

"I'd rather go bald!"

It was like that the rest of the day, and into the night, until Terrance was more than slightly drunk. "I can't do those late night deals anymore. Dad time is rough. I gotta get my sleep when I can." Both ended up calling it an early night.

The next day the two toured the area, finding a boat to rent and doing a simple sail out into the blue-green waters, like the old times of five long years ago. Erick had tested his arm, his skill, and his trust, and all had been successful. Terrance had made it easy for him. The evening before Terrance had to fly out, the two had sat at a local watering hole, eating ceviche, plantains, and beans, while swilling it all down with beer. "I could get used to this, I'll tell ya that for free," Terrance said as he downed a thin filet of lime coated snapper. "Listen, man, you gotta find your next thing. And I don't mean sailing solo around the world, dumbass. If you want to sail, then sail, come back to Florida, we'll put you up, the kid will love to see you, and you haven't even seen our baby girl yet. Come be the crazy uncle in the fancy car. Get a windsurfer, hell, get another cat, I don't know, but don't just sit here and get pickled in lime juice."

"I know," Erick picked at a mashed plantain. "It's just…"

"Yeah…" Terrance repeated the unsaid words with his eyes. "I don't know what to tell you about that. Maybe put yourself in the paper again. Look, I'm not that guy. Sheila and I pretty much settled for each other, and it isn't like either one of us prowled around. I'm not the most handsome guy in the world. So I don't know what advice to give you. I mean, it seems like…" he paused, hating to say it, "if she wanted you to find her…"

Erick said nothing, but nodded softly, looking at the sand covered floor.

"Maybe give someone else a chance."

"Yeah," Erick said, "someone else."

CHAPTER TWENTY-EIGHT

December 2000
Falmouth

Eliza tied her running shoes up as she sat on the bed. It was just easier and quicker to get dressed at her apartment than to go to the workout gym in Woods Hole and change there. Winter was setting in on Cape Cod, which meant cold, wet, short days, with ice and snow coming in the next month or so. It was already too cold to go for a run, so she spent time in the mornings on a treadmill. The mornings were quieter, with only the die-hards who took exercise seriously, and weren't there for chitchat.

Eliza had taken a year off from work in 1998 for a sabbatical, in order to follow Erick on his races. Her superiors had been encouraging of it. "After five years, a lot of people get burned out, doing the same work," explained her immediate supervisor. "This is a good career for you, but you need to see it from the outside for a while, know what you are missing. We lose too many people after five to seven years. I try to encourage a year off, or at least a position abroad for a time." It had been too easy, like they didn't even want her, even though they had said they did.

Eliza hadn't known where to go after Erick's accident. She was less than welcome at home. She knew her father would have a daily "I told you so," on his lips, and would encourage her to find a nice man who worked at the processing factory, who went to church on Sundays and Wednesday evenings. The thoughts made her cringe. Eliza had been down that road before, and it didn't work out well. Instead she headed back to Falmouth to stay with co-workers and re-establish her job there.

Eliza didn't say much about what had happened to anyone. She kept the end of her relationship tight inside her. Even as she grew closer to her friends again, Eliza simply said that she and Erick had different ideas on their relationship.

Perhaps it was the exotic nature of a young woman traveling the world, a picture of both cuteness and scientific intellectualism, experienced, wild, even, that made Eliza become an appealing target for the men at work. The various sciences, engineering, biology, and technology didn't exactly create an air of sexiness for the women who worked there, and the men were even less appealing. Scientific curiosity in one man's mind looked like nerdy monomania to Eliza. Plus, the cold weather brought out the layers of coats and dumb longshoreman stocking caps, pale skin, extra weight. "This place is nothing like Mallorca," Eliza said as she got out of her Camry, new to her, but used in the wrong way before she bought it. Eliza shook the thought from her head. It wasn't fair to compare the two places, and she really, really, didn't need that now.

Eliza showed her ID to the woman working the early morning desk at the gym before going to the multi-use room to stretch. The gym was warm, with a small pool and hot tub that no one used except for the occasional aquacise class. Eliza had given up swimming in it and soaking in the hot tub as soon as someone else decided to get in with her. At least running on the treadmill gave a sense of focus, a Do Not Disturb sign as she ran, eyes forward, not bothering to see who was near her. Eliza went to the weight room with rows of treadmills and stair steppers that no one was using. She chose the one farthest from the door and programmed her morning run. It was just a fifteen minute jog, usually not much more than two miles. Eliza could go faster and farther, but that wasn't the point.

A mile in and Eliza was starting to feel awake and loose. The morning workout wouldn't come close to exhausting her. This was like coffee, just a reason to get out of bed and out of the house, away from her roommate, away from anyone who wanted to engage with her. Eliza saw herself in the mirror, still in track pants and a t-shirt. No sports bra, no shorts, it was too cold outside for that. That's what she told herself. Eliza could see the few others that were up early, the usual not so crowded crowd. An athletic red haired woman that Eliza recognized but never spoke to was on a weight machine. She was the opposite to Eliza in most ways. Pink and white skin, bright fiery red hair, thickly built, not slim, but powerful, a feminine version of a football team's tight end. An older man who lifted light weights and jogged for hours, Eliza wondered when he ever got his work done. Two more men would be coming in soon, a pair of pals who made too much noise for early in the morning, seemingly to tag team their entrance to overcome the shyness that they had singly. But the two barely spoke to anyone else. Eliza liked them because they seemed afraid to speak to her.

Out of the corner of her eye, Eliza could see the glass window of the front desk, far beyond the pool and workout room. She saw the woman there talking with someone, just out of view. Then the figure walked by to the men's locker room. Even from the distance, through windows and empty space, she recognized the man who came in. The dark hair and beard gave him away. Michael Canlon, a doctoral student who had come in the year Eliza had taken her sabbatical. "God," Eliza said, looking around at a place to escape, "Why is he here now?"

Eliza had moved back in the late summer. She had tried to fit in as well as she could. Most of the graduate students and researchers had bonded over group work, trips to sea, or lectures. Eliza had still been getting reacquainted with her friends, and hadn't even had much of a chance to meet new researchers. Michael had arrived to finish his doctoral dissertation. At 34, he was older than the graduate students, but had fit in with the crowd because they were all in the same boat, a different one than the professors and post doctorates. He had almost immediately shown an interest in Eliza.

Her friends had encouraged Eliza. They had known Michael, saying he was fun, outgoing, always with a smile on his face. He got along well with most everyone. When he began paying special attention to Eliza in their social free time, it seemed like a good match for the two. A kindhearted and smart man, fairly handsome, especially compared to the other academics, single, Eliza's coworkers were more pulling for him to become a couple with her, rather than the other way around.

Eliza had felt like she had given in, but Michael had been a nice enough man. They held hands when they went out to local concerts. He didn't pressure her into drinking, and understood she didn't want to be around someone who drank too much alcohol. It took weeks of friendly socializing, but Michael had worn Eliza down with a quiet charm.

He was handsome, Eliza had to admit. The clean cut dark hair and growing black beard, just a week old stubble in the early fall gave him a look of ruggedness, while dark eyes softened his face with a bit of kindness.

Eliza felt like she kept having to explain to him she wasn't ready for anything serious, every time they went out on a date and he got closer to her. Evenings on walks had Michael leading Eliza to dark and private spots where he wold pull her close to kiss her. Eliza would reciprocate, until Michael would pull her close, too close, too forceful, hinting at wanting more.

Her roommate would occasionally be asking if she had slept with him yet. The plain and nerdy group of marine biologists and scientists, especially the younger graduates and undergrads, hid a seething side of rampant sex, especially on any sea going voyages where boredom often led to the introverted kids from high schools and the science labs of colleges getting a wild release when they were finally free with their own kind. Eliza found their hedonistic adventures unappealing. She had been the popular girl in high school, which meant she didn't fit in as well with this crowd. Eliza felt the pressure to fit in. She also wondered what was wrong that she was dating a man but wasn't entirely physically attracted to him.

It was early December when she had finally acquiesced and accepted a visit to his apartment to spend the night. Dinner and then a bit of TV was about all the foreplay Michael had needed as the two undressed on the sofa. Eliza had been uncomfortable from the beginning. What had shocked her most was just Michael's lack of appeal to her. He had undressed to his boxers, plain loose blue cotton, just dumb excuses for underwear. His chest was hairy and dark, with coarse curls in a mat that matched his face and head. Eliza had been repulsed, not just by his body, but by what she was about to do. "I can't do this," she had told him. Michael would claim he was in his beginning throes of passion as he tried to keep her close to him on the sofa. He pulled on her wrist, and it twisted as Eliza had wiggled her way out from his grasp. She held her wrist close to her, grabbing her clothes as quickly as possible, only partially able to get dressed. But she had put Michael at a disadvantage. He had tried to hold her down for sex, even if only for a moment. Then she pulled her pants on, standing far from him and near the door, while he lay on his side, all dark and hairy, like a dumbstruck bear, only in his boxers. He wouldn't be able to stop her from leaving, Eliza thought. If he did anything, no matter what he told people, it would still be a stain on him. Eliza had seen the fear in his eyes as he had looked at Eliza's wrist as she held it close to her chest. She hadn't waited for pride and shame to fight out on whether to leave immediately or get fully dressed first. Eliza held her shirt close to her as she ran out the door. She hadn't even driven to his house. Eliza walked home alone in the cold and dark.

She had confided with both her roommate and her supervisor. Her roommate had been surprisingly supportive, while the supervisor had done nothing more than note the incident as a lover's quarrel. Her roommate commiserated, "We've been there, girl. I'm proud you got out of there and didn't go through with it." She sounded guilty for encouraging Eliza so recently before.

And now here he was, showing up at her quiet time, where Eliza could take out the morning stress. "This can't be a coincidence," she knew. Eliza looked around, trying to figure out a way out that didn't send her back by the front desk. The only place to go was the women's bathroom. Eliza turned off the treadmill, grabbed her bag and water, and began to walk toward the bathroom. She could hide inside, but couldn't get out without Michael seeing her. Eliza hated the idea of standing around in the bathroom for an hour until Michael left. But it seemed more appealing than talking to him.

So she ran.

Ten minutes later, Eliza was leaning against the wall. She was done pacing. It didn't help any. Eliza needed to get out, shower, and go to work. She jumped a little when the door opened, and the redhead came in. Immediately, the woman asked, "Are you okay?"

"Yeah… No…" Eliza didn't want to air her laundry, not here, not to a stranger. "I mean… Is that guy still out there? With the beard?"

"Yes… why?"

Eliza didn't like to lie, but didn't want to admit the truth, at least as she saw it. She had gone up to a man's apartment for sex and then turned him down. That's what someone else would say happened. And that was what happened, but … not. "He kinda had a thing for me. I had to turn him down. I just don't want to deal with it now."

"Girl," it was the same tone as her roommate over a month ago. "Say no more. You got a car? Your keys?"

"Yes."

"Well, that guy has been watching me in the mirror while he was running on a treadmill for the past ten minutes. I get it. I mean, I get it a lot. But usually it's a glance, not a constant stare." Her comment made Eliza more uncomfortable. She should have seen Michael differently. "Hey," it was as if the redhead read Eliza's mind, "sometimes it helps to look at a person through their reflection. I saw that look on your face now. Don't you do that.

"I'll get you out of here."

It took about another ten minutes. She came back to get Eliza, still alone in the women's room. The two went out through the offices and storerooms from the back while Michael was back at the front desk. The two young men were in an animated conversation with him, making sure his back was to the window and the workout room far behind.

CHAPTER TWENTY-NINE

August 2001
Marlowe Beach

"*Well, he's not broken.*"

Stupid voice in my head, that's not what I meant.

Eliza and Erick ran, foolishly, from the shower to the back walkway steps to the back porch to the back door to Erick's house. They had gotten dressed and tried to cover themselves with a single wet towel over their heads, but the hurricane was blowing hard now, sending sheets of rain sideways on them as they ran the short distance from the outdoor shower to the inside of the house. It was only forty feet, but by the time Erick had opened the door and let them inside, they were soaked. Not drenched, but wet enough to feel the cold of the air conditioning chill them. "We'll dry off quick," he had told Eliza, as if she didn't know. A coastal life, with tropical storms and hurricanes always on the doorstep, meant getting rained on was a part of life. If it started raining when you were in the ocean, you didn't get out. That was silly.

Erick went to get more towels for their hair, while Eliza watched the news on TV. The hurricane was moments from making landfall somewhere near North Myrtle Beach. The reporter stood just outside one of the big high rise hotels that glutted the land there, showing the strength of the wind.

"Ninety miles an hour," Eliza told Erick as he threw her a towel.

Erick scrubbed at his hair. "I can believe it. I think I just got more sand in there than I washed out."

"You just need a haircut," Eliza teased.

"Yeah, I probably do. Mom would like that."

"You'd look good with short hair." Eliza roughed up Erick's head with his towel and giggled. She was sorely tempted to grab his arm and squeeze him close, like she used to. But it seemed possessive, and it was too soon.

"*You just had shower sex with him.*"

Shut up. Just right now, let me enjoy the moment.

Eliza realized she needed it do just that. It was a moment. A bit of peace during a very long storm, so she did nothing but watch the blue hooded talking head with the microphone in a bag scream at a wet camera lens. The Weather Channel cut to their other reporter in Wrightsville Beach, where it was a cloudy white, but no rain, not yet.

"Lucky stiffs, they probably won't get anything there." Erick sniffed as he threw his wet towel on a wooden dining chair. "Look at that beach. I always liked Wrightsville."

"Did you ever think of moving there?" Eliza asked. After she said it, she realized it was a soft way of asking an important question. It was just a vague little ask, a daydream.

"No," Erick answered. It's crowded with vacation houses, too much traffic. I like Wilmington, but it's turning into just another city. If I want to live in just a city, I'll go live in Atlanta. Drink Coke and fly everywhere."

"Where are you now?" This was more into what Eliza wanted to know. What she really wanted to know was, "Where do you want to be?" but that would come. Maybe he'll just say it.

"Good question," Erick responded. Eliza realized he took the question not in the geographic sense. "I'm short terming in Florida. Sheila Creedy got me a place while I work on the cat. And I have my mailbox in Atlanta."

"Mailbox?"

"Yeah, I have an apartment there where I can stay if I need to when I'm home. I just need some place to send the bills. Mom goes over and gets my mail. She calls the place my mailbox."

This man is as settled as a jellyfish, Eliza's mind told her. She agreed with herself with an invisible nod. "You need to find a place to be," Eliza told Erick, looking away so as not to stare into his eyes and accuse him, or hint at anything. Eliza opened her mouth to continue, but Erick timed her out.

"Yeah, Creedy keeps telling me that. You want some coffee to warm you up?" Erick walked away before she could answer.

CHAPTER THIRTY

August 2001
Marlowe Beach

Erick had already had this conversation, too many times. Most of the time it was with his parents, who always wanted him back home in Atlanta, working for the business. Astrid could handle that, but Erick knew at some time, he would have to be more involved. But not yet. He walked to the kitchen to make a real pot of coffee. The rain came down in heavy buckets now, making the world outside seem green with water and tropical flourishes. It was a trick of the mind. The sky was getting gray and dark, with hints of an ashen blue. The ocean on the other side of the dune began to roar, and Erick knew it would be a slate gray with foaming white waves, all ugly with sea foam. "I'm moored, not on the hook."

Sailors refer to being at anchor as "on the hook," where they can pull up at any time and leave. Tied to a dock, especially in a gale, that meant you were stuck. It was as good a time as any for a cup of coffee. "Maybe a splash of rum, too.

Just don't get the mugs mixed up." Erick didn't ask how Eliza liked her coffee. If she did drink it, which was seldom, it either was loaded with chocolate or mixed with enough cream and sugar to make it a hot milkshake. Erick found some liquid creamer for Eliza, and just a pinch of sugar in a mug of black coffee for himself. He took a sip of Eliza's, just to make sure it wasn't too hot. The storm gods sent an extra gust for the lie.

Erick came back to the living room, TV still blaring, but this time a commercial, as Eliza looked around. "Same old place, huh?" he said. Erick tried to figure out the last time she had been here. Definitely before the accident. And not in the year they had traveled. He didn't even get home to the beach in all of 1998. So probably 1997, soon after they had gotten back together.

Eliza was looking at some of the photos on the old fireplace mantle. The smooth red brick hearth stuck out in hard rectangular shapes, horizontal bricks, so different from the soft floor to ceiling cypress wood. On it were two whelk shells, which were by rule of the beach necessary at all old houses. Matching duck decoy pictures faced each other. They had probably come with the place, Erick had thought, and never asked his parents why they were there. Then, strewn across the mantle and top of the hearth were pictures in frames of the family. It was a noticeably equitable mix of Erick, Astrid, and their parents. There was a shot of Conrad at the wheel of a race car. Astrid in a swing on a tropical beach somewhere, a teenage dream of a girl in a red bikini, all smiles and sunglasses. Erick and someone looking goofy as they sailed a small catamaran. Eliza picked up the photo in the frame. "Is that your friend?"

"Yes, that's Terrance. You met him, back in '95, when we did that sail up from Miami to Norfolk. We landed here. He's the reason I'm building my boat now. He pushed me to do it, back when I didn't have anything better to do. He's a nice guy. Nuts. But nice. He's got two kids now. One will be starting school now. Jeez, we're getting old." He took the photo from

Eliza, stared at it, and put it back on the mantle. "I still see him every month or so when I'm down in Florida long enough. He lives in Boca Raton."

"Do you want to move to Florida? When the boat is done?"

"Oh, God no!" Erick shook his head in disgust. "I've done Miami, and I don't need to do it again. I'd gnaw my own leg off to get out of that trap." Erick saw where this was going. "So, where are you now?" Erick wanted to know, but then, he still didn't really want to know. Not anymore. Erick had no desire to hear about how Eliza left him and went wherever she had gone. "No, I want to know, I just don't want to hear it," Erick told himself just after it was too late to take back the words he spoke.

"I'm back in Falmouth. I got my position at Woods Hole back."

"You like it there?" That was the leading question that Erick knew Eliza was trying to ask him, "and there I go asking it," Erick said in his head.

Eliza sighed. She didn't know what to say. "*Maybe the truth?*" her mind told her. "Nnnoooo…" she slurred. "Not really. It's just cold there." That was a good excuse, and technically true. "And to be honest, ever since I got back, I feel like I don't fit in there." That was more than technically true. "I like the work, but it's not home anymore."

"I get it," Erick agreed. "I haven't been home in years." He said it with a hint of inflection.

Eliza smiled. "That's a quote from a movie, isn't it? I can tell when you do that now."

Erick didn't answer, but paced across the room. He looked at the other pictures on the hallway. Little maps of the island, a few of his boats and cats, Erick and his sister growing up. Eliza was absent from the photos, even though there had been a time when she was up there, too. Astrid had a picture of her and her current boyfriend displayed. "That's what Mom would do,"

Erick recognized his mother's touch of ridding the world of anything from the past that wasn't in the present.

Eliza followed Erick. She knew the pictures by heart. Most of them, at least. They were bright and slightly blurry photos from the 80s and 90s taken by a point and shoot camera, with overexposed sand and bright gleaming colors. "You look happy here," she said of a picture of Erick on the beach.

"Castles in the sand, huh? Yeah, the beach is my happy place. There, and a boat."

"You ever think of coming back here?"

Erick paused, stopped, and looked at Eliza. That was what was going through her head, was it? Coming back here. To Marlowe. He didn't want to get into that discussion, even though it was coming. Erick deflected. "Do you know that quote, 'castles in the sand'? You know where that comes from?"

"No, but I can guess you're going to tell me." Eliza frowned. It was probably another film, she guessed. Eliza started to remember why she hated all Erick's movie quotes.

"I am. It's from a poem by Edna St. Vincent Millay. She says 'Safe upon the solid rock the ugly houses stand. Come and see my shining palace built upon the sand!' It's about the difference between a stable life and a temporary one. We can build an ugly house and be safe, or we can built a sand castle, have it crash down, and build something new." Erick left it at that. He wasn't going to explain any more of it to Eliza. He didn't need to explain it, or his choice, to anyone anymore. Erick turned, walked past her, and out to the back door. Even in this rain, he needed some air.

The rain came down in a torrent now, with heavy winds whipping across the dunes. The sea grass lay flat, like a short and dull politician's haircut. Erick could see the part in the scalp of the dune. Near his sundeck, now weathered and dark after being soaked by rain, a yucca stood guard with its narrow stalk flower upright even in the wind, like a palace halberd. The pointy leaves at the base trembled, though, as they filleted the wind coming over the dune. Erick opened the back door anyway, and went out onto the covered but unscreened porch.

The rain blasted him, even as Erick stood with his back to the wall. The sky looked brighter and clearer than through the salt rimed windows. It was gray, but a harsh daylight gray. The clouds moved over each other as they raced from the ocean to the shore. It reminded Erick of how the big sailing ships would force themselves along a path, not answering the helm for a change in course as the wind fought against the captain's will. The clouds just plowed ahead, great sky whales unhindered by pleas or wishes. The hurricane was coming ashore, and no man could stop her.

"Damn, Michelle," Erick said into the wind. It wasn't a curse, not in the sense of cursing the wind. A compliment. She's coming to shore, and there's nothing you guys can do.

Eliza stood in the doorway and laughed. "Come in out of the rain."

CHAPTER THIRTY-ONE

March 2000
Playa del Carmen

Erick watched as the athletic blonde woman walked topless across the tile floor of his condo. She only wore a simple bikini bottom, not even shoes, as she padded ever so softly over the smooth tiles. Her feet made tiny, delicate kissing sounds with every tread.

"You've grown pretty comfortable here since I met you," he said.

Sophie Pannier had met Erick five days ago on her first night in Playa del Carmen. Erick had lost track of how many nights it had been for him there. The two met at the tourist tiki bar near the pool of the big condominium complex. The main buildings were mostly for weekly vacationers, like Sophie and her cadre of girlfriends who came to Playa del Carmen to escape the cold spring of Illinois for a week. Erick had been passing by after a visit to the large, well equipped workout room, on his way back to one of the more distant buildings that seasonal vacationers used to come down for months in the winter.

Erick had taken Terrance's advice in a way and gotten back to some form of civilization, staying at the condo owned by his family's business for the higher end clientele to use when needed to schmooze a wealthy buyer. Or to rehab a racer in the winter. Playa del Carmen had an efficient and well run medical staff that could serve about any need to the expats, gringos, and the ultra wealthy who needed to get away to do cosmetic surgery or heal from various wounds, some of which might be detrimental to be seen in the U.S. All Erick needed was a bit of massage and some cardio and weight training.

Moving from the quietude of Costa Rica to the hubbub of Playa del Carmen in Mexico was a bit of a shock, but it also was a bit of what Erick needed. He was able to get out with other people, just talk and rub elbows, maybe bend one, too. And yes, meet a few women. Though that hadn't been as fun as Erick had hoped. Erick might still have been a handsome twenty nine year old, but he was still a twenty nine year old, heading toward thirty. And the bubbly college crowd of rich spring break girls, or the rich divorcees with stretched necks and no time to waste didn't appeal to him. Sophie, at twenty eight, saw Erick, the handsome easy going guy who looked like he knew where he was going and didn't bother to make eye contact with the flavors of the week at the bar, and was immediately intrigued. Erick had stopped for a drink because he knew this bartender on duty, and he could get an actual decent mixed drink from the guy, not a flowery pineapple with a bit of well rum thrown in. Sophie didn't need the nudge from her friends to say hi, but the whole group of them staring and smiling certainly drew Erick's attention.

Two nights later and she was visiting his condo in the quiet section of the resort. Now Sophie had moved in enough to walk around topless. Erick didn't mind one bit.

"I'm no better," Erick said to her. He waved his hands vaguely at his chest. He had no shirt and only beach shorts on.

"I can cover up if you like," Sophie said.

"No, I don't mind. Really." Erick wasn't trying to be lewd or puerile. In fact, it was almost the opposite. One of the many things he knew he was missing all alone on a Costa Rican shore was physical contact, the warmth of skin to skin, an intimate closeness that Erick needed. Feeling Sophie pressed against him, especially his torn chest, with her warm and long body had felt as healing as the preceding casual intimacy.

Erick had taken a bit of time to explain his life story, in the briefest of monologues, "Expensive cars, sailing, accident, therapy, blah blah blah…" was about all he had said, in a few more words. Sophie hadn't been shocked or even stared at his scar when Erick took his shirt off. Erick had been shocked, a little bit, in a good way, when Sophie removed hers for the first time.

Sophie had explained her life in only a bit more detail. "Single, girls week, getting out of Chicago, blah blah blah…" Then she explained she worked for a plastics manufacturing company with headquarters in Chicago. Neither person seemed to care too much about the backstory at the time. Five days and four nights later and the two had become comfortable. Erick was getting used to having a half naked woman in his house. It wasn't entirely what Terrance had suggested, but it was somewhere in the bigger picture.

Sophie looked over at a desk in the big condo that overlooked the ocean view sliding glass doors. It looked oddly mixed with a cluttered order. Pencils, a few rulers, a box with a compass, and a sketch pad. Everything was out, in its place, but the desk was covered with tools. A mess, but an organized mess. "What's this?" Sophie asked, picking up the sketch book. The most recent sketches were very neat line drawings of a long and thin catamaran, gliding over a flat line of water, as if it was skating on hot ice. "These are nice. I didn't know you were an artist."

"Engineer, actually."

"Oh…" Sophie said it like "ew," but held back on the disgust just enough.

"I know, I know, we're known to be kinda stiff."

"What are you drawing?"

Erick took the sketchpad, took a deep breath, and held it. In the moment, he knew that most of the time, almost all of the time, people just didn't care about these dreams and ideas, especially when he had to explain things. Especially engineering things. "It's part of my therapy," he explained simply. "My old mate, a best friend of mine told me, I need to find my next thing, my something else, is what he called it."

Sophie looked at the picture, "So, is art your something else, your next thing?"

"Kinda," Erick said simply. He waited, to see how Sophie responded. "You don't like engineering? I would think with your job you would see a lot of that stuff."

Sophie laughed, "I'm a mid-level regional manager; I run the interaction of plants and shipping. I don't do the design work. As a matter of fact, I avoid that like the plague, really."

"Well," Erick tried to play along, "I do, too. In a way. I…" he was going to start with "Look," but that was where everyone began when they wanted to explain something, something that no one cared about. And what Erick drew was different. "Um… do you like this picture?" Erick showed a detailed line drawing of a swooping catamaran, the sail small but filled. The drawing almost looked like it was moving.

"Yes, it's nice. I wouldn't call it art, but, well, it's close."

"What do you like about it?"

Sophie thought it was a trick question. She looked at Erick, who just smirked a small smile, saying it was okay, "Say what you want."

"It looks..." she turned the drawing to make the catamaran upright, "sleek? Happy? I'm not sure."

"You're right, it's happy." Erick smiled. "What you see and feel are what makes it, what it is. Does that make sense?" Sophie nodded, seeing Erick get excited. "Now, your stiff engineer friends would tell you about how the sail and the keel works and all that. Form follows function, and all that shit, right?" Again she nodded. "Well, this, from my eye, is function follows form. I'm starting with what is beautiful, sleek, like you said, and making it work. Truth is beauty and beauty is truth, and I'm starting with beauty.

"And she's a beauty."

Erick smiled at the picture, then set it down, and leaned over to kiss Sophie. She put her arms around his neck, her fingers grazing the scar before wrapping around his neck and kissing him back. "Well, I think you might have found your something else."

Morning went into day, and into afternoon, after the heat of the worst of the day, and the siesta that kept the heat at bay. Erick took Sophie out on the resort catamaran. It was a forgiving and generic craft, but Erick didn't mind. He wasn't racing anywhere. He barely even lifted a keel. Sophie had screamed as the cat rose up on one hull as it went faster and faster, so Erick lowered it back down immediately. After about fifteen minutes, he could tell how Sophie looked longingly at the beach. Erick knew there were people who just enjoyed sailing, and those who loved it. He turned the rudder and ran the boat to the beach, where Sophie's girlfriends waved for her to join them at the bar.

The next night, Erick and Sophie stood under one of the long line of identical palm trees that bordered the beach and grassy park that was the center of the resort. White lights reached up from the base of the trees to light them up at night, while casting long shadows of people as they strolled by.

"This has been a wonderful vacation," Sophie confided. She whispered into Erick's ear.

"It doesn't have to end, you know. You can stay a little longer if you want." Erick pulled Sophie close. She wore only her bikini top and a tight, long white sarong. It was the costume of choice for sexy twenty-somethings on holiday in Playa del Carmen, and Erick was perfectly fine with the outfit. He wrapped his arms around her bare waist, while Sophie lingered on his bare shoulders. Erick had put on a linen white button down shirt, but had barely bothered to button it, except to cover the lower part of his scar. That, too, was the expected look of any handsome slightly scruffy Americano man in all the commercials, and Sophie was perfectly fine with that, as well.

"If I had unlimited free time, sure. But I'm still just a cog. I'm a big cog, I turn a lot of things in the business, but I'm still a cog. Without me, things don't turn. And then they would just put another cog in my place. You understand?" Sophie couldn't come out and say it, but they had just met. She was attracted to Erick, and if it was another time…

"Yeah," Erick looked down at the sand, "I know, I get it. I don't understand, maybe, but…"

"You're a sail, you know it, you go with the wind, and you're lucky to be able to do that. It isn't like you're going to come to Chicago, as much as I would love that." Sophie kissed Erick, more passionately than she needed to. Her open mouth on his, closing her lips on his and pulling, her tongue running over his lower lip. "God, you are a handsome man," Sophie sighed. "I'd take you home in my suitcase if I could."

The night went by the same as the others, only with a greater sense of passion. As if the two were in more of a hurry, they intertwined silently, demanding more from each other than the relaxed desires of the past days and nights. When they were finished, as the dim ochre glow of the path lights that stayed on late into the night came through the curtains, Sophie lay naked halfway onto Erick's chest. He let her sleep, knowing she was exhausted from hours of more aggressive sex than in the nights before.

It was only a week, and Erick knew it was too soon to think he had fallen in love. Sophie was wonderful, beautiful, in his eyes, smart and successful. And she seemed to get him. He liked her, and Erick could easily tell that Sophie liked him. That was as good as they could do in a week.

But Sophie was right. Erick would never fit in at a big cold city that had only a lake, frozen half the time, winds that were bitter and blatant, in your face, never at your back. It would be weird, strange, a fish out of water, to be there. And Erick couldn't ask Sophie to leave what she loved. Any more than she would ask him.

Terrance had told him to give someone else a chance. "It's just going to have to be someone else," Erick told himself as he fell into a deep, warm, happy sleep.

CHAPTER THIRTY-TWO

August 2001
Marlowe Beach

The hurricane began in earnest by the afternoon, which both Eliza and Erick knew was a bad thing. Hurricane Michelle was fast moving, but large, which meant that no matter how quickly she came ashore, it would be a full 24 hours of rain and wind. The news carried on, with the location reporters all trying to find a place in the wind, not out of it, to show just how bad the storm was.

"It's not that bad," Eliza said, staring out from the front porch.

Erick came out with a glass of tea from a pitcher he had brewed. "Myrtle is getting it. It looks like Wrightsville is barely getting anything." He stared out over the front yard, just a long sandy plot covered in sharp sea oats and cacti, dotted with red gaillardia, Joe Bells, named after a brokenhearted man who seeded the coast with the plants after his love rejected him, like a lonely Johnny Appleseed. The wind turned all the flowers over, only to have them pop up for a moment's peace when the wind stopped whipping for a bare second. Most of the time they were invisible in the sea of rain and tall salt grasses.

"At least it's not raining in on *this* side," Eliza patted Erick, stupid boy, standing in the rain on the back porch earlier, on his chest.

"I couldn't see the horizon here," Erick said back, as Eliza took the tea from him, drank some, and didn't give it back. "When it gets this bad, I get a little nervous. No stars, no sun, no horizon, just wind. I just need to be outside, a little, you know?"

Eliza understood. When hurricanes came, everyone had the same ritual. You stood on the porch, then walked "out back," wherever that was, to see how windy it was getting. If it was raining a little, that was fine. When the wind picked up, you grabbed the trashcan before it blew away. But then the storm came in earnest, and the windows had to be closed. You felt a little cooped up. It was usually just the men, but they had to go out in it, "just to see." Eliza knew it was some strange male coping mechanism, to show off and prove the hurricane couldn't cow them into retreat. She had seen the same thing when she worked offshore on her research vessel. The men had to go out on deck to see the ocean as the ship pitched. She was happy to sit inside where it was dry, dead center, where the ship moved the least. She heard a lament from so many other women since she was a little girl.

"Boys are stupid."

Erick stared out in the rain as he watched the Intracoastal waters begin to pick up and flood the banks. "I'm glad I'm not out in this stuff," he commented. Then he went inside to get another glass of tea.

Eliza followed him. "No man against nature? Standing on the bow with the salt spray in your face?"

"That sh... stuff is overrated," Erick didn't even turn as he kept going to the kitchen. Eliza heard a cabinet open, a glass plunk on the counter, and the sound of ice being scoured up from the freezer. Erick came out with another glass. "I wish I had a lemon," he said. "No way, I've done that before. I like the wind, and a bit of rough seas doesn't bother me, but going into a storm, nope, that's foolhardy right there. You just have to button up and hope to stay upright."

"But you'd have a story to tell," Eliza said back. "I've got lemons over at my house."

"You wanna go get one?" Erick pointed with one finger, the others holding the glass, out the door to the garage and her house far beyond. "After what you just asked me?" He seemed a little incredulous.

"No," Eliza answered. "You can, though." She watched Erick, and saw that he just might do that. Eliza watched his face, as if Erick was considering whether this was a dare or a request. "Don't you dare go out for a lemon!"

Erick stared out of the kitchen window. It was now blinded by pelting rain, turning the glass green as the dull outside colors were bent into an ugly prism onto the window pane.

"Eliza, my dear paperwhite, we are most assuredly stuck here for the time being. As much as I tried and tried to escape, it seems you and Michelle have connived to keep me here." Erick put a free arm around Eliza and slowly twirled her so as not to spill their drinks. When she got halfway around, Erick let go and walked out of the kitchen. "But I'm not spending it stuck inside listening to the news."

Eliza followed Erick as he went out the front door to the porch. He sat down in one of the four rocking chairs that were pulled against the wall. Eliza took a smaller one and sat next to him. They watched the storm blow in sheets across the street as the whitecaps picked up on the other side of the road. Farther to the south, the road narrowed where there were no houses, and big riprap and boulders were placed to hold down the shoreline. Waves began crashing into the rocks, creating little mesmerizing splashes in the air.

Eliza shivered, even with the warmth of the day. The hurricane may have come up from the tropics, but the wind and rain made it cold.

Erick noticed, "C'mere," he set his tea glass on the floor, near the parallel lines of worn wood where the rocking chairs had carved their initials into the paint over thousands of back and forth motions.

Eliza got up and sat on Erick's lap, snuggling with the familiarity. She felt Erick shift, get comfortable, and grunt slightly. "I'm not hurting you, am I? And you better not be calling me fat!"

"No, and, *no*. It's just I think your hip was in my thigh a little. It's okay," Erick tried to pull Eliza close again. "And I'd still let you sit on my lap even if you were fat.

"Which you're not!"

"Good answer," Eliza laughed it off, but still stared at Erick. He probably would let her sit in his lap if she got fat. He'd probably run over in the rain to get a lemon for someone. He'd probably drive to the store in this mess to get a lemon for someone.

"So, you wouldn't like to be out in the storm, for real? Go out in this and show off? Haven't you ever done something to get someone's attention?"

Eliza saw Erick stare knowingly at her, his head angled down so he could glare at her through his eyebrows, even though Eliza was a head taller than Erick sitting on his lap. "You're kidding me, right? Of course I did. I did that with you. You knew that, didn't you?"

"You didn't fall off your boat in the sound just to get my attention," Eliza answered, then looked away. He did almost exactly that, over a decade later, and it got her attention, in the worst way.

"No, no, not that. Remember when I sailed in on that flotilla, the big promotional sail I did from Miami to Virginia? I put ads in the paper all week, and I made sure we landed right here at our houses."

Eliza remembered the big event. It was a big deal, ten or more catamarans sailing onto the beach on a leg of a two week sail. About half the island showed up to see it. "You did that, for me?"

CHAPTER THIRTY-THREE

May 1995
Marlowe Beach

Clear blue skies and a soft afternoon light graced the western sky over Marlowe Beach. It was a view that could only be seen from offshore, where ten racing catamarans skipped across the blue water. Half had made a turn to come about into the prevailing land breeze, while the first five continued past the finish line, marked with jubilant flags, alternating in white and silver. The first five finally came about, taking in a faster tack, so that all the boats would reach the shore at about the same time.

It wasn't a race, but a promotion. The boats were supposed to land simultaneously, with a little space for safety. The sailors knew this, and raced anyway. They had started from Fort Lauderdale, Florida, and would race to Virginia Beach, with frequent stops at any beach that wanted to see as many sponsor signs as they could possibly jam into the sand.

Today, the beaches were positively littered with big softly flapping banners of Penquin Island Rum and Sunstrom Autos.

"It looks good to the finish," Terrance commented, staring through dark glasses under a pink brimmed cap.

"All hail Salacia," Erick answered with a tribute to the Roman goddess of salt water.

"I think you just make these names up," Terrance said as he squinted onto the beach. "How do you know so many of these gods of the sea?"

"Salacia is the goddess of salt water, consort to Neptune, the god of fresh water. We all think of King Neptune of the ocean, but Salacia rules the seas."

"Yeah, yeah. But seriously, how do you know all that?"

Erick pointed. "You remember me telling you about my old high school girlfriend, and what went on with her father? He was sure I was a child of Satan, and kinda had her and the family a little wrapped up in all this holier than thou mumbo jumbo. After all that shit from him, I looked at all the other religions, just to see like how many there were, how many people thought they were the chosen ones. And while I was at it, I memorized most of the history and myths of the gods of the waters. It's pretty cool."

"You oughta write a book," Terrance laughed.

"Somewhere, out there, hopefully not in that crowd," Erick pointed to the shore where a large group of people stood growing closer with every wave they crested, "is that guy, thinking he's right and everyone else is wrong."

"I think you're winning. So don't worry about it," Terrance commented. He was sorry he asked, but it was something that Erick needed to get off his chest. They talked about a lot when they sailed, especially on this trip since it was not competitive, with shorter legs. Terrance already knew more about Erick's love life of the past five years than most of the women Erick had dated.

Terrance was right. Erick was winning. Erick had arranged this fun run from Florida up the coast with some big sponsors and most of his friends that he had sailed against in the past few years. Offshore catamaran racing had been in the doldrums from 1990 on when the old Worrell 1000 race had been stopped. Erick had never had a chance to do the race since he was still in college the last year they had it. Once in a slightly drunken fervor, he and some other sailors at the cat races in Miami said they ought to just do it themselves, like Michael Worrell did back in the 70s. Cooler and more sober heads prevailed in the morning, or afternoon, and instead of racing a 24 hour format up the coast, it was decided that they would do a fun run, nothing too dangerous. The sponsors from Penquin Island Rums saw this as a great opportunity to tie in with coastal restaurants. And a car company was always onboard to have their emblem on a spinnaker sail for the Sunstrom family.

And since it wasn't a race, even though it always was, the rest of the cats hove to, spilling just enough air to make sure that Erick and Terrance would race to the shore first on home ground. The landing point was just north of his house.

"Yeah," Erick agreed, "I guess I am winning."

The twenty foot long cat splashed to the shore in tiny foot tall waves to be met by the beach crew, which in this case was Archer Schultz, a burly man covered in dark hair and green shorts, who ran out to wrestle the giant cat to the beach with the ease of a strong man showing off at the sideshow. The boat almost lunged out from underneath Erick and Terrance as Archer gave his first pull. Cheers abounded for the local boy made good, as Erick stepped off the boat into the shallow waves that rushed the wet sand. He made a determined point not to fall over. Erick was the returning conquering hero, and there would be no photos of him doing anything other than smiling and waving.

The rest of the cats arrived with typical but lesser fanfare. The men and women that sailed all looked like beautiful worn and salted mermaids and mermen, a gift from the sea. But no one struck a pose like Erick did. He grinned his way through the local interview and posed for pictures, but his eyes were always scanning the crowd until he finally found Eliza.

She was beaming at him, but also a little coy. Or perhaps patronizing. As if her stare was patting him on the head, telling him he did a good job on his report card, now go tell your father. Erick didn't care. He hadn't seen Eliza in four years, and the last time was hardly a positive one. At least she was here.

"Considering I told everyone I was coming to bring everyone else, I guess they got the hint!" Erick announced to the crowd. Somewhere among the dozens of old friends from high school or summer jobs, someone had convinced Eliza to see Erick arrive. With one last picture taken, he hurried over. "Hey! You're here! I was wondering if you would be here!" Okay, hoping would be more apt, but wondering sounded less desperate.

"Of course! I didn't have much of a choice, really," said Eliza. It wasn't the nicest response, but Erick thought it was still fair. "Everyone else came out, Kimmy made me. She wanted to see you." Kimmy Teague was one of Eliza's friends from high school. Erick had long suspected she had a crush on him, but he only ever had eyes for Eliza. Kimmy was always happy to be the tag along girl. Now the roles were reversed. "Hey, Kimmy!" Erick waved at the girl, now a young woman, and a young man, younger than Erick, next to her. "You come get a picture with us! Come over to the cat!" He beckoned the two over.

Eliza was quiet for a second, then found her voice, "Erick, this is Lonnie, my boyfriend."

Erick had taken enough shots to the hull not to respond physically to this one. He put out his hand for Lonnie. Fair play,

Erick thought. “It isn’t like she’s just going to pine away for me after all these years. Still, this guy?” But to his face, Erick said, “Pleased to meet you. Come on, let’s get a picture. I haven’t seen you in so long. I’m so happy for you.” That’s what people say to the other person who wins the race.

Poses and pictures, and a bit of promotion, but the wind had gone from Erick’s sails when he had met Eliza’s boyfriend. He wasn’t even a “new” boyfriend. They had been together for almost a year, that Erick had gathered. It was decidedly humbling, because it wasn’t like Lonnie was overly striking, or handsome, really. Short brown hair, pushed forward, not quite as tall nor as thin as Erick, though probably heavier. Not ugly, but not good looking, or even noticeable in most ways. But he and Eliza seemed happy together. Lonnie didn’t even bother putting his arm around Eliza’s shoulders when the three talked. That was a power play in its own right.

Erick was ready to end this. He took the hint, a big one. “Hey, you should come to the beach party tonight! It’s at the Ramada ballroom, and the tiki bar outside by the pool. Penquin Island is pulling out the stops on the organs. It’ll be a lot of fun!”

Eliza frowned at the mention of alcohol, and Lonnie chimed in, “We’re not much on drinking, so maybe not.”

“No one will make you. It’s just a big dance. Tiki torches, candle lights, it’s not some teenage kegger. We’re responsible citizens now!” Erick poked at one of the other sailors passing by. “Right?”

“Yeah, I’m married with a kid,” the sailor threw out the bona fide with a smile. “When I’m not doing this, I teach woodworking and sailing to at risk kids in Fort Lauderdale.” Erick beamed. He couldn’t have picked a better example.

We’ll try,” Eliza said, and with that, the two walked away. Kimmy stayed a moment longer. “You shouldn’t be such a stranger. Come back to the beach sometime when you have more time. We’ll go get dinner.”

The sailors and crew took the time to secure the cats, then they rode to the hotel. They all needed some time to rest, shower, change into more festive apparel, and get the zinc oxide scrubbed off of them. Some had better luck than others. Erick had stayed in his house with his parents and sister. The beach house was quiet and empty compared to the crowd at the beach only an hour earlier, but it was nice to have a place to himself, even for just a moment.

Conrad took Erick to the hotel. Erick was dressed in more appropriate sponsor clothing, a crisp blue and silver button down shirt and pressed navy blue shorts. If Erick had shown up in a suit and long pants, they would have thrown him in the pool. They probably still will, he thought, but at least I'll dry easier.

Most of the sailing teams were down already, hanging out at the long bar by the pool. Contrary to the longstanding rumors and legends, most of the sailors were drinking soda or water, limiting themselves to one or two drinks for the night. The only thing worse than sailing with a hangover was sailing while mildly drunk. At least, it was foolish to do so when they were sailing under a sponsor's banner.

The invited locals poured in soon after, taking advantage of the open bar. Erick saw several old friends, promising to find time to get back home, even though he knew he was roped up in sailing for the next several months. "Maybe October, if the hurricanes stay away," Erick joked with one the kids he had once worked with, a boy named Timmy, who now was nearly 22, went by Tim, and was about to be a father. Tim nodded, hopeful still in his relative youth, and then went "uh oh," as he glanced towards the hotel doors that opened to the back courtyard. Eliza and her boyfriend Lonnie had shown up after all.

"Eh, what are you gonna do, man? I had my shot."

"Didn't you…"

Erick cut him off. "Yeah, I know, I told you what happened, but no one else, man, and certainly not Eliza. She's always been her daddy's girl. And this isn't the time, that's for damn sure. She's happy, and if I'm supposed to care, then that should be good enough for me."

"That's pretty cool of you." Tim had always been a little in awe of Erick, the older college guy that would hang out with him and give him a ride home in the summer in his badass car. Tim had grown, but the idolization still remained. "Still, I don't know about that guy. I've heard he's kind of a dick."

"Well, it's not my call. Not yours, either. Eliza knows herself best, and, well, it isn't like I have been around, or didn't deserve this in the first place."

"Not from what you told me," Tim answered. "Still, that guy's a dick."

Erick let the debate go. Tomorrow morning he would be on his way north on a catamaran into a cool and windy ocean. Maybe he didn't make quite the splash he had hoped with Eliza, but the party was going on, everyone else was happy, and the promotion was incredibly successful.

Erick walked through the crowd, patting a few backs to get through. The party always took time. Erick needed to find Eliza, just for the moment, to tell her he was happy for her. Erick caught her scanning the crowd he had disappeared into. The timing, as bad as it was overall, was somewhat perfect, as Lonnie had walked off, leaving Eliza alone for a moment. "Hey! You two made it. I'm so glad," Erick smiled his white toothed wide smile, a fake one he knew worked for the cameras and sponsors.

"Yes, well," Eliza looked around, as if she was either wondering if Lonnie would show up any second to save her or berate her. "This looks like the event of the night." Eliza barely made eye contact.

Erick couldn't help what had happened before to them. And he knew there was nothing he was going to do to break up a couple while standing around a hotel pool. The whole race had been an attempt to make a scene, but not that kind of scene. "So, you found someone you like, huh?" Erick glanced around, trying to find the missing Lonnie, just in case he had to make a quick and polite exit too soon.

"Yes," Eliza spoke more confidently now. "It's nice having someone who really has a sense of your same interests. We share a lot of the same beliefs."

"That's great." Erick agreed with her. And he knew Eliza was right. If the two of them are happy together, he can't wish for something less. Erick had no right or claim over Eliza. He never thought he did, and never liked anyone implying that they had some possessive type of relationship. Still, Erick felt a little hurt. Eliza had gone and fulfilled every teenage boy's fantasy of showing up at the high school reunion, rich, getting off the private plane, a beautiful blonde on his arm, and saying to his former crush, "And you are…?"

Lonnie showed up, just popped out of the crowd, and took Eliza by the arm.

"Hey, Lonnie, right?" Two could play at that game, joked Erick. "I'm glad to see you made it. It's going to be a great night. You two have fun together, okay?" And with that, Erick turned on his smile, turned on his heel, and walked away into the crowd of people.

While the sailors stayed relatively sober, the other guests were a mix of liberally libated, happy, and a few closer to soused. It was about time to get the promotional stuff out of the way before it all got wild, and the music got loud, and someone, namely Erick, got thrown in the pool. "It looks cold," he glanced at the smooth blue water. He had thought about begging the others not to, but that would only charge them up more. Terrance and his new wife Sheila were sitting with him, and he didn't want them, or more specifically her, to get caught in the watery melee. Terrance would take a few with him if he went, but the spouses were usually off limits unless they opted in. A couple husbands had wives sailing. They probably would help throw Erick in, and happily regret it later.

Erick stood up, and everyone shushed. “As always, I’ll keep it short. But tonight my speech is just a little longer. I want to thank Penquin Island Rum, and Noel especially,” Erick waved at the Penquin rep, “for helping to sponsor this party tonight, and for the entire event. They have been really good to us sailors and sailing for a long time now. We really owe them our thanks.” Cheers and glasses went up, the usual that happened every night.

“And of course thanks to our favorite car brands, and Alina Auffenberg in particular, who helped arrange their sponsorship. Automobile racing obviously has been good to my family, and they really helped make it possible for this jaunt up the coast. That compass has done a great job pointing us in the right direction.” Bigger cheers, knowing the family ties and local connection.

“And I know I would end it here normally, but of course, I have to recognize my home, my beach, Marlowe Beach, for welcoming us here.

“I grew up here. The sand means something to me. We all know this feeling.” Erick looked around the room at the other sailors. “We all have… a port, where our heart can rest, where everything is familiar and comfortable. This is mine.” Not cheers this time, but agreement. An understanding of how a person can love a place. “They say that heaven is just that moment when you are with your best friend, someone you love, because you earned it, and you are at peace, and everything is perfect. Five o’clock in the afternoon, when the tourists have left, mid August, just walking the beach,” holding your hand, he didn’t say out loud, “when everything is quiet, on a low tide, with those small waves that kiss and rush the shore…” Erick looked around, catching the eye of so many people who understood, both the sailors and crew, along with more knowing nods from the adults who were teens like he was just a few years ago. "When we would skimboard and scuff our knees on the pebbles, or sit in the empty lifeguard stand," he caught Tim's eye for a moment, and Tim smiled back at the memories of life on the beach when nothing really mattered, "Or snuggling in the sea oats when the winds came."

Erick looked around, and caught Eliza's brown eyes, just for a moment. Erick smiled almost a smirk, an acknowledgement of a good memory, before looking away. He had her brown eyes seared into him. They were open, but turned down, looking downward to an unsmiling face.

"This place has been my home. And while it has changed, for good and bad, it will always be special to me. And so my greatest thanks go to Marlowe, and my friends, and mates, that make it so special.

"Alright, enough melancholy, let's turn up the music and get someone to go ahead and throw me in the pool so you won't see me all teary eyed."

The music swelled, on cue, the lights went down, and the crowd moved in on Erick. They lifted him up, and took him for a ride around the pool first. As he neared the end of the circuit, he saw two figures leaving, Eliza being pulled away into the darkness, a glaring face looking back on a heaving crowd of loving and wild debauchery. Erick had to close his eyes and hold his breath before he hit the water.

CHAPTER THIRTY-FOUR

August 2001
Marlowe Beach

"Well, yeah… pretty much."

Eliza almost lifted herself off of Erick's lap. She pushed against his shoulders roughly to get her head away from his. The gray sky had seeped into the porch, even though it was only the afternoon, and she had to see in his face if Erick was serious. "All that? The race, everything?"

"Well, like I said, pretty much. We just kind of came up with the idea of doing a fun sail up the coast, me and a few mates of mine, Terrance, of course, with this idea that we would sail into a bunch of cool beaches, hang out like pirates, and move on. About five minutes into us talking about it, just bullshitting, ya know, I thought how I could maybe see you. I figured you might notice a bunch of us in bright catamarans sailing onto the beach and partying at my house. Then I thought of a few ideas how I could really get your attention.

And, well, this was after the Penquin Cup down in Miami and after I raced the Citizen's Cup in San Diego. It was a bit of a let down time for me. I hadn't made the America's Cup team, not that I expected to, but still.

"They hadn't done the World 1000 in years now, and we didn't think it was coming back. The weather was getting warmer and calmer, with easy seas, no storms yet. And we were always running into sponsors, or sponsors talking to us. It was, well, kind of easy, for them to throw a little money our way. We were already going to do it, and Penquin Island Rum was up for something that would look good on a poster. A big catamaran flying a spinnaker always looks cool at a beachfront restaurant."

Eliza listened to the tale, leaning away from Erick as he spoke. She tried to take in the whole of what he said. Organizing an entire sailing event on the off chance she would be on the beach that day. But the mention of sponsorships made her cold on the rainy, windy porch. Eliza wanted to ask more, but was afraid of the answer she might get, even though she knew what it would be. Just as much as Eliza had met someone else back then, it was unfair to think that Erick wouldn't have, too.

Eliza didn't realize at the time Erick would go to such lengths to get her attention, though. "You should have said something," Eliza said as she got up. They were getting wet and cold on the porch. "Let's go inside. It's starting to rain in out here." Eliza held her hand to catch the droplets that were being splattered to a fine mist by the front porch screens.

"Are you hungry?" Erick asked. It was a good distraction from the seriousness and reminiscence for both of them.

"Just a little." Eliza shrugged. "It's not like I've done much to work up an appetite."

Erick raised an eyebrow in accusation. Eliza stared back as blankly as she could. Their intimacy in the shower seemed to be getting farther away with every passing moment, like the way Erick blasted though his failed attempt at getting Eliza's attention years ago. It had been wonderful, but Eliza found the wonder to be the hard part. It almost felt like they were moving more toward an end, not another start.

"Alright, I don't have much," Erick changed the subject. "Macaroni and cheese? I have some boxed pasta, and I can make a roux, probably, to make it a little better. I think I have a frozen sausage in the freezer."

"I've got food over at my place," Eliza said.

Erick looked out the window, another raised eyebrow. "You know I'm not going to stop you," he told Eliza, "but, please don't. I'll never be that starving to send you out in this mess."

"It's just a little rain!" Eliza tried to joke her way out. That would be what so many people would be saying, trying to go out when the stores are closed, or rescuing a cheap chair that blew down the street. Erick had none of that.

"I hope you are kidding. I know it's not anything special. I can make it up to you later. I'll get scallops or something."

Eliza initially brightened at the suggestion. "That was for the future," she thought. A plan, maybe tomorrow, maybe next week.

"*Maybe never*," her head told her. "*That's what people do, make promises that they don't plan on keeping. 'I'll come down next week.' And then something happens and they don't come back.*"

"Mac and cheese it is, I guess," Eliza said.

"Hey, don't sound so excited," Erick tried to make some levity, but Eliza turned and left the room to watch the weather on TV. There were better replays of things blowing down the streets of Myrtle Beach than Eliza could see out the window, so she sat down and watched, eyes wide and wet. "Let me know if I can help." There wasn't much heart in the offer.

Erick clanged a pot and pan, ran water, ran a microwave, almost cursed, but held it back or under his breath. Eliza could smell the cheesy aroma, mixed with bits of garlic scent and mustard smell. She tried to ignore it, but the food began to smell really good. It was familiar, as any comfort food was, making Eliza remember being a kid and getting excited at the simple box meal they had often. But the scents coming out of the kitchen permeated the room, over the salt and wood. It was more than just the old box meal of pasta and powdered cheese.

When Erick came out with two bowls, Eliza saw why. Instead of just a pile of elbow macaroni, mixed into an orange goo, the pasta was covered with a thick cheddar sauce, and in it were slices of a Polish sausage, and bits of sun dried tomatoes. "It's the best I could do from a limited pantry," he simply shrugged.

"Just like him," Eliza thought. "He goes and makes some kind of magic, out of nowhere, like it's nothing." Eliza felt a mix of hate and loving admiration, "fitting, right now," she thought. A rumbling tummy won out over a confused head and heart.

"All I got is ginger ale, a Dr. Pepper, and some Diet Coke," Erick proffered both a can of soda and two bottles of a deep champagne brown elixir, his go-to drink for years now. "Or water."

"I'll take the Diet Coke," Eliza said. She began with a heaping forkful of the amazing smelling food after cracking open the can. With one bite, she couldn't help but talk with her mouth full."Ooouuhh… this is *so good*!" She emphasized the words like a teenager. "What did you do to make it this good?" She didn't wait for Erick to answer before taking another bite.

"It's just a roux, I grated some cheddar cheese and made a better sauce than those packet things, and I added some mustard powder and a bit of garlic. It gives it that sharpness that macaroni and cheese needs. No big deal."

Eliza just looked at him. "No big deal," she thought. "He whipped up fancy comfort food on the fly in a hurricane in an empty kitchen." Another mouthful, then, with food jammed into a cheek, she said, “You could brag a little about it, you know.”

Eliza ate while Erick watched, only nibbling on his, pulling out a tomato or a piece of the sausage to gnaw on at the end of a fork. Eliza had almost finished hers, and Erick asked, “You want some more?”

“Is there any more?”

Erick just handed her his bowl. “I’ll go get me some. Here, have this.” Erick took Eliza’s empty bowl to the kitchen before she could protest, but Eliza didn’t stop eating.

They finished lunch quietly. Eliza couldn’t just keep complimenting the food, and ran out of things to say. There were things she wanted to say, but they would be better said when she wasn’t trapped in Erick’s house.

After the late lunch, Eliza and Erick got bored watching the different news broadcasts, or staring out each window, front or back. On the open beach, with the houses empty and most of the population evacuated, nothing happened. Palmetto fronds were loosened and sent flying. They weren’t nearly as dramatic as Erick would have hoped. They mostly just flopped onto the road about ten feet from the nearest tree where they fell.

“Not much of a storm, huh?” Erick stared out the front window. The front porch was getting wet and shiny now. “I’d sit on the front porch and read, but wouldn’t want my book to get soggy.”

Eliza came to stand next to him. She looked out at the wind and rain. “It looks like it’s going to take its time, but this should be done tomorrow afternoon. C’mon,” She tugged Erick’s arm, “you gotta admit you love this here.”

“It makes me anxious,” Erick admitted. “I hope the boat’s okay,” They both tried to look across the street, but the rain was so heavy it was just sheet of white. The water had risen, with white waves pumping into uncomfortable lines that couldn’t flow evenly. They struck the banks and docks, ending too soon, only to be replaced by another wave behind them. There was no rhythm to the pattern.

Eliza shook Erick gently. “It’ll be okay. It’s not the first hurricane we’ve been through.” Then, she was quiet, but with an intake of breath, ready to speak again, but waiting, a little afraid to ask. “Did you really do all that for me?”

Erick turned from the mellow carnage of the hurricane just outside. “Of course I did. Things were going well for me. I wanted to show off. I was hoping you would see me and we could get back together. I just didn’t think it would take two years.

“You know,” Erick hesitated, “you never told me what happened with your boyfriend.”

“You never told me anything about any of your girlfriends,” Eliza’s tone was accusatory.

“I never told *anyone* about them,” Erick insisted. Except maybe Terrance. There was a lot to share when your world is the size of a sailboat. “I learned that lesson early. If you don’t want trouble, you keep your big mouth shut.” Again, he held back some juicy swearing that would have added emphasis, but would have bothered Eliza. “So, you told me he was some sweet guy that you had a lot in common with. What happened?”

Eliza didn’t want to talk about that. It wasn’t fair. If Erick kept his secrets, she should be able to, also. Erick had never asked, not once, about anyone Eliza had dated, or Lonnie, who had been more than just a boyfriend. But also much less. Erick never asked, and he didn’t talk about his girlfriends, but now he asked about Lonnie. Eliza never had mentioned him much anymore. He was one of the reasons she hated coming home to her family.

“He was the son of a friend of my father’s,” Eliza began.

“Oh…” Erick’s tone said everything.

“Don’t you start,” the last thing Eliza needed now was judgement, especially from Erick. “You weren’t perfect. You asked. If you want to know, I'll tell you, but don't do that. I can't stand that."

Erick, instead of arguing back, simply said, "You're right. I'm sorry. You don't need to tell me if you don't want to."

"I guess you deserve an answer." Eliza felt more and more like she wanted to tell someone. By the time she and Lonnie were serious, she had grown distant from her high school friends, and didn't have many people to confide in. That had been one of the problems. "We met at church. He was the son of one of my father's co-workers, who was a church layman there, and Lonnie was going to be a youth pastor. I liked him. He treated me well. Well, at first…" This was the tough part for her to admit.

"You're not saying he abused you?!" Erick balled his fist slowly.

"No, no!" Eliza tried to hold his arm, then let go quickly. "Not… that. Well, I think because he was going into the ministry, and his father was in the church, and my father… He was torn between wanting us to be intimate, and the morality of not sleeping together until we were married. I think he just got frustrated."

"That's not an excuse," Erick said. He had a low boil going on him now. Eliza could see his eyes narrow and lower. It was a strange side of him she had rarely seen before. Eliza knew Erick had a raw spot and extreme discomfort about men who tried to control or hurt women.

"I know… I know that now." Eliza still couldn't come to grips with the fact that she still blamed herself and made excuses for Lonnie, even years later. "But, he wanted us to get married, and me to stay here and be a wife, work at the ice cream shop, while he worked at the processing plant and the church. I wanted to go finish my master's degree. For a while, I thought about staying. But he became controlling, more verbally abusive. We disagreed on a lot of things, where we would live and work. I had my opportunity at Woods Hole, and he didn't want me to go. I think he didn't like me getting a degree and thinking I was smarter than him."

"When did you two break up?"

"I made my plans to go to Woods Hole and told him. I said if he wanted to he could come with me, or wait until I was finished. He didn't want either one. It was a big fight. My father sided with him. He said I was embarrassing the family. I think my father is still mad I didn't marry him."

"I can believe it."

"Hey, be nice."

"What?! I was agreeing with you," Erick huffed.

"Well, it's just something I'm not proud of." Eliza walked away and sat on the sofa. The droning of the TV helped blend in with the roaring sound in her ears.

"What about you?" An accusation might help her position. "I know you dated around. What about that Alina woman?" It was Erick's turn to squirm a little.

Instead of squirming, as much as Eliza hoped he would, he walked over to the fireplace and toyed with the photos. "There's not much to that."

CHAPTER THIRTY-FIVE

March 1995
Miami

"How do you like your eggs?" Erick asked, watching Alina stretch her long torso out of a not nearly as long t-shirt of his.

"Oh," she yawned, tired from the late night before, then smiled a distracted and uncaring smirk, "It doesn't matter. I'm not so hungry." Alina made it sound cute, flippant, and self-confident all at the same time, with her soft German High Swabian accent that worked well with her statuesque body and childlike face and blue on blue eyes.

"You need to eat, it's breakfast," Erick insisted. "Busy day coming up," which was not entirely true. It was Monday, and the last of the Penquin Rum races were done. Most of what was left was packing.

"You really care about your food, don't you?" Alina stood up in the middle of Erick's spacious condo, her body backlit by an early morning sun coming through the windows facing east. The light became a perfect halo for her, surrounding her creamy skin, illuminating her body, even the parts hidden by the cotton t-shirt.

She seemed almost American, Erick thought. Except she turned down breakfast after spending the night.

"Well, I'm more on the side of being a gracious host," Erick explained from the kitchen bar.

"You don't seem to be," It was probably lost in translation. Alina meant it was a surprise. A lot of the sailors would have been either fixing hangover cures or kicking out the woman they met the night before. At least that was her experience. The Americans were actually the least offensive in that respect. The French were the worst.

Or perhaps the Australians.

That's why she didn't sleep with the sailors.

Erick was different, though. The scion of a wealthy, very wealthy, supporter of the brand she worked for, he was to be kept happy, even if he didn't know it. Not that she slept with him for money. Erick was incredibly attractive, and Alina was drawn to him. But they were also both young, with plans ahead. At least she had plans. Erick seemed to plan for the next week. That could change.

Erick spoke up, "Terrance once said that I could chase a guy down for ten miles for stealing candy from a kid, but also cry if I didn't cook his eggs just right. Admittedly, he's right."

"Did you ever beat up someone for stealing candy?"

"No… but, well, let's just say I don't tolerate bullies well." He left it at that.

Alina took the note in stride. Americans, cowboys, sailors, some looked for fights. It wasn't something she was used to. But then, especially around race tracks, and a little bit less around boat docks, there always was someone trying to cause problems, and someone ready to bring in their version of a solution. To be fair, she saw similar things in Germany at race tracks. And in Italy. And in England. And… "*Doch*, the behavior is a little more universal."

Erick smiled about it, a small shrug, as if to say, "I do what I have to sometimes."

"Why don't you like bullies?" Alina asked, "or is it men who mistreat women? Something in your family?"

"No, no, no!" Erick insisted. The last thing he needed to be insinuating is that his father was abusive or sexually harassing women. "Nothing like that at all. It's more the opposite, really. My father adores my mom. I know, he gets out and goes away every weekend, and she drags herself along, because she's doting, and that's what she does, but my father is devoted. I've seen it in him. He listens, sacrifices, a lot, a lot more than you'd realize, for her, for me and my sister. There's none of that there. That might be more why I am the way I am. I always saw a healthy relationship, and my father especially taught me not to be mean, or cruel, or to treat women badly.

"You know when people say, 'I'm not perfect?' and what they mean is 'I fight with my wife, or I cheat on my wife, or I hit my wife?' Well, when I say, 'I'm not perfect,' I mean sometimes I forget flowers or can't get a reservation, or I don't shave.

"I'm not saying I'm perfect, either," he tried to laugh off his minor confession, "I'm just trying to be the best I can be. I've been through loss and failure and screwups. I've messed up before, but it wasn't for lack of trying. Sometimes you do your best and things still go wrong."

Alina laughed at the poor boy trying to catch up to himself. "Well, you certainly did your best last night," she came over and kissed him.

"This isn't going to get you into trouble with work, is it?"

"Well, I'm not going to tell anyone, but no, it won't."

Erick was almost relieved. Sailing all week before, seeing the women and girls that dotted the party spots, and watching the other competitors going out with bikini clad Miami attention seekers had been a bit much for him. The women pursued him, too, but Erick was still unsure, a little afraid of the sheer temporaneous relationship, of a woman coming up to his condo, not just a hotel room, and then expecting her to be gone in the morning. Miami wasn't his home, and while it was fun and wild, it sometimes was a little too wild, too loud, too much heat and sweat and shining suntan oil. Too easy to be hot and sexy.

But Erick needed a release. Unlike Terrance, who was a little older and wiser with a significant other that made him happy, Erick didn't have someone to go to. Not since college or high school. Especially now, with the Penquin Races done, and the America's Cup trials getting ready. Erick was already disappointed he would likely not make the America's Cup final team, but just being there, on a Citizen's Cup challenger boat, that was a claim in its own.

Last night had been a release. Erick just wasn't sure how released he was. Alina was attractive, certainly, as he stared at her body as she sat down for a breakfast she didn't really want. Alina could fit in with the travel lifestyle Erick would have to have if he was a professional on the international sailing circuit.

But Alina was also a business partner. She was there to promote automobiles, putting a logo on sails and hulls, when she wasn't an assistant at the car race tracks. She was young, but up and coming. Alina had her priorities. She wanted to move up and up in the promotional side of the brand.

And the businesses from Munich to Stuttgart didn't have an ocean.

CHAPTER THIRTY-SIX

August 2001
Marlowe Beach

Erick stood by the fireplace as the TV blared on. "There's not much to that."

Eliza pushed. She walked over and gave him a nudge, harder than he needed. Erick put his hands up to his chest and the wall to catch himself. She pushed too hard, both in the question, and physically.

Eliza looked at him, thinking she should apologize, then thinking he owed her an explanation. He didn't get to hide from this. "No reminiscing. You made me tell, now you."

Erick knew he owed her something, but there really wasn't much to their relationship. "Yeah, okay, not so rough, huh? I think Alina liked me more than I liked her. But she also loved her career more than she liked me. We, well, we didn't date, there was no time for that, but we were together for only about a month. She had to go back to Germany, and she wanted me to go with her. I wanted to go to San Diego and train. Places like that, San Diego, Hawaii, Australia, they were far away from Stuttgart, and the farther away you are from the head office, the less you get noticed. It doesn't matter how good your papers look, they are just papers. She needed to have people notice her. Not just one person." Erick almost looked sad.

"That sounds familiar," Eliza said.

It took Erick a moment to realize Eliza was talking about him, not her former boyfriend. "You don't have to be mean about it." It was a cold remark. Erick's gaze was past the stern fatherly scolding look. This was the abuse he didn't need, not now, not ever. "People sometimes have to put themselves first, you know. And other times, they might be working toward something bigger." He fingered a small box on the mantle, opening and closing the lid. "Sometimes they're just scared. And fear is a great motivator." He shut the box and turned to face Eliza.

Eliza said, "You're not afraid. I don't think you're afraid of anything."

"You'd be surprised."

"Really?" Eliza huffed. She was getting upset now, as she mirrored Erick's increasing frustration at her questions and doubt. "What are you afraid of?"

Erick was bored and tired. He'd already had this debate in his head, time and time again, since… "July of 1989," he remembered. And Erick promised he'd never say anything, especially to Eliza. He kept the promise to himself all but once, in a small fit, just a soft aside to another teenager he had known.

"And it's going to stay that way," he promised himself now.

"Right now, this," he pointed out the window at the raging hurricane. The wind would shift in a few hours. The wind blew hard from offshore, driving the rain and storm surge onto the coast. Erick couldn't see the waves behind the dunes, but he could hear the wind and crash of the breakers. The rain didn't blot out the grass on the dunes yet. It was still early on in the storm. The movement of Hurricane Michelle would mean that at some time the sound would get pushed out first, then, tonight probably, when Erick was asleep, the winds would change and push the Intracoastal Waterway and the sounds and bays beyond up and over the road. Erick didn't think it would get up to the house, but the change in elevation was only a few feet, and enough of a wind, with all this rain, meant he could be living on a much smaller island tomorrow morning. "I don't like being trapped. I don't want to be stuck here. I know I can't leave, but I don't want to be some poor deer pushed out of the lowcountry to be stuck on a hill with the cows and coyotes when the flood comes! Yeah, yeah..." he waved off Eliza's open mouth comment that stopped on her lips, "I know, it happens, we get stuck. You get stuck, I get stuck, I still don't like it happening. And I don't *want* to be stuck."

Erick walked to the back door, the old wooden entryway now closed and locked to stop the wind and rain from coming through the cracks. Little bits of wind whistled a high pitched cry through the old jam. The glass in the frame was old, wavy, and the water on top of it added an atmosphere of fantasy to the outside world as it distorted the view. The back porch had no screen to slow the deluge, and was getting soaked with rain.

Erick turned and walked past Eliza, who sat silent and still on the sofa. The front porch was wet and misty. The rocking chairs were now damp, moving slightly on their own. Only the ghosts were enjoying the gloomy weather. Erick turned again, went back toward the hallway to the garage, and out. It was the only place he could still be outside and relatively dry.

The wind swirled in magical mists, stirred by an invisible wand of a sorcerer. Erick said a quick apology to the Nereids. He wasn't one to shout at a pretty girl, one he liked, "had liked, a long time ago," Erick lied to himself. He apologized for that one, too. The winds didn't stop, but they did seem to take the rain more to the west. Something, a piece of old foam cooler, maybe, blew around the side of the garage and down the driveway. It tumbled and staggered, sometimes spinning like a wheel, other times laying flat and trying to slide like a hockey puck as it got stuck in the wet sand and trash on the drive. Finally a big gust grabbed it and sent it out into the street to be lost. It was just another bit of trash to be thrown away into the water and reeds.

The garage smelled. It always did. There was this strange underlying hint of bacon that Erick never understood. It was probably some of the old wood in the house. There was this sour smell, like a cooler left sealed up. Grease and oil, that was no surprise. And salt, lots of salt, the fishy smell of sea salt that you had to get used to. It wasn't pleasant at all. But it was part of the beach. It brought back memories of Erick going to the local fish mongers, who had a store that was permeated with fishy odors. Never rotten, but strong, too strong, and it was tough for him to go in and hold his breath for so long. The scent never left his memory, as he stopped by there in later years. The scent went from odiferous and harsh to a promise of scallops and dolphin for dinner. Erick took a deep breath as he stood alone in the garage. The salt air helped. Erick leaned against the back door. It was simply a piece of plywood painted green, with hinges and a hook to hold it closed. He let the wind push on the other side as the door and he breathed in and out together, calming in the heart of the hurricane.

CHAPTER THIRTY-SEVEN

August 2001
Marlowe Beach

The hurricane was at her worst and lingering, stalling out just over the coast in the late afternoon. The continued dull roar of a downpour was mixed with relentless wind. It no longer howled, whistled, and soared around the house. It was nothing less than a single-minded tempest.

The coastal beach houses stood against the hurricane, taking the battering as they had for years. The force of the winds of Hurricane Michelle just were not strong enough to batter down the walls or take the roof off of them.

Not that Erick's home was immune from damage.

Erick had come inside when he heard the banging noise of the door. The back door hadn't given way; Eliza had gotten frustrated at Erick and decided to go back to her house, the wind and rain be damned. She had been met with a deluge that forced her to shut the back door against the rain as it stung her eyes and pelted her face. Slamming the door felt so good, even as it felt as frustrating, being trapped in Erick's house, not being able to get back home, even though she was so close. Eliza opened the door, keeping the knob turned, and slammed it again.

And again.

On the third slam, one of the nine panes of rectangular glass finally gave up and broke. Erick had heard the noise but not the softer crash of the old glass as he came back inside from his chosen banishment to the garage. The wind was starting to shift and he was running out of space. Erick came in to find Eliza picking up a piece of glass from the floor.

"Feel better?'

Eliza glowered a determined slow burn at Erick. "You don't have to be sarcastic," she snapped. "I didn't mean to do it. This damn rain, I can't get out of here."

"I wasn't being sarcastic," Erick said in a softly paternalistic patronizing tone. "I know you didn't mean to. It's alright."

"And you don't have to treat me like a child!"

"I'm not!" This wasn't where he wanted to start back up. "We're cooped up together, and you want out. I get it. The glass is broken, it can't be unbroken, so there's no use me getting mad about it. That won't help. Here," he put out a hand, "don't cut yourself. That old glass is sharp." The piece that had fallen to the wood floor was a polygonal dagger, with a glistening needle point, just aching to stab someone. "I'll go put it in the trash." Erick pinched the thin old glass delicately, pointing the wicked edge down and away as he carefully carried it back outside. Down the hall he called out, "Don't touch the window. A little rain won't hurt, but I am not taking you to the clinic in my Jeep."

Erick knew he probably deserved that. He was a little annoying when he tried to fix other people's problems. Eliza was a little pissed off, frustrated, and the storm didn't help. "She just doesn't see things my way right now."

The trash cans were fortunately nestled into the corner of the garage and the house, so they hadn't blown over, even as the winds tried their best to get at them. Erick never got to move his Jeep to put the cans inside the garage. He lifted a cover slightly and tossed the shard in with a dull clink. The rain and water off the roof poured down even in the few seconds he was outside as it splashed off the top of the lid. In less than five seconds, he was soaked through yet again.

Once inside, Erick left his shirt on, unwilling to go through another shirtless bout with Eliza right now. "Anyway, I gotta fix the window," he sighed inwardly. Some discarded cardboard, a packing knife, and copious amounts of masking tape did the trick to stop the rain from coming in, for now, until the paper was soaked through. "Which will be in about five minutes," Erick thought, looking out the other panes of glass. "But that's not a problem right now."

He dried his hair with the towel left over from his shower, not so long ago.

"I'm sorry," Eliza said again.

Erick just waved his hand. "It's not the first broken thing in this house. We'll fix it tomorrow." One more reason not to escape as soon as the sun came out, Erick thought. "Or I'll get someone to do it, I dunno. It's not a big deal."

It was to Eliza. "I'll pay for it."

Erick wanted to tell her to forget it. It was a piece of glass. An old, original piece, but a piece of glass, still. It wouldn't cost much. But it would be something Eliza feared would hang over her. Something that was her fault, even though, really, it wasn't. It was his, and Erick knew it.

"Maybe you can come over when they fix it, open the door or something. How about that? I won't be back here any time soon."

Eliza let the statement hang, trying to let it go, along with what she had done. She walked away to sit back down, this time in the soft recliner that Erick's mother seemed to like more than anyone else. Eliza tried to get comfortable in the cushions, but couldn't. She sat upright, grabbed the TV remote, and changed the channel.

The regional news had live coverage of the storm, too, but at least it was a different color. Oak Island was getting some decent ocean flooding. A reporter stood on the Yaupon Pier, talking about the waves hitting the beach. Then they threw it to the studio, which passed it on to other locations, before making it to Marlowe. A reporter stood in the pouring rain, barely seen from a drenched camera, on the western side of the bridge, reporting that flooding had covered both sides of the bridge onramps. "Access to the coastal area, as well as leaving if you are there, is not possible at this time, say the local emergency management leaders in Bodin."

"Yeah, I coulda told her that," Erick smirked.

"Why do you not like it here?" Eliza finally asked. It wasn't the exact question she wanted to say, but it was a good start. Maybe it was an easier one to say, and easier to answer. Eliza knew why she didn't like it. Not anymore.

"I wouldn't say I don't like it," Erick answered her. "Actually, I love this place. I always have. This place was home to me. Even with all this," he waved at the winds outside, "the island, the wind, the cold winters, this is beautiful.

"But it's still an island."

"We're all on islands. I lived here."

"It's… it's not, well, …" Erick stammered. "You have to understand. Everyone knew me. It's not a brag," he shook his head at Eliza's planned protest, "wait, let me finish. Everyone knew me, but they knew their version of me, their idea. Everyone had this expectation of me. I could have done anything I wanted. I lived in 'Stuttgart Castle,' and I was expected to live like royalty. At least, this is what I heard, all the time. Remember, I was just a kid, a teen. I could have done whatever I wanted, and failed at it, and done something else, and failed again. And I would still have my castle." He waved his hands in mock praise, a false *yadah* at the walls and ceiling. "My family was rich, and could do no wrong, and I was expected to be a prince."

"And you just wanted to be a knight, huh?" Eliza tried to hide her contempt at Erick bragging about his wealth.

"No!" He almost screamed, then paused, gathering himself. "I wanted… to be…" he had to breathe, slowly, so he didn't seem like he was blaming Eliza. "I wanted to be an engineer. What I'm doing now.

"I liked designing things, drawing them out, seeing how they worked, and make them work more beautifully, if not better. I always liked that. I know it sounds stupid, no one likes engineers, but that's what I wanted to do."

"I never knew that. You never told me."

"I never told anyone, except my parents, sometimes. And I didn't tell you because I didn't want to when I met you. People would have made fun of me. I got enough shit from people who thought they knew better what I should do. Especially when most of us had no idea what we were going to do when we graduated high school, or college. If you didn't go to work at the plant or on a fishing boat, you were a snob, but if I didn't take advantage of my parents, I was stupid. Because everyone wanted the money I had."

"But why couldn't you do that? Be an engineer. You could have done that, followed your dreams."

"Here, you mean? That's the point, what would I have done here? Design boats over at the shipyard, next to the cannery, down a dirt road? 'Build me a yacht with a big Carolina Flare!'" Erick said in the deep mocking voice of a local fisherman. In a different voice, "'Now build *me* one, but bigger than his!' 'It's going to cost more.' 'Well, make it different then.' 'How?' 'Make mine blue!'"

He stopped the mock debate between two made up men for a moment and looked at Eliza. "I didn't want to do that, do the same thing, over and over. I didn't want to be a prince, or a knight, or some knight errant, tipping at windmills with my father's money. I wanted to be sailing and designing boats, going from Fort Lauderdale to Newport or Mystic, then to San Diego and Long Beach. I was going to be the guy who showed up with the fast stuff, the clipper, I was going to break records and break hearts." That was a bad turn of phrase to use. Erick had actually done that.

"But here, everyone just thought I was going to ride my father's coattails, drive around in fancy cars, and be a car salesman in Atlanta. Or Raleigh.

"Or settle here."

Erick knew that was the real question Eliza wanted to ask. But Erick still wasn't ready for that one. Not now, not soon, and maybe not ever. Sometimes you just kept secrets. Big or little. The secret of why Erick had left and not come back wasn't big, why he initially didn't come back, but it was pretty big for the two of them. But there was no way Erick was going to let that secret out. If Eliza didn't know now, then she hadn't been told why Erick had moved on, and Erick wasn't going to be the one to tell her now. Erick just had to make sure Eliza never asked.

Erick beat Eliza to the punch by asking, "So, I spilled. Now, you. What about you? Why aren't you still here? You could have stayed, but you didn't. You could come back. What about it?" Erick knew some of the answers already. It may be a little cruel to make Eliza face up to them, but the alternative was less appealing.

CHAPTER THIRTY-EIGHT

August 2001
Marlowe Beach

"I told you already. I tried it. It didn't work." Eliza said quietly. She wasn't used to talking about her failed relationship. It was easier to hide or pretend it didn't happen. That's what she learned to do.

"You told me one part, and it was the abridged version, at best. I know there's more to it, and you know it, too. If I say it to you, you'll get mad and say I'm accusing you. You're not admitting anything to me. Just to yourself." Erick pointed at the rain curtains outside, the flooded driveway to a flooded road. "I'm not going to shout it to the world or anything. No one is going to hear me. Not here." No one would care what I said anyway, Erick thought. Erick wasn't a native, not a local, not anymore, and since he didn't work for a living, in their eyes, Erick's opinion wouldn't matter.

Eliza's opinion mattered. Erick knew it. He knew it mattered to her, and Eliza needed to say it, confront it, and hopefully do something, no matter how hard.

"Why do you not want to come back? You left, why not come back? Here," Erick tacked on the last word, a little qualifier to make him not sound desperate.

"You know why..."

"I said that. You know, too. Just say it."

"I'm never going to escape my family." Eliza looked at the floor.

Erick immediately felt guilty for making her say it. "But if I had…" Erick thought as he kneeled in front of Eliza. "Hey…" Erick started to touch Eliza's knee, then pulled back. This was not the time.

Eliza agreed, as she turned away from him in the big soft chair. But she didn't get up or walk away. "My father wants what's best for me, what he thinks is best. And I can't do right by him. Not unless I do what he says.

"He was mad when Lonnie and I broke up. Or when I left him. We weren't just dating. Lonnie asked me to marry him. I wasn't ready."

"Did you want to?" Erick felt like there was a brick in his chest as he asked the question.

Eliza paused, holding her breath, looking around and away for anything that would help her. The hurricane pinned her in the house, and the walls closed in even further. Her heart beat a little faster as a lump formed in her throat.

"No…"

It was an easy admission, because she already knew the answer. But she could never say it, not to anyone. "He was nice, we had the same values, and my parents liked him." Erick looked away at that comment. Eliza noticed, but continued. She wasn't in the mood for soothing Erick's hurt feelings now. "He kept saying he wanted what was best for me, and my father kept saying that Lonnie was what was best for me. We were supposed to get married, have our parents buy us a house, and I would have kids while he worked at the processing plant.

"You know, I had a girlfriend from ECU that was dating this guy that moved here. He was a sweet guy, liked to fish, go out in his boat, and he worked as a cook at the Fish Market. She told me how nice a guy he was, but she didn't want to marry him and live here. 'I don't want to live in an unheated shack,' she told me. I felt like that.

"And it wasn't Lonnie, not really. It was," another hesitation, but this one was easier to get through, "everything. I was supposed to follow in my father's footsteps, but at the same time, I was this little girl that wasn't going to work at the seafood company unless I was a secretary. Which is what my father wanted. He wanted his little girl close.

"I could have done something, anything! I was happy even when I was working at the ice cream shop in the summer during high school! But that, being married to a man that worked morning to night, making dinner, being a mom, answering the phone for my father, it looked like a road to nowhere."

Erick had seen that path taken all too often on the islands. A lot of little fish in a little pond, and the big fish in the little pond, that got elected to town council, or became the police chief, and when they shouted the little people jumped. Some of those people had tried to shout at Erick, in their own way, when he was younger. It's part of why he left, too.

Eliza looked at Erick, his face a mask of sadness and disgust. Eliza felt sad, as well as a lingering anger, "*disappointment*," her voice in her head told her, at Erick. Eliza sniffled, trying to keep her brown eyes from welling over.

Erick looked back, that brick that was aching his chest now slamming him in the back of the head for asking her all this. He listened, though, and understood. Erick thought, "I could say, 'sounds familiar.'" It was a dark shadow of the same reason he hadn't followed his father's wishes, and had run off to the sea. But it wasn't the same. His father had pushed Erick, even offered bribes, let's face it, Erick knew, but Conrad Sunstrom had never actually forced Erick into a job, or a relationship. It wasn't the same, by a long shot.

Erick again felt like he needed to touch Eliza, just put a hand on her knee. His palm wavered over it, gripping and releasing air. It was a habit, a near involuntary action that people had when they cared. The idea of putting pressure on a wound, especially a wound of the heart. Erick wanted to suck all that pain away from Eliza, if only he could, but he couldn't touch her.

Eliza saw him linger over her, and took his hand, then laid it gently on her knee, and squeezed it there. Then she slid off the chair, down to Erick and wrapped her arms around him. She held on too tight, trying to break him, nestled onto his shoulder.

All Erick could do was to put his arms around her back and hold her up as the two teetered. Eliza's ear was nuzzled up next to his lips, but Erick wasn't about to tell her "It will be alright," because he wasn't going to lie to her, not right now.

It took a moment, as Eliza finally uncoiled herself with a sniff. The rain outside had darkened the house, and with the confessions, neither had thought to turn on a light. "Now what do we do?"

Erick looked over her shoulder at the broken glass from the door, and the big window with pelting rain behind it. When pirates faced a gale, they found a hurricane hole, tied up, started a fire with some driftwood, and waited it out. Usually with a bottle of rum between them.

"We go with the wind," he answered. "And hope for a nice, soft beach."

CHAPTER THIRTY-NINE

August 2001
Marlowe Beach

"Maybe I should go."

Eliza felt very uncomfortable at the moment. After their shared confessions, Eliza felt like there was more to be said, and all this did was open up more old wounds for her. "*Good thing you didn't say that out loud,*" said her mind, "*You're getting better at this.*"

"Aw, c'mon," Erick looked out the window. The winds were starting to change. The water was already over the banks of the Intracoastal, and the road was slick, filled with trash and palmetto fronds. He immediately tried to correct his incredulous tone. It sounded condescending as it escaped his lips. "It's pouring out there, and I have lights, TV, I can cook us dinner."

"You barely have any food here," Eliza said back. It felt good to correct him, after baring her soul and admitting her fault. "*Not your fault*," reminded her mind. That was a good one.

"You have better?" asked Erick.

"I've got lots of stuff over there."

"You don't have to go. We've got power, TV, music, books, and I'm sure I can whip up something. You don't need to go out in this. It's fine here."

As if to add to the discomfort, a distant pop sounded far to the north. In a moment, a blink of the eye, the power went out in the house.

Eliza had to laugh. "You were saying?"

All Erick could do was shake his head. "Seriously?" He raised his head to the heavens, above a ceiling, roof, and a roiling cloud cover thick with rain. Then, Erick tried his best to spin it. "See? It will just be dark and lonely over there. Here we've got…" Erick heard the words coming, "each other," and immediately corrected himself, "light, adventure… Okay, I don't know. I'm going to get a couple hurricane lamps. If you want to go, who am I to stop you." He jerked a thumb at the back door. "Just, be careful, huh?" Erick set off to open closets to pull out his oil lamps.

Eliza didn't know he would call her bluff. "You got a flashlight or something?"

Erick nodded but said, "Yeah, but where's the fun in that? You gotta set the mood." He carried out an old hurricane lamp with a deep yellow oil and a half burnt wick. "If we just use flashlights, how will the ghosts find us?"

"Don't say that," Eliza scolded him. There just might be a few out there in the storm. "Not like I'm going to be able to sleep through the night, anyway," she thought.

"There's another one, a lamp, not a ghost, in the back room," Erick pointed to the little guest room behind the fireplace. The porch had wrapped around the house originally, until a little room had been closed off, making space for a folding bed and a dresser. Eliza walked into the room to find the other lantern.

Inside were several of Erick's trophies set on shelves installed on the walls. "Wow! Hey, how come you don't have your trophies out in the living room? Or upstairs in your room?"

"Well," Erick almost yelled from the kitchen, "I didn't really want them out, like I was bragging. Not all of them are really memorable."

Eliza looked at the trophies and medals. Many of them were first place awards, and not just stuff from high school or college. A big Penquin Rum flag was folded up behind a gaudy trophy. Several large cups were lined up in order on a high shelf, all first place winning awards, as far as she could see in the dwindling light. One smaller cup, more a low bowl on a black base said Third Place. She read the race name, and realized it was the race in Spain where Erick had been injured. They must have run the race anyway, with him in the hospital.

"They gave me that," Erick appeared in the doorway, holding a box of wooden matches.

"They still ran the race?" It seemed cold hearted to run a race after two sailors had been so badly injured. Eliza flashed back to the moment, something she desperately had tried to forget. It seemed so cruel, thoughtless.

"No," explained Erick. "We were, I think first in the qualifiers, maybe, and the top three boats race in the finals. But our boat was broken, and we didn't have a full team, of course. And no one else wanted to fill in our spot. Well, I bet the New Zealanders did, but no one was going to let them. They canceled the race and declared us third. It seemed like the fair thing to do since we really couldn't compete for first.

Eliza made a sad look on her face. "You wanted to know why I don't put these things out…" Erick knew his mom had put the trophy in the room. He didn't even see it until he had gotten out of the hospital in Mallorca. "The lamp is over on the table." He turned and walked out without another word.

Eliza stood still for a moment, counting silently in her head just to give Erick a few steps. She set the trophy down and picked up the hurricane lamp instead.

"You know," Eliza said once the lights were lit, "I've got more food over at my place. I know it's raining, but if you want to, you can come over." It was a hopeful invitation. Eliza felt like there were too many memories floating around in Erick's old house right now.

"Like what?" Erick asked. He dipped his match in the remnants of a glass of melted ice.

"Well, I've got lots of frozen dinners. Dad likes them, so… I mean, just because you can't cook here."

"How would you heat them up?" Erick called from the kitchen where he put the dirty glass.

"We can put them in the micro…wave…" Oh, yeah, Eliza realized.

"You know how when the power goes out and you go to the bathroom and just habitually throw the light switch?" Erick came back out, grinning.

"Well, I might have some peanut butter," Eliza said. Islanders kept peanut butter on hand just for occasions like this. There was always peanut butter and saltine crackers around.

"Have a little faith, my little sea oat," Erick answered. "Peanut butter? I have peanut butter. I can do better than that."

"Unless you have a gas stove hidden somewhere, or a generator, I seriously doubt that. You're not going to cook something on your car engine, are you?" It seemed like something Erick would do, and probably do well. "He's probably already done that before." Eliza thought.

"No, I did that once," Erick answered her thought. "It made my car smell like fish. Lesson learned. No, I'll figure something out." He stared at the open pantry door, where there were mostly ingredients, and nothing fresh that needed refrigeration. "You like tomato soup?"

"Like a can?"

"Can?! What do I look like, a hobo?" He actually did. Erick hadn't shaved in days and was starting to look tired and more than scruffy in the darkening evening. "No, I'll make something. How about tomato soup and grilled cheese?"

"I'll believe it when I see it."

Erick shooed Eliza out as he grabbed a white candle from the top of the pantry shelf. "But I wanna watch," Eliza was curious how he would do this. Erick seemed determined to keep his secret.

It took a good forty five minutes, but Erick came out with hot tomato soup, and melted cheese on a pile of multigrain crackers. "It's actually gazpacho, but I heated it up," he explained as Eliza sipped the tangy broth.

"This is," she had to admit it, "really good. It's definitely not canned. You gotta show me when we're done."

The two ate by lamplight. It was less romantic than candles in silver holders. The flames danced only softly, protected from the drafts that tried to seep through the windows and broken door glass. Little bits of smoke tried to escape the glass chimneys, only to be caught on the edges. They darkened the rim of the lamps until the smoky tops blended into the encroaching darkness.

After dinner, Erick tried to take the bowls, but Eliza swiped them away from him. "No, I gotta see what you did. Show me, and I'll do the dishes."

Erick led Eliza into the kitchen to show her his makeshift gourmet stove. "Okay, I had to improvise a little," he explained. "I used some of Mom's Italian tomato paste," he held up an empty tube, "and some broth, garlic, the rest of those sundried tomatoes, a cucumber that looked like it was on its last legs, olive oil, onion, a bit of vinegar, and some of this What'sThis'Chere sauce." He held up a brown bottle of the Worcestershire sauce. "I cut up a candle and put them into that muffin tin and made a stovetop to heat it up. I had a little bit of that cheese left, and used some extra Parmesan cheese on the crackers since I didn't have bread. It's pretty much just a hot gazpacho."

"I don't believe it," Eliza stared at the dirty pot and still smoldering candles.

Erick blew out the last of the flickering flames, sending the kitchen into momentary darkness. "I've learned to improvise."

Eliza stared at Erick's silhouette in the dark. It was just a shape in front of the dark gray of the windows that were still being splattered with rain. Erick was so recognizable to her, even in a black profile line. Eliza waited in case an angelic glow came out from behind Erick. It wouldn't surprise her if it did.

"See? If you can do this, I think you could do whatever you want, even back here."

"What?" Erick chuckled, his face finally coming into focus as Eliza's eyes adjusted to the darkness. "Open a restaurant? A Denny's or something? I'm no cook. I just like a decent meal." He walked up to Eliza, a gray ghost in the old dark house, then bent his shoulder to pass by and get back to the light of the living room.

Eliza followed Erick to the front windows as he looked out the door. The hurricane had passed on to land somewhere to the south. She could tell. The counterclockwise rotation had started to shift from the direct east to the south. It meant the water from the Intracoastal would flood soon.

"No," Eliza tried to continue the conversation. "I'm saying you could do anything you want here. It's a great place to live, it's beautiful, normally," she curled the word with an upturned lip into a snarl, as she blamed the hurricane for setting a bad example. "We've got friends here, history, And you admit it. You like it here. You wouldn't have come here now if you didn't."

Erick sighed and turned to her. He desperately wanted to take Eliza's hand and pet it, like they did in the old movies, when it was time for pity. "Or when they say goodbye," Erick thought. But he kept his hands to his side, then, to be sure, stuffed them in his pockets.

"What about you?" Erick asked, not sure if turning the tables would be a good idea. "Why don't you move back?"

Eliza was ready for the question this time. She had already admitted her struggle to connect with her family. "I want to, but you answered your own question. Just like you, why would I come back? What would I do here? You don't want to build fishing boats, I don't want to work for my father. I don't want to…" this part started to flummox Eliza as she thought in her head, "Get married and have a kid? Be a housewife?" Those weren't the answers Eliza wanted to say back, but they were the right ones. "Be married to a controlling and unloving man who expects me to do everything for him when he's home," was closer. Eliza continued quickly, "stop having to do…" what I want, Eliza thought. Now she was getting closer to the real answer, and she realized how much it mimicked what Erick had said. "I haven't had the chance yet to do for me. I don't have a boat to build, Erick.

"I want to be part of this place," Eliza waved at the wind. "But I'm young, I'm a girl, my father is the power in the family, I haven't found what I can offer yet. You've got that chance."

"Daddy's money," Erick sniffed.

"No!" Eliza grabbed his arm and shook it, just to jostle the insult out of his brain. "No, I didn't say that, and I don't mean it. You have something. Look at what you can do. Sure you could do a lot if you took advantage of your name, but you could do something on your own. You're creative, skilled, look at all the things you've done already. I haven't had those chances, not yet. I made a few mistakes," Eliza hated to admit it, but it was coming out now. "And those mistakes set me back. And I don't know if I'm going to get over them. It's a little scary…"

Erick stood there and listened. “I’m sorry,” he said as he pried Eliza’s grip off his arm, then took her hands in his. “I shouldn’t have said that. You never saw me that way, the rich boy.”

“No, but you sure were handsome soaking wet.”

CHAPTER FORTY

June 1997
Marlowe Beach

May hadn't been much fun on Marlowe Beach for Eliza. It really never was. When she was younger, May only meant that school still had a month to go, with exams coming, but high school sports and social events were over for the season. Summer hadn't started then, nor had the wild circus of tourists that laid the town wide open with the fun of beaches crowded with people during the day and the bright lights of late night mini golf and trinket shopping. For all the horrible things people said about the tourists, they brought the island to life.

Now, for Eliza as an adult, May had been even more dull. The bars and clubs that titillated Eliza's girlfriends as teens, but had scared her with their hidden closed doors and loud music, would open in the late spring to the college crowd. Eliza was no longer quite part of that scene. Many of her friends had moved away and not come back. The people she was still friends with on the beach had moved on and up, getting married or at least having serious relationships, so staying out late dancing wasn't always in their plans.

June didn't get any better. Marlowe was a family beach town, and not really much for the twenty-something crowd of social interaction that Eliza was starting to crave. She had left Woods Hole for the summer, needing a break from her final work on her Master's degree. Eliza was happy to be in a warm climate, where she could tickle her toes in warm sand and people talked with less of a grating accent. But she was a bit of a fish out of water. Eliza had been feeling lonely for weeks now, and was hoping for something exciting to happen.

An early morning rise and a run on the beach probably wouldn't deliver much in the way of excitement. Eliza got up early to stretch, then go for a jog on the wet sand shoreline of low tide. "No one out but me and the sunrise fishermen," Eliza said as she made her way down the sand dune to the beach. Her big running shoes felt like boots in the soft, moving sand, but she needed the support on her ankles. "Plus, I look cute in them," she told herself. "Not that anyone is going to see me but the fishermen." Eliza thought about the old men, who couldn't sleep through the nights, waking up early to spend their retirement sticking frozen shrimp through hooks and wading out into the water to catch bluefish. "At least they're happy," Eliza realized. She counted five fishing poles in the distance to the south. To the north would be more, along with a few early risers who came to take photos of the sunrise or walk their dog. The south was the more appealing choice.

Eliza ran into the morning sun. At least it was a warm day. June warmed up fast, with the wonderful Gulf Stream running just offshore bringing warm air with the warm water. The ocean would already be warm enough for swimming, and Eliza planned to peel off her shoes and shorts to go for a quick swim after her run was over.

Two miles, each way, out and back. An old shack, just a bit of shade, a popular hangout for the escapist stoner crowd thirty years earlier, was Eliza's target. The structure really was only some old wood pilings and slats for shade. No walls, no benches, just a bit of shelter in the heat, and a pretend hiding place from prying eyes. She and Erick had occasionally snuck off there when they were young. By that time in the 80s, the beach was really too crowded to hide from anyone, but it had been fun to pretend.

Now it was just a mile marker, slowly falling down in the sun, rain, storms, and wind. Eliza turned and headed back.

The beach was quickly getting busy. Not summer crowded busy, not yet, but just enough that there were people out, pretending to check out the waves like it meant something to the tourists from Pennsylvania and New Jersey. "The little one foot morning waves would be great to surf, if you were doll sized," Eliza laughed at her joke, imagining the tourists shrinking down to miniature on tiny surfboards before getting caught up in the little washing machines that came ashore.

Eliza knew she was getting close to her home when she could see her house standing tall on the dune. The big brown wood structure stuck up at weird angles, all blocky and polygonal. The stairway window, big, round, stood out like a giant dark eye, a periscope looking out over the seagrass.

Just before it, tucked in a little swale, was the castle. The Sunstrom Stuttgart Castle. It was big and fancy, old, but restored to its coastal glory. Since the Sunstrom home sat low behind a dune, it still looked tiny compared to Eliza's house that stood tall on top of the dune. But the Sunstrom beach house was full of color, all greens and soft yellows and browns, a blast of a natural palate, compared to the boring wood brown over her whole house. Eliza had only been home a few weeks, but had seen no light or action in the house the entire time. She had stopped even looking for a fancy car in the drive.

"The last time I saw Erick was two years ago, when he was making his victory lap up the coast. Back when I was with

Lonnie." She shuddered at the reminiscence. "Erick hadn't even been jealous. He said he was happy for me."

Eliza bounced along, her feet barely leaving a print as she attempted to sneak up on the sand with every step. She found herself staring not at her destination, but the house next to it. "I haven't been inside that place in years," she realized. Eliza wondered if the Sunstroms had changed the old interior over to something modern and new. Eliza could imagine Erick's mother insisting that she have a new modern kitchen. Or maybe she was just imagining someone else doing what her own mother dreamed of.

Someone came out of the cut in the dune by the house. Thin, young, male, definitely not Erick's father, not a sister or mother. The blond hair, the loose t-shirt, the baggy white shorts, Eliza recognized her former boyfriend, even though she had seen him all of once, not counting the photographs reprinted in the local paper, in the past nine years or so.

Eliza didn't know what to do. There was nowhere to hide on the beach, with the sun rapidly rising, no longer orange and yellow but quickly becoming a white hot ball in the sky over the ocean. She just decided to stop, right there, about fifty feet from an old and overweight fisherman who seemed like he was only there to stab and drown worms. Eliza wouldn't be surprised if the man cracked open a cheap can of beer this early in the morning. He would be almost no help in hiding her.

Eliza watched Erick from afar. He was still a long way off. "Maybe he doesn't see me," She hoped. Erick threw down a towel and took off his shirt. "Yes, that's definitely Erick," Eliza knew now. Still trim and fit with those round shoulders and powerful legs, Erick's shape was unmistakable even from a distance. He looked one way, then another, and seemed to stare right at Eliza.

Eliza turned away to stare out at the ocean, stretching a calf muscle just to have something to do. She watched out of the corner of her eye, keeping the fat fisherman, who glanced at Eliza as he cast, between her and Erick. Erick was stretching, too, waving his arms to loosen his shoulders. Then he plodded casually into the water. "Like walking into the party," Eliza marveled at the confidence the boy still had, even when he had to know no one was looking.

"Except me," Eliza knew.

As he began to swim out, Eliza took to running again. While Erick was out, swimming in the sparkling morning, racing the porpoises and skates in the flat, glassy green water, those long arms propelling him like he was born to the water, Eliza would run past, head down, and go straight up the dune so she wouldn't have to speak to him.

"Or, maybe, go to the next access so he doesn't know it's me and I'm at home," she thought. "Just keep running, then work my way back down the beach road." Eliza saw how that wouldn't work. "He'll know I'm home sooner or later. And I'm not going to let him hold me hostage in my house while he shows off for the tourist girls on the beach. It's my beach, too."

Eliza ran on, wondering if she should slow and wave to Erick, out in the water. Or just pretend she didn't notice him, and if he got out of the water, she'd be surprised. "That part would be true," Eliza thought.

Eliza had no more than a quarter of a mile to decide. As she got closer, Erick seemed to turn from the deep water past the low sandbar offshore and swim to the breakers. Before Eliza got even with him, Erick was up and walking in with the waves. He waited and let the waves carry him forward instead of them slapping him down to fall in the wash. "He has to be so darn graceful, doesn't he?" Eliza wondered if she hated him or admired him more.

"Eliza? Hi!" Erick moved from his beach model strut to a sloppy jog in the low waves. No one could run in the water and look good. "Not even this guy," Eliza almost laughed. After her previous thoughts, Erick now looked like a happy dog chasing a stick into the water.

"Wow, it's great to see you! You look, well, you look wonderful. I was wondering if you were around." Erick stood there, dripping wet, tanned, a morning's worth of facial hair, still thin, with a hint of muscle over an impossibly smooth abdomen. Eliza looked at Erick, wondering how he could look that way, and then say *she* looked wonderful. Eliza shook her head from the childish reverie.

"So do you," Eliza answered. She realized that she actually meant it. Erick was smiling, happy. Yes, he still looked great, but it was this happy puppy look, running toward her like some goof, out of the water, calling her name. "Have you been home long?"

"Heh, no," Erick shook his head, getting salt water out but onto Eliza's chest and swim top. "Ooo, sorry, let me get my towel." Erick wandered up the beach to where his shirt and towel lay crumpled in a pile. He shook the sand off and threw it around his shoulders, rubbing the soft purple cloth over his back, head, and arms. "No, really, I just got here today, about an hour ago. I drove overnight so I could see the sunrise, but I was so freakin' tired I fell asleep on the sofa and just woke up. I came out for a swim to wake up. I thought that was you running. You cut a pretty recognizable figure."

Eliza didn't say that she thought the same thing when she first saw Erick on the beach.

"Are you living at the house now?" Erick asked.

Eliza answered, "Oh, no, I'm on summer hiatus, a break from Woods Hole Oceanographic Institute. I'm finishing my Masters and just needed some time off.

"You're not living here on the beach anymore?"

"No, well, right at this moment, yes, but really, I don't have a home. I stopped my lease when I came home. It's expensive to live up there." Eliza spun herself lazily in the morning sun. "I'm as free as a bird!" It took a moment for her to realize that the question Erick asked was a leading one. No, she wasn't living here. No, she had no home, because, no she wasn't tied down or married with a job and kids. "No, I'm not with Lonnie anymore," Eliza realized she said it without saying it. But she said it. Erick may have been a stupid boy, but he wasn't dumb.

"Hey, that's cool, you're like me. A little bit of freedom never hurt. Gives you a chance for an adventure." He worked his shoulder and arm. Eliza noticed a small band over Erick's elbow.

"Are you hurt?" she asked.

"That? No, it's just the leftovers of a bump I took." Erick acted like it was nothing as he bent his elbow.

"What happened?" Eliza pictured Erick ready to tell the story of how he fought off a shark from attacking some dumb blonde while lugging pirate treasure over his shoulder.

"What can I say? I'm an idiot. Some dumbass, uh, sorry, some guy left his cooler on the dock behind me and I tripped over it. My elbow swelled up for a week when I hit it on the dock. I probably should make up a better story, huh?"

"No," Eliza said, "I like that one." She laughed a deep and soft singsong laugh. All of her fantasy, and Erick tripped over some beer.

"Wow, I haven't heard that laugh in a while," Erick smiled back at her. "I should trip and fall more often."

Eliza was delighted. Erick wasn't some larger than life merman coming out of the waves. He was as much a klutz as anyone. It made him all the more human. And appealing.

"So, you gotta tell me about life in Falmouth. You know, I was near there for a week. If I had known, I would have come to see you."

"Not much to tell, really. It's interesting, but it's mostly a lot of compiling data and information right now. I teach an undergrad course. Nothing as fun as tripping over coolers. What was it, Bartles & James, or Zima?"

Erick laughed hard at the joke. Coming from Eliza, it was a surprising contemporary reference on alcohol. Erick sniffed, salt water running out of his nose. "Probably Natural Light, knowing those guys. Zima? What, you think we're made of money?"

"So, what are you up to now? What brought you back to the beach?"

"Well, you mean besides seeing you?" Erick joked and continued. "I got an offer to go train some younger high school sailors, a few in college, all amateur, but looking to compete in the future. It's someone with the new IACC, training kids for the America's Cup future. There's an old Stars & Stripes at Hilton Head, so I'm going down there in about a week to spend some time training them. It's great money, and I can use it to do some summer races in the Caribbean. I just gotta make sure my arm works."

Erick looked over Eliza's shoulder, at her house. "Are you staying here at your place? Is this where you are for the whole summer?"

"Yeah," Eliza tried to put forth a bit of mock suspicion. "Why?"

"Well," Erick scratched at his wet hair, feeling the bits of sand embedded in his scalp. "I'm here for a week. You, uh, you got any plans?"

Eliza looked at Erick as he rubbed the back of his head with a towel. "Is he flexing his arm for me?" Erick's right arm curled up and behind him. "Oh, I hope not." Then Erick shook and rubbed an ear to get water out, looking somewhat silly in the process. "Nope, probably not." Eliza put her hands on her hips and spoke. "No, nothing much. Most of my friends here are either working or staying at home. My parents moved back to the house on Bodin when Tommy moved out. The cold winters were too lonely for my mom. And, honestly, I don't really want to move back in with my parents, even for three months. What are you doing?"

"I'm filling in time while I got it. I'm going up to Wilmington to hear a band I like; it's some guys from Chapel

Hill. I'm meeting up for a sail in Southport. Me 'n a couple mates are going up to Wrightsville to surf. I know a guy there that opened a Mexican restaurant. Stuff like that. If you want to come with me, I'd like it. It would be nice to have," Erick paused, ostensibly wipe some salt water off his face, "you around. To hear your stories. You look a lot better than my friends do."

So, guy friends. That's what he meant. Hopefully. "What the heck," Eliza thought, "It beats listening to my parents. Or having anyone showing up, well, having Lonnie show up, at my door."

"I'd like that. I'm up for a bit of an adventure."

"Great!" Erick almost seemed giddy. "I have to finish my workout. Well, I barely started, but you know what I mean." Erick stammered his way through some sort of attempt to end the conversation before Eliza had the chance to realize what she agreed to and take it all back. "I, uh, I will be out here for a few hours, if you are around later this morning. I'm going to get cleaned up afterward, but if you want to go get dinner, I don't have any food here yet. I need to go to the store today, but we could go out to eat for tonight, if you want."

Eliza watched Erick as he began to back away, headed toward to the ocean, throwing his towel back into the sand. He was making distance from Eliza like he needed space for her answer not to wound him so bad. "Sure, that would be nice," she answered. "We can go to the pier for shrimp, if you want." Eliza smiled as she watched Erick begin to beam with those bright white teeth. He was not going to have to swim out to sea and drown himself after a rejection. Eliza silently begged for Erick to walk backwards into the water and fall into the little waves. While it didn't happen, she was not really disappointed.

Six days later, Eliza sat across from Erick at an intimate table for two at a local beachfront restaurant. The big dining room was in an old beach hotel, built seventy years prior, and served both the high and mighty and the meek and mild ever since. A small candle burned between them. The table was wedged close to one of the myriad windows that opened to the sand where people would play volleyball during the day, or dance to outdoor cover bands in the evening. Right now the side of the big restaurant was empty, though the dining room was full. Eliza paid little attention to her barely touched plate, because Erick was staring at her as he reached across the small table to hold her hand. The week had been great, and Eliza was more than a little dismayed that Erick was leaving in two days. He planned to come back, but then head off to far flung islands in the hot Caribbean soon afterwards.

"This has been so much more fun than a month with my parents. Ugh, and my brother," Eliza testified. "I'm glad you asked me out."

"Oh, yeah, not as much as I am," Erick shook himself from this dreamy reverie as he stared dumbstruck at Eliza over uneaten burritos.

"You sure you have to go just yet?"

"I need to," Erick sighed. "This is a bit of a big deal. And I've already gotten a place in Hilton Head. One of my father's friends has a condo in the harbor that I'm using. You ever been there?"

Eliza shook her head, wondering if Erick remembered mentioning the island to her years ago.

"It's really pretty. The beach houses are all hidden by these big twisted trees and palmettos everywhere. Nothing like this, where the houses are all out in the open. Like they are keeping secrets." Erick squeezed Eliza's hand.

While the two had spent all but one evening together the past week, they had not gone to any lengths to tell their local friends, or Eliza's parents, that they had been spending time together. It was still too soon to say they were dating. But to Eliza, they were. Erick still seemed like at any moment he expected Eliza to disappear or say she didn't want to do this.

"Do you remember our prom date?" Eliza reminisced. "You were joking about driving off to Hilton Head Island, just running away."

"Ha," Erick smiled. "I shoulda done that. I got an uncle that runs a classic car garage there. I could have gotten a job there while you sat on the beach."

"Our parents would have killed us," Eliza giggled.

Erick laughed as he turned away to stare out the window.

"Yeah."

Eliza poked at her plate, pushing a big pepper around but not lifting it. She stared pointedly at her food, then said, "You know, I still have never seen Hilton Head."

CHAPTER FORTY-ONE

August 2001
Marlowe Beach

Eliza had fortunately put her inquisition on hold for an hour. Erick didn't really want to get into that more than he already had. Eliza was bringing out too many feelings, just like she always did.

The hurricane had settled into a horrible dull roar outside, with the south winds rising. There was no more street light to see the water, but Erick knew it was rising. It had to be over the bank and into the street, maybe even into the driveway. The open parking space in front of the old house was filled with a good inch or more of water just from the rain. It gave Erick the suggestion of a pool in the front yard. "Who would want that when you have the whole Atlantic Ocean in your backyard?"

"Do you want me to stay?"

Erick was pulling out an old flashlight, hoping his father had kept the batteries new and clean, and that they weren't corroded. He wanted to see if he could shine the light down the driveway to see if the sound water had crossed the road.

"Huh?"

"It's late," Eliza said. "I probably should get home before it's real late."

"I just figured you'd stay here," Erick said. "You can sleep in my sister's room if you want. You don't need to go out in this. We've got light, company, this storm will be bad all night. We might as well share it. I'd be worried all night anyway." Now I'm worrying about her. Great.

"Thanks," Eliza said.

No debate. No polite "You don't mind." Just "Thanks."

"She's getting to you," he told himself.

"This girl had sunk her claws into me from the moment I first saw her. Now she wants me to move back here. I need to go to bed so tomorrow can come and she and I can leave." Erick looked down at the flashlight, which he shone directly in his eyes. "Well, the light works."

Erick opened the front door and shone the light into the darkness. Myriad white lines coursed through the beam, dimming it some, but Erick could still see to the end of the driveway. There was water forming at the entrance. Not so little waves, about six inches high, were sloshing into the seagrass and drowning Joe Bells in the dark. "The road must be flooded. I hope I can get out of here tomorrow morning."

"It'll be fine. This isn't much of a hurricane," Eliza was only halfheartedly comforting Erick. "Is it so bad that you have to stay another day? I'm actually glad to see you."

Erick was getting tired. The drumming rain and darkness mixed with the boredom of being in the same room all day. He had not slept much in days now, and his body chemistry was getting shot. "Sleeping on a sofa last night wasn't a good idea," he remembered. Not much of anything that happened recently seemed like a good idea. "Well, you know where I live. You could have found me any time. No, I really need to get out of here." To do what? Erick wondered. He switched off the flashlight and closed the door.

"I didn't know where you were," Eliza corrected him. Until yesterday, she had no idea if Erick was still alive, to be honest with herself.

"All you had to do was ask."

"Ask who?" Eliza said it too fast. She felt defensive, unsure where Erick was going with this.

"Well,… me. My parents. I'm still friends with a few of the guys around here. You could have asked someone."

Eliza knew she could have, but didn't want to. She hadn't wanted to know just how Erick felt.

How he felt with a giant tear across his chest.

With a torn up heart and broken ribs.

Or how he felt when he finally awoke and found her gone.

And the two years since, when she never said a word.

"I could have," she agreed softly. "I'm sorry I didn't."

To Erick, the apology seemed small. He knew it was tough for someone to apologize, and usually he just accepted them, forgave, moved on, with a "No problem," and the notation in his head to forget whatever it was.

But Eliza hadn't been there when Erick woke up. Or when he was trying to heal. And now she was just back in his life, one more time. Getting stuck in his head with those beautiful brown eyes, not looking at him, no matter how much he wanted them to.

"Why didn't you?" Erick needed to know. He wanted to accept her apology, so he could move on and forget this person. And definitely not move back to the island. Or ever come back again.

Eliza tried her best to gloss over a greater admission of guilt. "I guess I just wasn't ready." The words seemed hollow, vague, dispassionate. But she had heard them before from Erick. At least something like it.

"No, really, why didn't you call? Eliza, maybe you don't owe me. But you have to understand. It's been two *years*. I've been through hell after you left. I woke up, and my parents had flown across the world to be there for me. There were people from the team, strangers, but not you. And then when I was going through rehab. Or stuck in a cabin in Costa Rica. I wanted to sail away and never come back. I'd just like to know."

Eliza looked everywhere but at Erick. The back door, out into the dark winds, enticed her. She finally met his gaze. "I was there. I was there first," Eliza was almost getting angry now, remembering what it was like. "I waited for you at the hospital where no one spoke English and wouldn't speak to me because I was just 'the girlfriend.' Like I didn't matter. That German woman knew more than I did.

"And I didn't know if you were going to wake up or not. I didn't know if you were going to die or not. It just seemed like everything else, everyone else, was important.

"And I wasn't."

Erick felt an ache in his chest. It was a physical throb, coursing across him. His neck and back tightened, pulling across his ribs. The rip across his chest hadn't hurt in years; now it felt like he was being split in two.

"You meant everything to me," he insisted.

"It felt like you loved every boat you had more than me!" Eliza answered back. "Every time you had a chance to run off somewhere, you did. And you took me with you right up until it was time for you to do what you wanted. You would go off and sail away. Well, that time, I didn't think you were going to come back! I just couldn't handle that anymore. All the bad things that happened, my family, all the expectations people have of me, they were nothing compared to knowing you were torn apart like that, knowing that I was going to be alone."

"You wouldn't have been alone. You didn't have to leave me there like that."

"Why not?" Eliza felt like she was competing with Erick, all their history, and the wind outside as the house shuddered with gusts. "You left me. You left me first! I had to see you leaving, not coming back, not finding me, not for years.

Eliza cooled from an angry steam to soft cold blooded accusation.

"I learned it from you. You did it first."

CHAPTER FORTY-TWO

June 1989
Marlowe Beach

It felt weird that college was out for Erick, but his girlfriend still had more than a month in high school. His freshman year at UNC hadn't been the fun adventure for him that most 18 year old new adults were having. It didn't help that he was only 17, still technically a kid, and didn't even have a car, when he started classes. It was weird. And lonely. The only benefit he imagined was that at least he focused on his classes and got decent grades. Being on the Dean's List had gotten him praise from his parents and a notice in the local paper. That and fifty cents would get him a can of Coke.

UNC had at least been close enough to get a ride home on occasion. The three hour drive was much easier than the six hours from Georgia Tech. It was the only reason Erick had decided to go to school in Chapel Hill rather than Atlanta, so he could be a little closer to home and Eliza.

Erick had come home, and immediately called Eliza, who wasn't allowed to come over. She had moved from cheerleading to track and field in the spring, so she had practice, and still had homework after all that.

Eliza had to ask Erick to prom that year. Since he didn't go to school in Bodin anymore, it was technically up to her. Erick hadn't held the rituals of high school in much esteem when he was going to school there. It was a stepping stone to college and bigger things. No one cared what you did if you were a "peaked in high school" guy, as far as Erick was concerned. But he dressed up in his best suit, went to the dance, and was as happy as he could be to be out with Eliza, even if he was surrounded by a bunch of weird and desperate boys and giggling girls.

The parties afterwards seemed dull. Erick had to suffer through the endless comments of how they looked so good together, how he must be happy to see Eliza again. Yes, he was. Now just let us have a regular date, he wanted to scream at the thin, oddly shaped kids that didn't seem nearly as weird the year before. Eliza seemed like the only one that still looked familiar to Erick.

June rolled around, and while some of his friends were back, many were working, and there wasn't the same freedom of years before. Erick took a job at a surf shop. Eliza worked at an ice cream and hot dog stand. Erick insisted on having as close to the same schedule as Eliza, just so he could try his best to take her out to the movies. Her curfew tainted much of their plans.

When Erick got around other boys, life got worse. Too many had the same thing to say, "You two are going to get married, aren't you?" And the girls were more "You make such a cute couple!" When he explained that he was still 18, and didn't even have a real job, there was the inevitable example of some couple they knew, from an older brother, or just rumor, of how this wonderful high school romance moved into wedded bliss and they were happily married at 21 or something. Erick pointed out that this mythical couple was only 21, give them time.

Erick had discussed this with Eliza at the end of the last school year. "Look, I don't want to get married. Not now at least. We're still in high school. You still have years of high school left! Let's just get to college first."

Eliza had nodded in agreement, but Erick could tell she had a hint of disappointment. It wasn't like he didn't have feelings for her. He was just unaware of how he really felt. "How do you expect a teenager to know if they are in love?" Erick liked the way he felt when he was around Eliza. They were happy together, even when they did nothing. Just sitting around. Especially when they did nothing.

But then came all the comments and teasing and little taunts. "If you aren't going to get married, can I date her?" Erick heard that too many times. How could someone who said he was a friend say that? And then say it again and again. Others were worse, coming out and saying that Eliza was up for grabs while he was gone.

Erick didn't want to get married out of high school. He didn't want to be married in college. He didn't want Eliza to be married in college. It wasn't just the weird feeling of a teenager who has to go around in life being both an adult and a kid, where they manage a household, make car payments, take the trash out, while at the same time riding bikes and going to the movies to make out in the back of the theater. There was a strange stigma to that among college students, which would only be worse in high school. Erick's bigger concern was the perception of being sedentary, the view that adults who marry settle down, wild dreams crushed to day to day reality. Getting married meant closing a door on what each person wanted to do with their lives, and move into doing what they both had to do. It was a bad idea to Erick, but he could get by. He could join his father's business and everything would be fine.

It would be different for Eliza. She was young, too young to be engaged, much less married. Erick had a nightmare of seeing Eliza in her wedding dress as the two got married, a borrowed bit of white prom dress that didn't fit on her thin body. He had forgotten so much of the dream, for good reason, he thought. Erick had this terrible concern that her father was standing behind them with a weapon.

All Erick wanted was to date Eliza. To be normal, typical, like everyone else, go to the movies, out to eat at the local Mexican restaurant, to stare across the table over the glow of one of those silly green sea glass polished candles with the white mesh around it, just to look at her smile at him. Erick had his moments with Eliza, and he wanted more of those.

But all he heard was either commitment or abandonment. One or the other. One often led to the other. "I'm just eighteen. I shouldn't be in this position." Nothing made Erick happy, except the rare occasions he and Eliza got to go out. Even going out on his sailboat or swimming on the beach seemed to have obstacles thrown in front of them. Eliza's father seemed to find ways to make sure she was busy whenever Erick was home. The two of them rarely found a moment to be truly alone. Either Eliza's parents were around, at least her mother on most occasions, or Eliza was with her friends from school or church. The whole idea of them having a life of teenagers, a high schooler or college student, meant to Erick that he wasn't going to tell Eliza she couldn't do things with her friends, but Erick felt like telling her just that, to spend more time with him. Erick felt bad when he wanted to make demands, which made him want to stay away from Eliza. It just wasn't right, to ask Eliza to give up her life.

Erick had no idea how to solve the problem. He couldn't appease all the other kids who kept insisting they get married, as if that was some sort of solution. Letting her date other people while he was away would be miserable. Erick felt like he was missing out on his life since he wasn't dating anyone at college. Not that he wanted to. No one appealed to him like Eliza.

At the end of June, one of Eliza's girlfriends, Jenny Willis, came in to the shop while Erick was working. Jenny was a wonderfully tempestuous girl, a bony redhead that wore all green like a springtime sprite. Erick always liked her, even when she drove him a little mad with her flighty change of emotions. She blew in like the wind, and Erick never knew just what she was going to carry in with it. Erick loved her dearly and secretly because of the carnage she always seemed to bring with her.

"My dad says I have to get a new bikini," she said in a strange mix of dejection and joy. "He wants me to get one that's less 'bikini' for a pool party."

"Well, I'd help you, but I guarantee you'll know what you are looking for better than me. I can get you ten percent off, if it's expensive. Best I can do."

"Not half off?" Jenny joked.

Erick laughed. It may be a common joke, but still funny. He watched as Jenny took suits from the long wooden bar that held them by the hundreds. She had long, thin, tanned hands, with rings scattered across them in no particular order. Some were simple gold filigree, others seemed so gaudy with big green plastic emeralds that they looked like she got them from a gumball machine.

"Hey," Erick asked, "Can you do me a favor? I want to get Eliza a gift. I was going to get her a cute ring, just a little silver something, but I don't know her size. Can I borrow one of yours? Just to size it? I'll give it back next time I see you."

Jenny smiled a glinting, knowing smirk. "A man that knows rings comes in sizes, he isn't just looking for a gift."

"Don't you start with me," Erick said. "C'mon, I'm trying to do this right."

Jenny took off a simple gold ring from her ring finger. "Sure, I'll help you. It's not valuable. It's just gold plate."

"I'll give it back to you in a few days. Next time I see you, okay? Just don't tell Eliza."

It was to be more than a few days. Erick left the ring sitting on his dresser until he had a free day to drive to Barefoot Landing in North Myrtle Beach. He realized that a rich boy showing up at a town jeweler to get even a cheap silver ring would end up on the local coconut telegraph. The drive to the neighboring state and its tourist meccas was only forty five minutes, anyway. He had Jenny's ring sized, "It's tiny, a 5.5. That's pretty small," commented the salesperson. Erick shrugged. He didn't need to add any comment. Eliza's fingers were small and thin. And Erick didn't care about any judgement from someone whom he'd never see again. Erick picked out a complex silver ring, a delicate twist of intertwined rope that looked nice. He rode back home, looking forward to seeing Eliza and giving her the gift.

It wasn't an engagement ring, not even close. And that was what he wanted. Erick hated the notion, and the name, of a promise ring, but it was closer than anything else in meaning. It was a placeholder, at best. Just a gift, but a nice one. Something for Eliza to fiddle with and remind her of him. Erick hated the simplicity of saying so, but he still said the words to himself, "It's the best I can do right now."

It was an agonizing week of never being alone with Eliza. Erick just wanted a moment, just a breath, away from her friends, his friends, coworkers, his parents, her father, "ugh, her *father*!" Erick swore. Just a moment to have a right moment. Eliza deserved that. A look over a cheap candle and a fancy burrito, a soft hand to hold, a moment of "I've got something for you, sweetheart," to hand her a token gift where the thought really counted more than the price. Erick would have bought Eliza anything in the world, if she asked for it. But the only thing either of them wanted was to be with each other. The ring was a sweet but poor substitute, but it would do.

Erick went over to Eliza's home. He had given up on finding the right moment, and figured he would just dangle the ring out to her, or slip it into her hand when they tangled fingers in a delicate kiss on her back porch when no one was looking.

Unfortunately, Eliza wasn't home. Her father welcomed Erick in even after Erick insisted he would come back another time. He didn't want to wait. Erick had felt more and more uncomfortable with each visit to Eliza's house, as if he was less welcome. Erick walked an adult's life, even at only eighteen, expected to suddenly change his life to be a man, giving up joy and freedom. He always had this feeling that Eliza's father saw the step from high school to a working man, not to further education in college. Erick was the rich college student, dating his sweet innocent little girl now.

Then he went and ruined it all by calling Erick "boy."

"You and Eliza are pretty serious, aren't you, boy?"

Erick didn't like where this was going. All the battles he had already with his peers were one thing. Coping with a girl's father, on his turf, with a leading question like that, Erick squirmed. That was probably the idea.

"Oh, uh…" Erick didn't know what to say, "I really like her, if that's what you mean." Erick hesitated. He didn't want to add, "But…" because it sounded like a qualifier, a limit to his feelings, as if there could be an option. "We just want to be able to date, go play mini golf, go to the movies, things like that. It's been kind of hard, with work and everything." Erick tacked on that qualifier. It wasn't a blatant accusation, but Erick could let it linger. Her father hadn't done anything to help the two, that was for sure.

"You just like her, huh?" Her father orbited the living room slowly, making a point to end up by the wood stove insert. Over it hung the de riguer weapon of choice of most island men of Butch's age, a 12 gauge shotgun. "You aren't thinking of anything more?"

Erick wondered just where this was going. If it was some sort of threat about the two of them having sex, well, it was too late for that. And Erick had no intention of getting Eliza pregnant if he could help it. They were teens, in love, and also with the usual wild desires and weaknesses that come with the age. But Erick had no plans of knocking Eliza up to possess her.

Erick wondered if this was some hypocritical judgement on Butch's part, but Erick wasn't about to try to do the math at this time. Erick didn't really care, especially with Eliza's father lingering around the gun rack.

"Uh, I mean," Erick was in an uncomfortable position. If this had been anyone his own age, he could have stood up and told them off, tell them to mind their own fucking business. Anyone even close to his age, if they were implying some insult to Eliza, he would have picked them up by the shirt and shook the shit out of them, banging their head to the wall to beat some sense into them.

But there is a big difference between an eighteen year old boy and an old leathered fisherman in his "Forties? Fifties?" Erick had no idea how old the man was. Not that it mattered. Eliza loved her father like any daddy's girl ever did, no matter what he did or said. Erick, even if he ever wanted to, and he didn't, couldn't raise a hand, finger, or even his voice to the man. If there ever was a way to forever and ever ruin what he had with Eliza, it would be to go against her father.

"I mean, we're still kids. I want her to have a chance to be a teenager. I want that for me, too. I'm not asking her to spend every moment with me. I just want us to have a chance to be together." Even as he said it, Erick wondered if "be together" was a good choice of words.

"I want that, too. What you said. For my daughter," Butch emphasized 'daughter' with a caustic lilt in the island brogue. "She needs to have a chance to be a child." He again emphasized the word, hinting none too quietly that Erick was robbing Eliza of her life. "She needs to be around her friends more.

"I know you have been thinking about the two of you getting married. I think it would be a good idea to get that out of your head now. Get it right out."

Erick was stunned. He felt the pressure of the small box in his pocket. That wasn't what he wanted. Erick wondered how her father got the idea. People will talk. Eliza's friends, when he wasn't around, saying things around the house, when they think her father isn't listening. The general gossip of kids in school, going home to parents who work for her father. A nod and a wink, a bit of misunderstanding, from one friend to another. A soft mention of how young they were when they got married, by Eliza's mother. "He's rich, he would be a good provider," one that Erick had heard before.

He had left the gold ring, that cheap bit of Jenny's costume jewelry, out on his dresser, and never returned it. Had his parents seen it? None of this was what Erick wanted. None of it was true.

Well, some of it was true.

Erick stood quietly, a soft cold sweat forming, not helping his case in any way with the man who looked like he wanted to take down a gun, pump it for effect, and point it at Erick.

Then maybe pull the trigger and end the problem like he would with a cottonmouth snake in the water.

Erick wondered what would happen if this man killed him. Not how his mother would cry, his sister would break, his father would suffer in cold dread. What would Eliza do?

"I don't want to get married." Erick said the words coldly. It was true.

"That's what I thought." Eliza's father took a step back from the wood stove and mantle. And the shotgun.

"I think it would be a good idea if you gave Eliza some space. Don't you? Maybe you two don't see each other for a while. Let her be around people her age, more her type."

Erick merely nodded. He suddenly had a very strong desire to go to the bathroom.

The final bit of good fortune in all the bad was that Eliza's father nodded at the door, indicating Erick could leave.

Two weeks later, with a sizeable donation, and a commitment to attend second semester summer classes, Erick began his next year of college at Georgia Tech, a much more distant university from the tiny island of Marlowe Beach.

CHAPTER FORTY-THREE

August 2001
Marlowe Beach

"I just wanted to get out of this place, with you! We were supposed to stay together. Then you just left."

Eliza felt the pressure boil off. She finally said it. It may have been a little thing, just something stupid from when they were teens. Kids do dumb things. Eliza did dumb things when she was younger. She still did them, sometimes. Her mind tried to talk to her, "*That's not quite fair*," but the remnants of the roar in her ears overcame the whisper in her mind.

Eliza had never brought it up before. She just chalked it up to Erick being immature, just a stupid boy at the time. Eliza had been afraid that if she said the words, the magic would disappear and their world would become real.

"And boy, has it," she thought.

Erick stood with his head down, his hand resting on the mantle, to hold himself up. "You're right," was all he could say. Because she was.

"You never told me why. Was it just because I wasn't good enough for you? I was the little high school girl, and you were ready to move on to college? Or you just couldn't settle for me? You couldn't be tied down to a little girl on an island? What was it? Why is there always some other place you have to be?"

It was a fair argument. Eliza had felt the storm of emotions, seeing Erick back, his injuries, that horrible scar he wore, and whatever else was wrong with him. She fell back in love, or just fell, Eliza didn't know. And the whole time Erick is begging to be free. "*He just got here, and he's always looking for a way to escape. He's not going to change*."

Eliza just stared, exhausted. Tears welled up, filling her eyelids, lit into fiery little pools by the soft flames of the hurricane lamps. Eliza squinted, holding back the tears. She wasn't going to give Erick the satisfaction, not for this. The sweet, easygoing, always right, ready with a gourmet meal and a kind word in a hurricane Erick. He didn't get to play the sympathy card, like she was some weak teenager again. She had already cried about this, more than once.

"Well?"

Erick looked at Eliza, then away, at the mantle, his photos and little shells and treasure boxes collecting dust because no one lived in the house long enough to clean it regularly. When Erick looked at the wall, Eliza sniffed as silently as possible and wiped her eyes with a sleeve balled tight into her fist.

CHAPTER FORTY-FOUR

August 2001
Marlowe Beach

"You were the first, and only, girl I ever loved."

It was easy to say, because, now at thirty years old, a man who had been around the world, who had created things, failed, succeeded, picked up the pieces, and yes, almost died, Erick could look back at the poor little sixteen year old boy who saw Eliza's face for the first time and felt his heart flip and crush so wonderfully and terribly that he lost all sense of everything else in the world and crashed. He had fallen, literally, so hard, that for a moment, nothing mattered. If he had drowned on that day, Erick knew now, it would have been a life well spent, just by seeing Eliza, that first time.

And every time after that.

"If I said I was crazy in love with you, it would be a lie. Because I wasn't crazy." Erick felt this was the final confession, but he knew there were things he couldn't say.

Some things go to the grave. It was the other side of being an adult. Not a teen, not a kid, who could blurt out the hurtful words and expect forgiveness later on. Eliza deserved the truth, but she also deserved only some of it. "I was scared. I was sixteen when I met you. I hadn't dated anyone seriously, even high school serious. Flirting, girls who liked my car or my surfboard, that stuff was about as far as I had gotten. I was a kid.

"And after we were together, everyone thought we should get married. And that terrified me. I wanted to do something with my life. I wanted you to have a chance do something, make a mark, or even just be happy with yourself. I didn't know what that was, because I was still a kid. The thought of you, wandering around the school, being asked about our 'honeymoon,' can you imagine? There were teachers there who weren't married yet!"

Erick opened and closed the little wooden box on the mantle. His mom had given it to Erick when he was only twelve. She called it "the box of broken dreams." Jane had told Erick, "Take all the dreams that don't work out, and put them away in here. Put the pieces away, the broken ones that can't be mended. It's hard to forget a bad dream or a wish that didn't come true, so you need a place for it to sit, so it won't bother you the next time." By now the box rattled with more than a few things, enough that Erick wasn't sure what they all were, or stood for in his past. Erick had started to fill it with every token that didn't mean success, but realized it would get filled up pretty quick. Erick had decided to forgive himself for some of the failures, just to make sure he always had a little more space in the box. He hadn't put anything in it in over two years, but he knew there were two rings bouncing in there somewhere.

Erick looked back at Eliza, wanting to tell her more, in hopes that maybe a bit of redemption or forgiveness would come his way. But that was too much of a burden to pass on to Eliza. She was right, in some ways. He had left her.

“I didn’t try hard enough then. I was a kid, and I was scared.” Erick tried his best to say the word ‘scared’ not as a description, but a transition. He couldn’t say “I was scared off by your father…” Just saying he was scared would have to be enough. “I didn’t know any better. I wanted to fight for you, but I felt like I would be fighting everybody and everything, and I wouldn’t win anyway. And things would have only been worse.”

“Worse?” To Eliza, it wasn’t a good choice of words.

“We would have drifted, settled.” Erick had seen it with other couples who didn’t try, just expected things to work out. “You would have wanted me to be home every evening. I would have been some lowly George Bailey guy in an old house wondering what the world is like. We would have been plain, miserable, and in love. I know it. And I didn’t want you to be miserable with me.

“And I know, instead I took you to far flung Spain and almost killed myself just so I could have you tag along with me because I was in love with you and with competing, and I wanted the best of both worlds. I wanted to succeed and us get married and chase the wind. And that would have been unfair, too. You didn’t deserve that, either.” Erick watched as the flames of the hurricane lamps softly waved in agreement. “I burned like some wicked candle, too hot, too bright, always starving for air but letting the wind almost blow me out.

“I told you a long time ago, I was sorry, and I’m a screw up. And I still feel like it now.”

CHAPTER FORTY-FIVE

July 1988
Marlowe Beach

Summer evenings got thick and still on Marlowe Beach. Summer was wonderfully fickle with its winds, sometimes blowing down the marsh grass in waves, other times just a teasing breeze that creates hopes and wishes for a bit of cool air, only to take it away in a moment of held breath.

But it was always hot.

The best thing to do when it got hot, according to some, would be to find the coldest air conditioner that will create an arctic climate in a closed room. But kids knew better. The best thing, the real best thing, was to embrace it.

Erick and Eliza lay flat on the opposite sides of the trampoline of Erick's cat. They stretched out lazily, only their hands barely touching, fingers delicately intertwined just enough to keep that desperate physical contact that two teens silently in love had to have. The catamaran was beached on a low island across the Intracoastal Waterway from their houses. Only the stern moved, still slightly afloat in the water, giving the little sailboat a restrained drift back and forth that lolled the couple's heads in a satisfying way. Above them, the mast stood empty. Only a thin line and pulley led up the spar. The little pulley *tink*ed against the mast in an almost regular chime. Above the mast was only the clear dark sky and myriad stars twinkling thought the heat.

Erick and Eliza laid still, feeling the mix of heat and thick still water above and below them. If they moved, they would feel the thin veil of sweat that covered them. So they lay still, only their heads bobbing side to side, while Erick's fingertips played piano on Eliza's knuckles, and drew out little hearts on her palm.

"If I could stop a moment, just bottle it up and live it forever, this would be it," Erick said. It was a daring statement for a teen. He could have picked any intimate moment the two have had, or some deeply held and strange fantasy with Eliza in her bikini nestled up with him, but he chose this.

"Really?" Eliza said it not in surprise, though she was. It was sweet, and touching, but also unexpected. She rolled over on her side, intent on asking just what Erick had thought, in a more delicate way, "Not on the beach, or sailing off to nowhere?" But as she turned, her heart warmed at the notion. It may not be an overly romantic moment, or something steamy or passionate. It was just a moment, soft, of the two of them together.

Erick turned to face her. Eliza was barely lit in the mix of lights, the soft green and red on the bow and the normally brighter white light on the stern that Erick had covered with a towel to dim it to a glowing candle. Beyond that were the distant street lamps, the yellow-brown glow of lights inside the beach houses that dotted the barrier island. Eliza's face was barely lit but Erick knew it well enough that he could keep his eyes closed and see her if he had wanted to. "Really."

Erick was about to explain when Eliza slid across the center of the trampoline to wrap her hand around Erick's neck and kiss him delicately. It was no precursor to intimacy, not in the open, even in the dark of night at 9:30 in the evening in the summer. It was just a kiss to seal his mouth. He didn't need to explain more. Eliza was telling Erick that she got it.

Erick kissed back, then lay his head on the taut trampoline, looking at the stars. "One day, Eliza, I'll buy this old island and build you a castle, a real one, not like that place," he nodded over his reclined head. "A big castle in the sand, and we'll sit on the top at night and watch the stars and satellites go past us. And if anyone wants to get to us, I'll raise the drawbridge and let the alligators out."

CHAPTER FORTY-SIX

August 2001
Marlowe Beach

Eliza had said what she had wanted to say for years. She needed someone to blame, and Erick had always been better than anyone else. He was even easier to blame than her father. Her father at least had reasons. Butch grew up in this narrow minded town. Erick should have known better. They grew up at the same time,

Now Erick goes and admits the whole thing was his fault, "like it was all his fault or something," Eliza thought. "Where do I go from here?"

Erick must have been thinking part of the same thing. He was glancing around the room, between the two oil lamps and the dark spaces, wondering where he could escape to. The rest of the house was dark, and the rain had turned, coming thicker and harder from the south, a continual bucket pouring out of the black clouded sky.

"How come you couldn't have been a little less sorry?"

Erick stared at Eliza, almost puzzled, but mostly sad.

"How come you couldn't have been a little less sorry, and a little better?" It was an accusation, but a sad one.

At least this time, Erick didn't have an answer. He was running through them in his head. "I should have been." "I was only a kid." "I *am* sorry." They all were fruitless. He couldn't turn time back. Neither could Eliza.

"You're right, and I deserve that. And I've known it for years. And I have been trying to do better ever since then."

Eliza watched Erick as he stood in the dark, near the front windows, the rain pouring and wind whistling in the background. Hadn't he always been "brave?" No, confident, assured, comfortable. Unbreakable. Well, not unbreakable, but hard to break. Brave, too, admittedly, but not reckless. "Sometimes reckless," Eliza realized.

Now he just looked sad and broken. Or cracked. Eliza pictured the scar across Erick's chest. A crack across his heart.

All this blame Eliza had hidden inside herself, and letting it out hadn't helped any.

"I just wish you would have told me this… sooner."

Erick slunk back, deeper into the shadows. He sat down heavily into a chair by the window. He looked defeated. Eliza had wanted him to feel that, but now that she saw Erick like that, the victory seemed Pyrrhic. She had wanted Erick to feel the loss she had felt. But Eliza didn't want to hurt him. Not anymore, at least. When she was younger, it might have felt good, or appropriate, but not now. It was too late to take back.

"I'm sorry," Eliza said quielty. "I went too far. I was hurt back then, and I needed to hurt you back.

"Do you want me to go?" Eliza stared out into the darkness and storm. This time, she really meant it. No matter the weather outside, Eliza didn't feel right staying in Erick's home. It was taking advantage of him after she had torn into him like that. "I'm going to go home." Eliza got up and walked to the back door, ready to wander out into the rain.

"Wait! Don't go!" Erick was up and following Eliza before she got to the door, but he didn't stop her. Eliza undid the bolt and opened it, exposing herself to the night. The winds blew the rain sideways from the south. The door opened to a soaked back porch, with a sopping wet mat that was twisted into the corner. The weight of the water had kept it from blowing away.

The rain fell on the south side of the porch. It couldn't reach all the way to the door, though it poured onto the walkway, invisible in the blackness, only a harsh drumbeat on the wood slats. Beyond the screen door was emptiness, a small spot where the rain currently failed to reach, no matter how hard the wind tried to blow it there. If Eliza went that far, it was only one more step into the storm. It was a commitment. The rain would pelt down, the wind would blow her hair into madness, she would be soaked in steps, and she would have to find her way to her house through the night of the hurricane. It was only hundreds of feet, a path she had once memorized long ago. Eliza once thought she could do it with her eyes closed. Now she might have to.

"Wait! Don't go out there!" Erick had made it to the door, ready to reach out and grab Eliza from the winds. But he wouldn't. Erick had never once held her that way. He had hated even holding hands when they had lain on the sofa together. He felt like he was pinning Eliza down. Erick had told her so, back when she was only fifteen. He would reach out to hold her, keep her safe, make sure she didn't fall over the side of his boat, pull her from a wave, but he had never stopped her.

"Don't go out in that!" Erick almost begged. "Please, don't go. Stay. You can still stay here tonight."

Eliza looked from the darkness to Erick, only a few feet away, lit by the closer hurricane lamp. It should have been an easy choice to stay where she was dry and safe from the hurricane, but Eliza had that strange, desperate feeling. It was always there, one that the locals felt after being cooped up for too long, the desperate need to run out of the house at any sign of letup in the rain. It was worse on the rare occasions that the eye passed over, and clear skies appeared. She urgently wanted to be outside.

"Don't go."

Erick pleaded with Eliza. She looked back, almost expecting to see Erick, teenage handsome smiling Erick, twirling a foot in the sand, with his hands stuffed into his shorts pockets, with his dumb grin. But it was just the same Erick, older, the adult, kind of sad, kind of begging, kind of sorry. He drooped in the lamp light as he stood there.

"Please, don't go."

Eliza felt the wind and rain and cold salt air. She shut the door to the winds, leaning against it, just for the support of knowing there still was a way to escape. Just in case she changed her mind.

"Don't go, stay here. Tonight. Like I said, you can stay in my sister's room. Or you can stay down here, in my parents' room, if you like. I won't bother you. You can leave in the morning, when there's light. Okay? In the morning?"

Eliza simply nodded. "Upstairs," she said. She wasn't going to sleep in Erick's parents' bed. Even with the wind circling the house, the second floor always seemed safer to people during a hurricane. The fear of flood was always worse than the fear of winds and rain.

"Upstairs," Erick agreed. He handed Eliza the closer hurricane lamp, then gathered the other and his father's old flashlight. The two walked up the stairs, their shadows cast on the walls as they marched up the old wooden steps, creak by spooky creak. The house whispered against the shrieking hurricane outside. As strange as the lights and shadows were, Erick trudged up with solemn comfort knowing it was just a house, not haunted. If there ever had been any ghosts in the house, Erick had never shaken hands with any of them.

Erick handed Eliza the flashlight. "In case you have to go to the bathroom. Don't worry about waking me. I'll probably sleep through this. I'm exhausted." He was as likely mentally drained, but definitely tired. Erick hadn't slept in a familiar bed in a long time. He had barely slept at all.

Eliza didn't bother looking around Erick's sister's room. It was almost empty, like a guest room now. There was nothing familiar or feminine in the room anymore. It was just a room with a made bed, which made it all easier for Eliza to want to get into bed. She kicked off her shoes and planned to sleep in her clothes, just to be more ready to get up and leave first thing in the morning. Her clothes still felt old, worn, wet from a storm, even though they were mostly dry. Eliza gave in and undressed, leaving her shirt on, as she climbed into the bed. Then she got up and turned the hurricane lamp wick down until the light went out. Eliza went back to bed and climbed into the stiff and perfect sheets. Exhaustion won over anguish, and she fell into a fitful sleep. The last thing she heard over the whistling of the wind was Erick's door creaking shut.

CHAPTER FORTY-SEVEN

August 2001
Marlowe Beach

Only fools thought a hurricane blows over in a day. They are huge storms, easily bigger than the entire state of North Carolina. The worst of the storms may only last a day and a night, but they wander in, bang on the door until it opens, and live in your house for a day. Then they finally clear out, much later, leaving the remnants, high winds, cloudy white and gray skies, scudding rain, made worse with the floods and puddles and dirt and broken branches and fallen trees. The day after a hurricane was still the day of a hurricane. They may lose their strength after falling onto land, then hurry away at high speed to terrorize the Midwest with floods, or course northwards along the coast to torment New England. They leave so that they don't have to stick around and pick up the pieces of all the things they broke.

Erick woke up with a start. His east facing bedroom looked out over the ocean, and he would have seen a churning Atlantic covered in white foam if the big Bermuda shutter hadn't been closed. Only cracks of white light beamed through the edges, showing little bits of dust in the air, fragments of the blankets and sheets that were twisted around as he rolled in his sleep, plagued with nightmares of birds pecking at him to pull off his sins.

Erick grabbed his clunky diver's watch to see the time. The fashionable Omega Seamaster was meant for debonair spies, not exhausted people with morning breath. The power was still off, and the clock by his bed sat dully, a useless plastic thing. Erick nodded to the device as he rubbed his eyes, "Me, too, bud," he said to the shiny black screen, "I wish I could make time stand still like you." Erick blinked his eyelids open, clearing the sticky crud with a deliberate squint. Erick felt his beard, scruffy, and slightly wet from sleeping with his mouth open. He had been exhausted, and slept the sleep of the dead. Erick was usually up with the sun, or earlier, but today, with the darkened room, and cloudy skies outside, the sun hadn't come in to welcome the day. He had slept until 7:50.

Erick got up slowly. It was more habit than difficulty. He had always been careful not to strain the cut on his chest. The stitches and glue that had held Erick together for so long felt so delicate when they were on him. Erick had been afraid he would split back open, so he had been terrified of using his abdomen to crunch himself up and out of bed. Erick had developed the habit of rolling over onto his right side, then up on an elbow, then a knee, and finally a careful push up. It had been a long time since he had needed to do it that way, or even really felt like he had to. It just became a ritual on the morning after a long night.

But once up, he rose quickly. Erick pulled on his shorts from the night before. He didn't have any more clean clothes. Erick may have had a few t-shirts somewhere, but a sloppy t-shirt from three years ago was not the dress code for the morning. The shirt from the night before wasn't any better, but not worse. He just needed to get dressed.

Erick padded out of his room, looking at his sister's door, still closed. He hadn't heard Eliza get up, but the way he had slept, she could have banged the door shut while singing and he may not have noticed. But Eliza probably would have left the door open. Erick slipped into the bathroom. If Eliza wasn't up, all the noise from the bathroom would wake her. Erick had always heard both the noise and the complaints from Astrid, depending on who went in the bathroom early in the morning or late at night.

Erick did a disappointing and truncated version of his morning toilet. Looking in the old medicine cabinet for a razor and only finding a slightly rusted disposable from a year before, he quickly gave up on any hope of having a clean shaven face. A tube of toothpaste served as a bit of a refresher for his mouth and teeth as he licked a drop off the tip of the tube, then wiped his teeth with a towel. Then he splashed water in his face like in the old movies he watched. Erick was surprised how much it helped. A softly burbling wash with some soap was about the best Erick was going to get.

He hadn't looked outside yet, so Erick opened the window and pushed out the big shutter with its white prop. The shade opened to a dull but bright white morning. The clouds were still overhead, covering the sky. But they were white and rolling, not gray fur shaved off a beast. The ocean was a sea of huge white waves, each ten to twelve feet tall, all with horribly organic patterns of bubbling white foam, hiding the gray-green color just beneath them. The beach was covered in seagrass, blackened from being soaked in the salt water. Trapped in the tangles were mounds of algal foam. The whipped cream fuzz blew in giant piles, but it was an ugly ecru filled with salt and dead sea life. Erick always admired the ability of a hurricane to cause such mayhem on the shore. He wondered what had washed up in the middle of the night.

But he couldn't wander out to the beach, not yet. It was still raining, certainly, but Erick needed to be there when Eliza woke up. "If she didn't leave already," Erick wondered. Erick went out of the bathroom, into the hall, and opened the other shutters. The big new house to the north sat high on the hill, still sealed up. The dull Camry sat in the same place it had for days now. If she had gone anywhere, it hadn't been far, and she was walking. "Unless she stole my Jeep," Erick laughed. He pictured Eliza, wind in her hair, soaked from the rain, driving through the deep puddles of the beach road in his open topped Wrangler.

Erick went down the stairs as quietly as he could, but the stairs creaked like little rats, giving away his every step. "Finks," he told them. "When I come back, I'm going to replace all of you. What do you think about that?" Erick wondered what he meant about coming back.

Erick had missed the house, even with its squeaky stairs. He liked the view, even through a storm. He missed having old friends, even though he hadn't seen most of them in years.

"Go ahead, say it," he told himself. "Yeah, I missed Eliza, too, even though she was more trouble than it was worth."

Eliza must have still been in bed. She wasn't downstairs, and the doors were still locked. The house was too quiet, with no power to make the compressors from the refrigerator run, or even the soft almost undetectable hum of the lights and clocks. It also meant there was no coffee. "Ugh," Erick thought. "Coffee..." he said it in a mocking zombie voice, but he really could use a very strong cup of java right now. His mouth was still pasty and his head was still in a bit of a sleepy fog. It was too early to figure out how to make a cup over a candle. He needed a cup of coffee to get his mind working to figure out how to make a cup of coffee. "To hell with it," he gave in, picking out a mug, "I'll have to make do." It meant opening the fridge, which had stayed cold enough, and the freezer, which had, kind of. Erick was happy to see the sealed plastic sandwich boxes of frozen shrimp had stayed mostly solid. It meant they wouldn't spoil and smell, if the power came back on today. He grabbed a handful of ice from the box, threw the cubes in the mug, and quickly shut the freezer door. A can of Dr. Pepper from the fridge was a poor substitute, but it was loaded with caffeine, something he wouldn't get from ginger ale. "And I'm not about to drink Mountain Dew for breakfast anymore." Erick rubbed his chest. This time from the memories of heartburn as a teen.

Erick sipped his drink, barely tolerable, but at least fairly cold and refreshing in a mouth that tasted like paste, not that Erick had ever tasted paste, and stared out the back windows. The hurricane had passed, and all that was left was the annoying remnants, dreary rain, light winds, compared to the huge gusts of the day before, and damage. The beach would have some erosion, there would be palmetto fronds and pine needles everywhere, water would have pooled up and it would have to go somewhere, just not anytime soon.

Damage.

Erick set the mug down and looked at the sea grass, still there, now barely moving and weighted down with rain. The sun would come out later, dry the fine knife edge blades, and the sea grass would spring back up, full and green.

He heard the stairs squeak behind him. "Okay, I won't replace you guys… yet." he whispered to the house.

Eliza walked quietly up behind Erick. He glanced over his shoulder, tried to give Eliza a soft smile, but had to stifle a very demanding yawn. He laughed a little, knowing how bad a face he just made.

Eliza smiled a little, too, and patted Erick on the shoulder, just a little bit, a little contact. It was as close to an apology or forgiveness as either would be able to get to this early in the morning. A pat on the back and an acceptance. It was pretty good for before coffee.

Eliza picked up the mug and sipped it. “Ugh,” she almost spit it out. “What is this?” she complained, wondering if she should swallow it or not.

“Dr. Pepper, you can drink it, don’t worry,” Erick laughed a little louder now.

Eliza wiped her mouth as she gulped down a sip. “No coffee?!”

Erick put his hands up to take in the still house. “No power. And no, I haven’t figured out how to make coffee over a flashlight, or on my engine block. This was the best I can do.”

“It’s still early. Hopefully they will have the power back on.” Eliza looked at the coffee mug in her hand, then set it down on the table. Dr. Pepper for breakfast was a little too much for her. She looked out the back window with Erick at the thin rain splattering the walkway and sundeck on the sand dune beyond. The wood was darkened and soaked from a night full of rain. The sand below the walkway was scarred into a dark brown coarse pebblescape of tiny craters where the raindrops had beaten it down. Eliza knew that beneath the wet crust would be dry sand. Walking through it would mean breaking the layers, getting the wet sand stuck on her feet, then getting coated with the soft white sand beneath. It was an awful feeling, tracking the sand everywhere. It was impossible to get off without a hose or running faucet. Even the thought of the discomfort gave Eliza wonderful shivers and chills. It was yet another price to pay for living on the coast.

“Are you going to wait to see when the power comes on? Or leave as soon as the rain stops?”

“I’ll go once the weather clears. I gotta get back. I have so many things to do. What about you?”

“I better get back. If I stay too long over here, once the bridge is open, my father will come looking for me.” Eliza looked through the walls to her house, up on the hill. "If he comes over and finds me here…"

"And me here," Erick added. He had no desire to have any conversation with Butch either. Even the pleasantries, if there would be any, would mean a delay. Erick quickly went from a desire to leave to something approaching desperation. He opened the back door, just to let the fresh air in. The house had smelled of burnt oil and old wood. It needed to be opened and freshened up. It didn't hurt to have a way out, as well. Both Eliza and Erick welcomed the warm wind even as it still carried the remnants of the hurricane with it.

"Once…" Erick was interrupted by the pop of sound. A light came on, followed immediately by the buzzing whir of the refrigerator compressor, ready to get back to work now that it had power. The TV clicked on, then off. Erick turned it back on, ready for relative good news of rain ending and clear roads.

"You could stay," Eliza said, staring at Erick as he moved around the room. She stood still in the center of the room. "Why are you in a hurry to get away from here? I'm going to be here for the rest of the week. Maybe we could talk, you know, a little more, about our plans."

Erick stared at the TV, though he didn't hear it. Hurricane Michelle had passed over the coast in the night, and had picked up speed quickly while losing her power. It was already a tropical depression turning north over Raleigh. She still had rain in her, but the fight had gone out of the storm. Erick looked up.

He liked the way the island looked after a hurricane. It was more natural, with the trees fallen, the pine needles covering the inland areas. They always smelled wonderfully pungent when a car ran over them, searching for the road beneath. On the beach, once the storm had fully passed, a high pressure would race in to take her place. With it would be high blue skies with thin wispy clouds. The ocean would churn, then get blown out to a flat blue glass, with long, low waves that rolled for hundreds of feet until they barely kissed the shore. The beaches would be temporarily empty, flattened by wind, with only the detritus of the hurricane washed ashore. No footprints, no men desperate to get away from their families, no old ladies collecting shells, not even the surfers who wanted to claim to be the first out on the water.

The beach was a beautiful place, Erick thought, looking at Eliza, who still waited for an answer to a question that wasn't really what she asked.

"I'd like to, really, but… I've got to get back to work. I don't know what I would do here. I love it here, but I'd be alone. I don't really fit in anymore. I'm not a native, hell, I'm not even a local anymore. I was always the Prince of Stuttgart," Erick waved at the house, his ancient castle.

"That's not true," Eliza came close, "and you know it. You have friends here. There are people that like you. You could do whatever you want, and you don't need to be in any particular place to do it."

"Then why be here?"

Eliza looked at him, sad for a moment, then she changed to a disdainful frown. "Jerk," she thought, but didn't say. "There's a reason to be here. I just want to know if it's a good enough reason to you."

Erick knew what Eliza was saying. He looked down, smiled a half smile, trying to be charming, but not really succeeding. Erick did it better when he knew he was the most handsome man in the room, and could grin in a pretend timidity while basking in the applause. Erick said nothing for a moment. He tried to pick his words carefully.

"It's too bad you didn't stay when I had my surgery."

Eliza looked quizzically at Erick. "Why?'

"You know, they had to put an anchor on my chest, and make sure I wasn't torn apart on the inside. It was pretty bad, the wound. I got lucky."

Eliza didn't say anything. She hadn't been there. Being reminded that she left him in a foreign hospital wasn't the answer she had wanted.

Erick continued. "They cut me open, not much, admittedly, but some. Then they sewed me up, from waist to shoulder." He traced the scar under his shirt as a reminder. "Now, I've got this big scar here. It's healing up. It looked worse, believe me. It looked pretty bad, and I couldn't move well for a long time. I was afraid I'd rip the sutures out, or split back open. I've healed, and the scar has gotten softer. It will always be there, but it's better. It still itches some." Erick scratched at it out of habit.

"I'm sorry I…"

Erick put his hand up. "That's not what I'm saying. Whenever I take off my shirt, people are going to see all the scars and wounds I have had. They aren't going away. But when those doctors cut me open, I just want you to know, that I'm sure they saw your name already stitched on my heart."

Eliza felt the tears well up in her big brown eyes, and she wasn't even worried about if Erick saw them this time. Erick walked toward her and placed his hands gently on her shoulders, waiting for permission for anything more. Eliza slipped her arms under his and squeezed. She didn't worry about how hard. Erick didn't mind this time. The rain slowly stopped, and so did the hug.

"I just wanted you to know, that if I had the ability to stay, I would. I don't have a place here. I really don't anywhere. You have this place, you have, well, wherever you are.

"You were already perfect. I wasn't. I had to practice at it, and I still haven't gotten it right."

Eliza could only listen. Telling Erick that she wasn't perfect either wasn't what he was talking about. Eliza needed to listen at this point. She saw herself, trying to talk to other people about what she wanted, trying to talk to her parents, her brother not trying to listen.

"I get that, even if I could disagree, and, maybe, I don't." Eliza looked up at Erick, who looked tired, worn, unshaven and beaten by the storm and the night. "I just… You need to keep practicing, I'm just asking… Don't you want to do it with someone?!"

"With me," Eliza didn't say but didn't need to.

"I just want to be good enough. It's something I need to think about."

The rain left within an hour. Eliza walked back over the dune to her house, still sealed off from the world with the modern hurricane shades. Another hour later, and Erick had driven his Jeep up the drive. He looked anxious and ready to run. "He's probably nervous that my father will drive up and block him in." Eliza wondered why Erick was still afraid of her father, then she realized she was just as worried.

"The roads are cleared all the way to 501. I can get back to Atlanta today."

"Are you sure you want to go now? You might run into some more rain. That thing isn't going to keep much water out. Why don't you stay for lunch?"

"No, I gotta get back to Florida soon. I need a shave and a good night's sleep back at the apartment, then back to the grind." Erick smiled a soft, sad smile, as if he was hoping for something to happen that wasn't going to. He yelled from the Wrangler, "I have your number now." Erick picked up his cellular phone from the net pocket of the passenger seat. The little Nokia was new, easily portable, though useless on the island with poor cell service. "You need to get one of these! Never lose touch!"

Eliza shook her head and smiled back. It was too expensive for her to own a cell phone. She hadn't had anyone she wanted calling her, anyway, with the minutes and charges for texts. "Be careful, then," was all Eliza could add. Erick wasn't going to jump out and come running to the door and take her away. Eliza watched as Erick backed up the Jeep and drove down the driveway.

"Don't go," she said quietly.

Erick drove down a mostly empty road, toward the bridge. Only a few cars were out. He tucked a Braves baseball cap on his head. With his sunglasses, the cap, the new vehicle, and his several days of beard growth, as Erick glanced at himself in the rear view mirror, he knew no one would recognize him. Erick diligently stared straight ahead as the old Ford pickup, occasional police cruiser, or worn down hatchback drove past in the opposite direction.

CHAPTER FORTY-EIGHT

August 2001
Marlowe Beach

Eliza should have predicted just how the rest of the day, and the rest of the week, would have gone. It didn't start well, and went downhill from there. To Eliza it seemed like it was mere moments for Erick to leave her, alone, with the task of taking down the hurricane screens, then Eliza's father pulled up in his pickup truck. Admittedly, he hadn't heard from his daughter in two days during a hurricane. "It's their fault for disconnecting the phone now that they didn't live here anymore," Eliza said to herself at some point in her father's interrogation.

Eliza wondered if her father had seen or recognized Erick driving away, but Butch said nothing about it when he had pulled up to the house. Eliza wouldn't even offer up the fact until the next day, when she revealed, simply, that she had seen Erick at his house next door. Her mother was quietly cool, not wanting to ask anything personal, because that might mean

Eliza having to admit something personal. And no one wanted that. Mila simply said, “How is he doing?” But the implications in the tone were there. Was Erick successful? Rich? Did he take over his family business? Was he still the problem boy that took their daughter away? Was he with someone else? Eliza knew her mother’s skill in “just asking.”

Her father had been less tactful, and even less thrilled. “That boy is trouble.” Those words meant more, too. Erick was not controllable by Butch, not any more. He caused problems for Eliza, and Butch was the one who always had to fix those problems, even when Eliza never asked. It was as much a testament to Butch’s faith in Eliza as it was in his judgement of Erick.

It took a while for her parents to pry it out of her, but Eliza finally said she spent the night at Erick’s home because it felt safer than being alone in the storm. The judgment on that was as swift as it was quiet. Eliza went from “We just watched TV and talked,” which was technically true, to “It isn’t like we slept together or anything,” which was also true, technically. When her parents didn’t believe her, even as they said nothing more, Eliza slowly realized she just didn’t care what they thought. A few more days and she would be back in Woods Hole, away from her parents’ judgment and demands.

While she was home, Eliza delivered several sets of her sustainable seafood guide to local restaurants, along with a more engaged and chatty conversation with the managers and chefs. Eliza was pleasantly surprised to see the restaurants preferred both locally sourced and commercially viable foods over having to offer the more exotic, far flung catches that high end dining prepared for high end clientele. The easier to access, and by that, cheaper, fish, offered as a responsible substitute, would save the restaurants money, and make them look good at the same time.

At first, it was just pleasantries and not much else, until Eliza introduced herself. Eliza Rhodes, marine scientist.

"Rhodes?" was often the response, with a knowing look. The local restaurants recognized the name. It gave Eliza clout, even if it wasn't in her own right. If it was implied that the local seafood industry supported her initiative, well, all the better for Eliza. The initiative was a good plan. Eliza didn't really care how it got implemented. When she had first started the guide, Eliza had noted how her name wasn't attached. Now her name, and by association her father's, was making it successful.

The drive back north was not nearly as dreadful as Eliza had thought it would be. It gave her time to think. Eliza may have ridden her father's coattails, but it was as much her name as his, and the idea, the guide, was all hers. It would be a yearly guide, ongoing, even something that may live on without her, if Eliza ever wanted to get away from it.

Eliza's thoughts turned to Erick. The drive was long, with empty stretches of hollow interstate that offered no distraction from her wandering mind. Eliza retold the last few days in her head. All that she and Erick had shared, her questioning demands for him to see a different life, perhaps one with her, again, back home in North Carolina. "Then why am I leaving?" she wondered. "Trying to escape my parents."

Why was Erick leaving her? Why didn't he stay? "Trying to escape… me?"

By the time she got halfway and had to stop for the night, Eliza had already convinced herself differently. Erick was not trying to escape. He was trying to avoid. A night in a Holiday Inn outside of Baltimore lying on a typically plank-like bed while watching a movie had Eliza's mind wandering. Mostly wandering back a week before, as she looked for something better than a rerun of Friends on cable. The Americanization of Emily was on Turner Classic Movies. While it was unappealing as a war film, the drama and romance hit a little too close to home for Eliza. She wondered if Erick was watching it at the same time. Or more likely he was feting sponsors or dancing with bikini clad models.

"*That's not fair.*"

Eliza had no one to deceive but herself and maybe James Garner as he struggled with Julie Andrews on the TV screen. Her mind argued back at the thought of Erick being a wild playboy, unable to turn down any offer of sexual encounters thrown at him. It's not fair. Eliza hadn't seen Erick in over two years, and then over the course of two nights they had sex in the outdoor shower, "that was pretty hot," Eliza had to admit to herself. "*And you threw yourself at him, remember.*" Well, he certainly didn't mind, she did remember that. Then they argued and fought and Erick apologized. Eliza tried to remember if she ever said she was sorry for leaving him in the hospital.

"*You've had two years to do it.*"

Then Erick left her. He had to get back to his life. All the arguments Eliza had made, all the questions about staying back at the coast. But she never actually said for Erick to come back to her. And Eliza went on with her life.

She told her parents about seeing Erick, got that out of the way, and didn't really care anymore what they thought. Eliza got her guide promoted, which was a good start, something successful that she had done herself, even if she piggybacked her father's name.

"*It's your name, too, you know.*"

And now Eliza was halfway back to her home in Falmouth, back to her job, a career that was going somewhere, and she was becoming less and less attached to her parents.

She had a settled place, something to put her name on, and she was no longer looking for her father's approval.

"That's just what Erick wants. That's what he's doing, too."

This time it wasn't her quiet conscience speaking to her deep inside her head. Eliza was telling herself, almost out loud. "I don't need much convincing to tell myself I'm right."

"*Yeah, only when you're wrong.*"

Eliza turned the lights off and fell half asleep to the glow of the black and white movie on the TV. Only when the war explosions woke her back up did she turn the television off, then roll onto her side and fall into a deep, mostly comfortable sleep. Eliza felt like much of her life had been resolved in the week of the hurricane. If only she could figure out what to do with Erick, if anything.

The next morning, after a non-committal selection of the various breakfast offerings in the hotel, Eliza left for the rest of a long day's drive. With so much less on her mind, Eliza had more time to think about Erick, and where he might still fit in with her life. That was the first realization Eliza had on the second day of the journey. She definitely wanted Erick back in her life.

"When I get home, I'm going to call him," Eliza had his cell phone number, but hadn't used it yet. She wasn't going to make a long distance phone call on her parents' phone for them to have Erick's number, nor even the few dollars charge that they could hold over her the next time she came back. She would call on her own line, at her own time.

It was a long, slow drive back to Massachusetts, made longer the more Eliza looked forward to getting to her house. The words she wanted to say raced through her mind, over and over, trying to work some way to get Erick to come up to see her. Eliza wondered just how Erick would respond.

Finally, after navigating the long interstate corridors up to and through Providence, then into the tight corners of Falmouth, Eliza arrived at her shared rental house. She tried her best to be patient, unloading her bags and even considering going back out for dinner. It was a little after five o'clock, after all. She checked her mail, piled up by a thoughtful housemate. Then Eliza glanced at her phone, pretending to just see what messages she had, not because she was desperate. The light on the answering machine blinked all of twice. "I've been away for over a week, Only two calls," Eliza was a little disappointed. It also meant there was little to answer for.

If it had been the movies, the first call would be some nondescript reminder with a male voice stammering "Uhh... Ms. Rhodes, this is uh Sam with Speedy Dry Cleaners to tell you your coat has been ready and you can pick it up," or some sort of nonsense. It heightened the tension. Only then, after a loud beep, would come the important call.

Eliza didn't live in a movie.

The first call was Erick's voice, plain and clear, confident, but still sweet, coming through the small speaker as the little cassette spun. "Hey, Eliza, it's Erick. I know you aren't home yet, but call me when you get back. Let me know how the drive went. You have my cell phone number. I carry that with me, so call me any time, even if you just want to say hi. Bye."

It was that simple. Erick already took the first step. After all they went through, there he was. At least, there was his voice,

Eliza didn't even bother listening to the next message.

"Well," she said as she picked up the phone, "if you insist." Dinner could wait.

CHAPTER FORTY-NINE

November 2001
Boca Raton

October had no surprises, no treats, for Erick, but no tricks, either. It felt strange to him to enter into fall without going through the motions of the change of the season. Though it wasn't really different from years before. "It's not like I've been home for Halloween in years. Hell, I haven't even been in the U.S. for, like, three of the last four times." Erick had missed, not by longing for, but actually not been around, Halloween for a long time.

September had left him without many options for travel, especially by plane, and with the catamaran finished with the build, he only needed to test the designs. The retail version, cheaper, easier to sail, was fun, fast, but obviously commercial. The racing design was lighter, with a less forgiving twin hull, more brutal and aggressive and scary.

Fun.

When Erick realized he needed months in Florida to test his cat, as well as make contacts with builders, he went ahead and rented a nondescript condo outside of Boca Raton for the month. Besides his clothes, the dull inland apartment was filled only with the typical rental furniture of the transient businessperson. He could have gotten a nicer high rise on the beach, with nicer interior, but all Erick really had to have was a bed and shower. Everything he needed, Erick bought in a bulk visit to the local chain pharmacy.

Looking around his condo as October rolled around, Erick realized he had nothing that made the place his. There were no Halloween decorations hidden in the attic. There was also no attic.

"There's not many kids here, anyway." Erick made a point to remind himself to get a pumpkin and a box of full sized chocolate bars. What few kids he might get at least deserved a decent reward for going to a stranger's door. "And if there's only one kid, well, they're definitely getting a treat. I'm not eating those things all by myself."

Erick couldn't afford to snack on Snickers bars. The whole month was dedicated to taking the catamaran out to see how it would work. For Erick, it actually meant sailing it until it didn't work. It was his idea to sail the boat past its limits to see what broke, just to make sure. The problem he had was that the cat just wouldn't break. Sailing to the limit just took the cat to the ragged edge, where it sat. Unless Erick made the boat tip over, or just did something that no one would ever choose to do. It was surprisingly forgiving, even flying a hull. The cat simply worked the way Erick designed it.

Now was the time for promoting the design, in order to seduce backers and builders. Which meant not only selling the design, but selling the image. It meant selling Erick's image, too. So he was out, every morning when the sun was soft and the skies were clear, taking the two final prototypes out for a modeling contract that included Erick hiking out with his pretty blond hair and tanned face. “And the name,” he told himself, “Don’t forget the name.” The Sunstrom surname was recognizable across cities in the south, as decals were placed on luxury vehicles as they drove up and down Florida, Georgia, and South Carolina.

Erick had scoffed at naming the boat after him, but had not come up with any better ideas. That part, the marketing, the business side, felt a bit empty, especially when he and Terrance entered Erick’s condo, still a stark white with no artwork on the walls. Life was imitating art. Erick had argued that he neither had the time, nor the need.

The fun nightlife and ritual celebrations of the city, the parties of Miami, the need to meet and greet at the exclusive Boca Raton Yacht Club, where the money flowed, along with the alcohol and bombast, were the passages Erick had to travel now. Erick knew the men he saw well. Many of them owned his father’s cars.

But the parties and meetings left him empty. Erick was lonely in a city full of celebrations. He could go out any night he wanted, and it wasn’t as if he didn’t have the attention of women when he was out. The nightlife clawed its way into his life, and Erick clawed out, continually begging off the late night club crawls with the insistence of needing to be up with the sun. A morning on the water or visiting the beach appealed so much more than a loud evening out with dance music that he just didn’t enjoy.

“I’m happiest when I’m on the water,” Erick kept telling himself. But he wondered if it was entirely true. “I’m happy… or maybe satisfied.” Erick felt comfortable when he sailed. The images he received, turned into promotional work, posters, showed him on his boat, unsmiling, but confident. A rugged sailor mixed with a James Bond confidence and a surfer body. “But, no, I’m not smiling.”

He smiled when his phone rang.

Eliza called, occasionally wrote, and the two just talked about what they were doing. And then the calls in both directions got a little less. Eliza was out on her ship more often, then in the office, and she wasn't at home until late. She didn't get a chance to call, or answer the phone. She had told Erick she was going to bed at 9 o'clock now. Erick actually understood the appeal of an early night in, even if it meant they didn't talk as much.

So, on a rather sad and pathetic afternoon over at Erick's condo, Terrance looked around at the undecorated but neat room, shook his head, and said, "You gotta get out of here."

Erick had tried, halfheartedly, to defend his bachelor pad. Then he looked around at how sad, clinical, and pathetic it really was. "What have you got in mind?"

"Sheila wants you to move in with us. You need a bit of family friendly relationships in your life. And you need me to shake the shit out of you on occasion. And secretly, I think Sheila wants to be your mom."

"Thanks, Dad," Erick joked back. But he accepted. Even though his lease ran through the end of October, Erick left the week before Halloween so he could spend it with Terrance and his family at their home.

It took only a week of costumes and pumpkin carving, running through the neighborhood dressed as a pirate, for Erick to brighten. Another week of being well fed by Terrance, distracted by Sheila, and constantly kept in check by their five year old son, and Erick felt not only like his old self, but slightly better. "You just needed a family," Sheila noted one night as they sat on the back patio, sipping wine and rum.

November was still warm. Florida in November didn't lend itself to the crisp autumn breezes that most people look forward to with the coming of fall. Nor did the weather call for soup and pumpkin and the hearty foods to fatten up for the winter. Sheila insisted the three go out for dinner. She had sold a rather gigantic home, and was ready for a celebration.

Terrance had no desire to argue. With the kids tucked away at Terrance's parents for a thrilling evening of hide and seek and occasional diaper changes, Sheila, Terrance, and Erick went out to a high end restaurant for a dinner that would look nothing like a farmhouse fall meal.

Erick followed his rule of getting what a restaurant was famous for, and in this case they visited a steakhouse, which meant he chose to forego any seafood for a delicate filet. Terrance ordered a New York strip so bloody Erick thought it might still moo and wander off the plate. Sheila chose an equally rare prime rib over a cloud of mashed potatoes and barely steamed green beans. The menu choices looked delicious, even though it was somewhat mainstream for Erick's normally risque palate.

Even before the meal came, as Erick picked at what looked more like only a decorative salad of bitter greens, Sheila spoke up over a large glass of very dark and very expensive wine. "I'm glad you got out of that condo. No one should be living there. That's where people go to die. Slowly."

"It wasn't that bad," Erick tried to argue, but he knew Sheila was right.

"No," Sheila shook her head, swallowing hard to not choke on the rich dry red. "I mean, the people who live there, they give up, start dying a slow and long death. They die of boredom over the next fifty years. I don't want that to happen to you."

"Alright, yeah, I admit I've been in a funk. I'm just lonely, I think. It's been nothing but work," Erick waved a piece of lettuce on a fork dismissively.

"You're not lonely," Terrance joined in. "You could have all the attention you want. I think there are three divorced women who watched you go by when we sat down." Terrance looked around expectantly. "I could ask around, if you want."

"No!" Erick laughed, but worried Terrance might mean it. "I'm not going home with anyone here. I'm not that lonely."

Sheila huffed. "Like he said," pointing a finger armed with a sloshing wine glass like a gun at her husband, "you're not lonely. You miss Eliza. There's a difference."

Erick looked away, then down. He didn't have a smart answer for the accusation. "Because she's right," Erick thought. "I admit it, I'm a little happier when I talk with her."

Terrance snorted and Sheila scoffed. "You light up for a day after you get a call from her," she said. "You need to do something about that. Have you told her you miss her?"

"No, mostly we just talk about work, and the weather."

"Seriously?" Sheila was getting a little mad now. "What is wrong with you?!"

"Yeah, man," Terrance wasn't going to side with Erick on this one. He knew which bed he was sleeping in. "What's wrong with you?!"

"I just…" Erick looked around, hoping his steak would show up and distract from what was looking more and more like a planned ambush. "I don't know what to say. She's always busy, and she's happy. She's doing her work. It's something she's proud of. It's not like I can interrupt her, go up there on vacation. She's gone two weeks out of every three on a ship, and working from morning to night. I don't want to interfere."

"Does she?"

Sheila posed a pointed question. It wasn't something Erick had thought about. When they had been together back home, Eliza had beaten around the bush about Erick moving back home, but she had never said anything about coming back herself. Not that Erick had ever asked.

"Well?"

"Well… I don't know."

"Well, maybe you should ask her." Sheila took another sip. This was going to be a two glass night, if Erick kept up with the stupid woe is me attitude.

Erick didn't say any more. Terrance let the discussion rest. He knew how far to push Erick. This was far enough. Erick needed time to cool from the simmer of accusations. The steaks came, and Erick was happy for the table to have something else to busy themselves with rather than his potential love life. "Lack of potential," Erick thought his hosts would probably correct him.

The three ate gravely, silently at first. Erick gave his compliments to the dinner, and thanked his hosts for getting him out, even if it was steak and not scallops. "I have to admit, this is very tasty."

Terrance took a long, red slice of meat and shoved it gracelessly in his mouth, chewing the tender slice and swallowing under the judgy glare of his wife. "It's good enough to eat."

Erick felt his phone in his pocket begin to buzz and vibrate. "I'm sorry," he said hastily. Erick didn't like to show off the phone. Talking at dinner seemed attention seeking and rude. "I've had it on in case, well, you know, the cat and all." He pulled out the phone as it rang a second time and looked at it.

Terrance glanced, too. "Speak of the devil, and she will appear!" Eliza's name appeared on the glowing screen.

"I'll talk to her later," Erick began to put the phone away.

Terrance grabbed at it as Sheila said, "No, dumbass, answer it! Talk to her!"

"No, I…" Erick didn't want to be rude to his friends when they were out.

Sheila reached across the table and grabbed the phone from Erick. "Talk with her!" The phone rang again. "Tell her you miss her."

Erick stared at his two friends, who were stone faced, humorless, severe. Then Sheila pressed the answer button. "Hey, Eliza! It's Sheila and Terrance. Erick is just coming back.

He really wants to talk to you." And she handed the phone to Erick.

Erick glared, then took the phone. "Hey… No, you're not interrupting…"

Sheila pulled a pen out of her purse and began scribbling on the paper cocktail napkin from her wine glass. She tried handing it to Erick, who waved it off. Erick was attempting to listen to the idle introductory conversation that Eliza and he would always have. Sheila got insistent, fluttering the note at Erick. He took it and looked.

"Tell her you miss her."

Erick nodded, but said nothing for a moment. He was trying to listen to Eliza while Sheila pestered him. Erick crumpled the napkin and placed it back on the table. "Yeah, no, I'm starting to do the promotional work now. I need to send you the pictures. They're pretty cool... Okay, yeah, pretty hot, it is nice here. I'll send one with a nice sunset to decorate your place… Yeah, I'll be in it."

Sheila took the napkin and unfolded it, then underlined the words she wrote. "Tell her you miss her!" she hissed at Erick softly.

Terrance agreed as Erick looked at him for support. "Tell her," he mouthed.

Erick tried to smile as he got up. A little distance would let him talk more freely, without the distraction, so he wandered to a corner of the bar, away from the fuming Sheila. As Erick left, he, and the other tables around them, heard her mutter, "Tell her you miss her, you piece of shit."

Once Erick was gone, Sheila looked at her husband and said, "I'm glad you weren't that much of a dumbass."

"He comes by it naturally," Terrance agreed. The final comment got a few laughs from the surrounding tables.

Erick stood alone in the hallway between the entrance of the restaurant and the bar. The conversation flowed, as always. It was the same one they had already had a few weeks before.

Only the temperature had changed. But Erick didn't mind. He laughed and smiled even though no one could see him. Even though Eliza couldn't see him. His steak would get cold, and he wouldn't care. Erick leaned casually against a wall near the bathrooms. "It's been better, staying with Terrance. Sheila is a bit of a mother hen," that was an understatement on this night. "But, you know I've been a little bored and lonely here... No, it's not as much fun without you around."

Eliza had joked about her being the life of every party. "Miami needs me to brighten it up, like I do up here. It's dull without me."

Erick thought about what Eliza said. He knew she was joking. Eliza couldn't move down; she couldn't even get time off for a weekend flight. It wasn't like Erick had tried very hard to visit her, either. The boat, the business, the lawyers, the old men with more money than they can burn. Erick had been walking in the badlands for weeks. Eliza, just her voice, brought a bit of solace to all the noise.

"Eliza, listen..." Erick had to catch himself from saying "I need to tell you something," because whenever someone said that, the 'something' was always something bad. But he didn't know how to preface what he wanted to say. Erick was sure that Sheila was just around the corner, listening, fuming, and glaring through the dark wood walls of the steakhouse. "I don't think it's that I'm lonely here, or bored. I think..." that's not good enough, "I know I miss you."

The curse of phone calls are that no one can see the visual cues, the soft smile or pensive frown that comes with the words. But Erick was sure he heard a soft sigh. "I miss you, too."

The two would talk, softly, for the next ten minutes. Erick was afraid to say much more. It might spoil the magic. Any asks about the two getting together would be met with conflict. They were both too busy, and too far apart. The words were good, not good enough, but good. Erick finally admitted to

Eliza that she was a part of his life that made it better. More importantly, he admitted it to himself.

Erick pictured Eliza on the other end of the phone, sitting in some old ornate house that she shared with a 25 year old graduate student, holding an ugly brown cordless phone up to her pretty brown hair. She was beautiful in Erick's mind. Her big brown eyes got all squinty and closed when she grinned. Eliza had been beautiful since the day Erick had first seen her.

But that wasn't what Erick liked in her.

Ten minutes later, Erick walked back to the table to sit down to an uneaten and mostly room temperature filet mignon. Before Sheila could comment, Erick said, "I told her. Don't worry."

"Good."

"Now what?"

CHAPTER FIFTY

December 2001
Boca Raton

The little Nokia chirped a tingling electronic cricket noise as it rang for Erick. He had slept in a little on Saturday, and now was only sort of up. It helped that he was alone for once. Living in Terrance and Sheila's home had been a godsend. Their son was over the moon excited to have Uncle Erick the Pirate at their house. Erick hadn't needed an alarm clock with the little kid around every morning.

But on Saturday, after a late Friday night, Sheila had to show a big mansion to a big kahuna client, and Terrance had taken his kids out to go on a play date. Erick enjoyed a soft moment alone in the big house, sipping fancy coffee with cream and sugar, not his usual black, just because he could. Sheila had a fancy house, with fancy food and drinks. No matter how wealthy Erick's family was, Erick had lived on the edge of simplicity, with the high end rewards only coming at the end of a race or celebration. "I could get used to this," he thought, realizing that this was exactly what his father had been trying to show Erick for years now.

The little cell rang. Erick wasn't expecting a call from the shipyard. He looked at the screen and saw it was Terrance, one of the few people for whom he would always take the call. "Hey, what's up? You need to be rescued from a bounce house?"

"Ha!" Terrance laughed. "No, it's fun, you should have gotten up with me. You don't know what you're missing." Erick pictured a blue plastic ball bouncing off of Terrance's bald dome. "Hey, since you don't have anything going on, I was going to tell you this yesterday, but didn't get a chance. There's a winter wooden boat show over at the marina by the lake today and tomorrow. Free sails, lots of boats, they always need someone to help crew."

"I'll check it out," Erick answered noncommittally. He wasn't sure if he really needed to leave the house.

"No, seriously, don't sit around watching ESPN. Go. And I've got something to show you. Sheila told me about something you might be interested in. I'll meet you there after three, okay?"

"Okay." That was all Erick needed to say. He never flaked out on Terrance. "What is it?"

"It's a surprise…" then Terrance clicked off before Erick could even snicker at the comment.

Erick drove the Wrangler over to Lake Boca Raton. The lake and access to the Intracoastal Waterway and Atlantic was filled with small and large daysailors, all circling in different spots, all having fun. They were mostly old wooden sailboats, along with a few old Chris-Craft motor boats trying to fit in. Lots of boats were doing free sails for people lined up to get on board an old sloop or work boat.

One beautiful boat sat tied up to the dock, with a middle aged man sitting in the middle of the open sloop. "Nice boat," Erick commented, "Why aren't you sailing?"

The man grinned a salted smile, crow's feet crawling down from his eyes into his cheeks. "Thanks! I was supposed to do the free sails, but I don't have a crew."

"Well, if that's all you need, I'll crew for you." Erick figured it would be fun.

"Have you ever crewed before?" It was a fair question. The guy didn't know Erick from Adam, and it was his boat, he was the skipper.

Erick stopped, and afraid he may look stupid with his mouth open trying to pick what might be enough of a bona fide for this stranger, he started at the beginning. "Well, I built a wooden dinghy as a teenager, I raced twenty foot cats, won five Penquin Cups, raced a World 1000, a TransPac, a Citizen's Cup, and the King's Cup in Spain." Erick figured the damn race had almost killed him and ruined his relationship with Eliza, might as well throw that in. "Oh yeah, I also have a new racing catamaran coming out that I designed."

"Damn," the man laughed out, "That's all? I should be sailing for you!"

"Permission to come aboard?"

"Permission granted!"

Erick introduced himself, "Erick," he said, deciding not to add a last name, just in case either his notoriety or jinx might have preceded him. "James," the man proffered his own first name and his hand.

Erick got the boat a little more shipshape while James welcomed his first passengers. It was a happily flustered late middle aged woman, a grandmother, but a younger one at that, with two young and antsy boys who were ready to jump in and probably through the wooden hull, if they tried hard enough. "Alright, you two fish sticks," Erick called to the little boys, "I gotta help you get in quietly and carefully, or else you'll scare away all the sharks!" The two squealed at that, but allowed Erick to lift them into the boat without shaking it into the depths. Grandmother was happy to get the two to calm down some, but was unsure herself.

"Are you sure this is safe for us? How long have you been sailing?"

Erick, in a quick glance at James, took off his baseball cap, placed it on his heart, and said, "Honest to God, ma'am, I swear this is actually the first time I've ever been on this boat. But it seems like it wants to float." James snickered as he gathered a line.

The afternoon went better than Erick thought. He enjoyed the simple sailing, in and out, letting kids handle the rudder, telling stories and joking with the passengers. James twice slammed the boat into the dock, so Erick volunteered to bring her in the next time. When he barely kissed the rub rail of the boat to the dock fender, James said, "You can keep bringing her in from now on."

Erick had almost forgotten that he was supposed to meet Terrance that afternoon. His phone didn't ring until 3:30. "I was running late. Ice cream, you know," Terrance explained. "Can you meet me at the dry docks, over by Nash Builders?" It was nothing more than a fifteen minute stroll through the afternoon crowd, then to a group of blue tin buildings, where boats were kept for repairs and storage. Terrance was waiting for him outside one tall building with the wide doors mostly closed. He had a sly smile on his face. "So," Erick asked, "what is the surprise you have to show me?"

"In here." Terrance walked Erick through the little office door.

Inside, standing on keel blocks, was a beautiful, long two mast schooner. It was clearly still in the works, but was mostly finished. The wide fin keel hung low like the upside down dorsal fin of a shark. Erick was properly impressed. Even unfinished, he could see this was a quality leisure cruiser.

"Steel hull, with a teak wood deck and cabins. Look at the cabin deck," Terrance pointed out the long flat space between the helm and the bow.

"It's low," Erick noticed. Usually the area was raised enough to give the interior cabins a bit more headroom.

Terrance nodded. He waved Erick to climb a scaffold to see the boat from the waterline. "This is a beautiful schooner, I tell you. The deck is meant to be a flat sundeck, so that you can walk on it, lay out, whatever. It's a useable space. See how it's flat, not tapered to the side deck and gunwale."

"It looks like an open main deck, almost. Like a pirate ship."

"Exactly," Terrance beamed. "I thought the same thing."

Erick looked up and down the boat, then asked, "Why?"

"Ha!" Terrance laughed. "You're gonna love this. This guy had the boat designed this way because he wanted a sailboat to motor cruise the islands. And he wanted a big flat deck where his girlfriend could lay out in the sun. He wanted her to have her own beach on the middle of the boat, where he could see her from the helm."

"That sounds about right for Miami, or Boca," Erick joked. "So he built this for his girlfriend. What's the rest of the story?"

"Well," Terrance laughed, "he built this so he could watch his girlfriend get an all over tan."

"Yeah…"

"Well… His wife didn't like that too much."

Erick laughed hard at that comment.

"Sheila found this guy, he's gotta sell his home, and the wife, now ex, definitely isn't letting him keep this. It's been sitting here, about done, for months. It's cheap, because she wants to hurt the guy, and no one wants a half finished boat. Only twenty five K."

Erick looked from the boat to Terrance. "Wait, so… you want me to buy this?"

Terrance shook Erick by the shoulder, then said, "Let's go on board." They stood at the helm, which was missing some of the equipment needed to pilot the boat. "She's an incredible boat, I tell you. Well balanced, a little weather helm, and it's not finished, but it just needs mostly the brightwork and the interior design, the bulkhead and fluff-n-puff, make it your own."

"My own?!" Erick was stunned. He thought Terrance was going to buy it and was just showing off. "I'm not buying this. I just launched my first cat. You think I want a shiny monohull?"

Terrance sat down on the cabin, dangling his long legs over the hatchway. "Look, man, you gotta," he was going to say "settle down" but that wasn't the right word for someone to live on a boat, "find your place where you can be content. With someone. I love you, Sheila loves you, the kids *adore* you. But you need your own home."

"You trying to kick me out?" Erick chuckled, wondering if he had overstayed his welcome. "I can move out. I thought you wanted me there."

"No, no no no," Terrance shook his head. "Almost the opposite. You like being with us, right? Sheila loves having you settled, not restless, not living out of your truck, or at that place, what does your mom call it?"

"The Mailbox."

"Yeah, the Mailbox. You've been great, a doting uncle, a great guest, you keep the house cleaner than I do, and you get out of the way without me telling you, all that stuff. That's my point. You're ready to find a home, something to do."

"My turtle," Erick commented, looking at the boat.

"I have no idea what that means, but if it's your reason for being, then yeah."

Erick looked over the boat. It still needed work, but it could be fast. And comfortable. It might be hard to sail single handedly. "I'd need a crew."

"That's the idea, dumbass."

CHAPTER FIFTY-ONE

March 2002
Falmouth

The big stern trawler *Albatross IV* made her way into the cold still air of Great Harbor, in Falmouth, Massachusetts. It had been a two week trip for Eliza, and it had been cold every single day of the trip. It had been a cold winter, but that was appropriate for New England. That didn't make the weather feel any better to Eliza. Now winter was close to ending, and March fought to break the icy grip. The long month wasn't winning yet. The trip was two freezing weeks of studying the catch of the Atlantic, mostly the north Atlantic cold water catch. Eliza kept hoping for a run to the warmth of Cape Hatteras to see her home state, but she was too often in her laboratory, or at her desk, going over data of scallops, crabs, and cod. This trip had only been off Massachusetts and other New England states.

Getting off the ship was a soft joy to her. Eliza had her sea legs, and usually enjoyed the two week trips, the camaraderie of other scientists and students, who liked to joke and party when off duty, though the wild freewheeling socializing of people who grew up introverted nerds was a little off-putting to her. On the way back, the rum locker was opened, as usual, and many students and scientists pushed their new freedom too far. More than one graduate student ended up leaning over the rail, regretting consuming too much cheap rum. And there were more than a few cries of passion from closed shared berths as the ship headed to home port. Eliza understood the desire to cut loose, but it wasn't in her nature to be so hedonistic. Sinful, her father would say. "He'd have a fit if he knew what was going on here," Eliza laughed inwardly about taunting her father with the descriptions. Eliza mostly found her co-workers intelligent but undesirable. She wondered if she just was jealous that they were having fun and happy.

It probably had more to do with her own anxious desire to get to shore.

Eliza waited patiently for the gangplank to be dropped onto the big ship. She needed to practice her patience. Two weeks at sea meant that she wasn't leaving a car at the port. It would be cold and dirty, maybe iced in, possibly a dead battery, so instead it was stored in a mildly heated carriage house at her rented house in Falmouth. She would need a cab to get home.

But once home, there was something to look forward to. Piled up, among the mail, and paperwork, were the few boxes of her life that she had stored and taped up, ready for shipment. Only a few things were still out on her desk.

She and Erick had started writing letters a month after their chance meeting on Marlowe Beach. First it was mostly just catching up, talking about each others' adventures. They were close to verbatim printed versions of the erratic phone calls they made to each other. Erick had shared how great his life was in Boca Raton, the testing of the new boat, as well as his father's plans for this year at Daytona and Sebring, as if she might care. Automobile racing was so beyond her ken. Eliza read the letters, hoping for a sign, some mention of a change of heart, a desire to come north, to keep her warm. But Florida and warm weather had held Erick in a grip. The water there never stung or froze. Eliza could see the appeal. Girls in bikinis, sunny days, parties at night… A warm weather version of the last night on the *Albatross*, only with much better looking people. Eliza looked at herself in the mirror and wondered if she would seem as appealing as the tanned curved women that Erick was seeing on a daily basis. "He never said anything about another girl, though," Eliza had thought as she read his letters.

No mention of if he missed her in the first few months, but no mention of anyone else, either. Erick mostly told stories of the family life of his friends that he was staying with. When he wasn't talking business.

The letters came and went, then they got more sporadic. Eliza wrote less and occasionally emailed. She was busy with work, compiling patterns of fish brain size, count of male and female crabs, the birth rate of lobsters. Erick had written less, too.

They still called, on occasion. Eliza didn't answer calls as often as she made them because Erick didn't call when he knew she was never at home. Erick was better at answering than she was, mainly because of his always on cellular phone. There was the one call, the time where he finally caved and admitted he missed her. And she caved and missed him, too. Eliza had admitted she was a little worried that the next call might have Erick take it all back.

The letters slowed to a crawl, with both of them being too busy, and the phone calls were sporadic at best.

But Erick started sending postcards instead. They wouldn't say much; the space was limited, and the privacy was negligible. But they were fun. Those postcards littered Eliza's mirror in the hallway and on her corkboard in her little office desk. Erick seemed to delight in finding the tacky and obtuse. Pictures of orange groves and big "FLORIDA" spelled out in images were the beginning. The retro feel of them had added a lot of color to the darkening skies of Eliza's late fall. Then came the novelty cards. First was the "Alligators have more fun in FLORIDA!" with a gator wide mouthed next to a tantalizing buxom wide hipped woman sticking her bikini clad butt out at the creature. Eliza shook her head in a bit of contempt, but laughed and kept the card. Another was a plain looking note that said "Here I am in Florida, and all you're getting is a stinkin' post card!"

Eliza liked the alligator on a sun chair being served a fruity drink by a skinny blonde in a bikini, with the gator saying, "So, what's it like up north?" Erick had labeled the two as "me" and "you." It at least put forth the idea of them being together. Erick had invited her down a few times, in a haphazard sort of way, "If you want to," he had said with a shrug she could hear over the phone. Eliza didn't help her case by telling Erick how busy she was, and then not writing back over half of November and the beginning of December. The postcards weren't much effort on his part, but Eliza realized that he was still doing more than she was.

Then Eliza had gotten three pieces in the mail between late December and early January, over the series of a few days for Christmas break that she had fortunately been home for. The first one was a pretty typical postcard, a dumb play on words, "The weather is here, I wish you were beautiful." "Ha ha, jerk," thought Eliza as she had first seen it. But the note on the back was as appealing as it was simple.

"The aquarium at Fort Fisher is looking for a marine sciences head. It's a bit warmer there, if you are interested."

The second postcard came two days later. It was an actual postcard from the NC Aquarium at Fort Fisher. The front was a less than unique design of the NC Aquariums, two spadefish in monochrome, along with a swimming hammerhead shark. But on the back, crammed in with Erick's scratchy print handwriting, it said, "I went by the aquarium when I was home. I figured you'd like their website and a reminder. It's a little warmer at Marlowe than Falmouth. Happy Holidays. Love, Erick." The words at the end got smaller and smaller as he tried to fit all of it into the limited section on the left side of the postcard.

Three days later was a letter from Erick. It was a tall manila envelope, which would have had the terrifying official feel of something from a law office if Erick hadn't scribbled her address in ink pen and drawn waves and a shark fin on the bottom. In it was a short note from Erick, "Just some more stuff to check out," and a dull color printout of a few pages showing the short and long description of the job at the aquarium. The highlighted yearly pay was marked with a pair of question marks. At $36,000 a year, Erick was unsure if that was good, or bad.

"It's more than I'm making now," Eliza had thought, "and a bit warmer," she smiled at her pale reflection in the mirror, half covered with the novelty postcards. Eliza was washed out, dry, with tiny wrinkles around her eyes from squinting through the cold bright sun. It would only get worse as winter wore on.

Eliza had given in; she didn't need much encouragement to apply. Woods Hole was smart, cutting edge, but she was lonely. Eliza still was uncomfortable with the men who pursued her, and the younger graduate students who expected her to cut loose. The strange New England brogue did crawl into her ear and scratch at her brain. As slow as the southern Atlantic North Carolina drawl was, with the strange almost Irish accent that the locals had, it was like sipping sweet tea compared to the continual "ahhh" sound that permeated the New England coast.

Eliza had filled out an application and later done a phone interview where someone recognized her last name. She didn't mind at all. A graduate of ECU, which happened to be the same alma mater of several other NC Aquarium admins, a masters degree and scientist at Woods Hole, and her father was the Rhodes who ran the regional commercial fisheries in the neighboring coastal community. It was a very late Christmas present, all the way into late February, when she got the offer for the job, with a question, "When can you start?"

Eliza had studies to close out, plans for shipping out on the *Albatross*, all of that took time. There was no chance of leaving during winter, or probably before winter was over. She had gone home in January for a short visit to make up for missing Christmas, and announced that she was looking for a job back home. It was met with joy from her parents. Her brother Tommy was less outwardly thrilled, still being the tough, stoic younger brother, but even he seemed to be happy she was coming back. When Eliza said she was going to look for apartments, possibly closer to Fort Fisher, there was a little backlash. Her parents assumed Eliza was just going to move back in with them. "That's not going to happen," Eliza thought, but outwardly she simply stated it would be easier and faster to live near Southport or Oak Island, near the ferry to Fort Fisher.

Moving to Southport seemed like the right idea. Until the next bit of mail came from Erick in midwinter. It was a longer, more intricate letter, explaining his plans with his new catamaran. He had business investors, a company in Marseilles, France, that wanted him to design and build for them, while they manufactured the boat. "France, the other side of the ocean. It might as well had been the other side of the world," Eliza thought.

Now March finally showed its brighter skies.

Eliza had packed her boxes, several boxes of clothes, a pile of pictures, a mix of some coffee mugs and souvenir plates, the usual mishmash of a single person living in a rental. There were useful items she needed to take home instead of getting rid of them and selling them here. Luckily, the house she shared was furnished, and, apart from a hammock chair and a rolling office chair, Eliza owned no other furniture, which meant she didn't need to ship anything big home on a moving truck. The bulk of her life were boxes of clothes, books, a computer, a tray of silverware, some photo albums, a bag of shells that she didn't really need but couldn't part with, and some CDs.

So Eliza stared at the boxes for the last night. Tomorrow the shippers would come. They couldn't come before because she had to be there to send the boxes out. All that she had left was a little bit of food. On her mirror and in her office were the postcards, the last line of decor in a quickly emptying house.

Eliza's plane tickets to Wilmington were on the top of her paid bills, along with the bill of sale to her car, just so she had the addresses to close out her accounts before she flew out. And the last letter, the fourth one, the one that had just come two weeks ago, with the one other item Erick had sent her. A simple photo of him with his new boat.

CHAPTER FIFTY-TWO

March 2002
Marlowe Beach

Winter had been kinder to Florida than North Carolina, but it always was. Winter was often just a whisper that far south, while much of North Carolina could be bitter, in a dry ice freeze, giving everyone pale and scaly skin. Erick felt out of place with his light tan and smooth complexion compared to the fishermen and dock workers around the industrial marina to the east of Bodin.

Most of North Carolina would freeze, while the coast could stay, if not tropical, then mild, tolerable, sufferable. If the money and work held out. The marina was a money maker for the town, and all the islands together. Even if someone didn't work at the marina, at the cannery, the commercial fishing boats, the ice house, or driving the big trucks, then they had family or friends that did. They spent their money at the grocery stores, the local shops, the gift stores for their kids, who knew "want" and "need" as a different meaning than an adult who made the hard earned money. The commercial fishing industry was a large underlying presence for the success of the towns and the county. Tourism may bring in the taxes, keep the beach shops in the black, but the industrial complex was a powerful backbone to help the islanders stand up straight.

So when the family that owned the commercial fishing licenses sold off the scallop fishing rights, it meant a big chunk of the industry was walking away, and the workers had two choices. Move with the ships or get a new job. Or go on welfare.

Erick had tested and proved his new catamaran was slightly faster than current designs. Not much, but a little, and a little was a lot in sailing. The little added up over the course of a race. It also had been slightly more stable on edge. He couldn't put it any farther over than any catamaran, but the new sponson design gave the cat more stability, with less drag in the water. The mast rake, the lead of the mast, and the new square top shape of the sail, shaped like an airplane wing, all factored in to creating both a fast and incredibly fun to sail craft.

It then caught the eye of enough builders that Erick started getting inquiries as to rights.

"This is my baby," Erick had exclaimed to Terrance back in Boca Raton as they looked over the growing pile of introductory letters, and a few insulting lowball offers. "I don't need another business taking over."

"I get it," Terrance had agreed, in principle, if not in practice. "You got skin in the game, and you want to keep control. But at the same time, this could be serious money they are offering, and you are going to need serious money, serious, I mean, big serious, backers, if you are going to go solo. And then, well," he shrugged, "you definitely *aren't* solo anymore.

"Unless you want to ask your dad." Terrance had known that would strike a nerve, especially at the start of the auto racing season.

"No, there's no need to do that," Erick shook his head. He didn't know if he was trying to prove something to his father, or just to himself. Or someone else. "I don't want this thing to move away from me. I don't want it taken out of my hands. I'm not too worried about the money. Yeah, it would be a risk, or it could set me up pretty well, but I really think there are people out there who would sail this design."

Terrance agreed, mainly because there was a pile of offers on his breakfast nook at his house saying so.

It had taken time, lots of phone calls, more lawyers than Erick had liked, and a face to face with a company manager that barely spoke English, but Erick had negotiated a deal with a Marseille boutique builder that was looking for a sport racing design to sell in Monaco. In exchange for the design rights and sales in Europe, Erick got to keep 60% of the brand, so he would not lose control over the design. More importantly, Erick got a backer with big pockets that at least understood boat building, and had the money to back it up. Erick kept some control, Marseille got access to a boat designer, and most importantly, the boats got built.

The best part was that Erick was in charge of the U.S. operations, which meant he could pick the best place to build the boats. Florida called, with its multitude of open slips and hangars, as well as the warm weather. But Erick had heard of the partial closing of the fishing industry in Bodin, and the plea for new business. There wasn't much that could go into the space. There already was a high end sport fishing boat manufacturer there, casting giant Carolina flares for rich offshore fishermen and the occasional commercial captain who could finally afford a loan to get their own yacht for charters. On the plus side, there was a skill set of people who knew how to work in fiberglass and plastic molds.

There also was the tax break. When the scallop industry, and the supplemental jobs like the tons of crushed ice and the long haul trucks, all dried up, the county and state almost threw blank checks out to reward anyone if they would come in and fill the empty space.

Erick didn't need to think much about it. There was the planning, the business side, all the initial equipment needed to be set in the big hangar-like buildings in the shipyard, the roads that needed to be repaired. All of the hard work that took time away from creating, from the actual *doing*, that Erick wanted to do. He wasn't a businessman, that was for sure. Anxiety, impatience, and he did not get along well.

But even with all the work, all the concerns, the business part, Erick didn't need to think about the decision. It meant going home. It meant helping out people, some he knew, many he didn't, to get them back on their feet. It also meant that he got back to his beach.

Terrance had been happy to get Erick out of his house. "I love you, man, but it's time you moved out on your own, son." It had been a fatherly joke from a guy that Erick would drink with and sail with, but Terrance was right. Terrance had become a dad to him. His advice became less "Don't drink that," and more "Do the right thing."

Erick had moved back to Marlowe Beach over the winter once the manufacturing was ready to start. He had written Eliza, surprising her with the news. The little postcards had been a fun flirt for him, but this was a commitment. Eliza had asked why Erick didn't stay, why he couldn't move back, and now, he was. He even found Eliza a possible job, or a career, really, up at the NC Aquarium. She never wrote back to tell him if she had applied. Whenever he had called, she was away, on a ship, or in her office, so Erick stopped calling. Eliza still hadn't opted for the necessary cell phone, and Erick wondered if it was the cost or the fact that it made for easier contact with him. "Or her father," he had thought.

The man would be a sticking point, Erick knew. Bringing new jobs to his world, the big factory that was now not as big, the marina without the big scallop boats, and the risk of more losses to come, hadn't sat well with Butch or the employees in the big industrial complex. Erick coming in with jobs, not as many but some, had been a lifesaver for several families. The old man didn't like Erick flying in with a big cape to save the day. "Tough shit for him," Erick had said to himself, while maintaining a neutral outward appearance whenever his photo was taken for the newspaper.

Eliza was still a conundrum. Erick had heard little from her in the past few months. She had finally admitted she had applied and interviewed for the job in February, but nothing much since.

"She's probably not wanting to say anything in case she doesn't get the job," Erick thought. He didn't care. He had a backup. But Erick was willing to wait and see. Then he was going to tell her of his other plan.

The first cats were coming out of the shipyard by February. It was mostly assembly/disassembly. The mast, sails, and trampolines were made elsewhere. The big kevlar sheets needed for the high performance racing versions were being made in a dedicated facility in Maryland. The simpler Dacron polyester sheets and nylon spinnakers for the commercial versions were made in Virginia and shipped to the factory. Erick wasn't about to trust the common Chinese polyester sheets to be the correct size, let alone strength. At least he knew who to yell at if something went wrong, and the trip would take hours in a car, not days in a plane. The sponsons, spars, and crossbeams were made in the factory in Bodin. The cat was assembled, mast attached, a test sail sheet raised, then the mast came down and the boat was wrapped up and shipped out, along with all her sisters, to far flung shops across the Gulf of Mexico, all the way up to Massachusetts and Canada.

Erick had a business, a design, a manager, an accountant, and a product. Once it all got going, he just had to sit back and watch.

"Not a thing I want to do," Erick had realized as soon as he had started the process. The other boat, the one Terrance had shown him, that was what he wanted to do.

North Carolina had frozen over the winter. Bodin had frozen. Now March brought the thaw.

Erick left the cluttered desk he had in his shipyard office, piled with useless papers that someone else would clean up, to go outside into the March sun. It was warm for early March. The push of the Gulf Stream up onto the coast helped. Most of the state would hope March would bring sun and warm weather, but in reality, it was always a long, cold, brightly bitter month. "But not today, thank goodness," Erick thought as he put on a cap and glasses. It was too nice a day for him to drive the short distance to the industrial docks. "I may need a bike for this place." Erick walked briskly from the shop to the still water of the industrial marina, farther inland than the sports marina with its gleaming charter fishing yachts. Soon enough, the trip would be to the far off fancy sport fishing center. Or perhaps the seasonal recreational docks in Bodin, where the rich boats tied up on day trips or stopoffs between Florida and New England.

Erick began daydreaming of other places on the coast that took in the sailboats that traveled the waterways of North Carolina. "Southport, or the inland side of Oak Island. Maybe Bald Head. Wilmington? Nah," Erick saw Wilmington as too far, too industrial. "Kure Beach? Wrightsville?" Both were on the waterway to Fort Fisher where the Cape Fear River poured out into the Atlantic Ocean. Any would do, depending…

Erick took his time, stepping over the old lines, around a pile of floats, a stack of crab pots that may never see the water again. He finally got to the boardwalk that wrapped the big industrial slips, where he had his new sailboat tied up. It still looked strange to Erick.

The boat was long, low in the water. It had that long flat deck between the two masts. The boat was still an "it" to Erick.

Boats were "shes," certainly, but to Erick, this one was an "it" until it got its name and christening. It had seemed like it was an open deck schooner, almost like it needed a big forecastle and poop deck. Erick knew a couple people who had pirate ships, some novelty ships with high decks and an open center where they could mount a few tiny cannon to shoot off. There was this one guy that had an actual pirate ship, a beautiful brig, up in Beaufort. The old man fancied himself a pirate, and even lived aboard. "The guy's twice my age, or more, and still lives on board," Erick shook off the idea. He liked being aboard a boat at sea, but when he was tied up to a dock, a home was preferable. Still, Erick wondered if he was going to be living aboard this thing. "Depends…" Depends on a lot, or just one thing. He still hadn't heard from Eliza, and didn't know what she was doing. Erick wasn't sure if she would want to live on a little sailboat, but she definitely wasn't going to live on a little sailboat tied up to the marina where her father worked. "Once the rest of the upgrades are done, I'll find a new slip." Erick promised himself.

The boat sat low in the water. It certainly was pretty, for a monohull. Erick had brought it up the Intracoastal Waterway under motor power. The sail system wasn't entirely installed yet. It needed some automation if Erick was going to sail it alone. He hoped that wouldn't be the case.

Erick planned that he could do day sails, maybe weekend trips up the Intracoastal. Or three and five day training runs, to teach kids how to work a sailboat. Let them live and work on the deck, camp out on the islands, catch their fish, be pirates in the ocean. He already had made plans for demonstration sails for the NC Aquarium, taking tourists out to catch shrimp and fish for educational events. Erick planned for everything.

Except a first mate.

There were plenty of mates on the islands, but not the one he wanted.

Erick looked at his watch. He was early. Seagulls circled lazily over the big marina, searching for a shell to crack open or a french fry to steal. "Poor little scavengers. You get a bad rap."

An old white pickup truck finally pulled up on the oyster shell and gravel road. It ground to a familiar halt, the tires crunching. It was a nondescript vehicle, even by pickup standards. When most fishermen owned the plain red and white Ford F-150s, this little Chevy S-10 was even more nondescript and austere. But it moved, and that was good enough for some. While some people used their cars as status, others saw them merely as a way to move from place to place without getting wet when it rained.

Nellie Spence was one of those people.

Erick had gone to school with her. She had been a year ahead of him, a strikingly popular and energetic teenage girl. Now she was in her thirties, with two kids, recently divorced by a loser of a man who took her money and her heart and ran about three miles before stopping. Now she did woodworking and art on the side when not working at the local seafood restaurant. She was a walking representation of what Erick wanted to fix on the island. "Fix isn't a fair word for her. She's not broken. Screwed over, yeah, maybe."

One of the things Nellie made was nameboards for decoration in the nautical themed restaurants and shops across Bodin and Marlowe. If a tourist family wanted to have their precious child's name carved in wood like on the bow of a ship, Nellie would gladly do it. There were many a "Miss Kathy" and "Jenny Sue" that went home to Pennsylvania or Ohio in the back of the minivan. The big nameboard might hang in a kid's bedroom for a year before they got tired of it, but the money meant that Nellie's kids would have an extra treat in the freezer that week. The tourists would never realize both the importance of the purchase, nor the quality of the work. Nellie was a skilled artist, and Erick knew it.

She had already delivered two sketches, one not the right size or shape, the other a misspelling of the name. The long, nearly transparent paper was crumpled up in the trash back in his office. The third one Erick had folded up in an envelope sitting near the cockpit of the boat. Erick wanted to go get it, but was afraid he would insult Nellie by comparing the drawn plan with the finished design. He had already told her twice that what she brought him wasn't what he wanted. But it truly wasn't her fault, really.

The first one he didn't notice the spelling. The board was too rectangular, the lettering too simple and small, with no flavor or emotion. "It should be softer, more, I dunno, loving." Nellie had laughed at him and pushed his head, but understood even though the description had absolutely no actual guidance for the style he wanted.

The second one was right, but Nellie had spelled the name wrong. "No, it's two words. I know, I know…" he had put up his hands in protest. But at the time, everything was still just on paper. It wasn't carved into wood yet. Erick had already paid for the work; he insisted, and Nellie didn't mind even as she protested.

Now, she was done. He hoped. Nellie got out of the little truck with a wave and a "hi."

"You ready to see this?" she asked.

Erick walked toward the truck.

"No, wait, you gotta let me surprise you," Nellie said. She reached into the back of the pickup and pulled out the long nameboard, still wrapped in old cloth and then paper and string. Erick liked that. She may have wanted to take good care of her work, but he thought a little bouncing around in the bed of her truck would give it character.

Nellie brought it over to the bow of the boat, where she sat the wrapped nameboard on a creosoted bench. First unfolding the cloth, she then whipped out a small silver knife to cut away the string holding the paper on.

"Damn, girl, you'd make a good pirate," Erick laughed as she slashed with her personal cutlass.

Nellie stopped and waved the little knife in a faux menace. "None of you fish head swabs over here better try to fuck with me. I'll cut ya."

"You swear like a pirate, too."

Nellie just giggled. Erick was happy to see her laugh.

The strings parted, the paper unfolded and there it was.

"What do you think?"

Erick beamed. "It's perfect. It's exactly what I wanted."

"So," Nellie handed the long plank nameboard to Erick, finalizing the contracted work, "Now will you tell me what it means? Like, I'm sure the name means something. You made me respell it. But what's up with the III?"

Erick scratched his head under his cap. "Tell you what. Help me put it on first. It's kinda bad luck before it's attached." Erick handed the nameboard back and stepped on the boat at the stern, near the helm. He dug out his power drill from the lazarette. With two clicks to the trigger to buzz the powerful drill, he was ready. "Hold it there," Erick pointed to two holes on the trail board, leading from the bow. A liberal dose of adhesive, two stainless steel screws, and the nameboard was attached.

"There, done. That was easy." Erick beamed at the nameboard. Now his boat was a she.

"Okay, Blondbeard, now, tell me the meaning of the name."

Erick looked at the nameboard and then Nellie. "Can you take my picture with it? I got my Polaroid over here somewhere." He walked to the stern and came back with the instant camera. "So, the name. Well, it's named after an old girlfriend of mine. You didn't know her. You graduated before I met her."

"Ugh," Nellie rolled her eyes. "Men."

“It’s okay, honest,” Erick defended himself. “We still talk. I named the first boat I ever built after her. It’s like it’s good luck. I hope.”

“So is her name Elizabeth? Why two names?”

Erick shook his head. “Yeah, I know. No, her name is Eliza. Eliza Beth. I think it was some play on words by her parents, but, well, it’s cute, like her.” Erick smiled as he lay down on the deck, just above the nameboard.

“Okay,” Click, whirr, the photo spit out and Nellie waved it in the sun. “So, that’s the name. What’s with the III? You said you named your first boat after her? Was there a II?”

“No, and I know you’re gonna hate this,” Erick winced. He was almost afraid Nellie would reach over the dock and smack him.

“What?” The word came out deep, hateful, but laced with adult contempt and a bit of a smile.

“Okay, I know I got after you because you spelled it ‘Elizabeth’ on the first two sketches, yeah? And, no, the first boat was just “Eliza,” that’s all. It’s still over at the house. I got to do some work on that thing. Anyway,” Erick tried to hurry along. Nellie made circles with her hand to speed him up. “So, you know that boat up in Manteo, that replica of the ship that brought the Lost Colony? Well, it’s a replica of the *Elizabeth*, probably named after the queen. And the replica is named the *Elizabeth II*.

“Now, sure, this is *not* the *Elizabeth*. It’s the *Eliza Beth*.”

“But what’s up with the III?!” Nellie wanted to shake him. This was taking too long, after days of demands and redos on the long wooden nameboard. “Get to the point, dumbass!” her face screamed without a word.

“Well,” Erick shrugged as he looked at the picture coming into view on the little Polaroid paper. The stuff was like voodoo how it worked. The picture was him smiling, one hand holding his head up as he lay on the deck, smiling broadly, while the other hand rested on the gunwale just above the nameboard. Erick would send this to Eliza the same afternoon to see what she thought.

"Third time's the charm."

About The Author

John Martell is the author of several novels set on the coast of North Carolina. A native of the state, John grew up and worked on the coast, familiarizing himself with the nuances of life on the ocean's edge. Erick's beach house is modeled on the beach house John spent every summer in as a kid, teen, and young adult. When not writing, he spends much of his time with his family, sailing, swimming, and diving on the coast.

www.ingramcontent.com/pod-product-compliance
Lightning Source LLC
Chambersburg PA
CBHW060541310726
48982CB00009B/1334/J

* 9 7 9 8 9 8 8 0 1 7 1 9 6 *